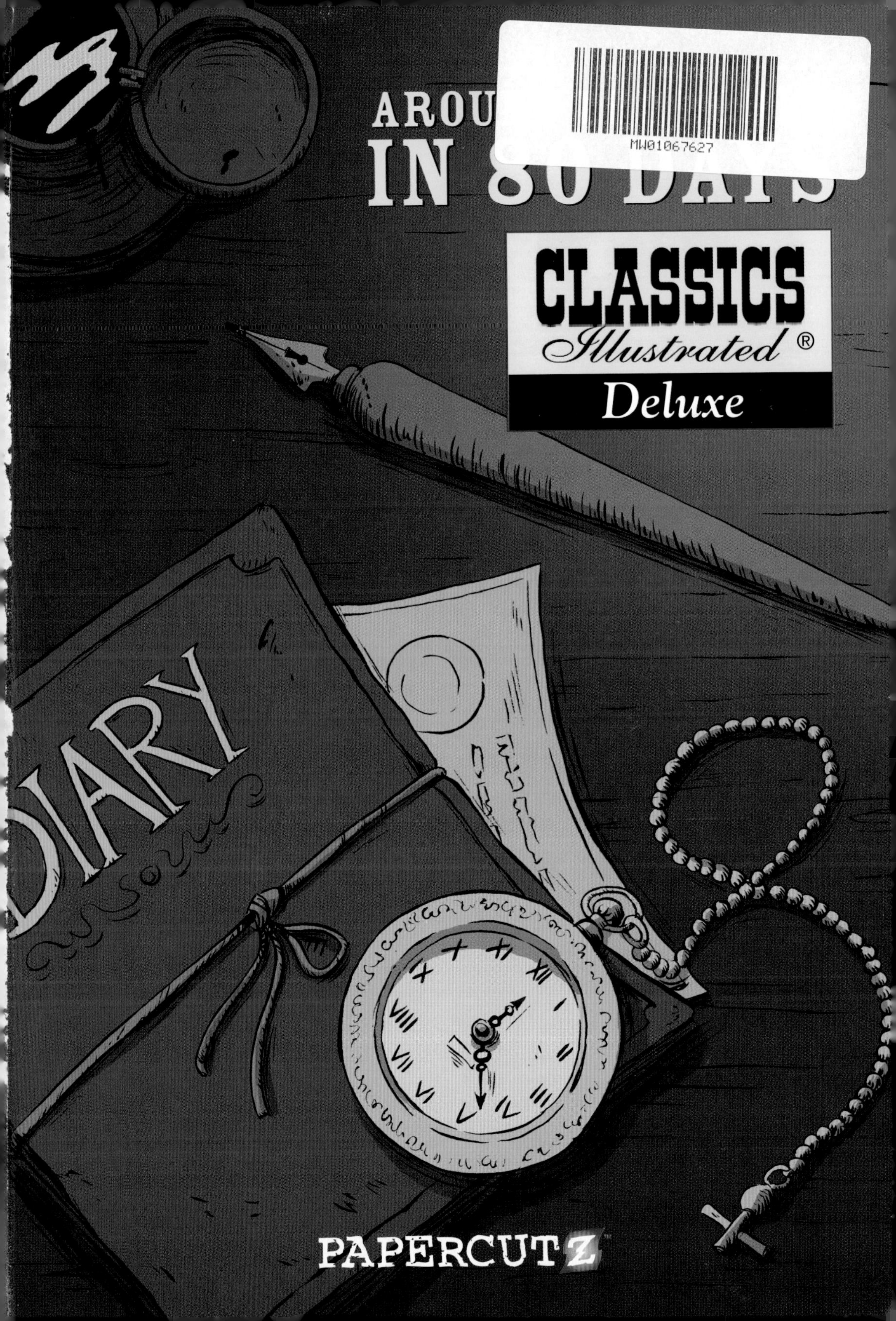
AROU
IN 80 DAYS
CLASSICS
Illustrated ®
Deluxe
DIARY
PAPERCUTZ

CLASSICS ILLUSTRATED DELUXE

#1 "THE WIND IN THE WILLOWS"

#2 "TALES FROM THE BROTHERS GRIMM"

#3 "FRANKENSTEIN"

#4 "THE ADVENTURES OF TOM SAWYER"

#5 "TREASURE ISLAND"

#6 "THE THREE MUSKETEERS"

CLASSICS ILLUSTRATED

#1 "GREAT EXPECTATIONS"

#2 "THE INVISIBLE MAN"

CLASSICS ILLUSTRATED GRAPHIC NOVELS AVAILABLE FROM PAPERCUTZ

#7 "AROUND THE WORLD IN 80 DAYS"

#3 "THROUGH THE LOOKING-GLASS"

#4 "THE RAVEN AND OTHER POEMS"

#5 "HAMLET"

#6 "THE SCARLET LETTER"

#7 "DR. JEKYLL & MR. HYDE"

#8 "THE COUNT OF MONTE CRISTO"

#9 "THE JUNGLE"

#10 "CYRANO DE BERGERAC"

#11 "THE DEVIL'S DICTIONARY AND OTHER WORKS"

#12 "THE ISLAND OF DOCTOR MOREAU"

#13 "IVANHOE"

#14 "WUTHERING HEIGHTS"

CLASSICS ILLUSTRATED DELUXE graphic novels are available for $13.95 each in paperback and $17.95 in hardcover, except #6 which is $16.99 pb, and $21.99 hc.
CLASSICS ILLUSTRATED graphic novels are available only in hardcover for $9.95 each, except #8-14, $9.99 each. Available from booksellers everywhere.

Or order from us. Please add $4.00 for postage and handling for the first book, add $1.00 for each additional book.
MC, Visa, Amex accepted or make check payable to NBM Publishing.
Papercutz, 40 Exchange Place, Ste. 1308, New York, NY 10005 * 1-800-886-1223

www.papercutz.com

CLASSICS Illustrated ® Deluxe

#7

AROUND THE WORLD IN 80 DAYS

By Jules Verne
Adapted by Loïc Dauvillier
and Aude Soleilhac.

PAPERCUTZ™
New York

For Abdelaziz Mouride…
L.D.

There, this trip around the world is finally finished. I'd like to thank those
who allowed me to bring this long voyage to a conclusion.
First of all, thanks to Cedric and Sophie, who lifted me up
and supported me in the bad moments.
Thanks to Sandrine and Mimi, for their good humor, their advice,
and especially for their graphic palette.
Thanks to Armelle, for her immense patience in understanding the life of a bédé author
and also for her precious help.
Thanks to Loïc for having shared this adventure with me.
I dedicate this book to Agathe and to all those who didn't doubt my abilities
for a single instant.

A.S.

"Around the World in 80 Days"
By Jules Verne
Adapted by…
Loïc Dauvillier – Writer
Aude Soleilhac – Artist
Anne-Claire Jouvray – Colorist, Pages 5-50
Aude Soleilhac – Colorist, Pages 51-142
Joe Johnson – Translation
Ortho – Lettering
Ortho and Chris Nelson – Lettering and Production
John Haufe and William B. Jones Jr. – CLASSICS ILLUSTRATED Historians
Michael Petranek – Associate Editor
Jim Salicrup
Editor-in-Chief

ISBN: 978-1-59707-283-0 paperback edition
ISBN: 978-1-59707-284-7 hardcover edition

Printed in China
October 2011 by New Era Printing LTD
Trend Centre, 29-31 Cheung Lee St.
Rm.1101-1103, 11/F, Chaiwan

Distributed by Macmillan.

First Papercutz Printing

October 2, 1872.

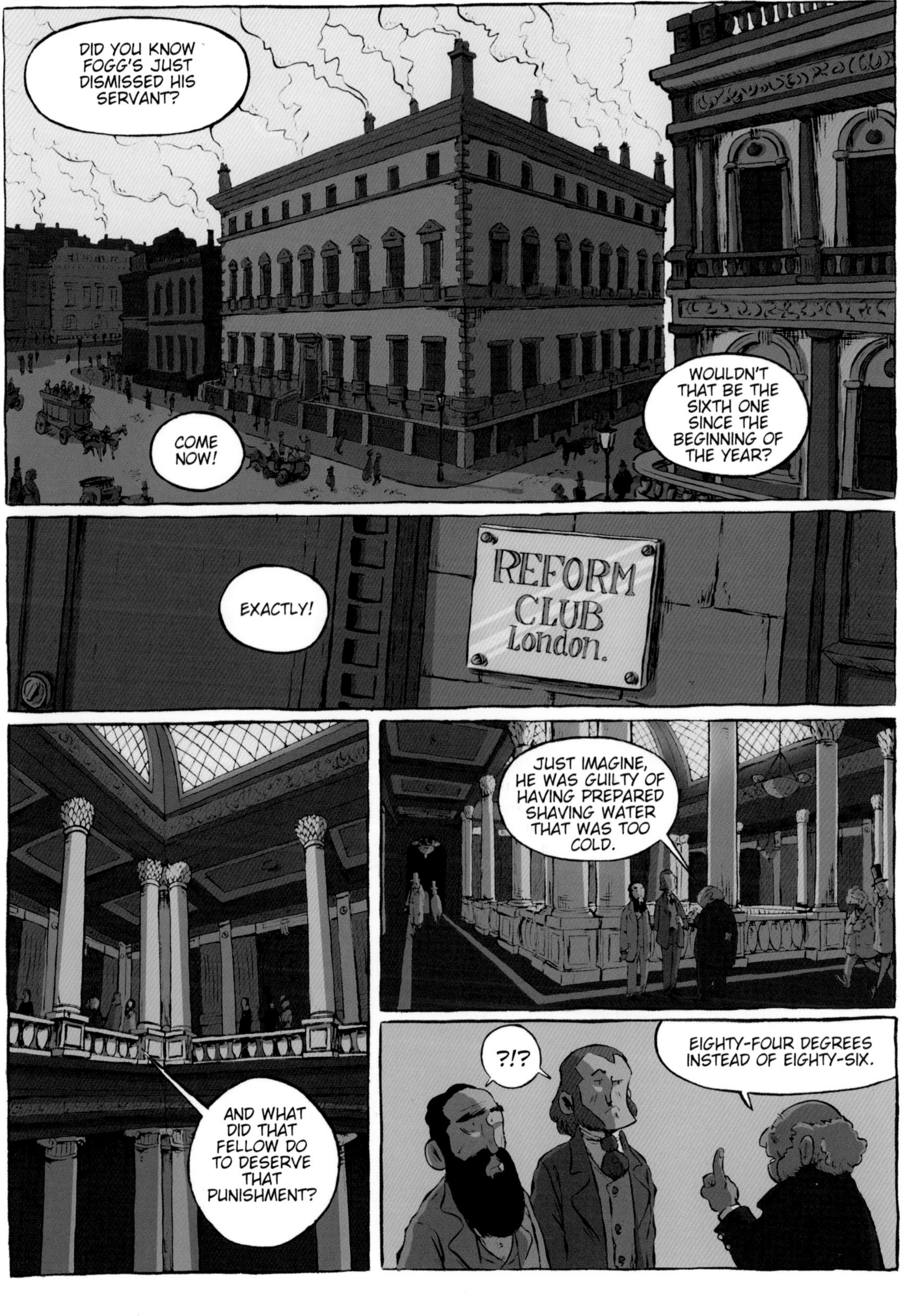
DID YOU KNOW FOGG'S JUST DISMISSED HIS SERVANT?
COME NOW!
WOULDN'T THAT BE THE SIXTH ONE SINCE THE BEGINNING OF THE YEAR?
EXACTLY!
REFORM CLUB London.
AND WHAT DID THAT FELLOW DO TO DESERVE THAT PUNISHMENT?
JUST IMAGINE, HE WAS GUILTY OF HAVING PREPARED SHAVING WATER THAT WAS TOO COLD.
EIGHTY-FOUR DEGREES INSTEAD OF EIGHTY-SIX.
?!?

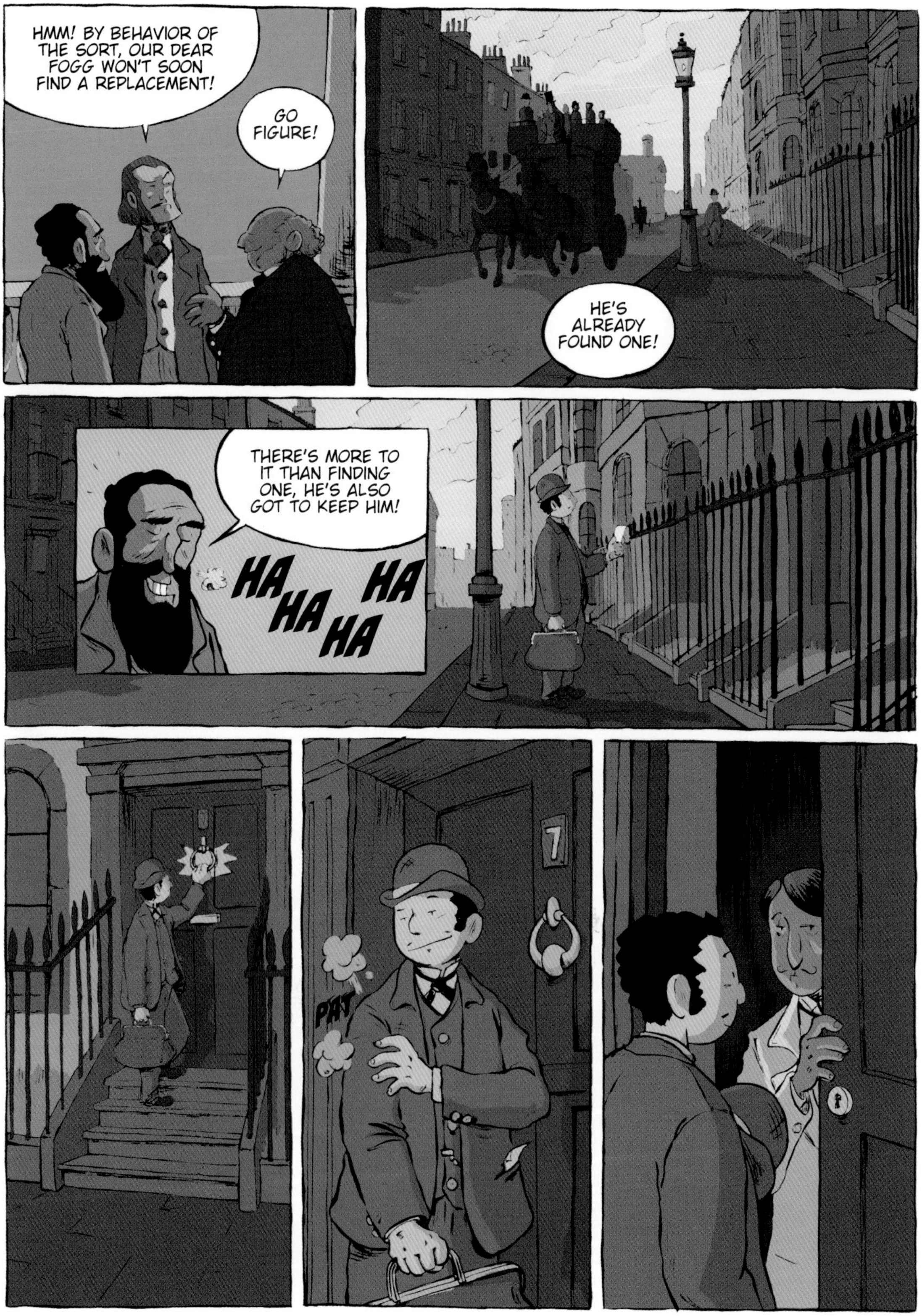
HMM! BY BEHAVIOR OF THE SORT, OUR DEAR FOGG WON'T SOON FIND A REPLACEMENT!
GO FIGURE!
HE'S ALREADY FOUND ONE!
THERE'S MORE TO IT THAN FINDING ONE, HE'S ALSO GOT TO KEEP HIM!
HA HA HA HA HA
7
PAT

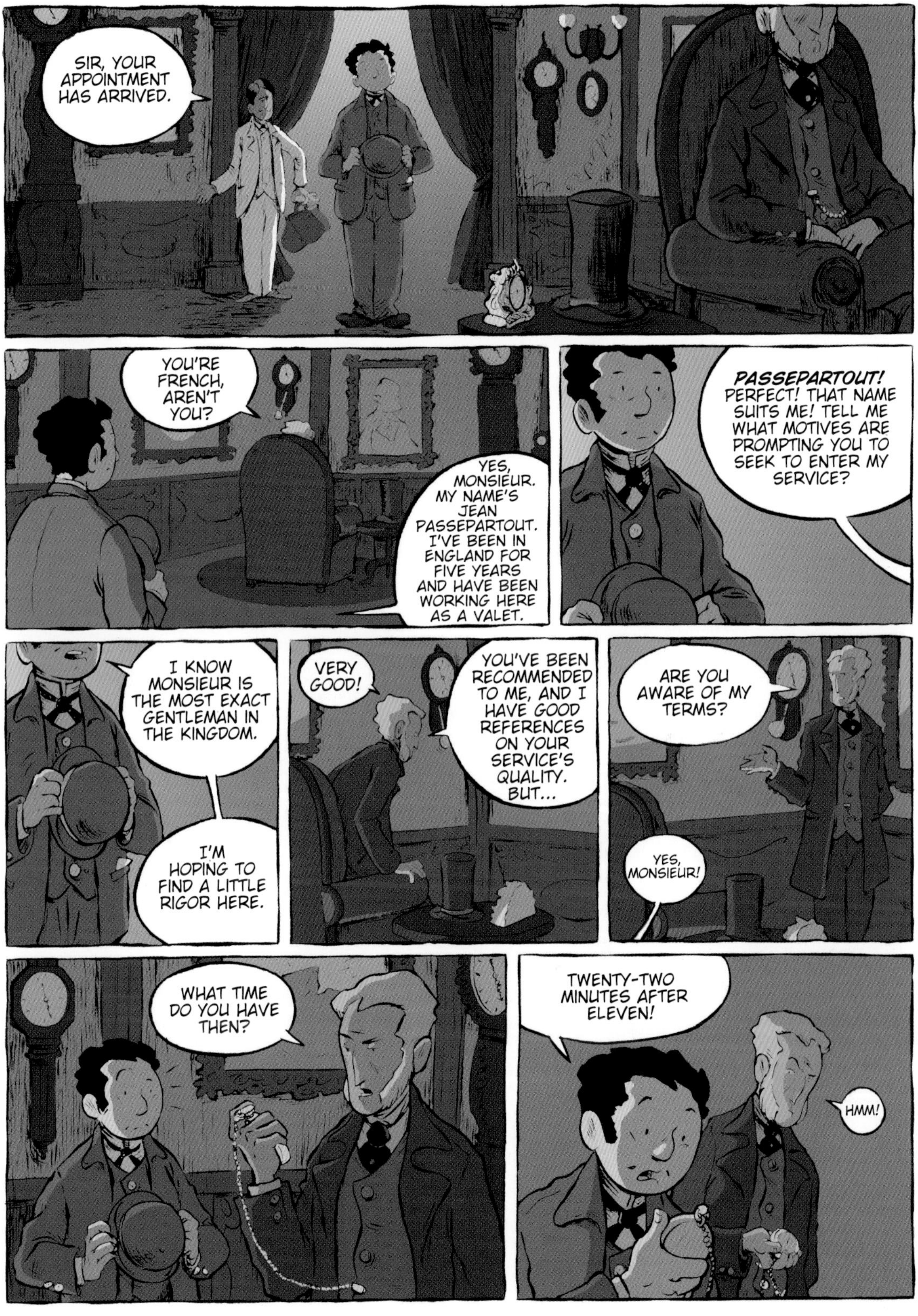
SIR, YOUR APPOINTMENT HAS ARRIVED.
YOU'RE FRENCH, AREN'T YOU?
YES, MONSIEUR. MY NAME'S JEAN PASSEPARTOUT. I'VE BEEN IN ENGLAND FOR FIVE YEARS AND HAVE BEEN WORKING HERE AS A VALET.
PASSEPARTOUT! PERFECT! THAT NAME SUITS ME! TELL ME WHAT MOTIVES ARE PROMPTING YOU TO SEEK TO ENTER MY SERVICE?
I KNOW MONSIEUR IS THE MOST EXACT GENTLEMAN IN THE KINGDOM.
I'M HOPING TO FIND A LITTLE RIGOR HERE.
VERY GOOD!
YOU'VE BEEN RECOMMENDED TO ME, AND I HAVE GOOD REFERENCES ON YOUR SERVICE'S QUALITY. BUT...
ARE YOU AWARE OF MY TERMS?
YES, MONSIEUR!
WHAT TIME DO YOU HAVE THEN?
TWENTY-TWO MINUTES AFTER ELEVEN!
HMM!

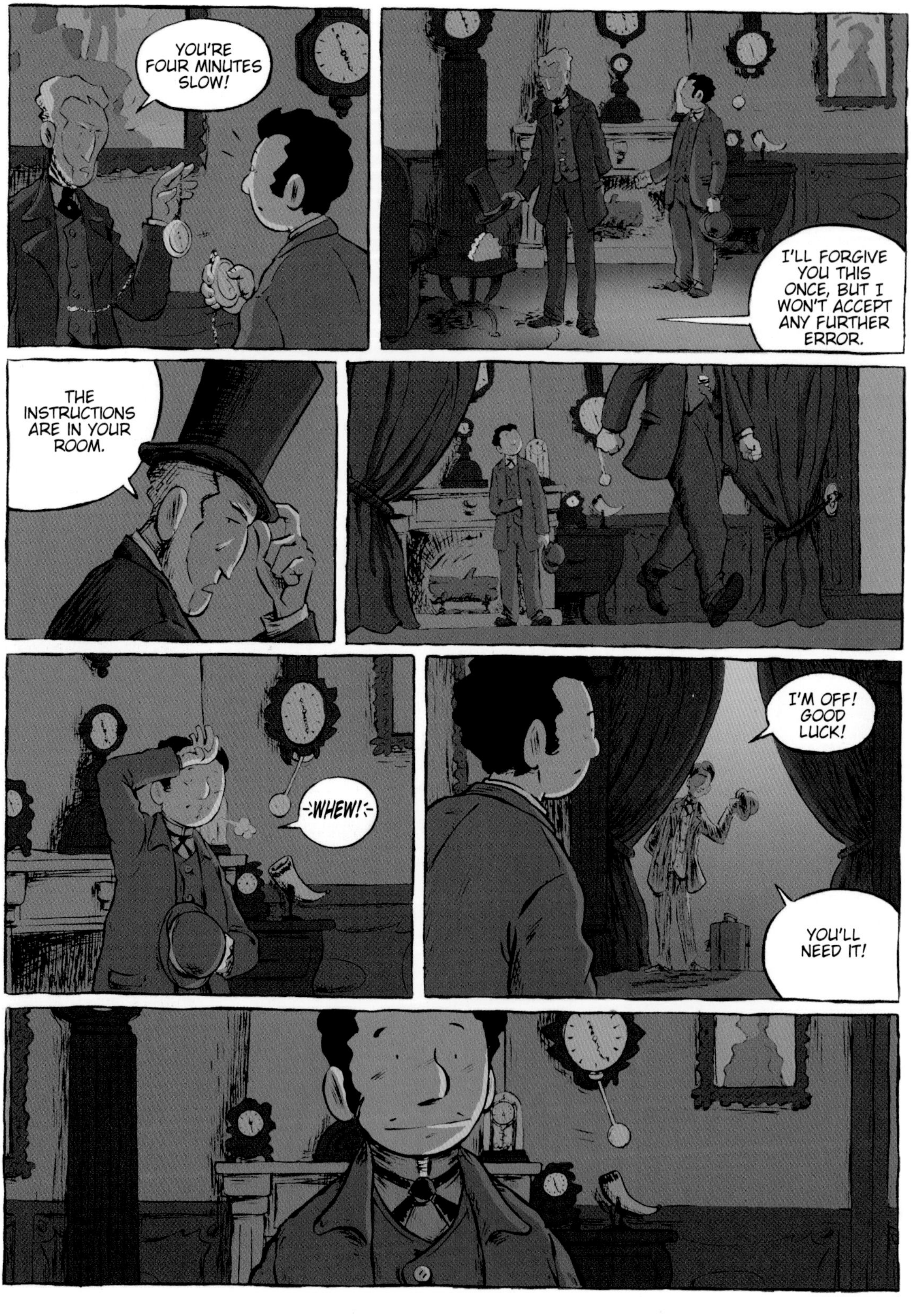
YOU'RE FOUR MINUTES SLOW!
I'LL FORGIVE YOU THIS ONCE, BUT I WON'T ACCEPT ANY FURTHER ERROR.
THE INSTRUCTIONS ARE IN YOUR ROOM.
WHEW!
I'M OFF! GOOD LUCK!
YOU'LL NEED IT!

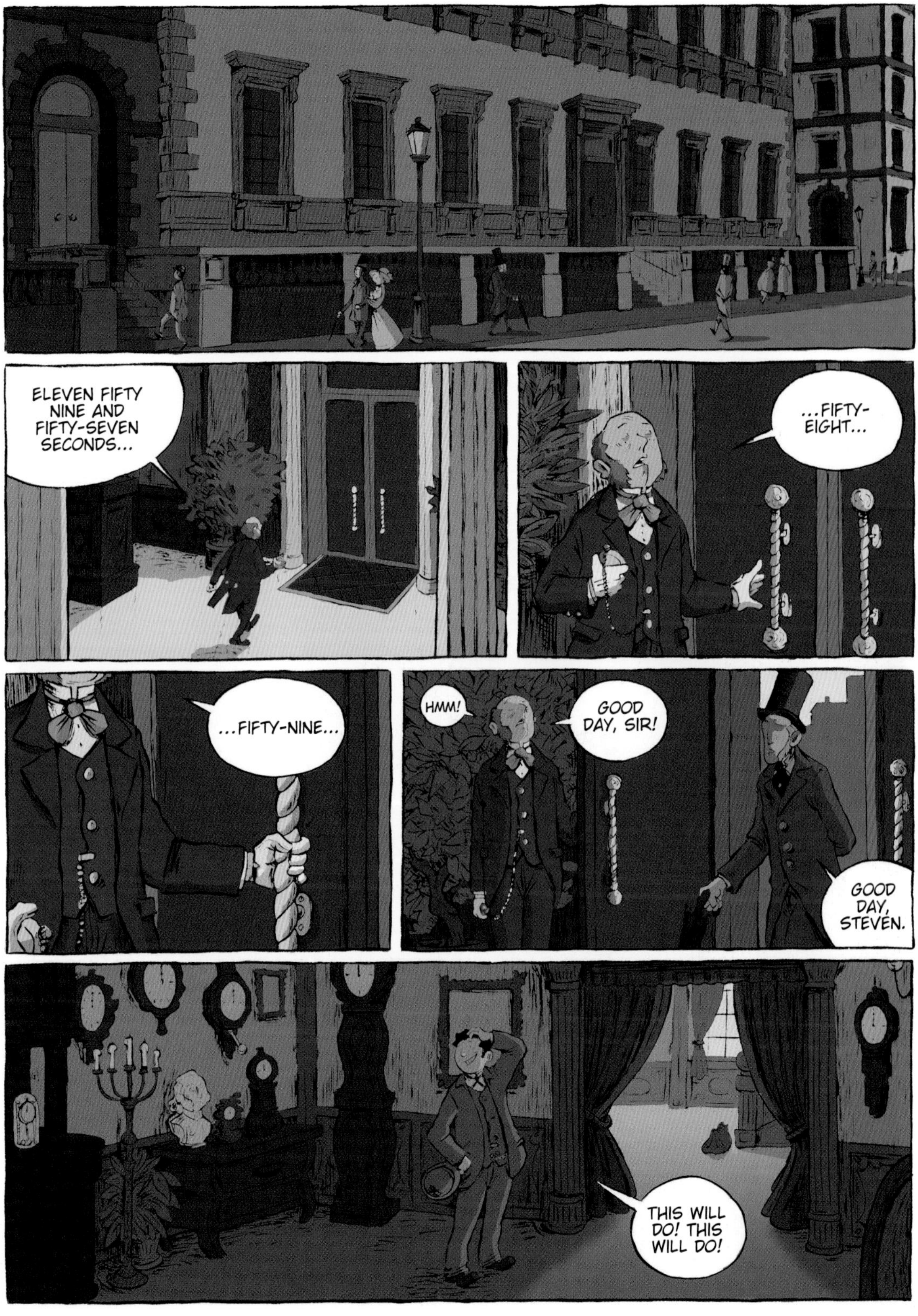
ELEVEN FIFTY NINE AND FIFTY-SEVEN SECONDS...
...FIFTY-EIGHT...
...FIFTY-NINE...
HMM!
GOOD DAY, SIR!
GOOD DAY, STEVEN.
THIS WILL DO! THIS WILL DO!

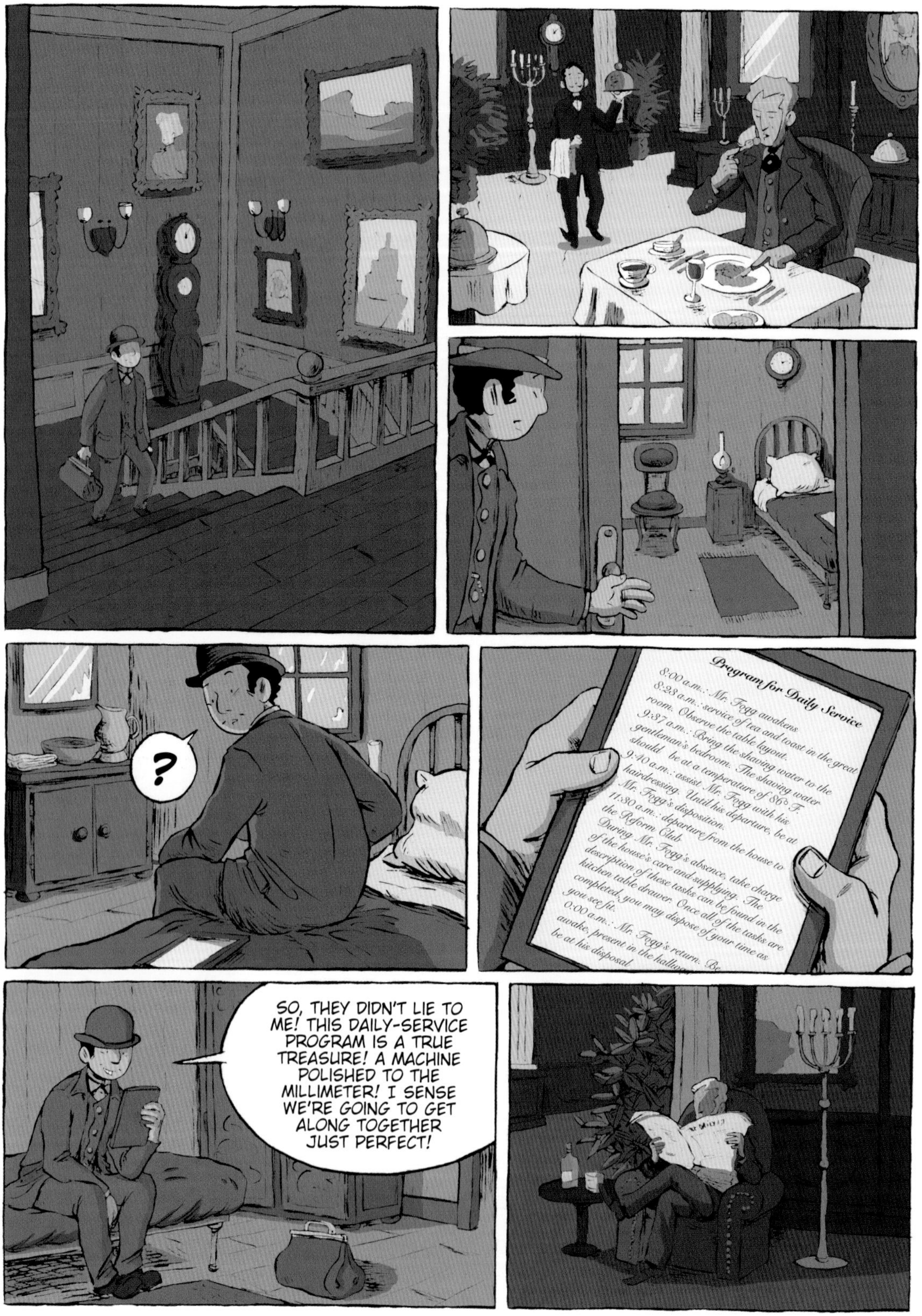
?
Program for Daily Service
8:00 a.m.: Mr. Fogg awakens
8:23 a.m.: service of tea and toast in the great room. Observe the table layout.
9:37 a.m.: Bring the shaving water to the gentleman's bedroom. The shaving water should be at a temperature of 86° F.
9:40 a.m.: assist Mr. Fogg with his hairdressing. Until his departure, be at Mr. Fogg's disposition.
11:30 a.m.: departure from the house to the Reform Club
During Mr. Fogg's absence, take charge of the house's care and supplying. The description of these tasks can be found in the kitchen table drawer. Once all of the tasks are completed, you may dispose of your time as you see fit.
0:00 a.m.: Mr. Fogg's return. Be awake, present in the hallway
be at his disposal
SO, THEY DIDN'T LIE TO ME! THIS DAILY-SERVICE PROGRAM IS A TRUE TREASURE! A MACHINE POLISHED TO THE MILLIMETER! I SENSE WE'RE GOING TO GET ALONG TOGETHER JUST PERFECT!

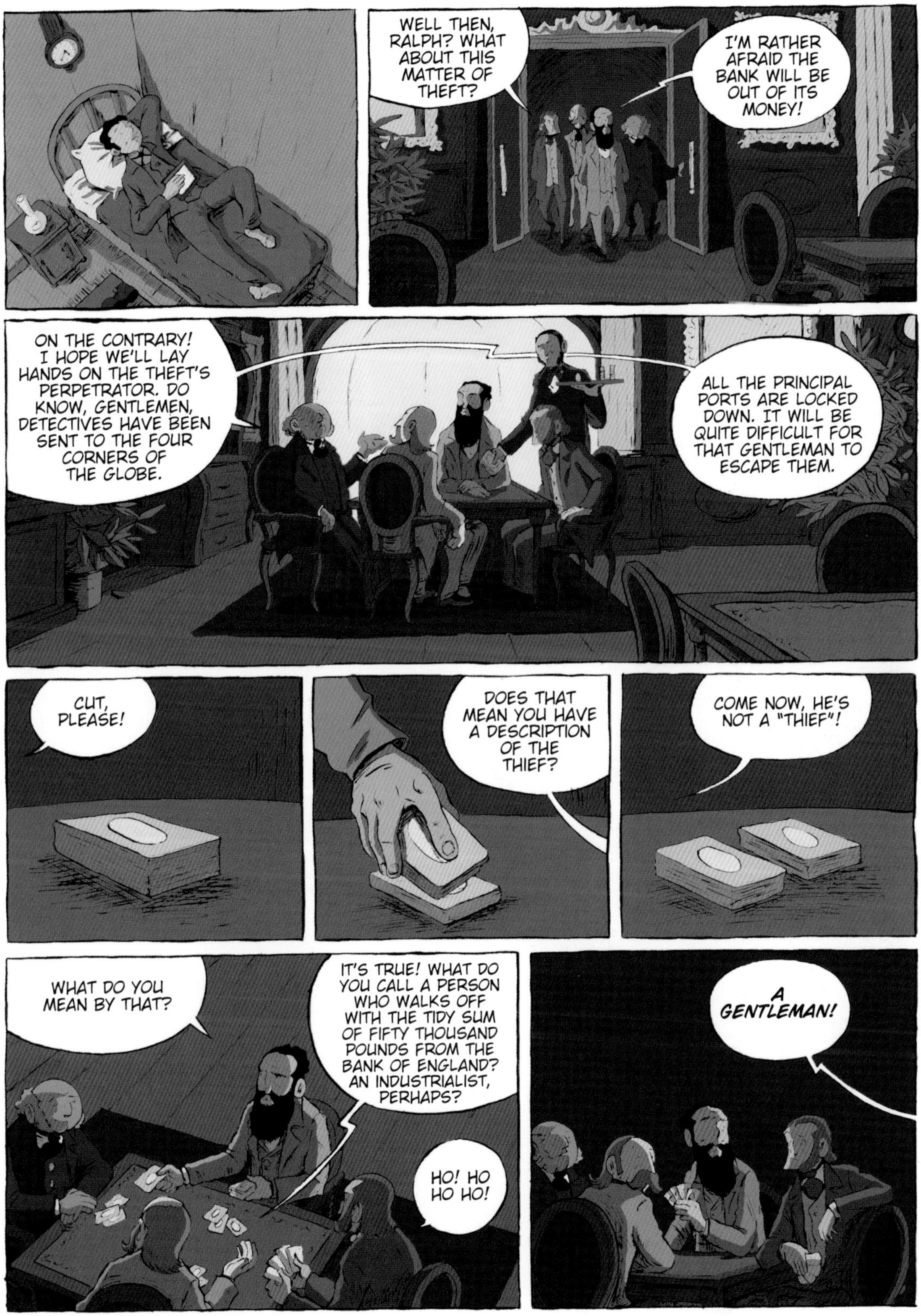
WELL THEN, RALPH? WHAT ABOUT THIS MATTER OF THEFT?
I'M RATHER AFRAID THE BANK WILL BE OUT OF ITS MONEY!
ON THE CONTRARY! I HOPE WE'LL LAY HANDS ON THE THEFT'S PERPETRATOR. DO KNOW, GENTLEMEN, DETECTIVES HAVE BEEN SENT TO THE FOUR CORNERS OF THE GLOBE.
ALL THE PRINCIPAL PORTS ARE LOCKED DOWN. IT WILL BE QUITE DIFFICULT FOR THAT GENTLEMAN TO ESCAPE THEM.
CUT, PLEASE!
DOES THAT MEAN YOU HAVE A DESCRIPTION OF THE THIEF?
COME NOW, HE'S NOT A "THIEF"!
WHAT DO YOU MEAN BY THAT?
IT'S TRUE! WHAT DO YOU CALL A PERSON WHO WALKS OFF WITH THE TIDY SUM OF FIFTY THOUSAND POUNDS FROM THE BANK OF ENGLAND? AN INDUSTRIALIST, PERHAPS?
HO! HO HO HO!
A GENTLEMAN!

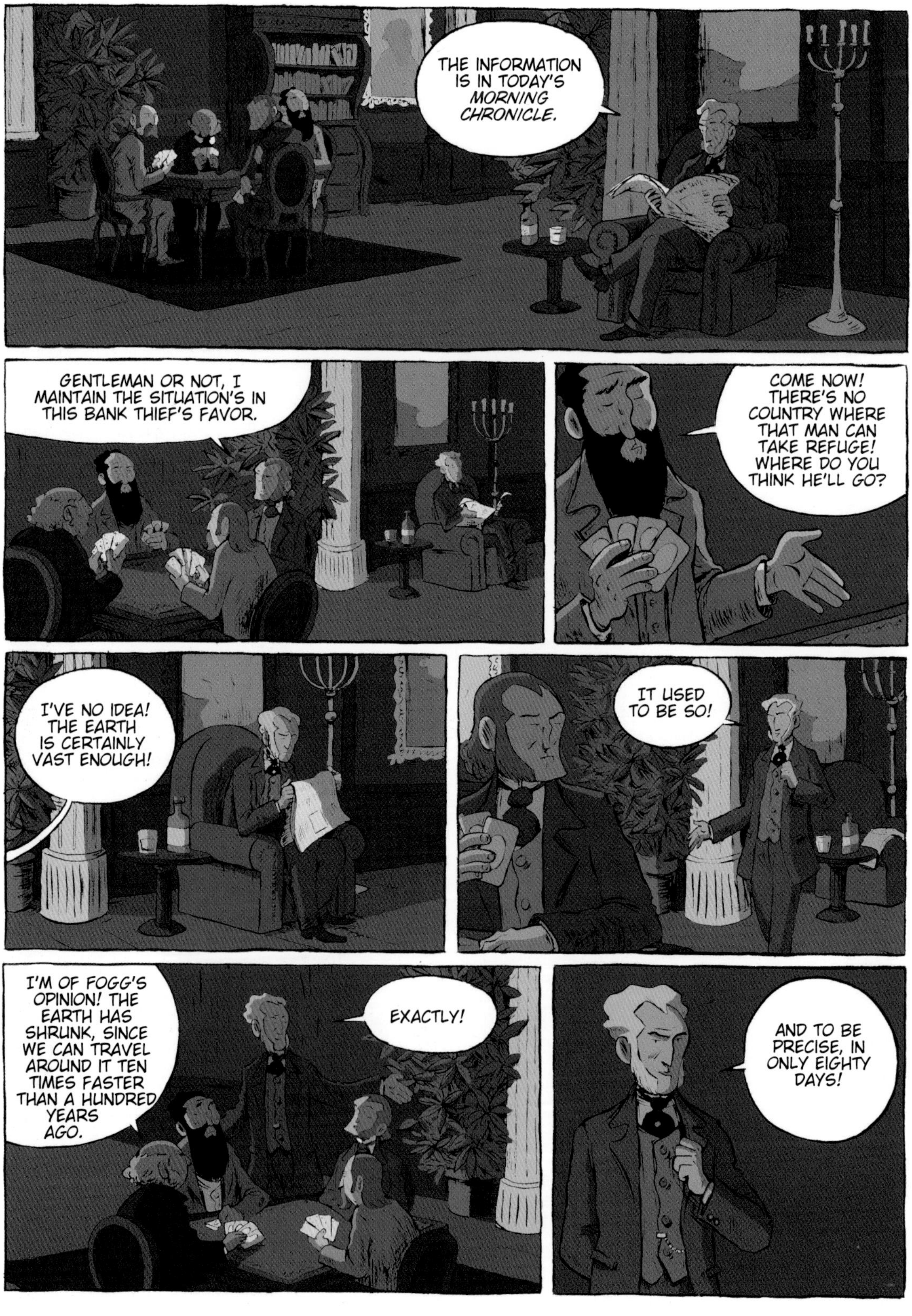
THE INFORMATION IS IN TODAY'S *MORNING CHRONICLE.*
GENTLEMAN OR NOT, I MAINTAIN THE SITUATION'S IN THIS BANK THIEF'S FAVOR.
COME NOW! THERE'S NO COUNTRY WHERE THAT MAN CAN TAKE REFUGE! WHERE DO YOU THINK HE'LL GO?
I'VE NO IDEA! THE EARTH IS CERTAINLY VAST ENOUGH!
IT USED TO BE SO!
I'M OF FOGG'S OPINION! THE EARTH HAS SHRUNK, SINCE WE CAN TRAVEL AROUND IT TEN TIMES FASTER THAN A HUNDRED YEARS AGO.
EXACTLY!
AND TO BE PRECISE, IN ONLY EIGHTY DAYS!

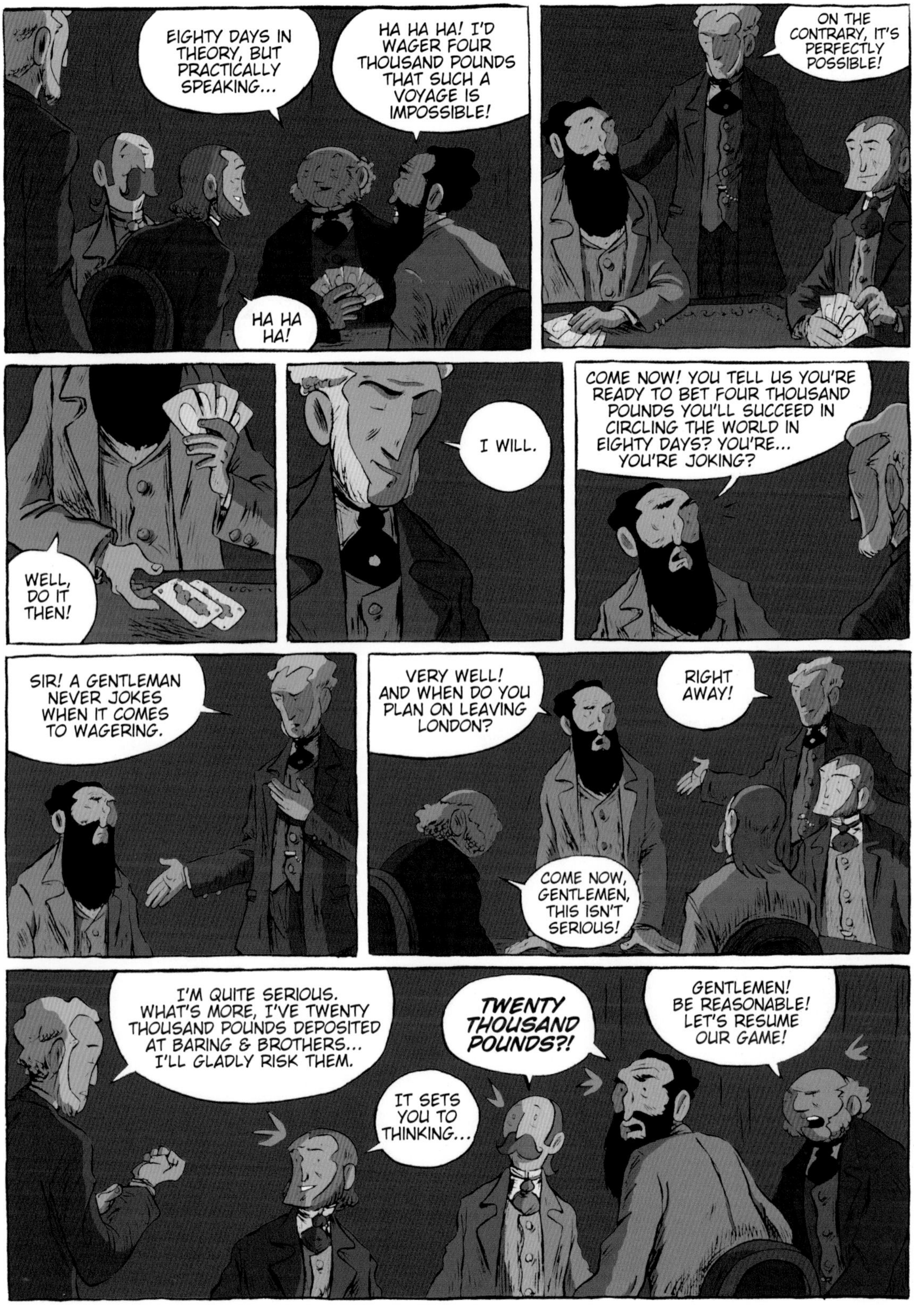
EIGHTY DAYS IN THEORY, BUT PRACTICALLY SPEAKING...
HA HA HA! I'D WAGER FOUR THOUSAND POUNDS THAT SUCH A VOYAGE IS IMPOSSIBLE!
HA HA HA!
ON THE CONTRARY, IT'S PERFECTLY POSSIBLE!
WELL, DO IT THEN!
I WILL.
COME NOW! YOU TELL US YOU'RE READY TO BET FOUR THOUSAND POUNDS YOU'LL SUCCEED IN CIRCLING THE WORLD IN EIGHTY DAYS? YOU'RE... YOU'RE JOKING?
SIR! A GENTLEMAN NEVER JOKES WHEN IT COMES TO WAGERING.
VERY WELL! AND WHEN DO YOU PLAN ON LEAVING LONDON?
RIGHT AWAY!
COME NOW, GENTLEMEN, THIS ISN'T SERIOUS!
I'M QUITE SERIOUS. WHAT'S MORE, I'VE TWENTY THOUSAND POUNDS DEPOSITED AT BARING & BROTHERS... I'LL GLADLY RISK THEM.
IT SETS YOU TO THINKING...
TWENTY THOUSAND POUNDS?!
GENTLEMEN! BE REASONABLE! LET'S RESUME OUR GAME!

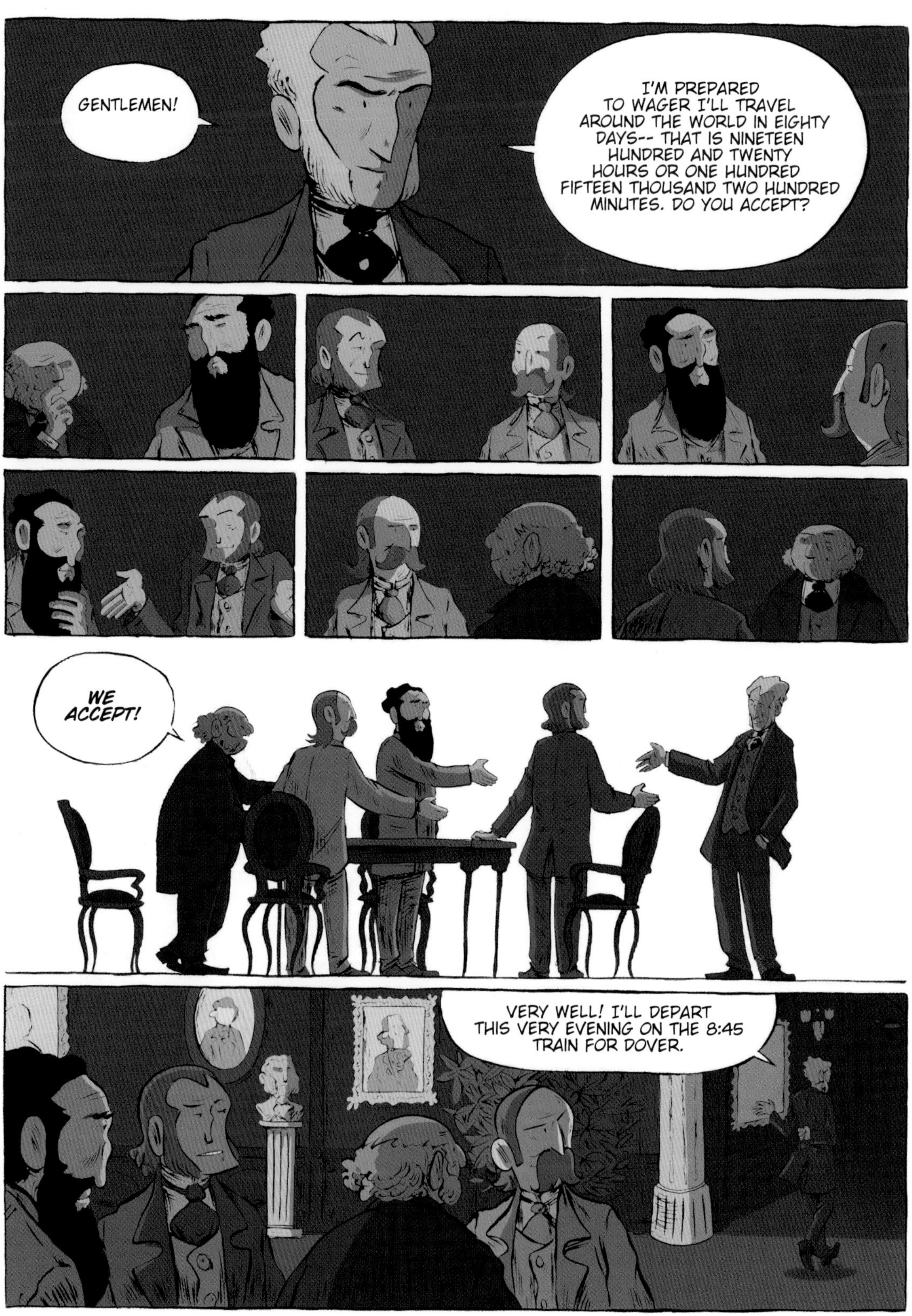
GENTLEMEN!
I'M PREPARED TO WAGER I'LL TRAVEL AROUND THE WORLD IN EIGHTY DAYS-- THAT IS NINETEEN HUNDRED AND TWENTY HOURS OR ONE HUNDRED FIFTEEN THOUSAND TWO HUNDRED MINUTES. DO YOU ACCEPT?
WE ACCEPT!
VERY WELL! I'LL DEPART THIS VERY EVENING ON THE 8:45 TRAIN FOR DOVER.

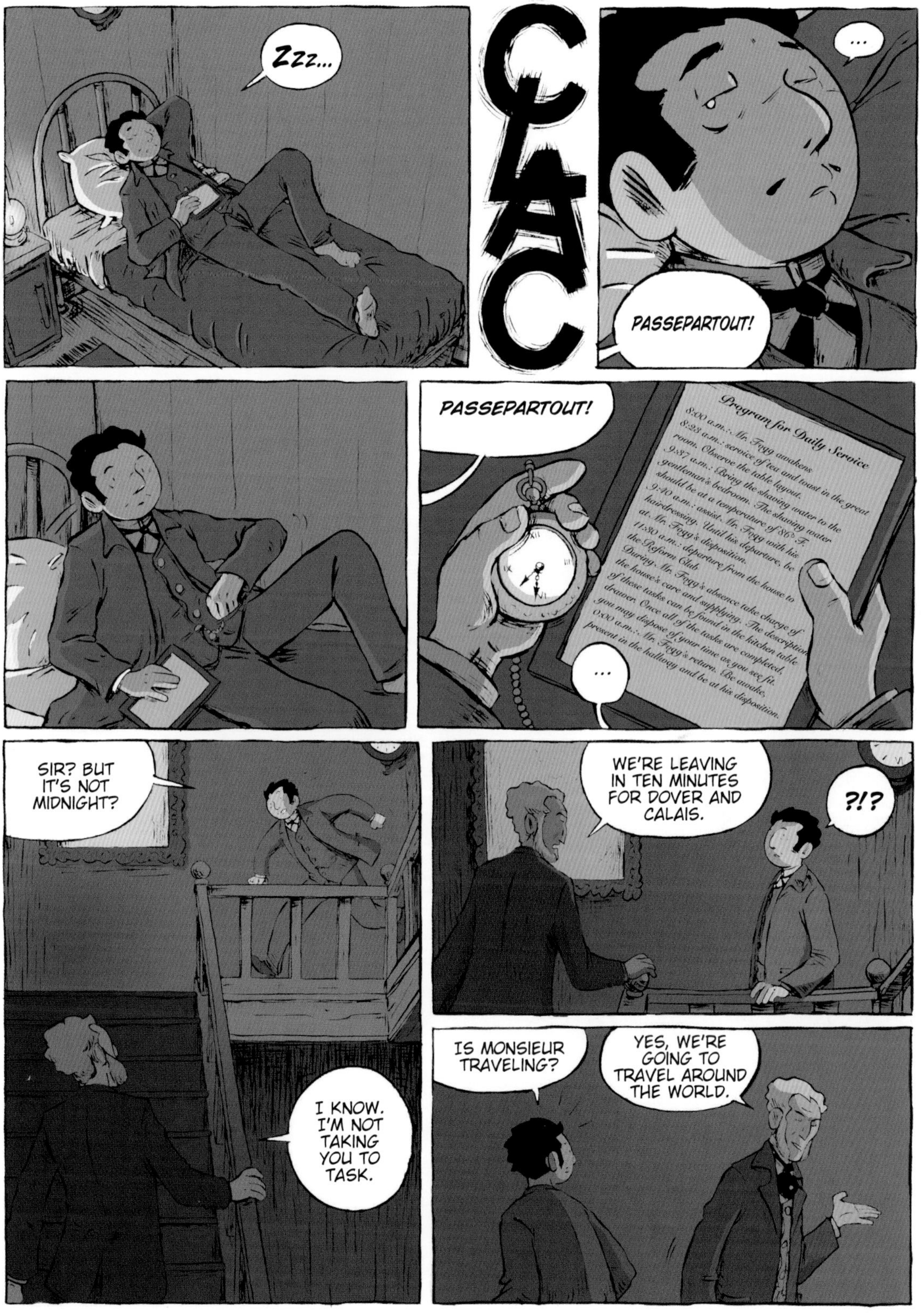
Zzz...
CLAC
...
PASSEPARTOUT!
PASSEPARTOUT!
Program for Daily Service
8:00 a.m.: Mr. Fogg awakens
8:23 a.m.: service of tea and toast in the great room. Observe the table layout.
9:37 a.m.: Bring the shaving water to the gentleman's bedroom. The shaving water should be at a temperature of 86° F.
9:40 a.m.: assist Mr. Fogg with his hairdressing. Until his departure, be at Mr. Fogg's disposition.
11:30 a.m.: departure from the house to the Reform Club
During Mr. Fogg's absence take charge of the house's care and supplying. The description of these tasks can be found in the kitchen table drawer. Once all of the tasks are completed, you may dispose of your time as you see fit.
0:00 a.m.: Mr. Fogg's return. Be awake, present in the hallway and be at his disposition.
...
SIR? BUT IT'S NOT MIDNIGHT?
I KNOW. I'M NOT TAKING YOU TO TASK.
WE'RE LEAVING IN TEN MINUTES FOR DOVER AND CALAIS.
?!?
IS MONSIEUR TRAVELING?
YES, WE'RE GOING TO TRAVEL AROUND THE WORLD.

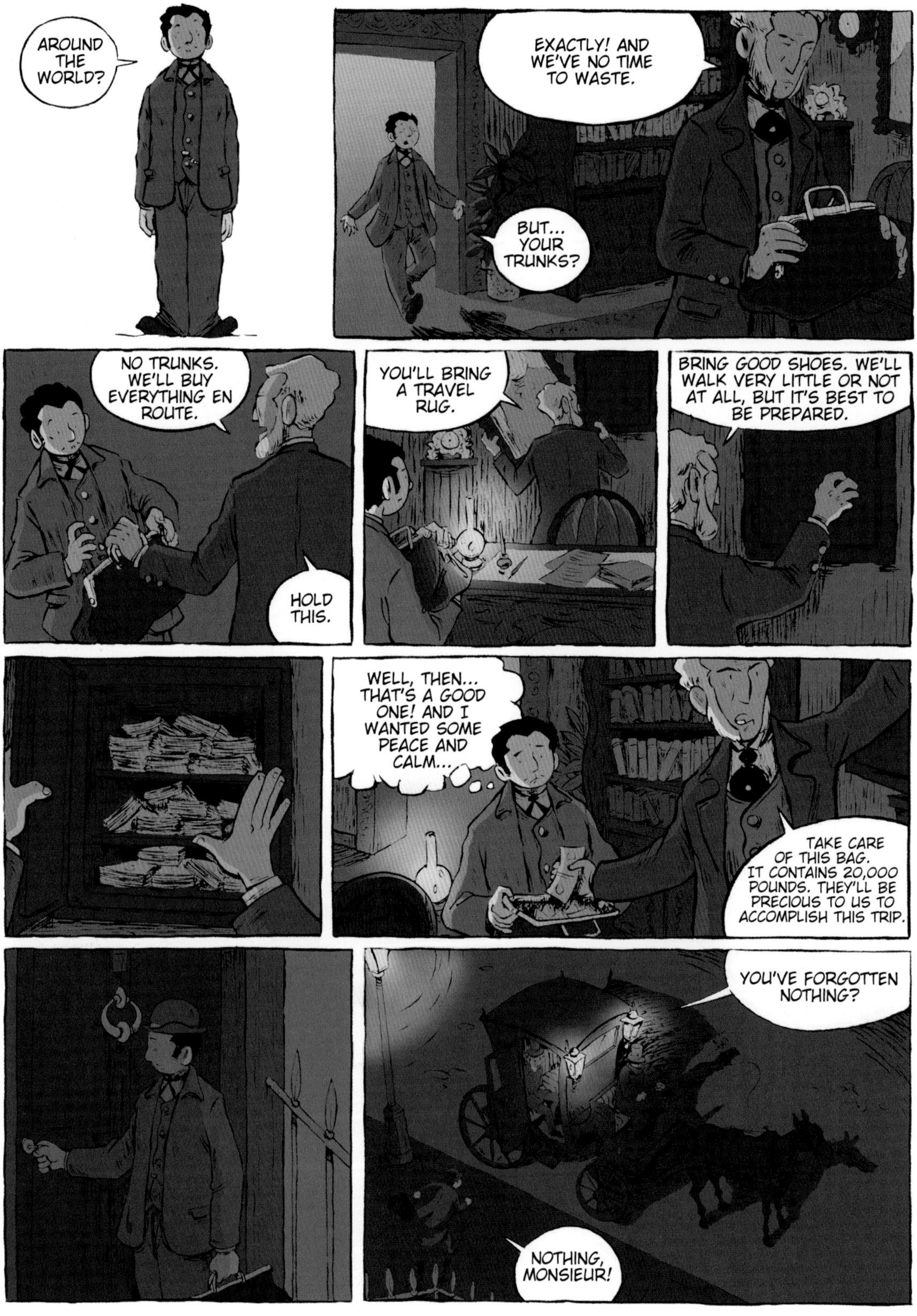
AROUND THE WORLD?
EXACTLY! AND WE'VE NO TIME TO WASTE.
BUT... YOUR TRUNKS?
NO TRUNKS. WE'LL BUY EVERYTHING EN ROUTE.
HOLD THIS.
YOU'LL BRING A TRAVEL RUG.
BRING GOOD SHOES. WE'LL WALK VERY LITTLE OR NOT AT ALL, BUT IT'S BEST TO BE PREPARED.
WELL, THEN... THAT'S A GOOD ONE! AND I WANTED SOME PEACE AND CALM...
TAKE CARE OF THIS BAG. IT CONTAINS 20,000 POUNDS. THEY'LL BE PRECIOUS TO US TO ACCOMPLISH THIS TRIP.
YOU'VE FORGOTTEN NOTHING?
NOTHING, MONSIEUR!

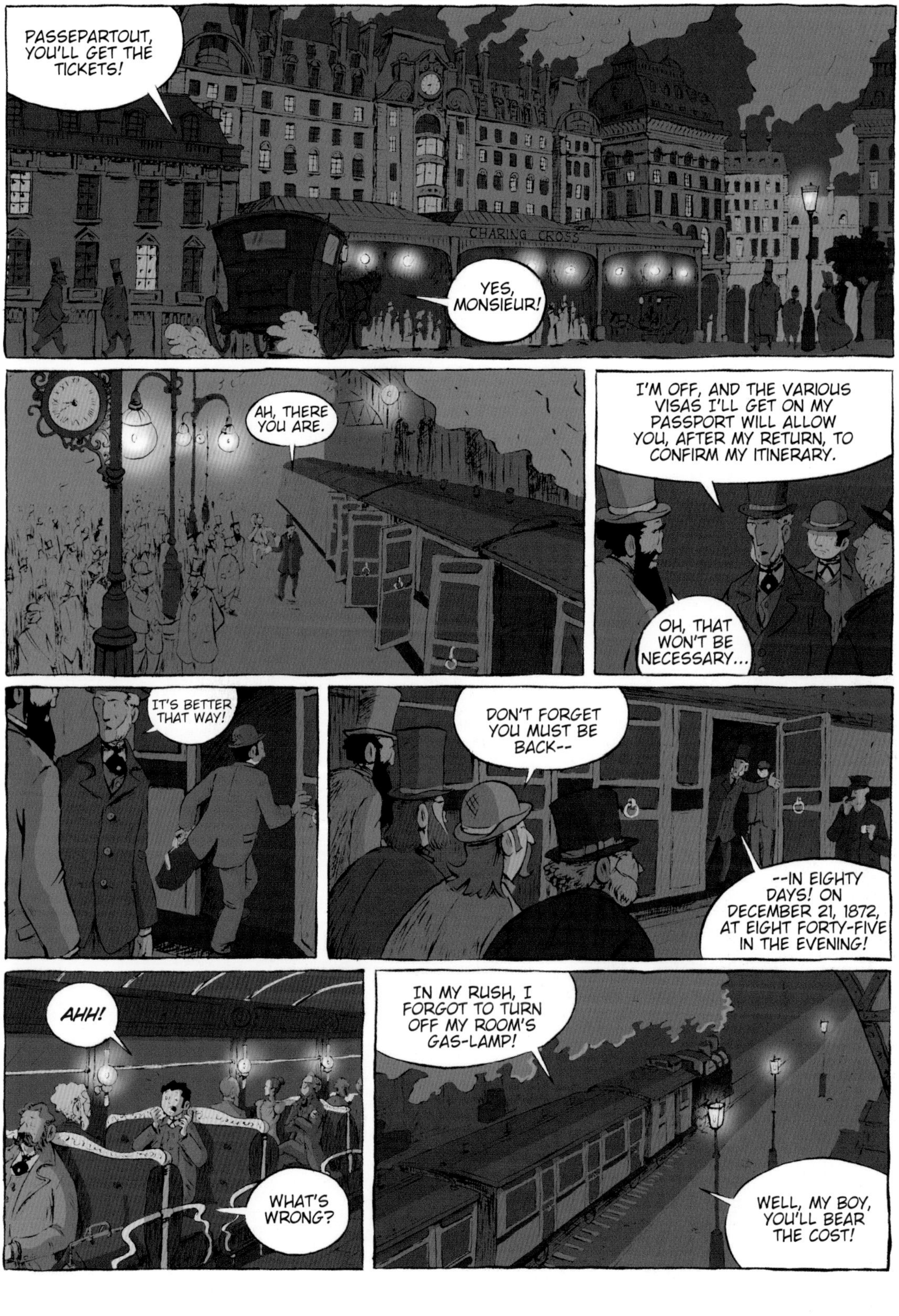
PASSEPARTOUT, YOU'LL GET THE TICKETS!
CHARING CROSS
YES, MONSIEUR!
AH, THERE YOU ARE.
I'M OFF, AND THE VARIOUS VISAS I'LL GET ON MY PASSPORT WILL ALLOW YOU, AFTER MY RETURN, TO CONFIRM MY ITINERARY.
OH, THAT WON'T BE NECESSARY...
IT'S BETTER THAT WAY!
DON'T FORGET YOU MUST BE BACK--
--IN EIGHTY DAYS! ON DECEMBER 21, 1872, AT EIGHT FORTY-FIVE IN THE EVENING!
AHH!
WHAT'S WRONG?
IN MY RUSH, I FORGOT TO TURN OFF MY ROOM'S GAS-LAMP!
WELL, MY BOY, YOU'LL BEAR THE COST!

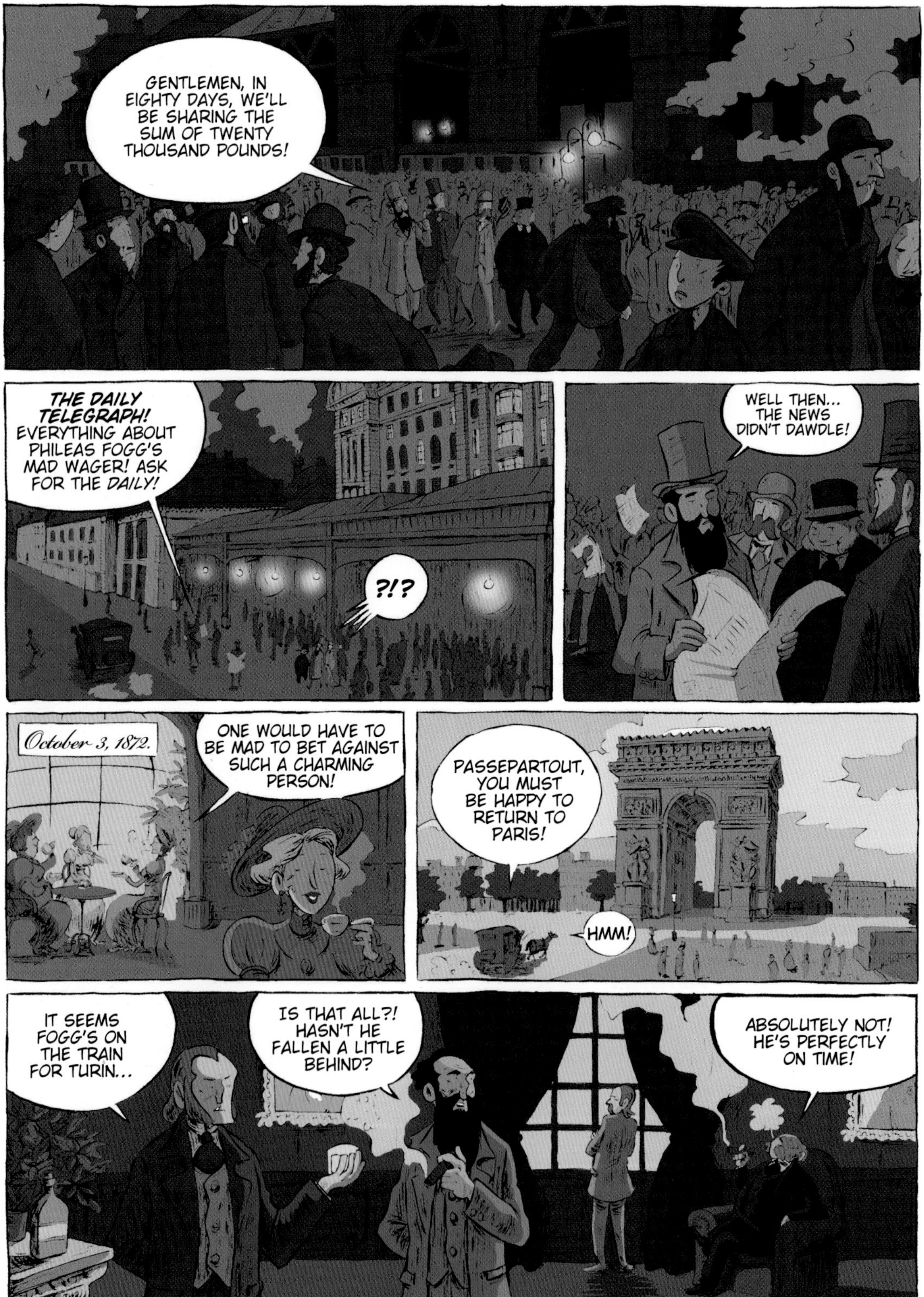
GENTLEMEN, IN EIGHTY DAYS, WE'LL BE SHARING THE SUM OF TWENTY THOUSAND POUNDS!
THE DAILY TELEGRAPH! EVERYTHING ABOUT PHILEAS FOGG'S MAD WAGER! ASK FOR THE DAILY!
?!?
WELL THEN... THE NEWS DIDN'T DAWDLE!
October 3, 1872.
ONE WOULD HAVE TO BE MAD TO BET AGAINST SUCH A CHARMING PERSON!
PASSEPARTOUT, YOU MUST BE HAPPY TO RETURN TO PARIS!
HMM!
IT SEEMS FOGG'S ON THE TRAIN FOR TURIN...
IS THAT ALL?! HASN'T HE FALLEN A LITTLE BEHIND?
ABSOLUTELY NOT! HE'S PERFECTLY ON TIME!

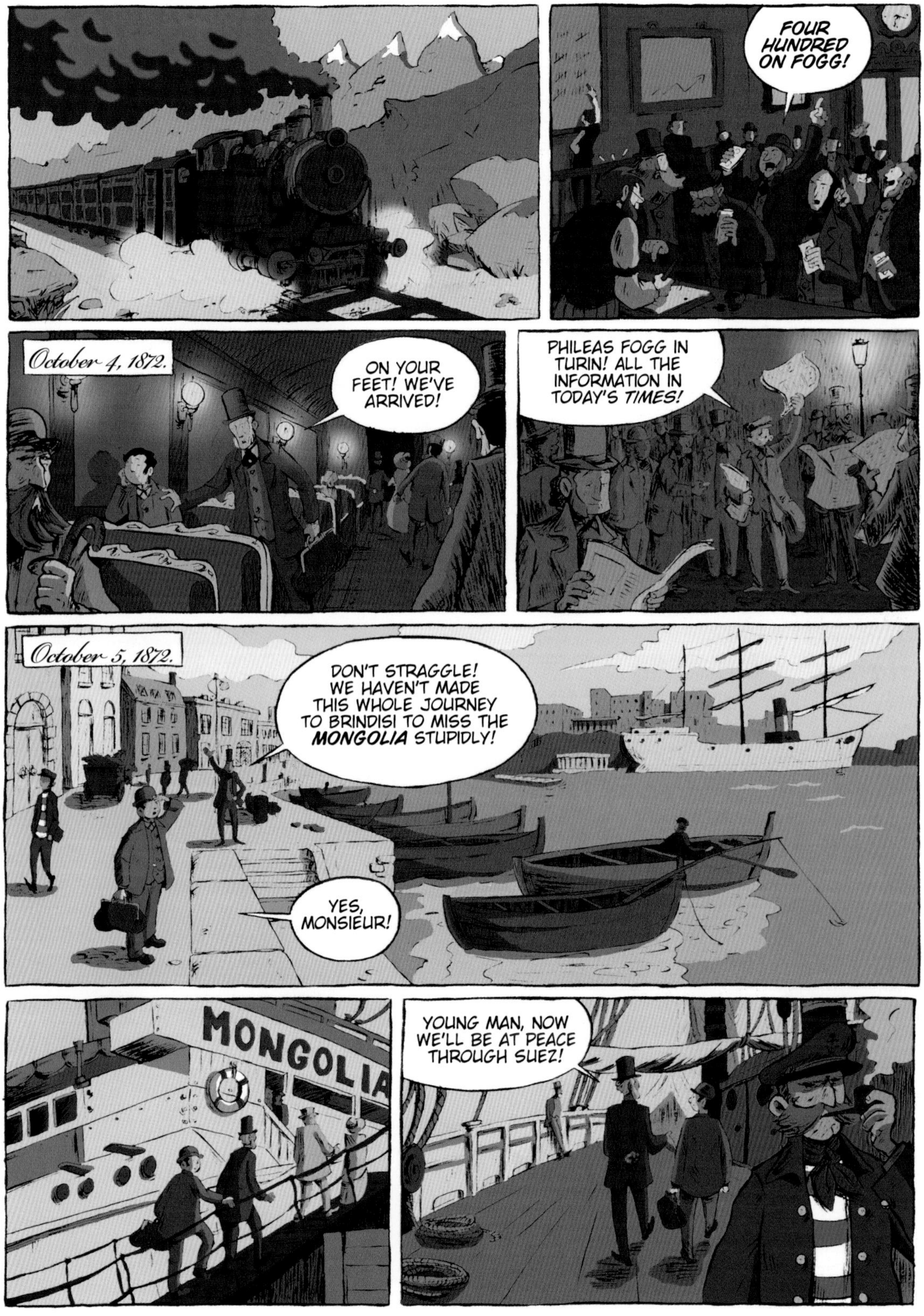

FOUR HUNDRED ON FOGG!
October 4, 1872.
ON YOUR FEET! WE'VE ARRIVED!
PHILEAS FOGG IN TURIN! ALL THE INFORMATION IN TODAY'S *TIMES*!
October 5, 1872.
DON'T STRAGGLE! WE HAVEN'T MADE THIS WHOLE JOURNEY TO BRINDISI TO MISS THE ***MONGOLIA*** STUPIDLY!
YES, MONSIEUR!
MONGOLIA
YOUNG MAN, NOW WE'LL BE AT PEACE THROUGH SUEZ!

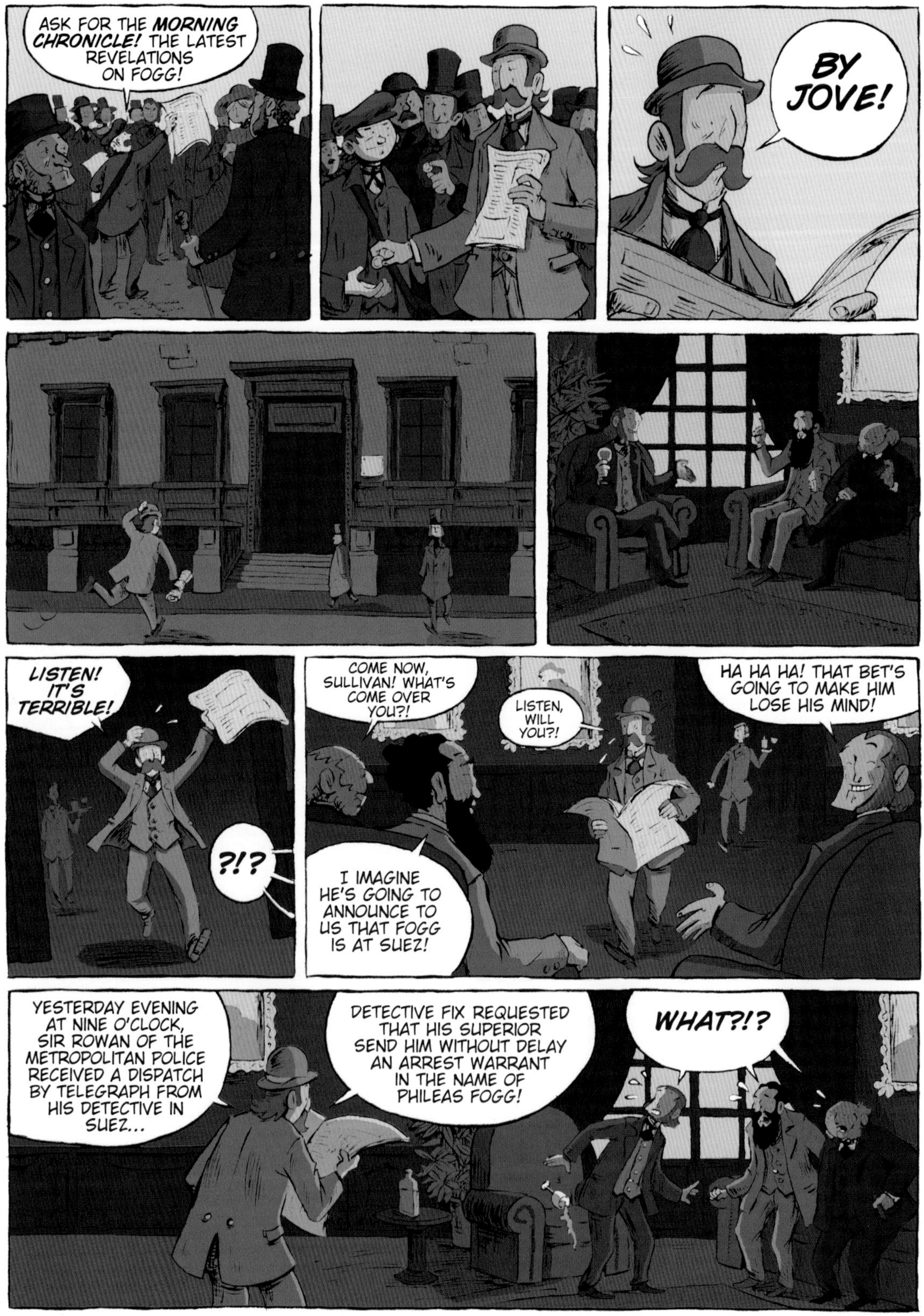
ASK FOR THE MORNING CHRONICLE! THE LATEST REVELATIONS ON FOGG!
BY JOVE!
LISTEN! IT'S TERRIBLE!
?!?
COME NOW, SULLIVAN! WHAT'S COME OVER YOU?!
LISTEN, WILL YOU?!
HA HA HA! THAT BET'S GOING TO MAKE HIM LOSE HIS MIND!
I IMAGINE HE'S GOING TO ANNOUNCE TO US THAT FOGG IS AT SUEZ!
YESTERDAY EVENING AT NINE O'CLOCK, SIR ROWAN OF THE METROPOLITAN POLICE RECEIVED A DISPATCH BY TELEGRAPH FROM HIS DETECTIVE IN SUEZ...
DETECTIVE FIX REQUESTED THAT HIS SUPERIOR SEND HIM WITHOUT DELAY AN ARREST WARRANT IN THE NAME OF PHILEAS FOGG!
WHAT?!?

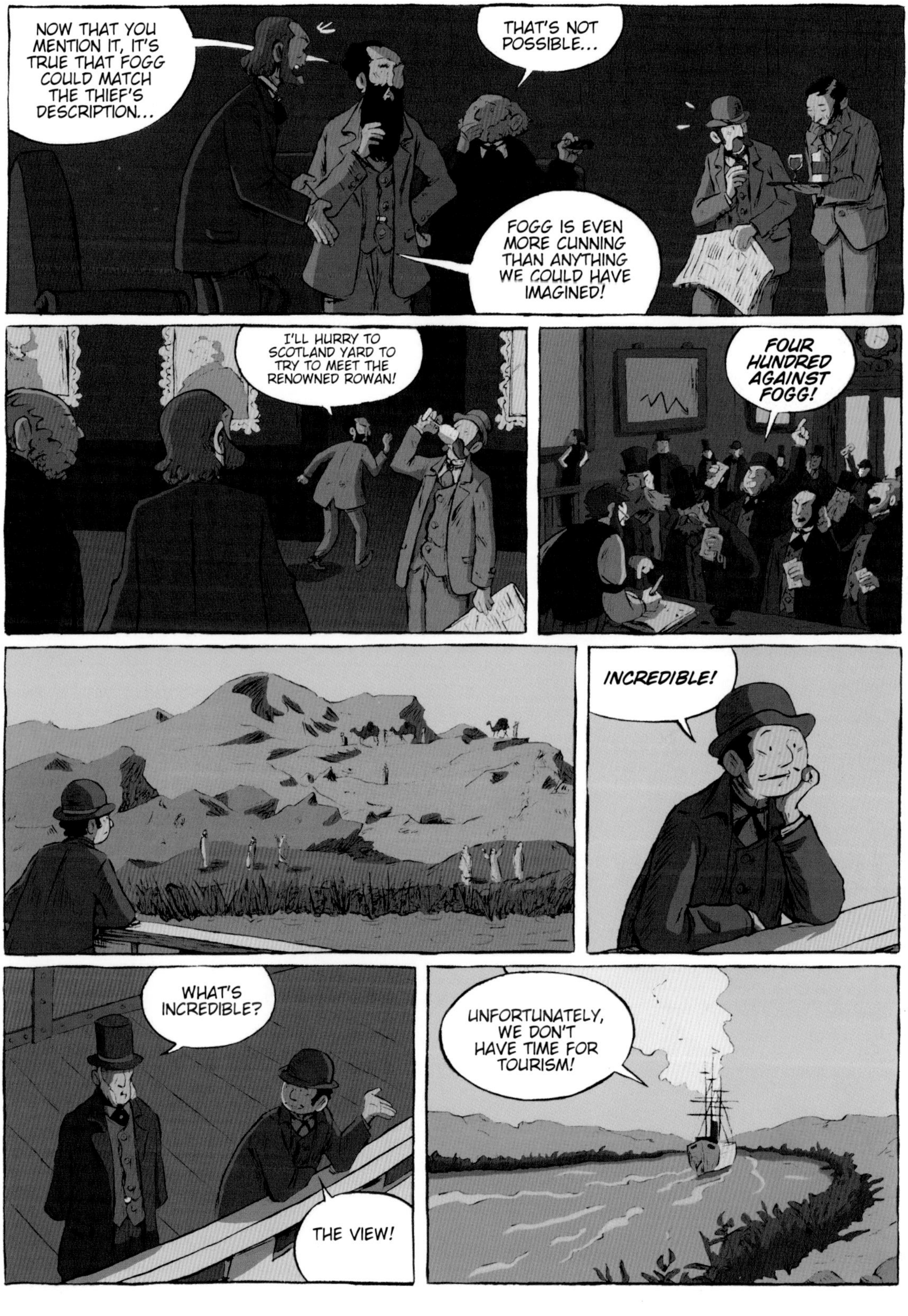
NOW THAT YOU MENTION IT, IT'S TRUE THAT FOGG COULD MATCH THE THIEF'S DESCRIPTION...
THAT'S NOT POSSIBLE...
FOGG IS EVEN MORE CUNNING THAN ANYTHING WE COULD HAVE IMAGINED!
I'LL HURRY TO SCOTLAND YARD TO TRY TO MEET THE RENOWNED ROWAN!
FOUR HUNDRED AGAINST FOGG!
INCREDIBLE!
WHAT'S INCREDIBLE?
THE VIEW!
UNFORTUNATELY, WE DON'T HAVE TIME FOR TOURISM!

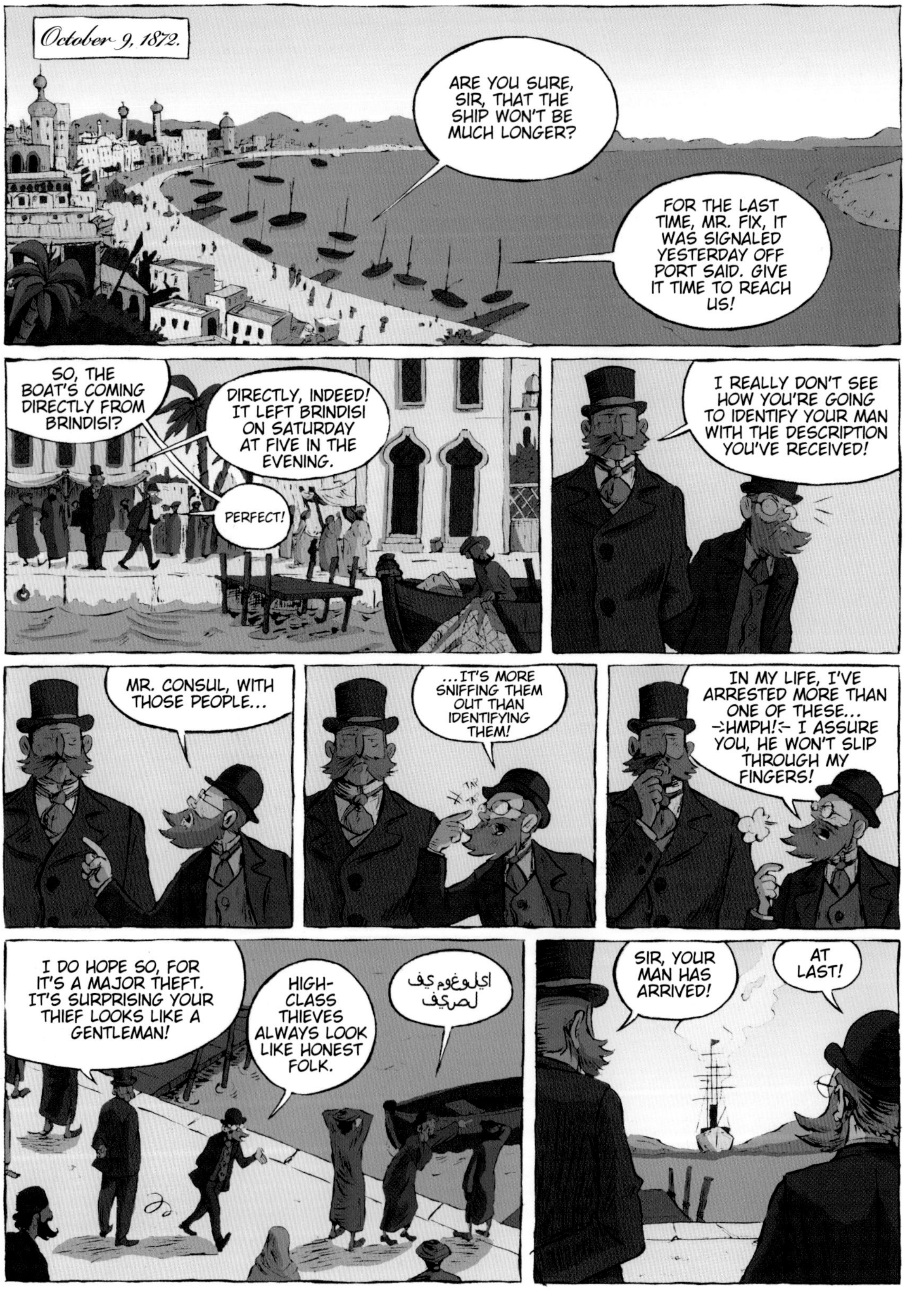
October 9, 1872.
ARE YOU SURE, SIR, THAT THE SHIP WON'T BE MUCH LONGER?
FOR THE LAST TIME, MR. FIX, IT WAS SIGNALED YESTERDAY OFF PORT SAID. GIVE IT TIME TO REACH US!
SO, THE BOAT'S COMING DIRECTLY FROM BRINDISI?
DIRECTLY, INDEED! IT LEFT BRINDISI ON SATURDAY AT FIVE IN THE EVENING.
PERFECT!
I REALLY DON'T SEE HOW YOU'RE GOING TO IDENTIFY YOUR MAN WITH THE DESCRIPTION YOU'VE RECEIVED!
MR. CONSUL, WITH THOSE PEOPLE...
...IT'S MORE SNIFFING THEM OUT THAN IDENTIFYING THEM!
IN MY LIFE, I'VE ARRESTED MORE THAN ONE OF THESE... -HMPH!- I ASSURE YOU, HE WON'T SLIP THROUGH MY FINGERS!
I DO HOPE SO, FOR IT'S A MAJOR THEFT. IT'S SURPRISING YOUR THIEF LOOKS LIKE A GENTLEMAN!
HIGH-CLASS THIEVES ALWAYS LOOK LIKE HONEST FOLK.
SIR, YOUR MAN HAS ARRIVED!
AT LAST!

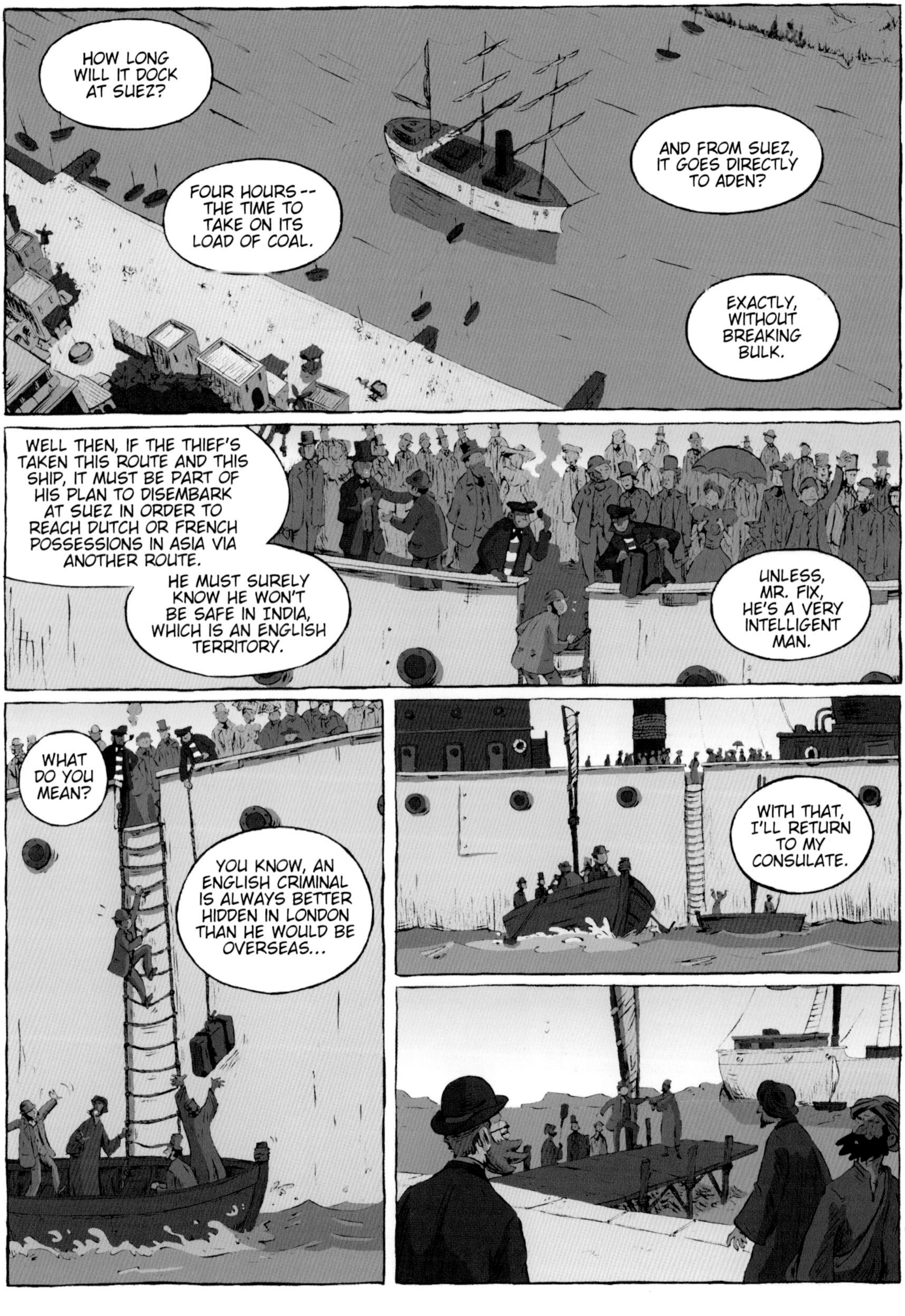

HOW LONG WILL IT DOCK AT SUEZ?
FOUR HOURS -- THE TIME TO TAKE ON ITS LOAD OF COAL.
AND FROM SUEZ, IT GOES DIRECTLY TO ADEN?
EXACTLY, WITHOUT BREAKING BULK.
WELL THEN, IF THE THIEF'S TAKEN THIS ROUTE AND THIS SHIP, IT MUST BE PART OF HIS PLAN TO DISEMBARK AT SUEZ IN ORDER TO REACH DUTCH OR FRENCH POSSESSIONS IN ASIA VIA ANOTHER ROUTE.
HE MUST SURELY KNOW HE WON'T BE SAFE IN INDIA, WHICH IS AN ENGLISH TERRITORY.
UNLESS, MR. FIX, HE'S A VERY INTELLIGENT MAN.
WHAT DO YOU MEAN?
YOU KNOW, AN ENGLISH CRIMINAL IS ALWAYS BETTER HIDDEN IN LONDON THAN HE WOULD BE OVERSEAS...
WITH THAT, I'LL RETURN TO MY CONSULATE.

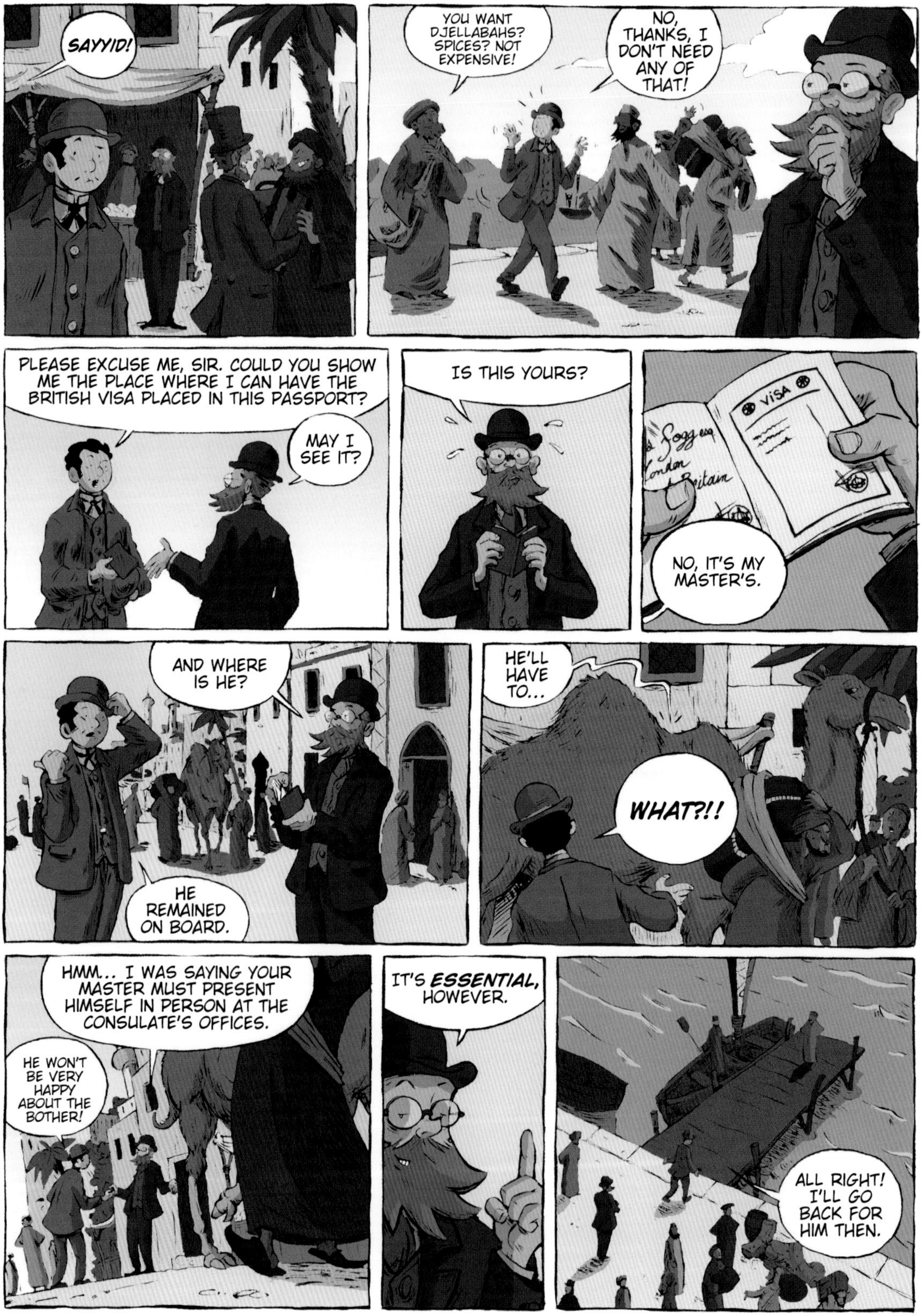
SAYYID!
YOU WANT DJELLABAHS? SPICES? NOT EXPENSIVE!
NO, THANKS, I DON'T NEED ANY OF THAT!
PLEASE EXCUSE ME, SIR. COULD YOU SHOW ME THE PLACE WHERE I CAN HAVE THE BRITISH VISA PLACED IN THIS PASSPORT?
MAY I SEE IT?
IS THIS YOURS?
VISA
NO, IT'S MY MASTER'S.
AND WHERE IS HE?
HE REMAINED ON BOARD.
HE'LL HAVE TO...
WHAT?!!
HMM... I WAS SAYING YOUR MASTER MUST PRESENT HIMSELF IN PERSON AT THE CONSULATE'S OFFICES.
HE WON'T BE VERY HAPPY ABOUT THE BOTHER!
IT'S ESSENTIAL, HOWEVER.
ALL RIGHT! I'LL GO BACK FOR HIM THEN.

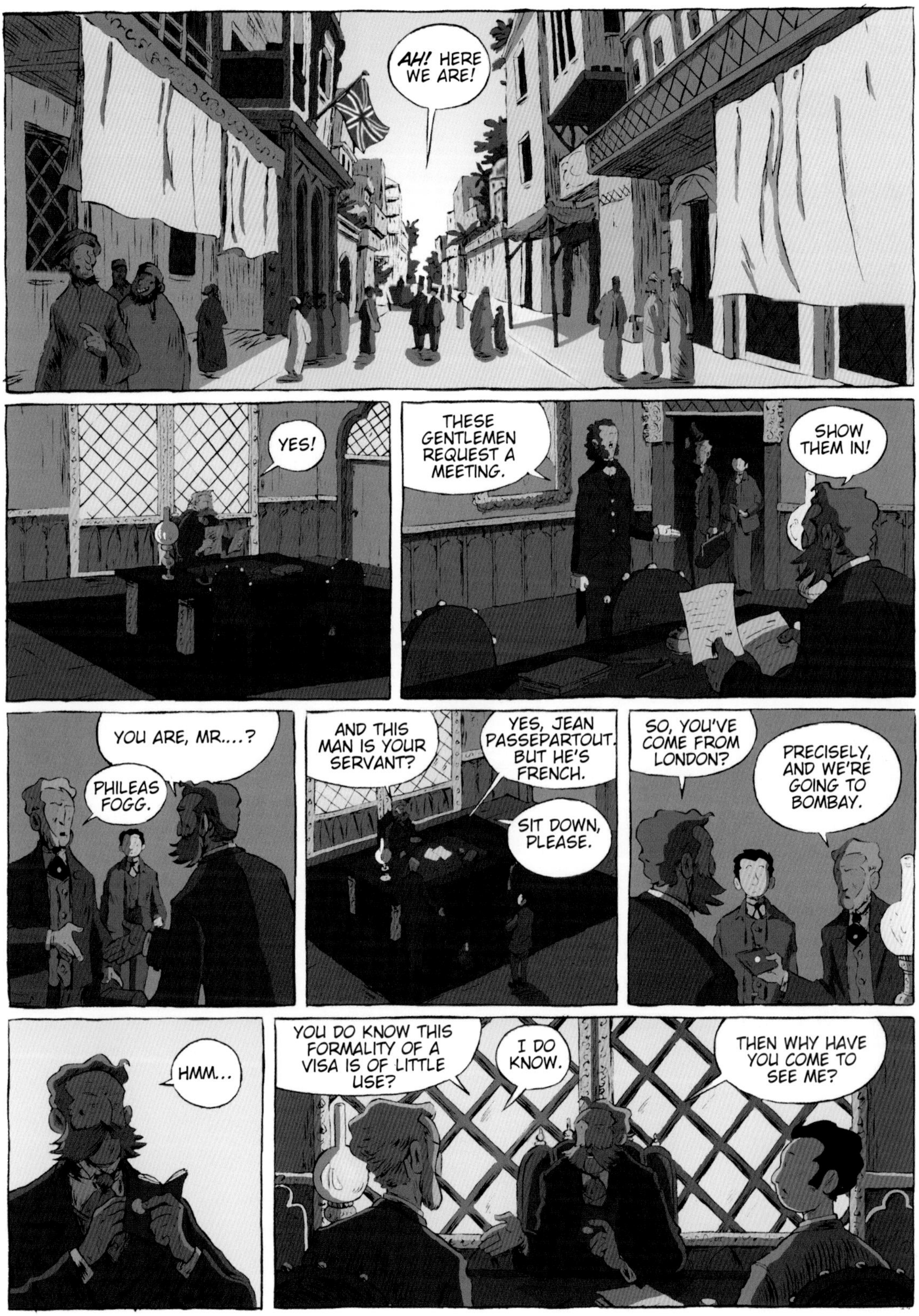
AH! HERE WE ARE!
YES!
THESE GENTLEMEN REQUEST A MEETING.
SHOW THEM IN!
YOU ARE, MR....?
PHILEAS FOGG.
AND THIS MAN IS YOUR SERVANT?
YES, JEAN PASSEPARTOUT. BUT HE'S FRENCH.
SIT DOWN, PLEASE.
SO, YOU'VE COME FROM LONDON?
PRECISELY, AND WE'RE GOING TO BOMBAY.
HMM...
YOU DO KNOW THIS FORMALITY OF A VISA IS OF LITTLE USE?
I DO KNOW.
THEN WHY HAVE YOU COME TO SEE ME?

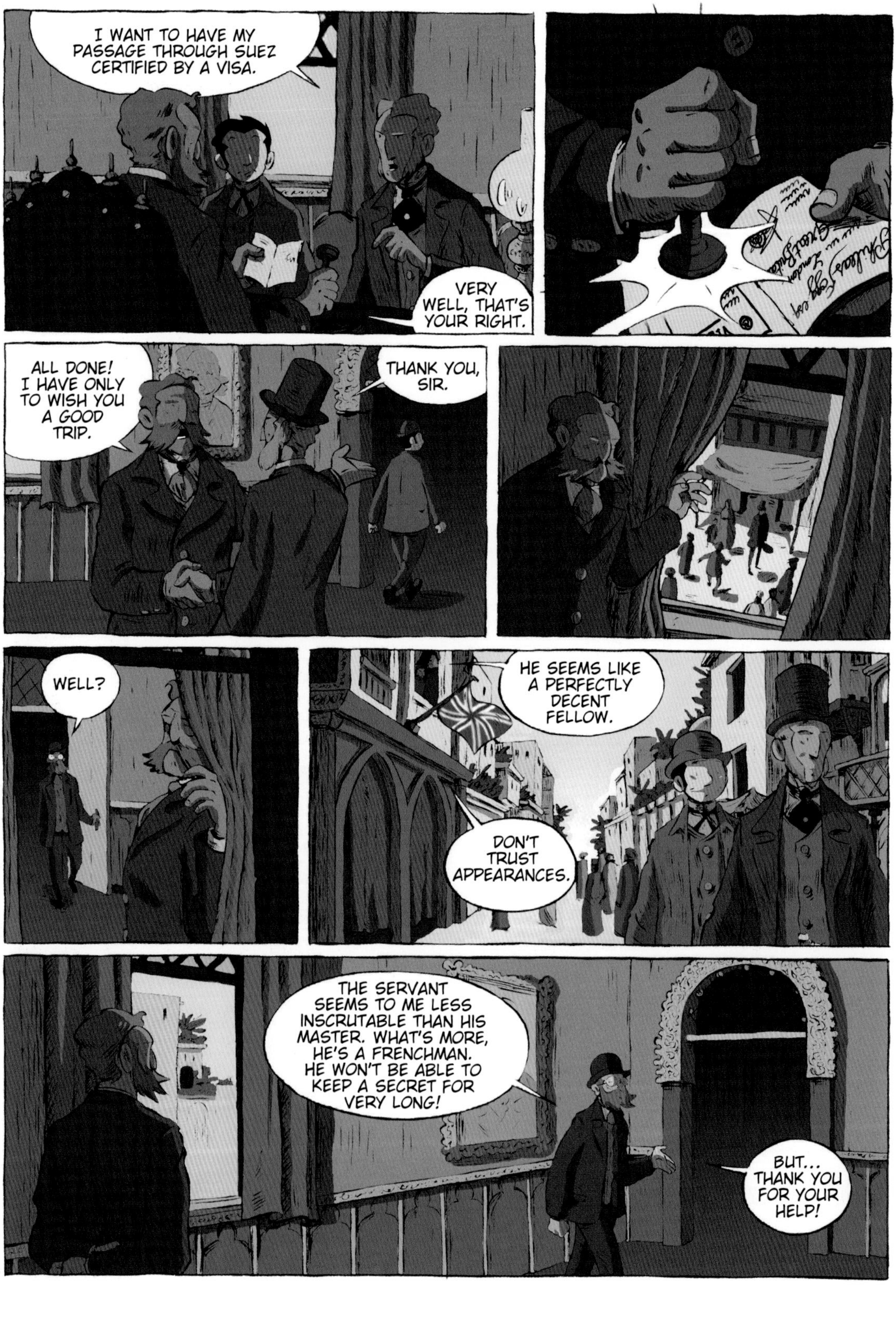
I WANT TO HAVE MY PASSAGE THROUGH SUEZ CERTIFIED BY A VISA.
VERY WELL, THAT'S YOUR RIGHT.
ALL DONE! I HAVE ONLY TO WISH YOU A GOOD TRIP.
THANK YOU, SIR.
WELL?
HE SEEMS LIKE A PERFECTLY DECENT FELLOW.
DON'T TRUST APPEARANCES.
THE SERVANT SEEMS TO ME LESS INSCRUTABLE THAN HIS MASTER. WHAT'S MORE, HE'S A FRENCHMAN. HE WON'T BE ABLE TO KEEP A SECRET FOR VERY LONG!
BUT... THANK YOU FOR YOUR HELP!

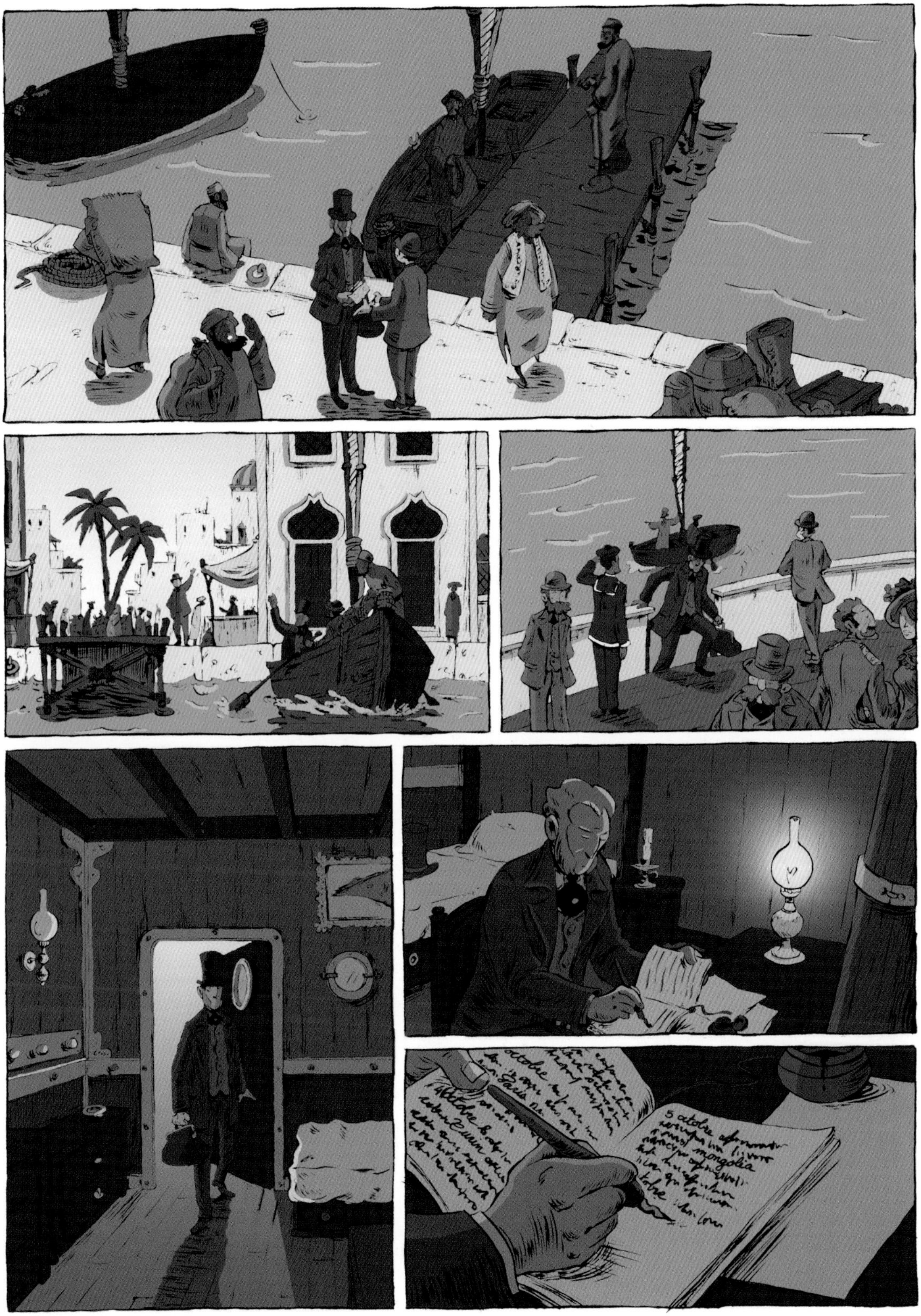
5 octobre

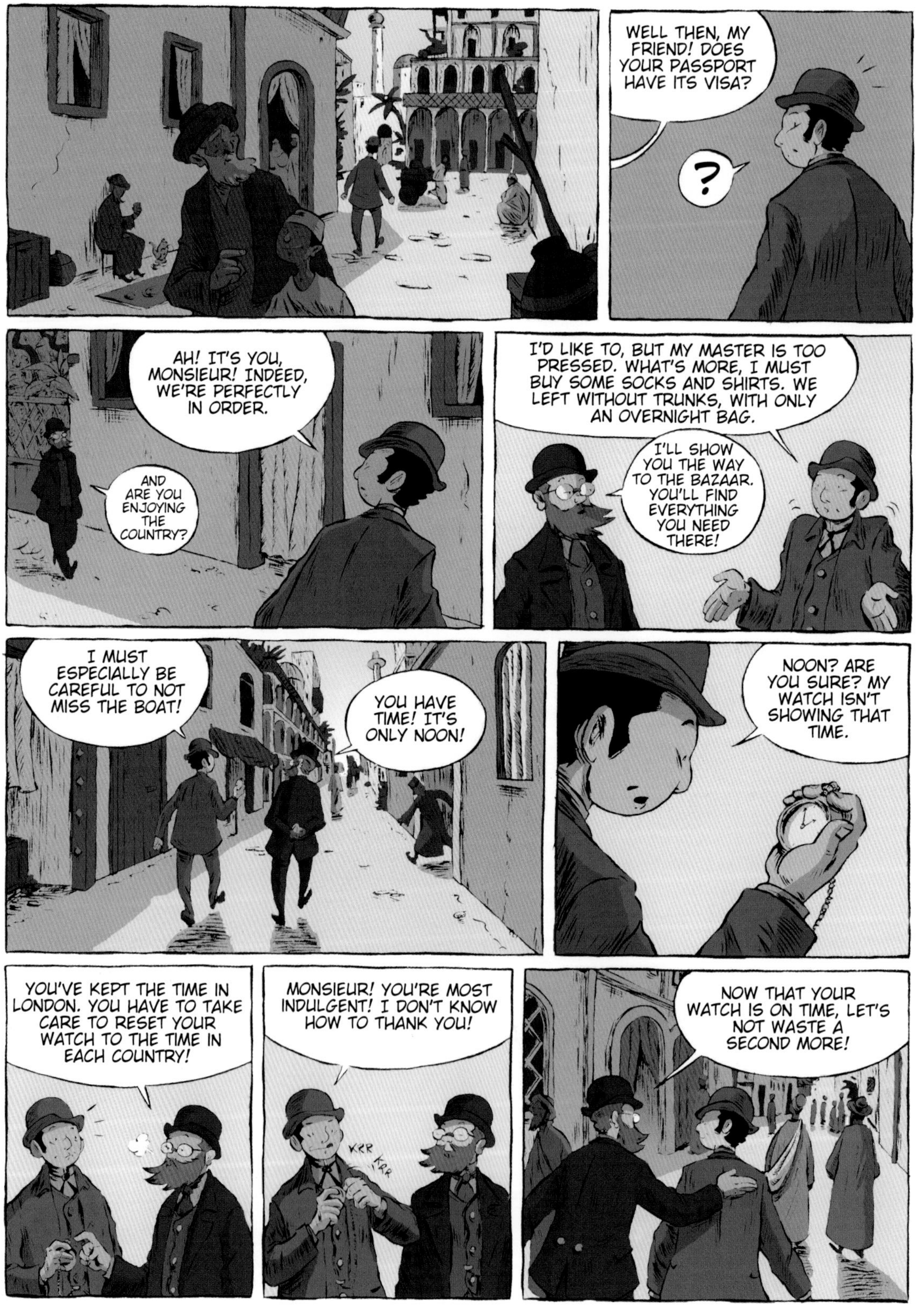
WELL THEN, MY FRIEND! DOES YOUR PASSPORT HAVE ITS VISA?
?
AH! IT'S YOU, MONSIEUR! INDEED, WE'RE PERFECTLY IN ORDER.
AND ARE YOU ENJOYING THE COUNTRY?
I'D LIKE TO, BUT MY MASTER IS TOO PRESSED. WHAT'S MORE, I MUST BUY SOME SOCKS AND SHIRTS. WE LEFT WITHOUT TRUNKS, WITH ONLY AN OVERNIGHT BAG.
I'LL SHOW YOU THE WAY TO THE BAZAAR. YOU'LL FIND EVERYTHING YOU NEED THERE!
I MUST ESPECIALLY BE CAREFUL TO NOT MISS THE BOAT!
YOU HAVE TIME! IT'S ONLY NOON!
NOON? ARE YOU SURE? MY WATCH ISN'T SHOWING THAT TIME.
YOU'VE KEPT THE TIME IN LONDON. YOU HAVE TO TAKE CARE TO RESET YOUR WATCH TO THE TIME IN EACH COUNTRY!
MONSIEUR! YOU'RE MOST INDULGENT! I DON'T KNOW HOW TO THANK YOU!
KRR
KRR
NOW THAT YOUR WATCH IS ON TIME, LET'S NOT WASTE A SECOND MORE!

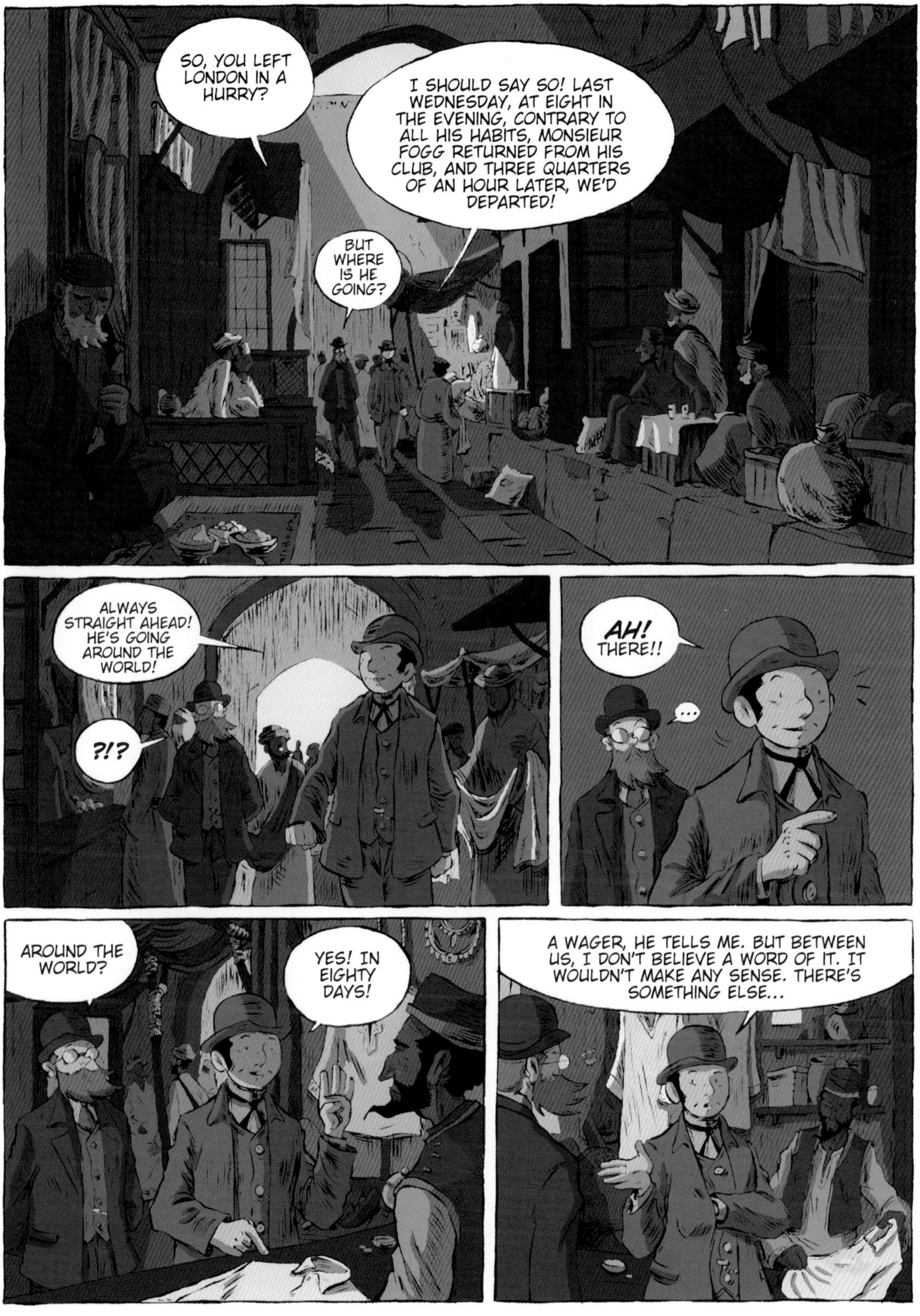
SO, YOU LEFT LONDON IN A HURRY?
I SHOULD SAY SO! LAST WEDNESDAY, AT EIGHT IN THE EVENING, CONTRARY TO ALL HIS HABITS, MONSIEUR FOGG RETURNED FROM HIS CLUB, AND THREE QUARTERS OF AN HOUR LATER, WE'D DEPARTED!
BUT WHERE IS HE GOING?
ALWAYS STRAIGHT AHEAD! HE'S GOING AROUND THE WORLD!
?!?
AH! THERE!!
...
AROUND THE WORLD?
YES! IN EIGHTY DAYS!
A WAGER, HE TELLS ME. BUT BETWEEN US, I DON'T BELIEVE A WORD OF IT. IT WOULDN'T MAKE ANY SENSE. THERE'S SOMETHING ELSE...

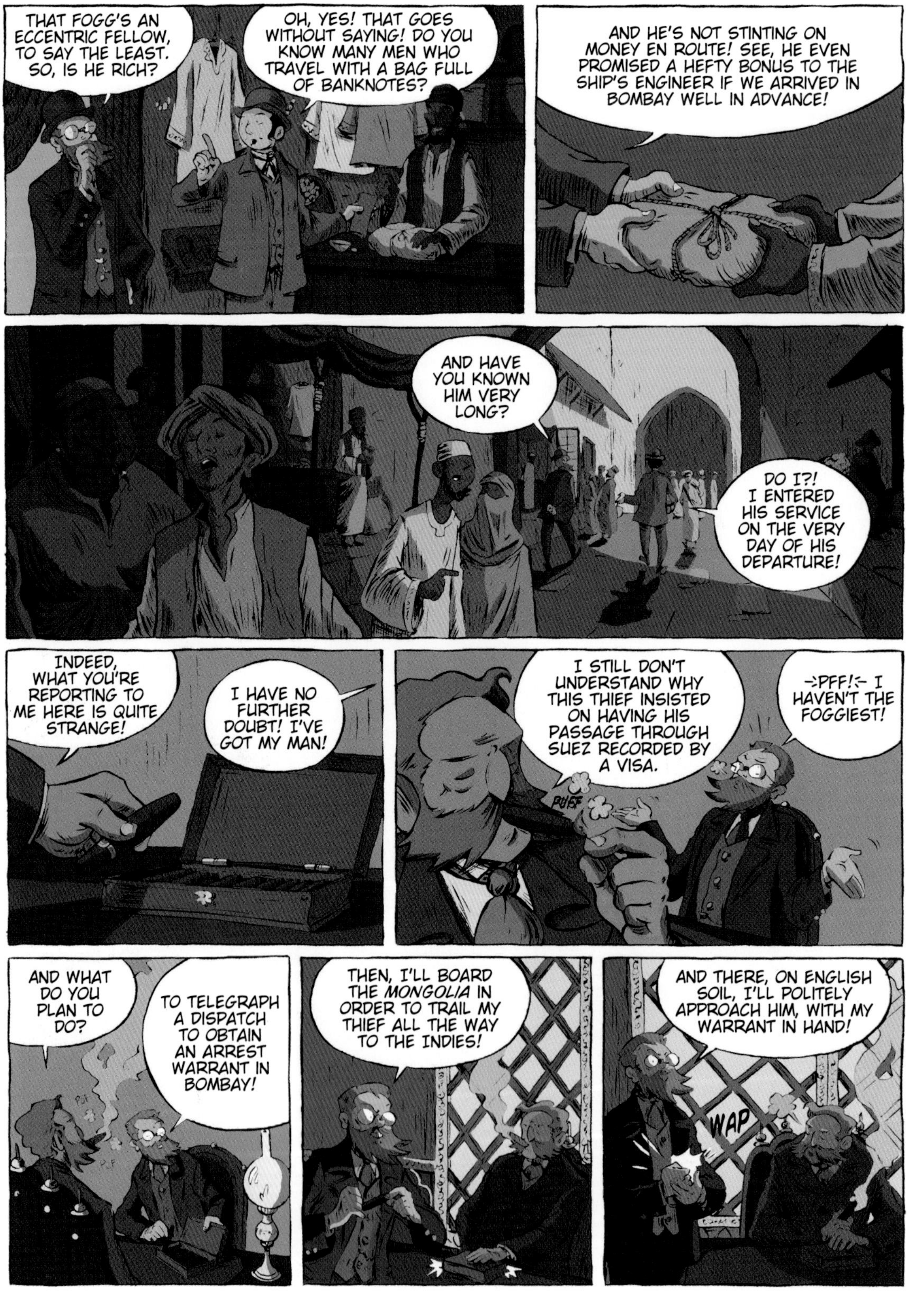
THAT FOGG'S AN ECCENTRIC FELLOW, TO SAY THE LEAST. SO, IS HE RICH?
OH, YES! THAT GOES WITHOUT SAYING! DO YOU KNOW MANY MEN WHO TRAVEL WITH A BAG FULL OF BANKNOTES?
AND HE'S NOT STINTING ON MONEY EN ROUTE! SEE, HE EVEN PROMISED A HEFTY BONUS TO THE SHIP'S ENGINEER IF WE ARRIVED IN BOMBAY WELL IN ADVANCE!
AND HAVE YOU KNOWN HIM VERY LONG?
DO I?! I ENTERED HIS SERVICE ON THE VERY DAY OF HIS DEPARTURE!
INDEED, WHAT YOU'RE REPORTING TO ME HERE IS QUITE STRANGE!
I HAVE NO FURTHER DOUBT! I'VE GOT MY MAN!
I STILL DON'T UNDERSTAND WHY THIS THIEF INSISTED ON HAVING HIS PASSAGE THROUGH SUEZ RECORDED BY A VISA.
→PFF!← I HAVEN'T THE FOGGIEST!
AND WHAT DO YOU PLAN TO DO?
TO TELEGRAPH A DISPATCH TO OBTAIN AN ARREST WARRANT IN BOMBAY!
THEN, I'LL BOARD THE *MONGOLIA* IN ORDER TO TRAIL MY THIEF ALL THE WAY TO THE INDIES!
AND THERE, ON ENGLISH SOIL, I'LL POLITELY APPROACH HIM, WITH MY WARRANT IN HAND!
WAP

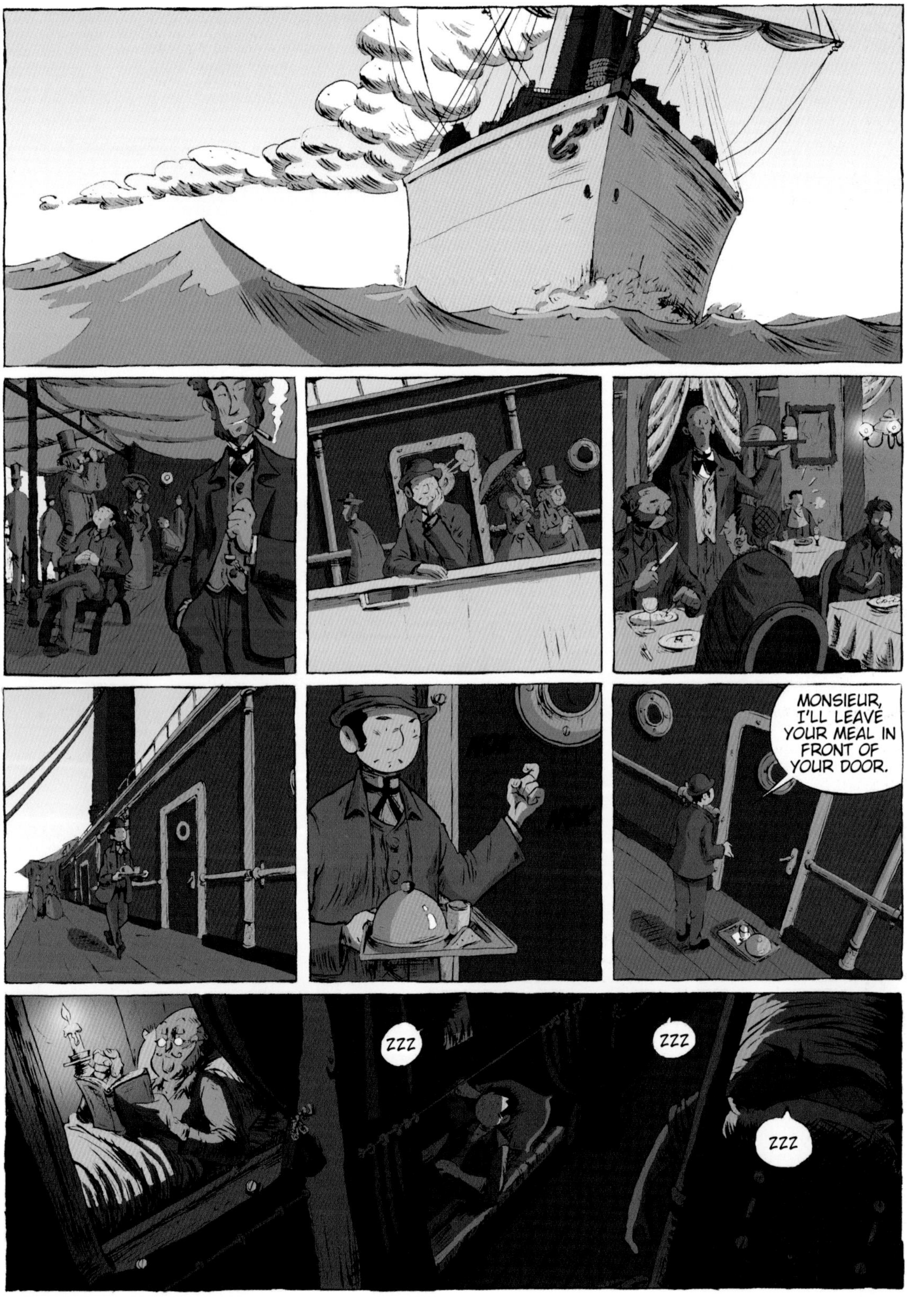
MONSIEUR, I'LL LEAVE YOUR MEAL IN FRONT OF YOUR DOOR.
ZZZ
ZZZ
ZZZ

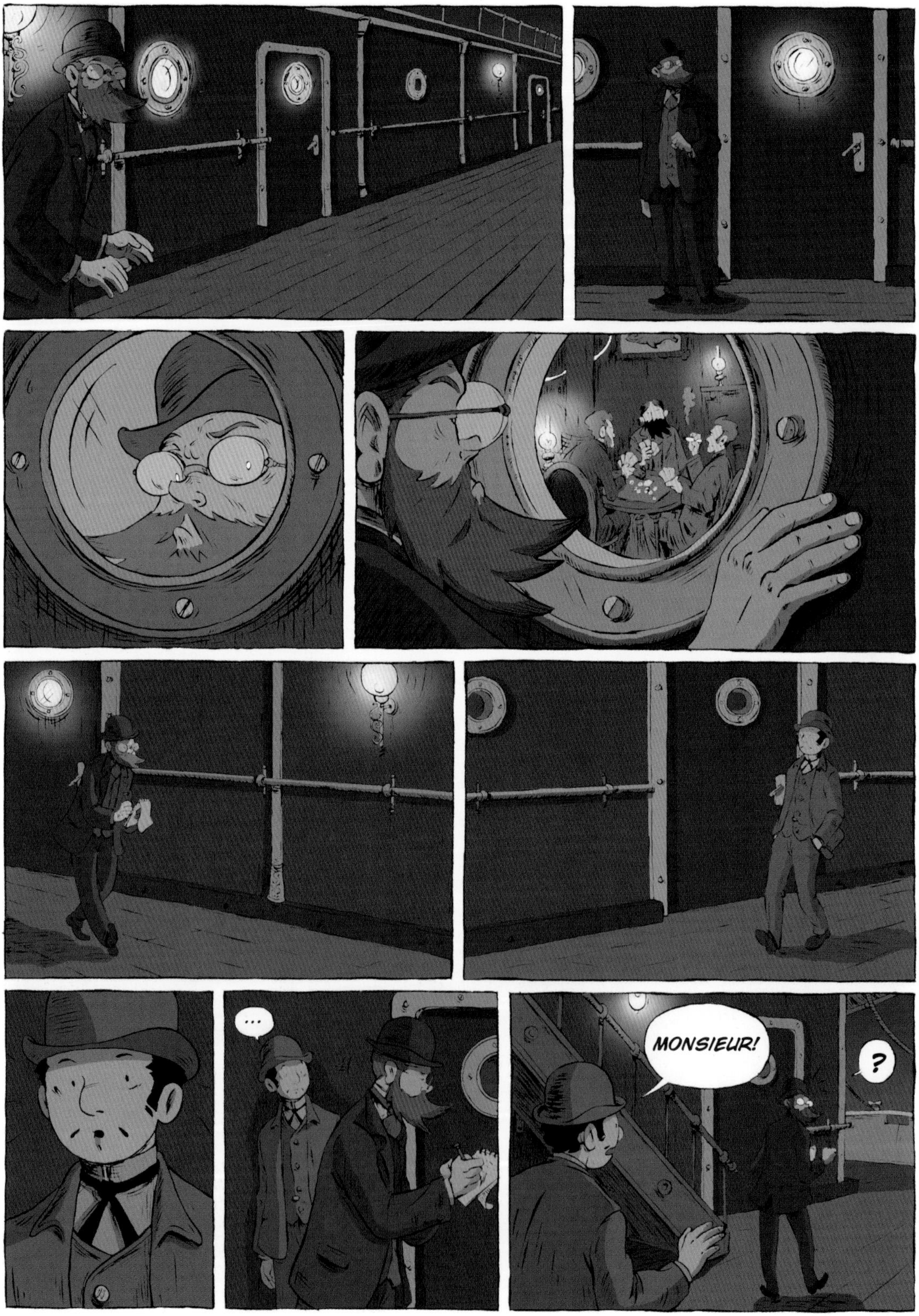
...
MONSIEUR!
?

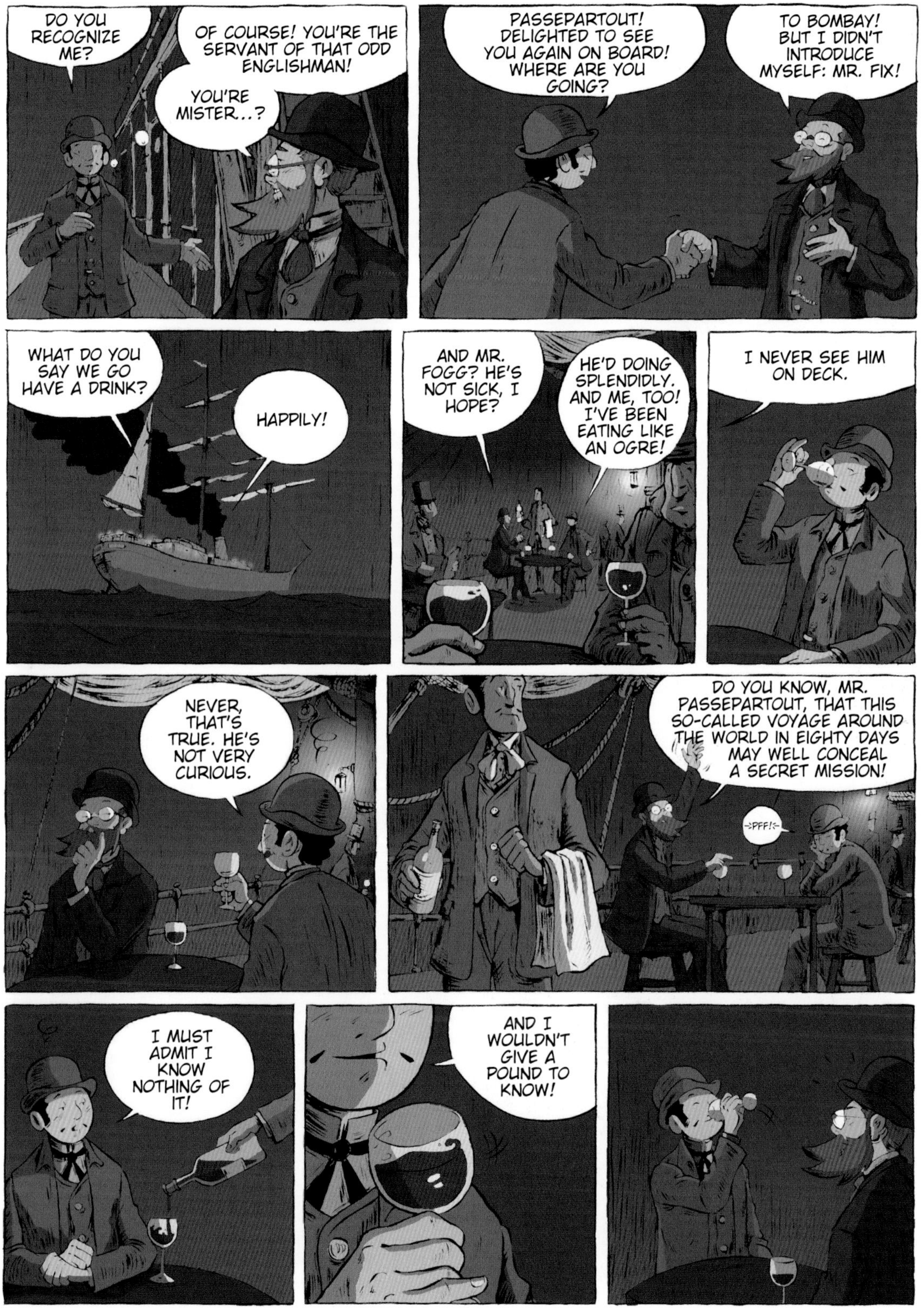
DO YOU RECOGNIZE ME?
OF COURSE! YOU'RE THE SERVANT OF THAT ODD ENGLISHMAN!
YOU'RE MISTER...?
PASSEPARTOUT! DELIGHTED TO SEE YOU AGAIN ON BOARD! WHERE ARE YOU GOING?
TO BOMBAY! BUT I DIDN'T INTRODUCE MYSELF: MR. FIX!
WHAT DO YOU SAY WE GO HAVE A DRINK?
HAPPILY!
AND MR. FOGG? HE'S NOT SICK, I HOPE?
HE'D DOING SPLENDIDLY. AND ME, TOO! I'VE BEEN EATING LIKE AN OGRE!
I NEVER SEE HIM ON DECK.
NEVER, THAT'S TRUE. HE'S NOT VERY CURIOUS.
DO YOU KNOW, MR. PASSEPARTOUT, THAT THIS SO-CALLED VOYAGE AROUND THE WORLD IN EIGHTY DAYS MAY WELL CONCEAL A SECRET MISSION!
PFF!
I MUST ADMIT I KNOW NOTHING OF IT!
AND I WOULDN'T GIVE A POUND TO KNOW!

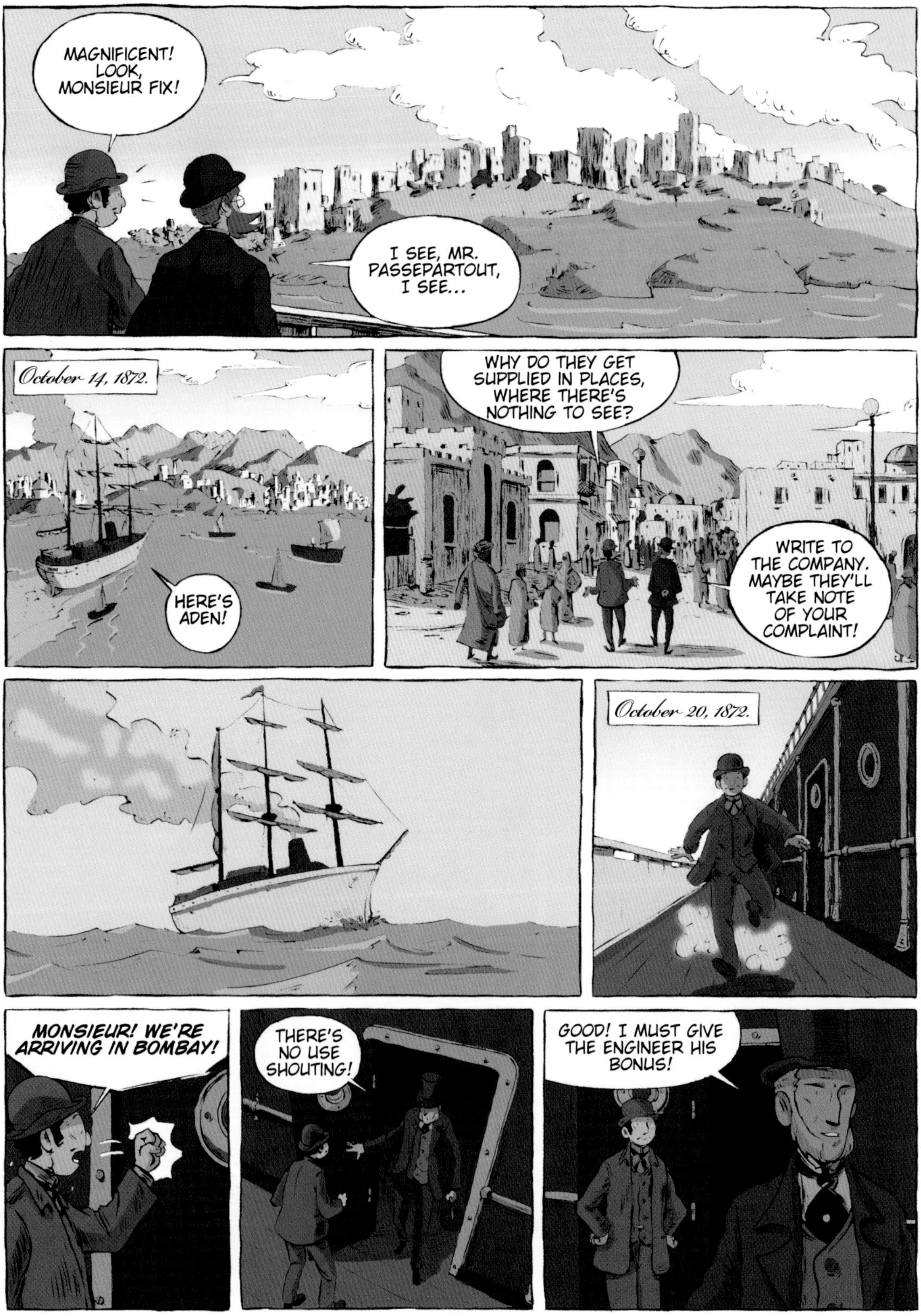
MAGNIFICENT! LOOK, MONSIEUR FIX!
I SEE, MR. PASSEPARTOUT, I SEE...
October 14, 1872.
HERE'S ADEN!
WHY DO THEY GET SUPPLIED IN PLACES, WHERE THERE'S NOTHING TO SEE?
WRITE TO THE COMPANY. MAYBE THEY'LL TAKE NOTE OF YOUR COMPLAINT!
October 20, 1872.
MONSIEUR! WE'RE ARRIVING IN BOMBAY!
THERE'S NO USE SHOUTING!
GOOD! I MUST GIVE THE ENGINEER HIS BONUS!

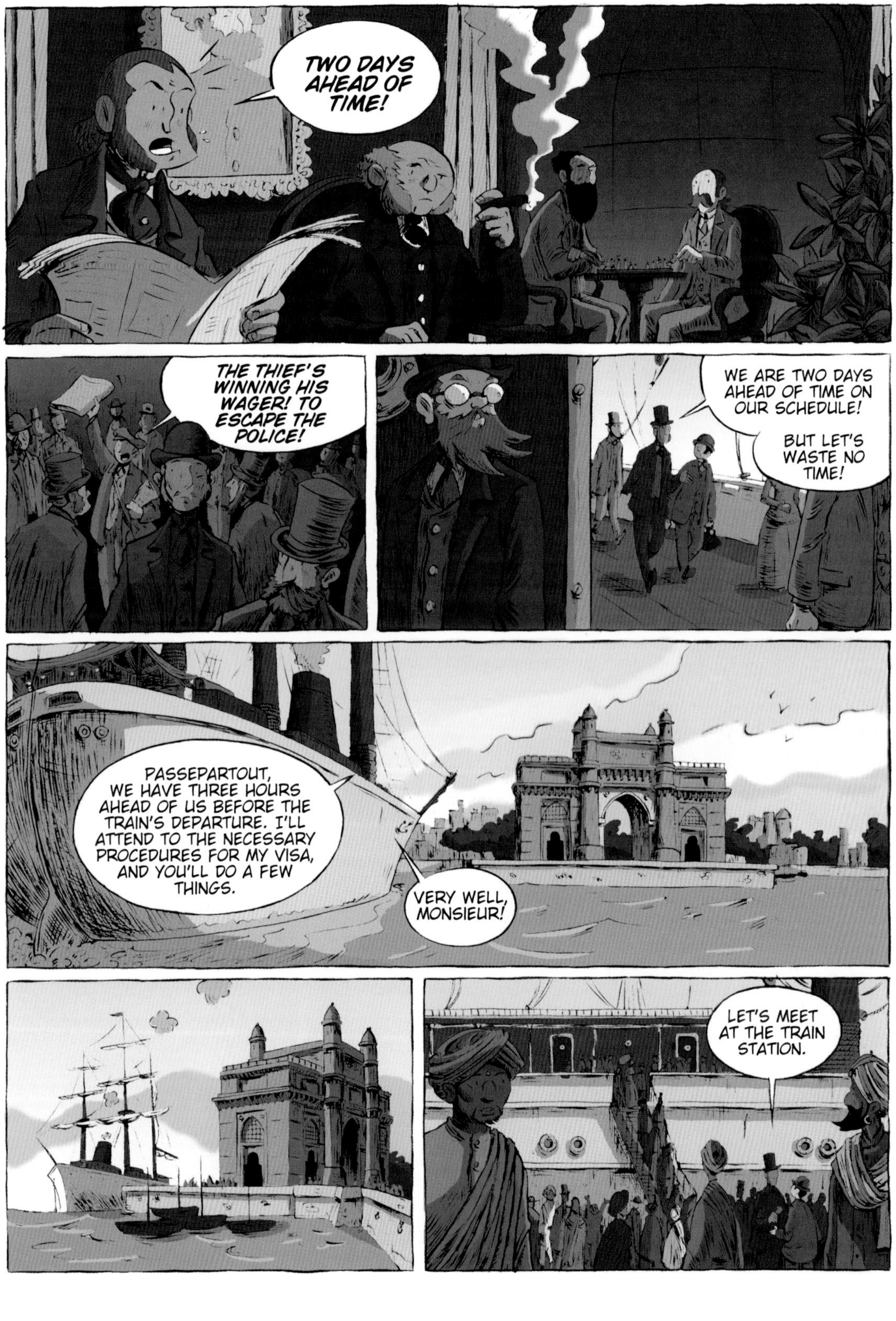
TWO DAYS AHEAD OF TIME!
THE THIEF'S WINNING HIS WAGER! TO ESCAPE THE POLICE!
WE ARE TWO DAYS AHEAD OF TIME ON OUR SCHEDULE!
BUT LET'S WASTE NO TIME!
PASSEPARTOUT, WE HAVE THREE HOURS AHEAD OF US BEFORE THE TRAIN'S DEPARTURE. I'LL ATTEND TO THE NECESSARY PROCEDURES FOR MY VISA, AND YOU'LL DO A FEW THINGS.
VERY WELL, MONSIEUR!
LET'S MEET AT THE TRAIN STATION.

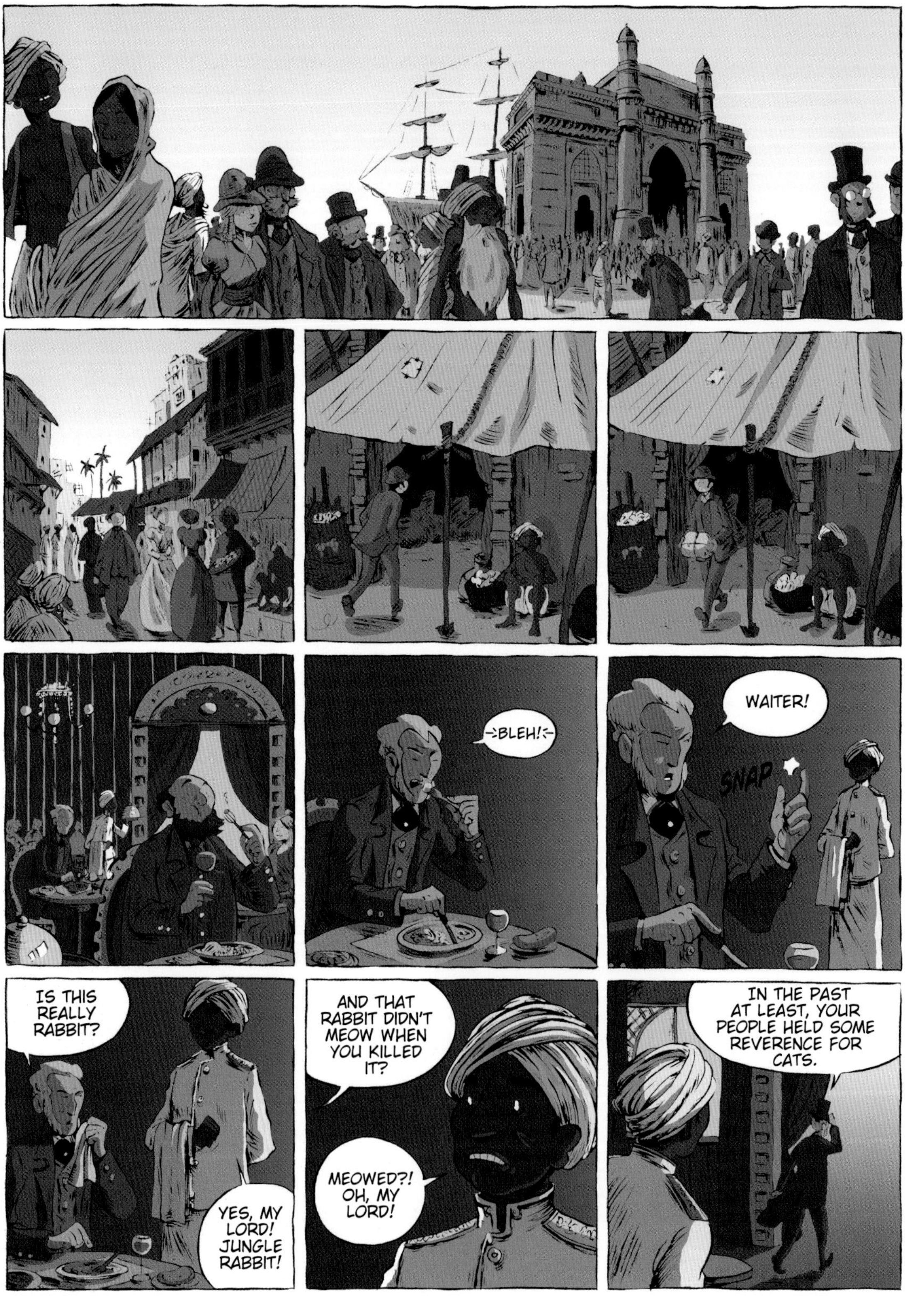
-BLEH!-
WAITER!
SNAP
IS THIS REALLY RABBIT?
YES, MY LORD! JUNGLE RABBIT!
AND THAT RABBIT DIDN'T MEOW WHEN YOU KILLED IT?
MEOWED?! OH, MY LORD!
IN THE PAST AT LEAST, YOUR PEOPLE HELD SOME REVERENCE FOR CATS.

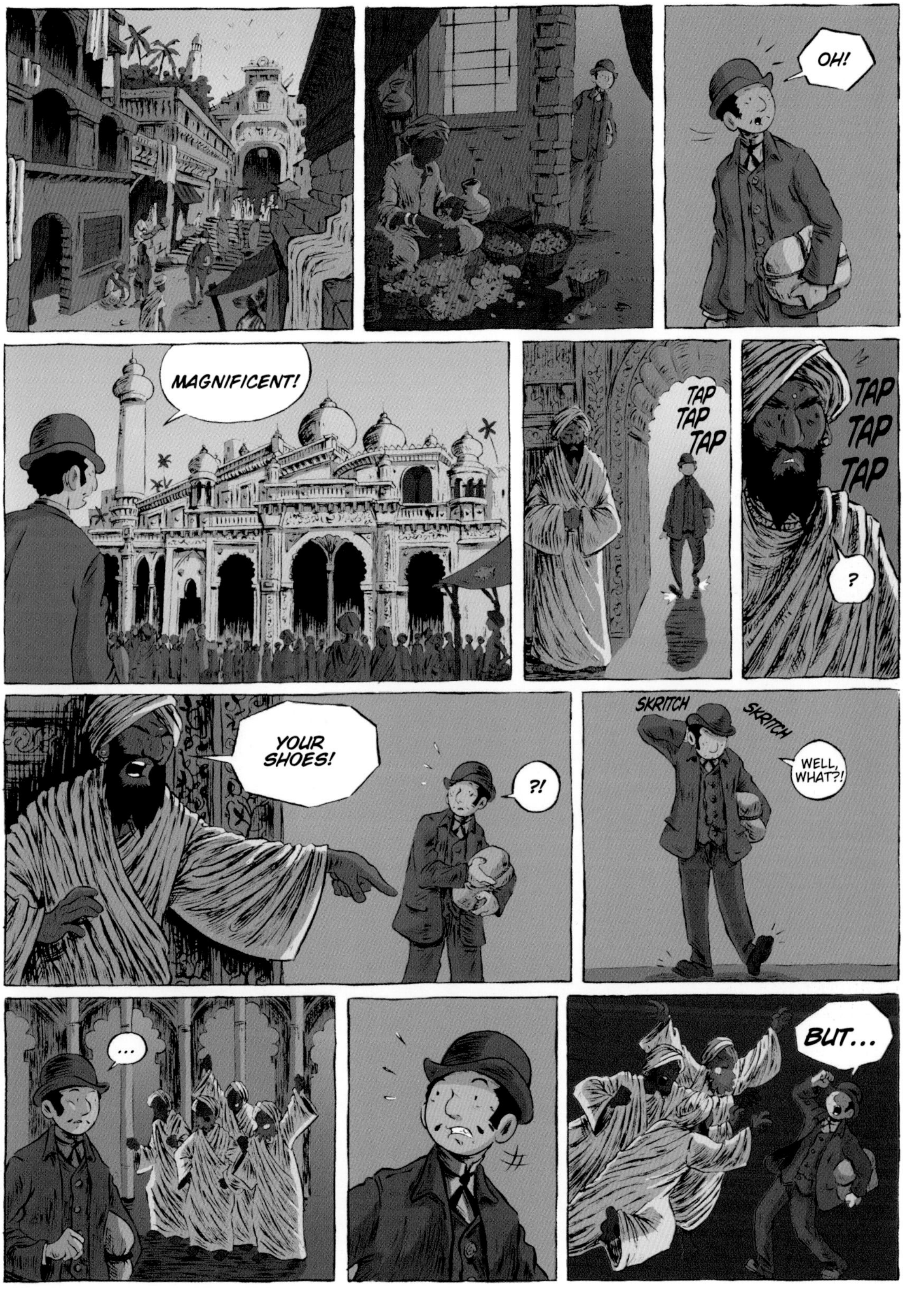
OH!
MAGNIFICENT!
TAP
TAP
TAP
TAP
TAP
TAP
?
YOUR SHOES!
?!
SKRITCH
SKRITCH
WELL, WHAT?!
...
BUT...

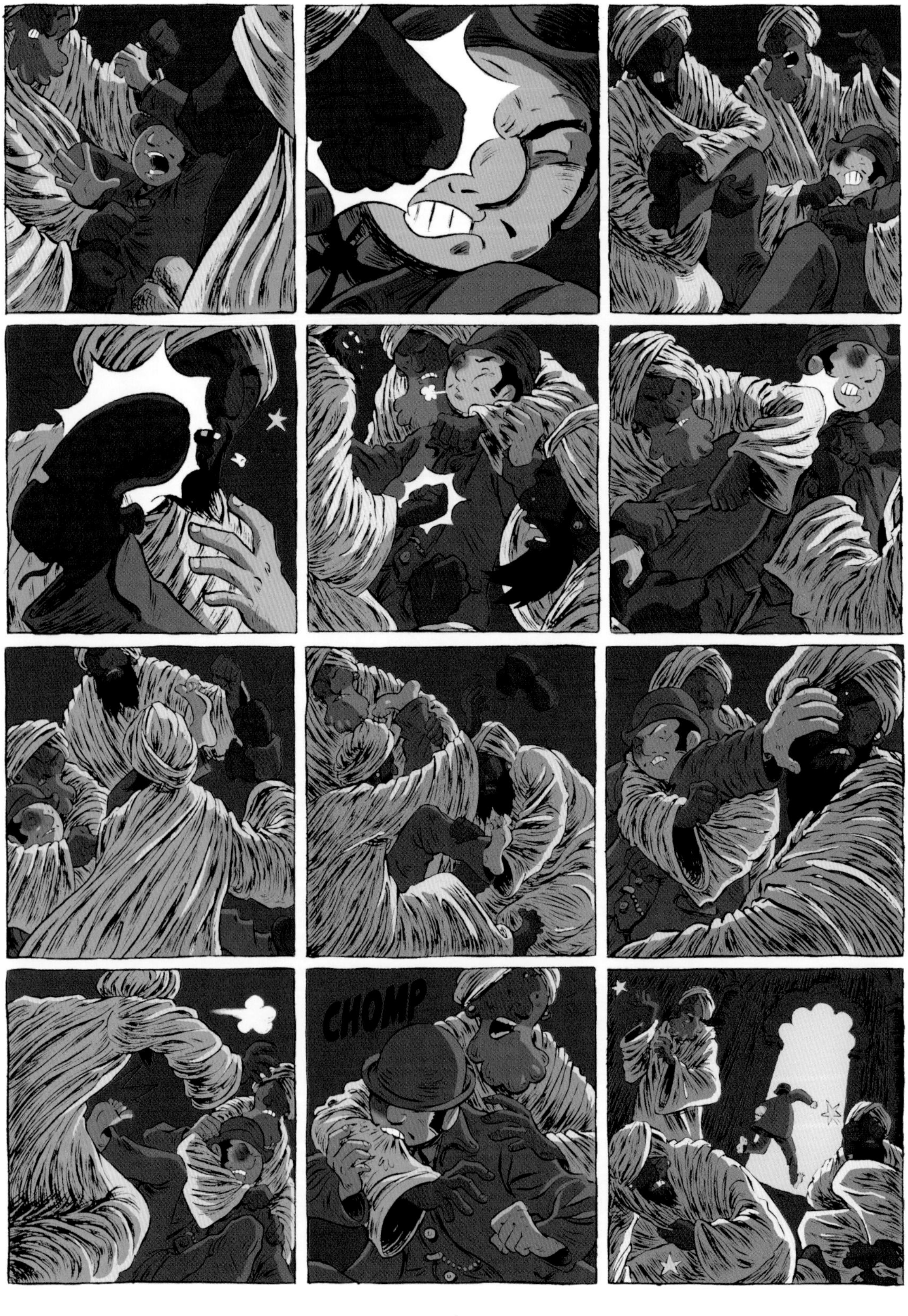
CHOMP

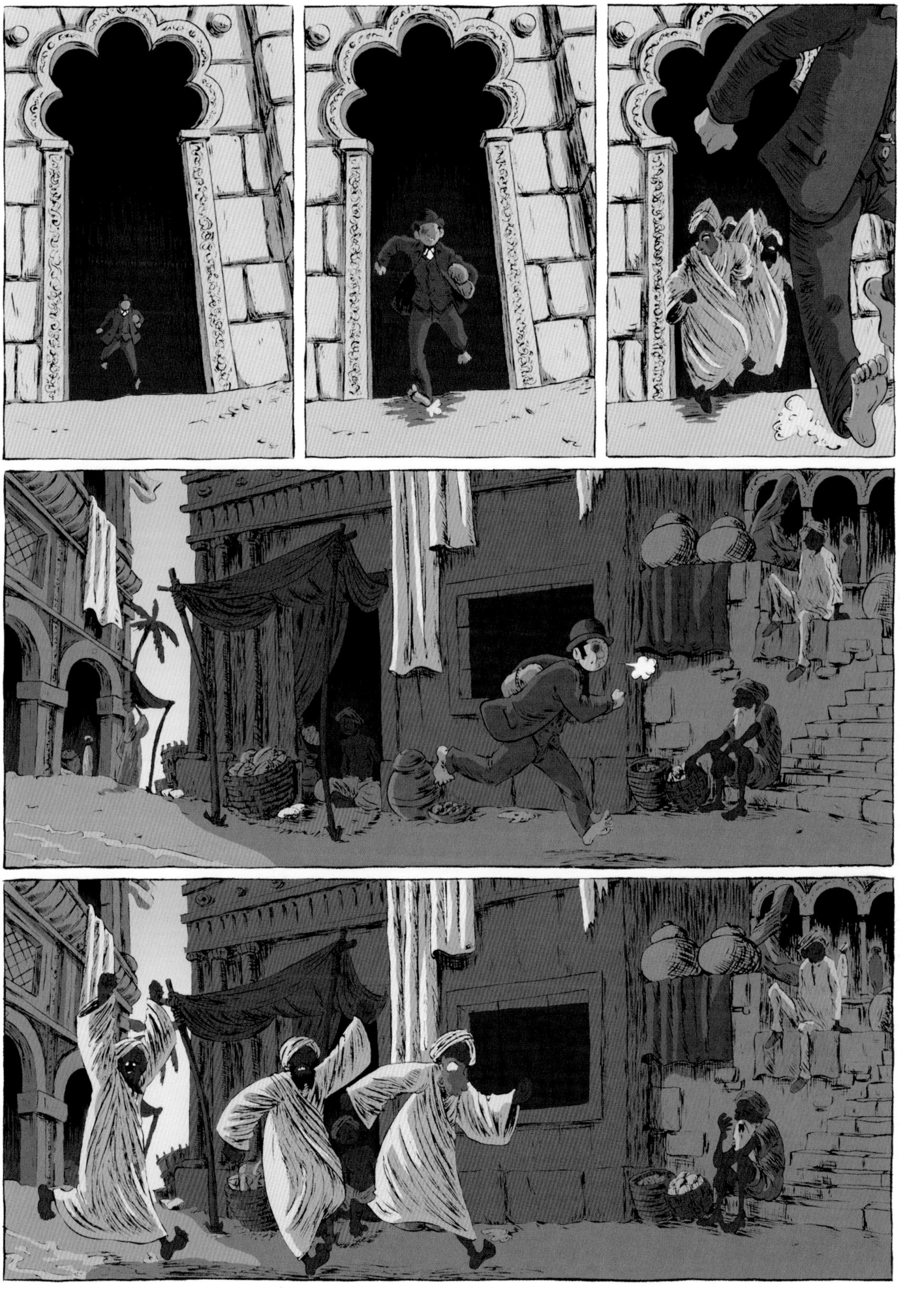

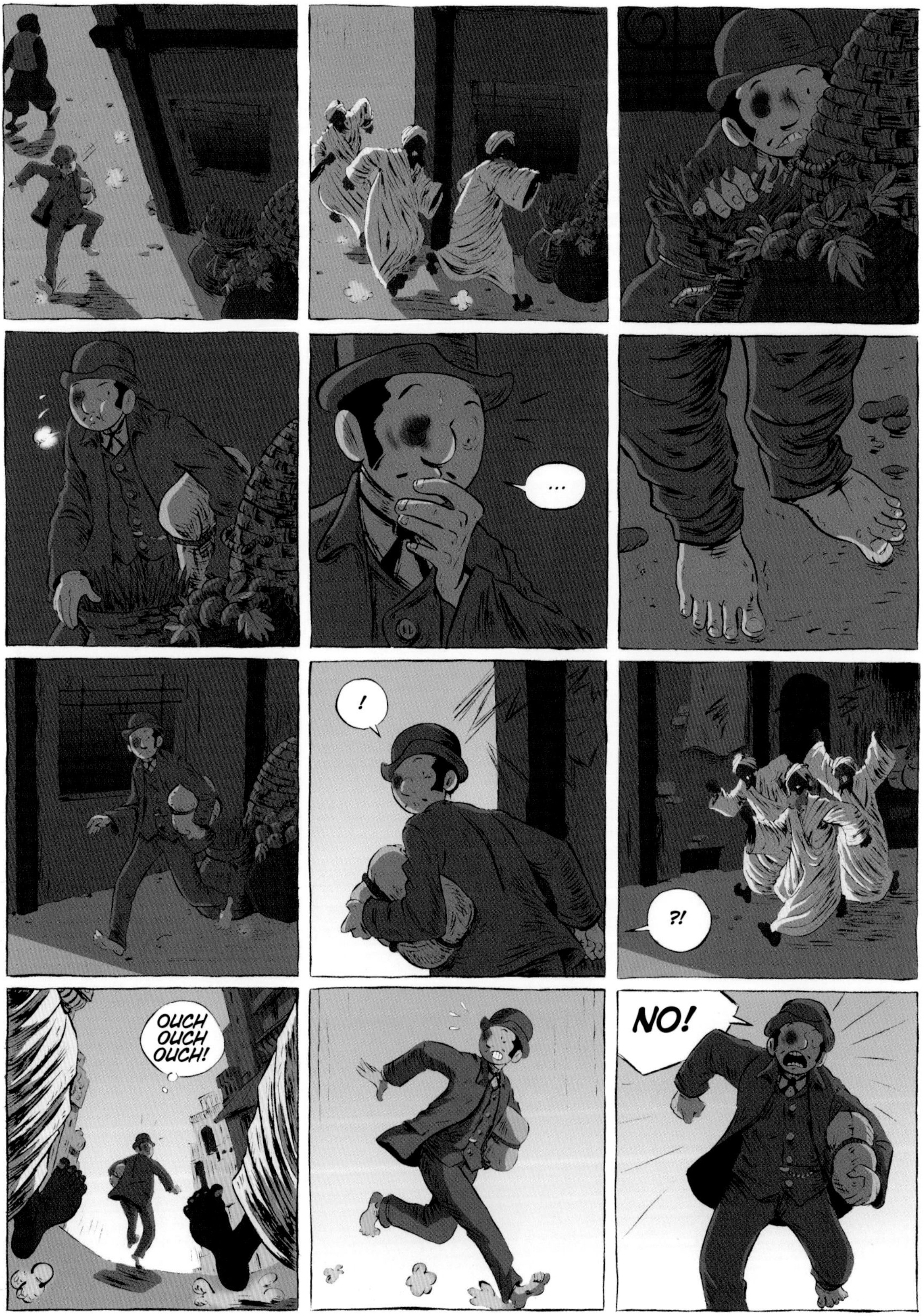
...
!
?!
OUCH
OUCH
OUCH!
NO!

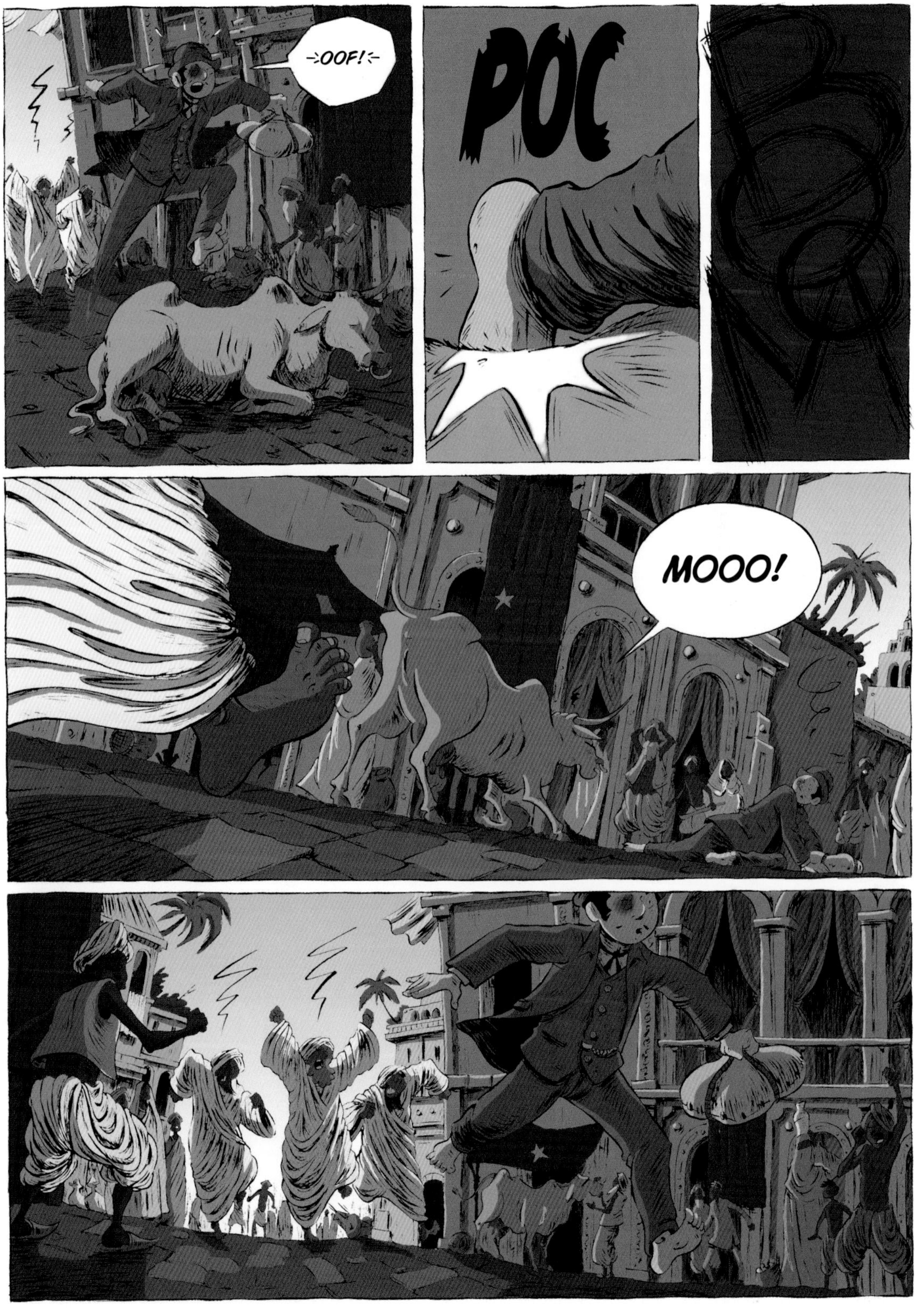
OOF!
POC
MOOO!

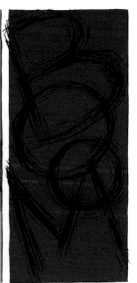

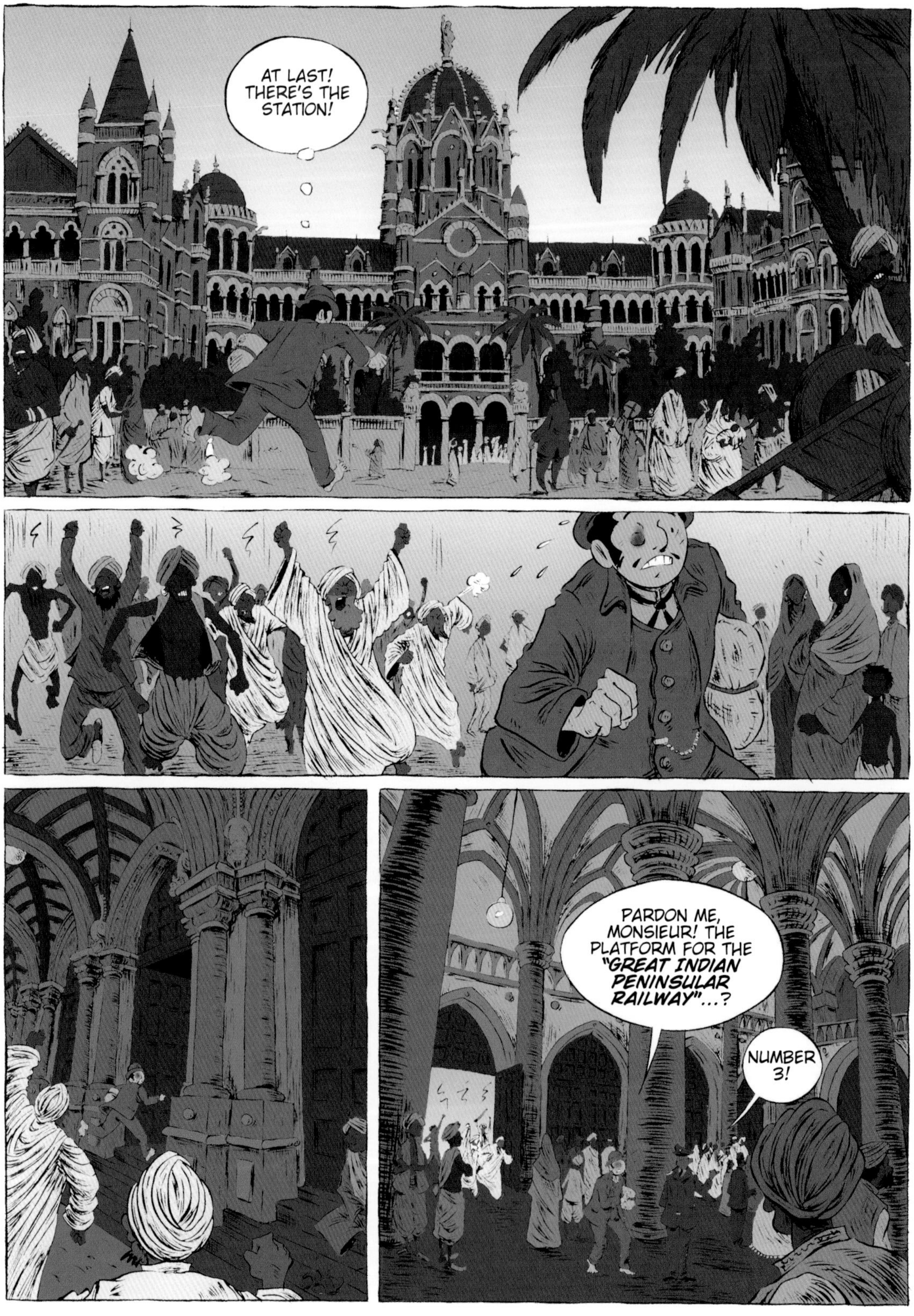
AT LAST! THERE'S THE STATION!
PARDON ME, MONSIEUR! THE PLATFORM FOR THE "*GREAT INDIAN PENINSULAR RAILWAY*"...?
NUMBER 3!

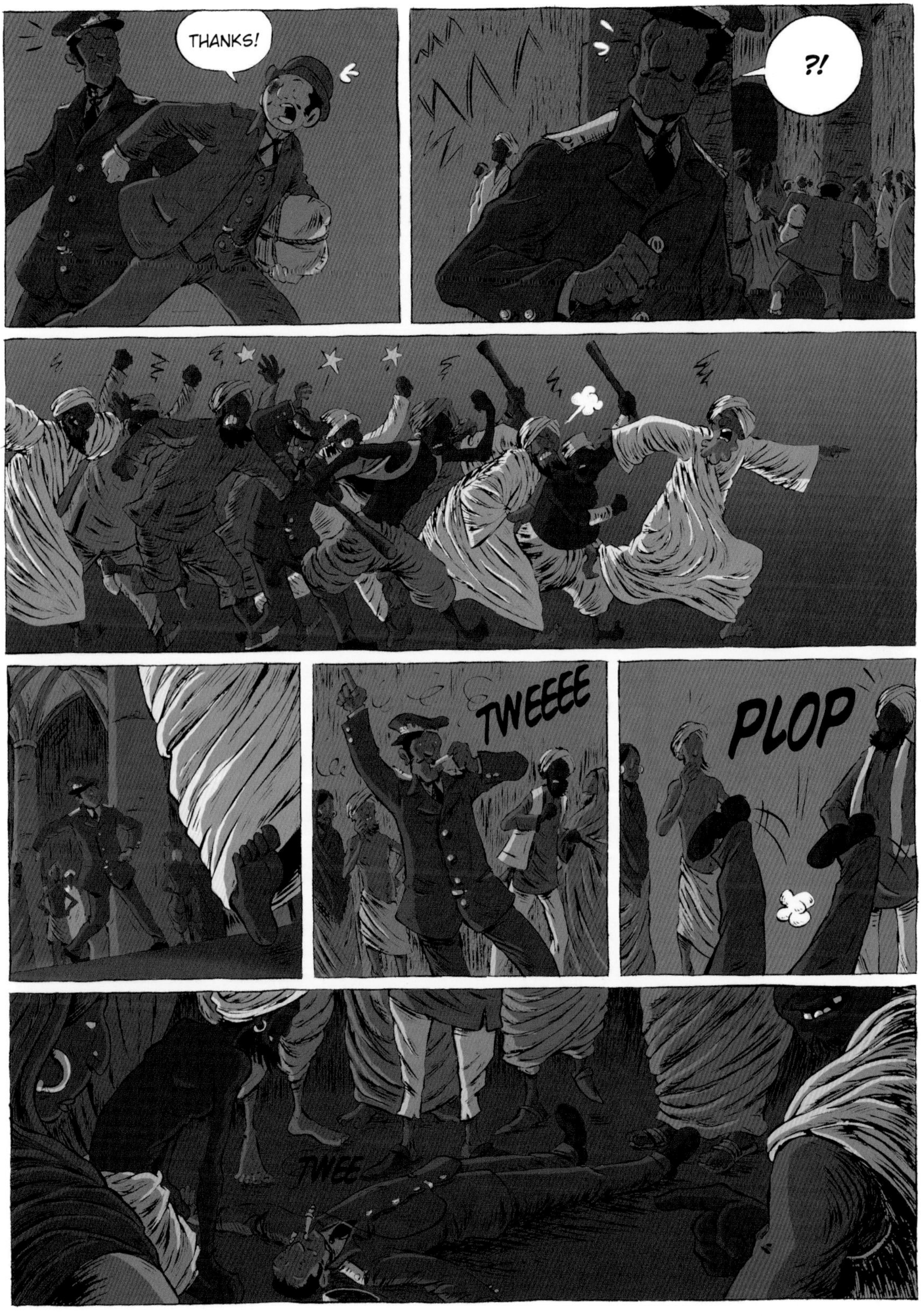
THANKS!
?!
TWEEEE
PLOP
TWEE

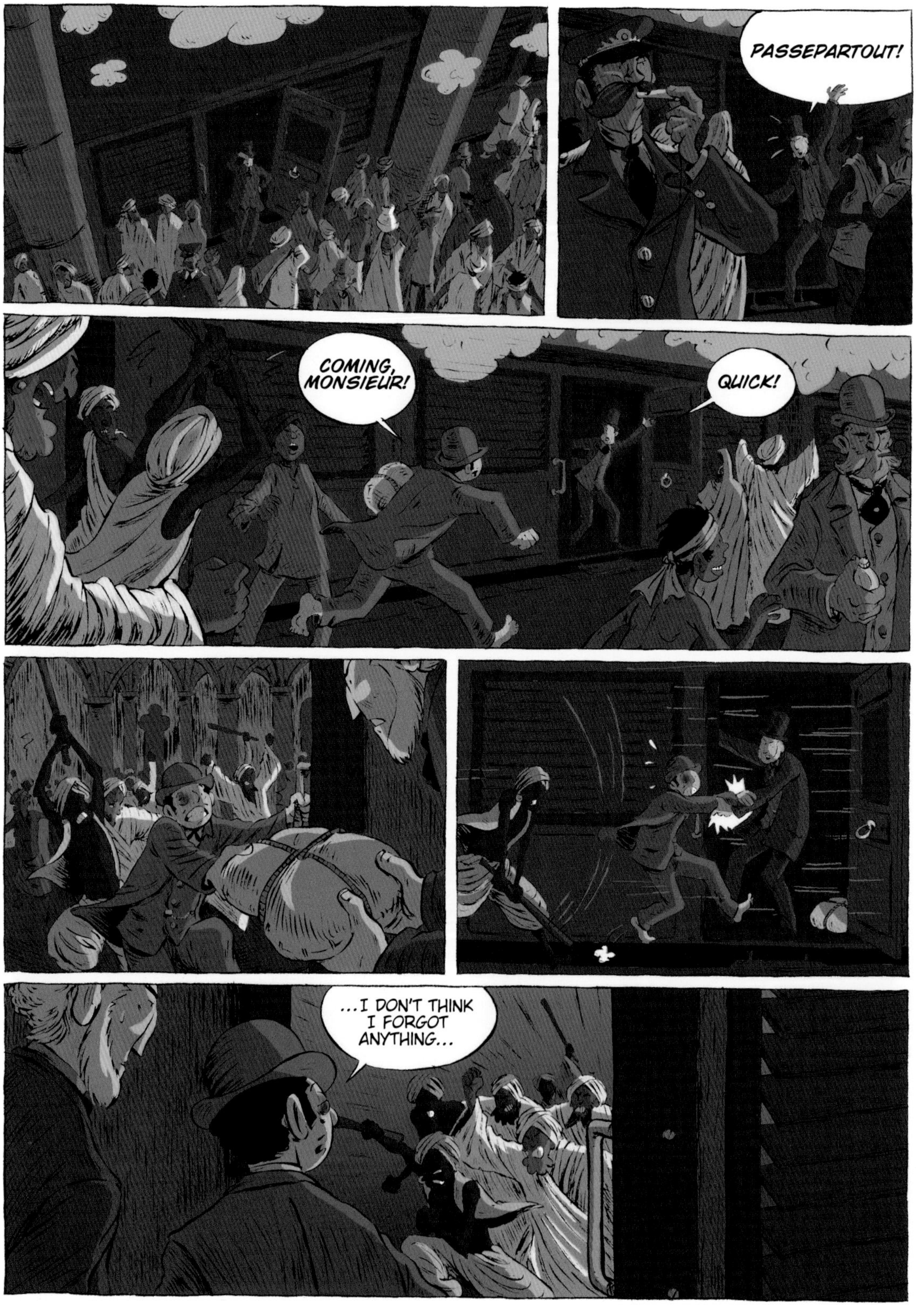
PASSEPARTOUT!
COMING, MONSIEUR!
QUICK!
...I DON'T THINK I FORGOT ANYTHING...

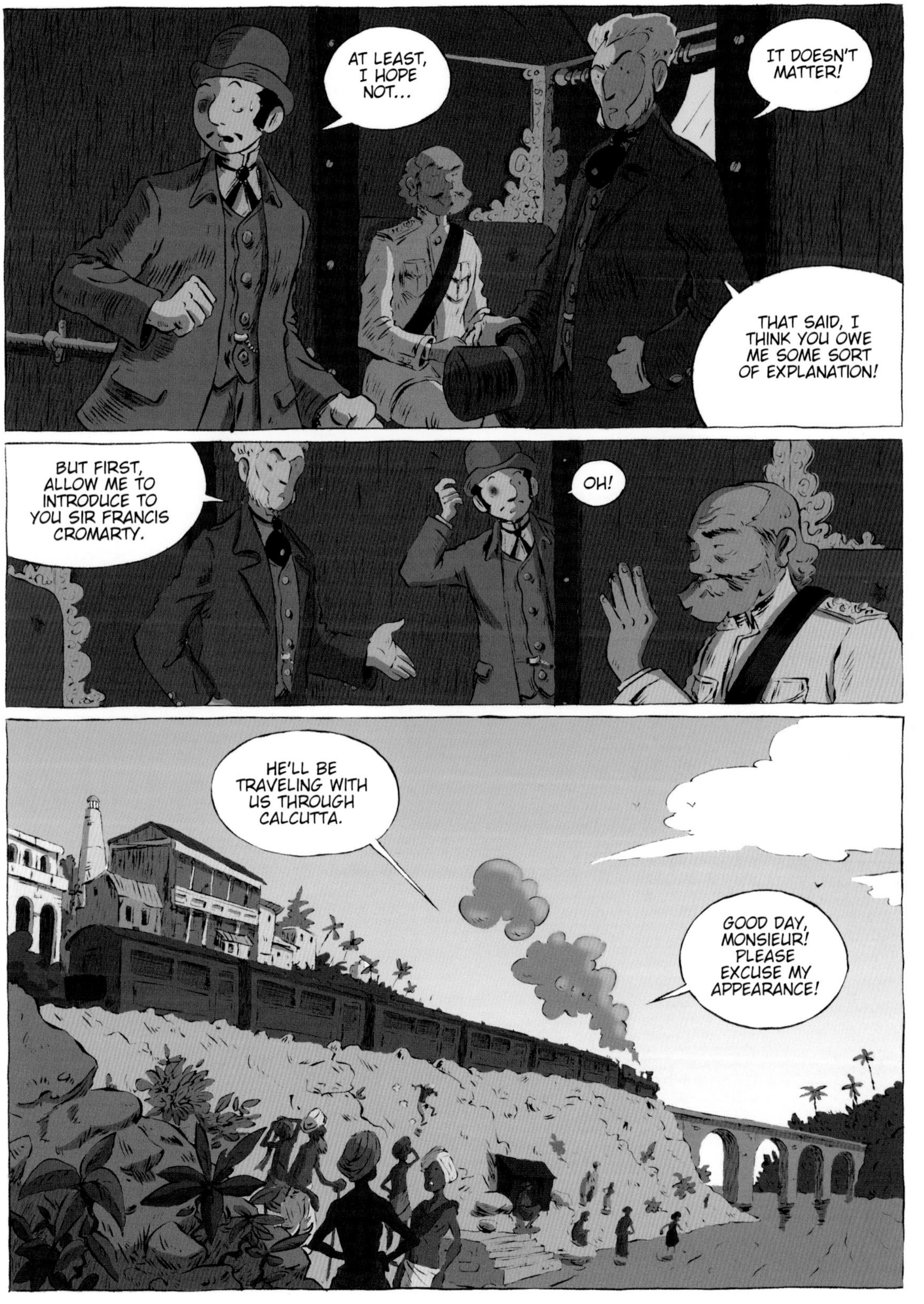
AT LEAST, I HOPE NOT...
IT DOESN'T MATTER!
THAT SAID, I THINK YOU OWE ME SOME SORT OF EXPLANATION!
BUT FIRST, ALLOW ME TO INTRODUCE TO YOU SIR FRANCIS CROMARTY.
OH!
HE'LL BE TRAVELING WITH US THROUGH CALCUTTA.
GOOD DAY, MONSIEUR! PLEASE EXCUSE MY APPEARANCE!

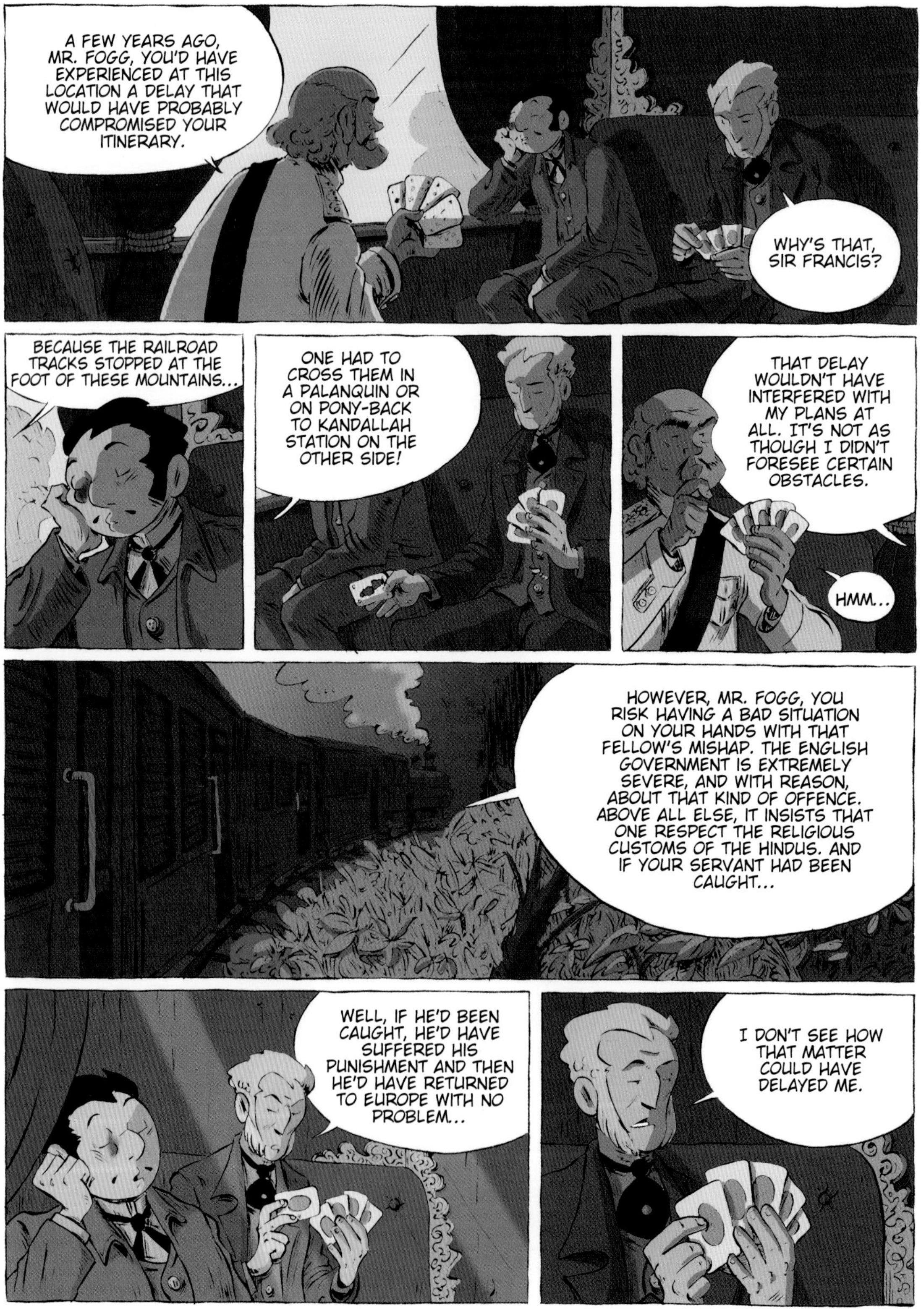
A FEW YEARS AGO, MR. FOGG, YOU'D HAVE EXPERIENCED AT THIS LOCATION A DELAY THAT WOULD HAVE PROBABLY COMPROMISED YOUR ITINERARY.
WHY'S THAT, SIR FRANCIS?
BECAUSE THE RAILROAD TRACKS STOPPED AT THE FOOT OF THESE MOUNTAINS...
ONE HAD TO CROSS THEM IN A PALANQUIN OR ON PONY-BACK TO KANDALLAH STATION ON THE OTHER SIDE!
THAT DELAY WOULDN'T HAVE INTERFERED WITH MY PLANS AT ALL. IT'S NOT AS THOUGH I DIDN'T FORESEE CERTAIN OBSTACLES.
HMM...
HOWEVER, MR. FOGG, YOU RISK HAVING A BAD SITUATION ON YOUR HANDS WITH THAT FELLOW'S MISHAP. THE ENGLISH GOVERNMENT IS EXTREMELY SEVERE, AND WITH REASON, ABOUT THAT KIND OF OFFENCE. ABOVE ALL ELSE, IT INSISTS THAT ONE RESPECT THE RELIGIOUS CUSTOMS OF THE HINDUS. AND IF YOUR SERVANT HAD BEEN CAUGHT...
WELL, IF HE'D BEEN CAUGHT, HE'D HAVE SUFFERED HIS PUNISHMENT AND THEN HE'D HAVE RETURNED TO EUROPE WITH NO PROBLEM...
I DON'T SEE HOW THAT MATTER COULD HAVE DELAYED ME.

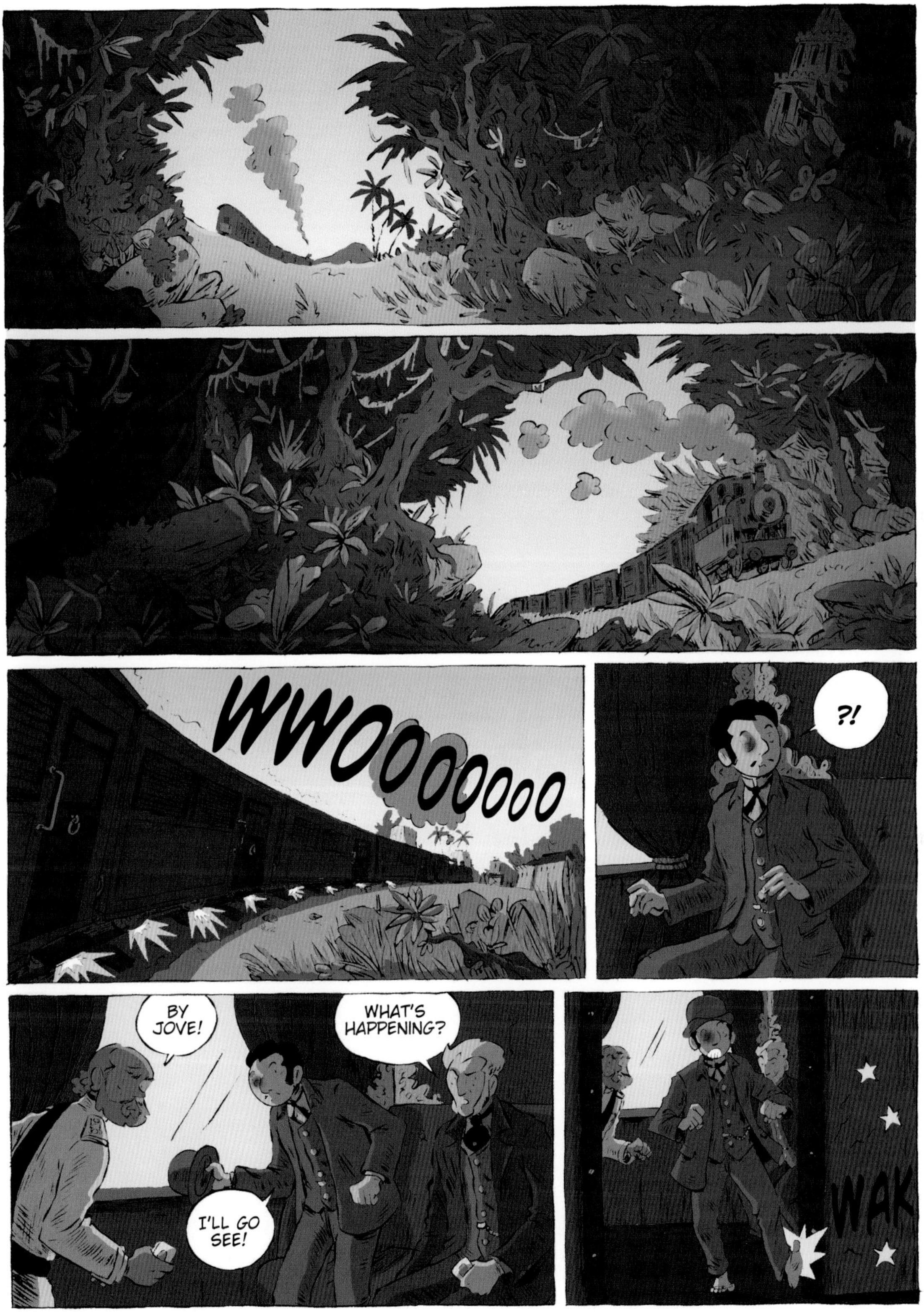
WWOOOOOOOO
?!
BY JOVE!
WHAT'S HAPPENING?
I'LL GO SEE!
WAK

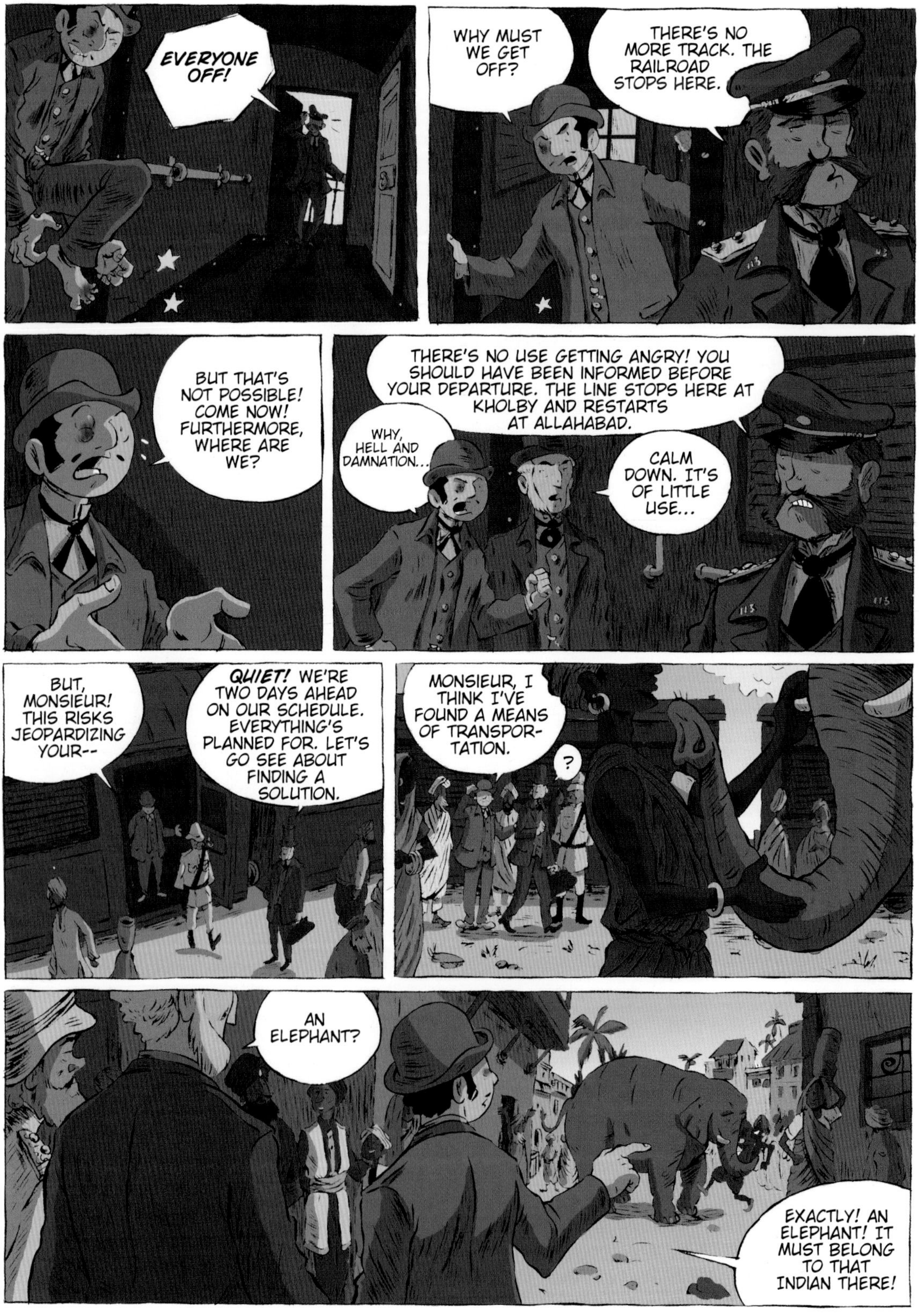
EVERYONE OFF!
WHY MUST WE GET OFF?
THERE'S NO MORE TRACK. THE RAILROAD STOPS HERE.
BUT THAT'S NOT POSSIBLE! COME NOW! FURTHERMORE, WHERE ARE WE?
THERE'S NO USE GETTING ANGRY! YOU SHOULD HAVE BEEN INFORMED BEFORE YOUR DEPARTURE. THE LINE STOPS HERE AT KHOLBY AND RESTARTS AT ALLAHABAD.
WHY, HELL AND DAMNATION...
CALM DOWN. IT'S OF LITTLE USE...
BUT, MONSIEUR! THIS RISKS JEOPARDIZING YOUR--
QUIET! WE'RE TWO DAYS AHEAD ON OUR SCHEDULE. EVERYTHING'S PLANNED FOR. LET'S GO SEE ABOUT FINDING A SOLUTION.
MONSIEUR, I THINK I'VE FOUND A MEANS OF TRANSPORTATION.
?
AN ELEPHANT?
EXACTLY! AN ELEPHANT! IT MUST BELONG TO THAT INDIAN THERE!

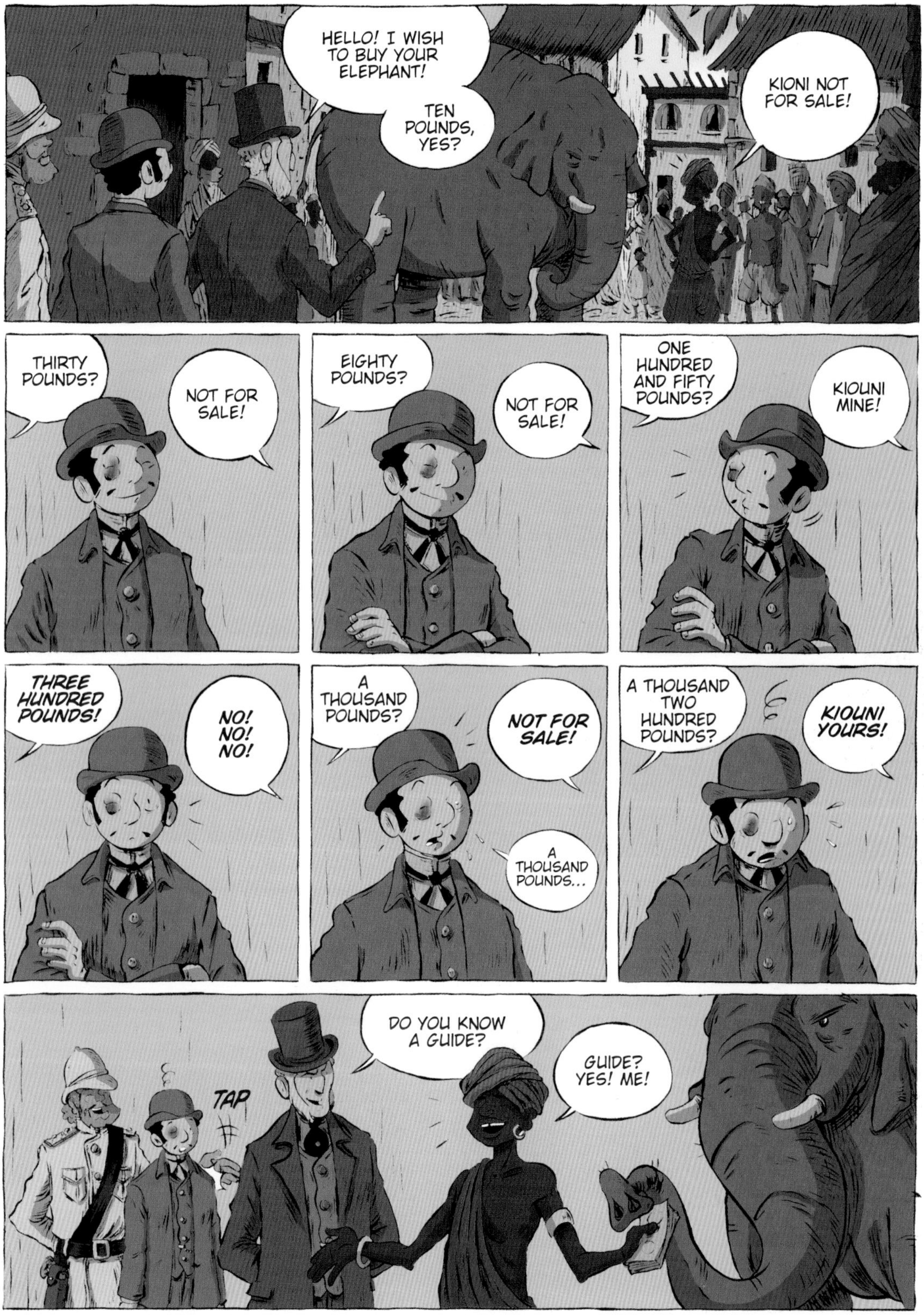
HELLO! I WISH TO BUY YOUR ELEPHANT!
TEN POUNDS, YES?
KIONI NOT FOR SALE!
THIRTY POUNDS?
NOT FOR SALE!
EIGHTY POUNDS?
NOT FOR SALE!
ONE HUNDRED AND FIFTY POUNDS?
KIOUNI MINE!
THREE HUNDRED POUNDS!
NO! NO! NO!
A THOUSAND POUNDS?
NOT FOR SALE!
A THOUSAND POUNDS...
A THOUSAND TWO HUNDRED POUNDS?
KIOUNI YOURS!
DO YOU KNOW A GUIDE?
TAP
GUIDE? YES! ME!

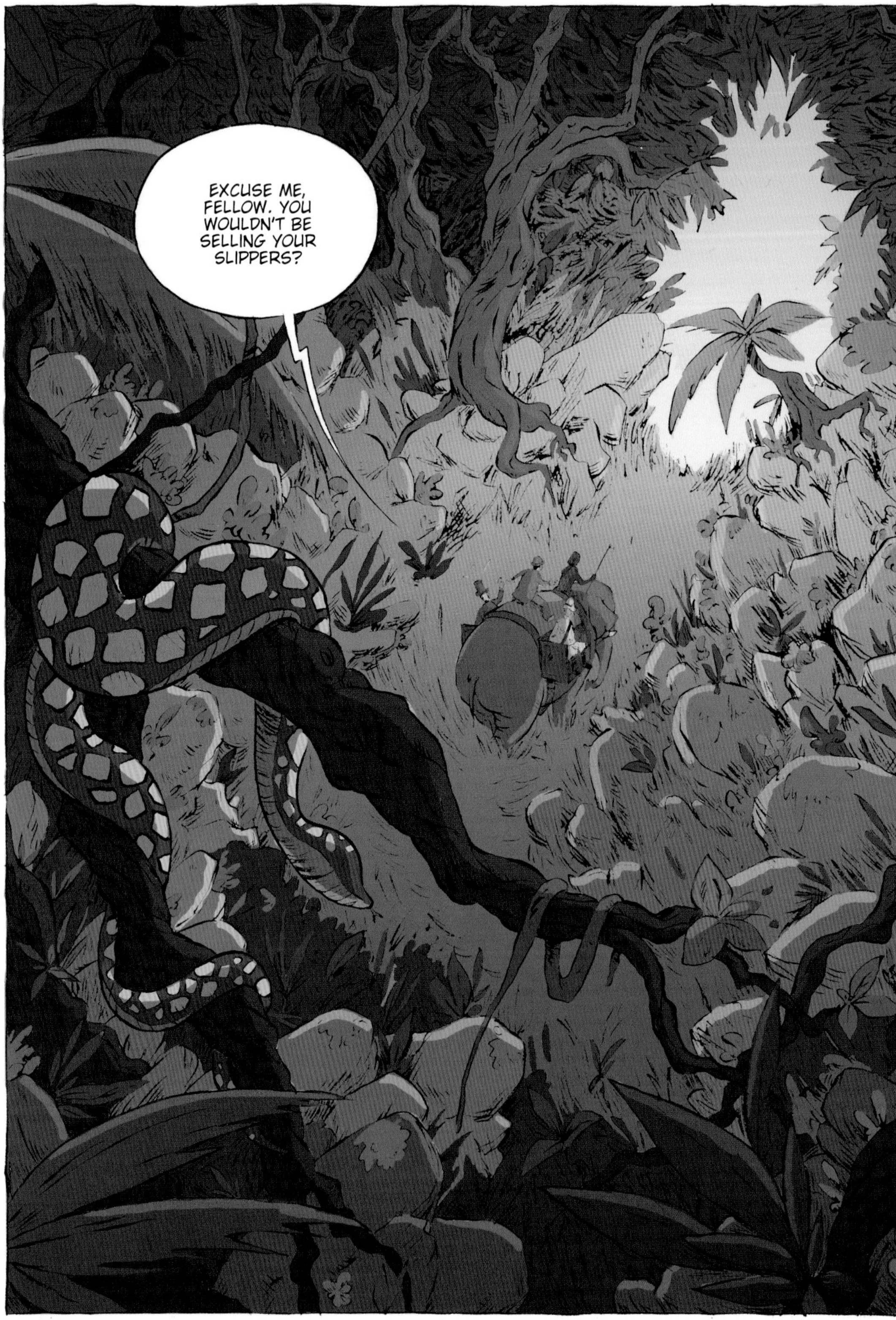
EXCUSE ME, FELLOW. YOU WOULDN'T BE SELLING YOUR SLIPPERS?

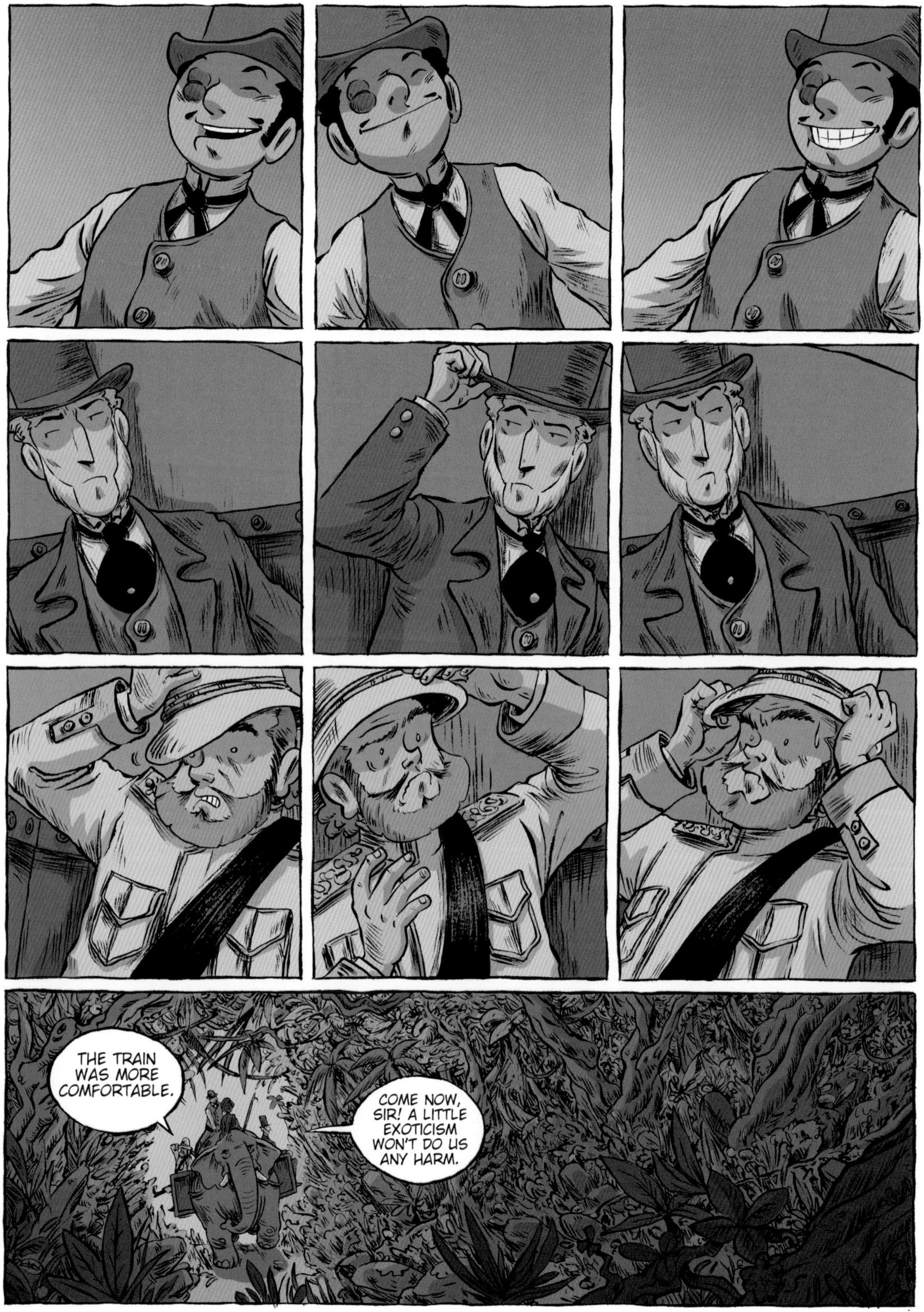
THE TRAIN WAS MORE COMFORTABLE.
COME NOW, SIR! A LITTLE EXOTICISM WON'T DO US ANY HARM.

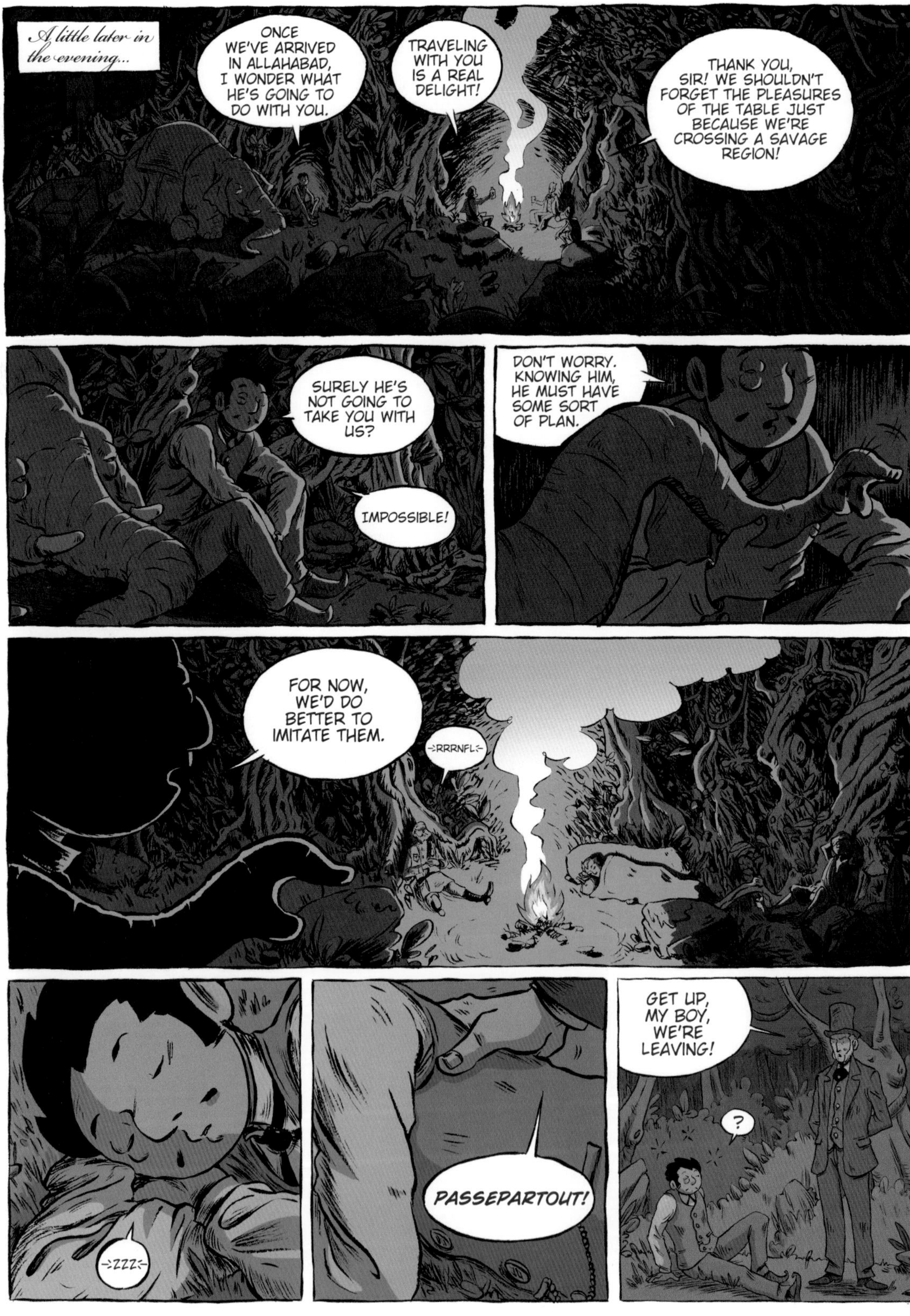
A little later in the evening...
ONCE WE'VE ARRIVED IN ALLAHABAD, I WONDER WHAT HE'S GOING TO DO WITH YOU.
TRAVELING WITH YOU IS A REAL DELIGHT!
THANK YOU, SIR! WE SHOULDN'T FORGET THE PLEASURES OF THE TABLE JUST BECAUSE WE'RE CROSSING A SAVAGE REGION!
SURELY HE'S NOT GOING TO TAKE YOU WITH US?
IMPOSSIBLE!
DON'T WORRY. KNOWING HIM, HE MUST HAVE SOME SORT OF PLAN.
FOR NOW, WE'D DO BETTER TO IMITATE THEM.
RRRNFL
ZZZ
PASSEPARTOUT!
GET UP, MY BOY, WE'RE LEAVING!
?

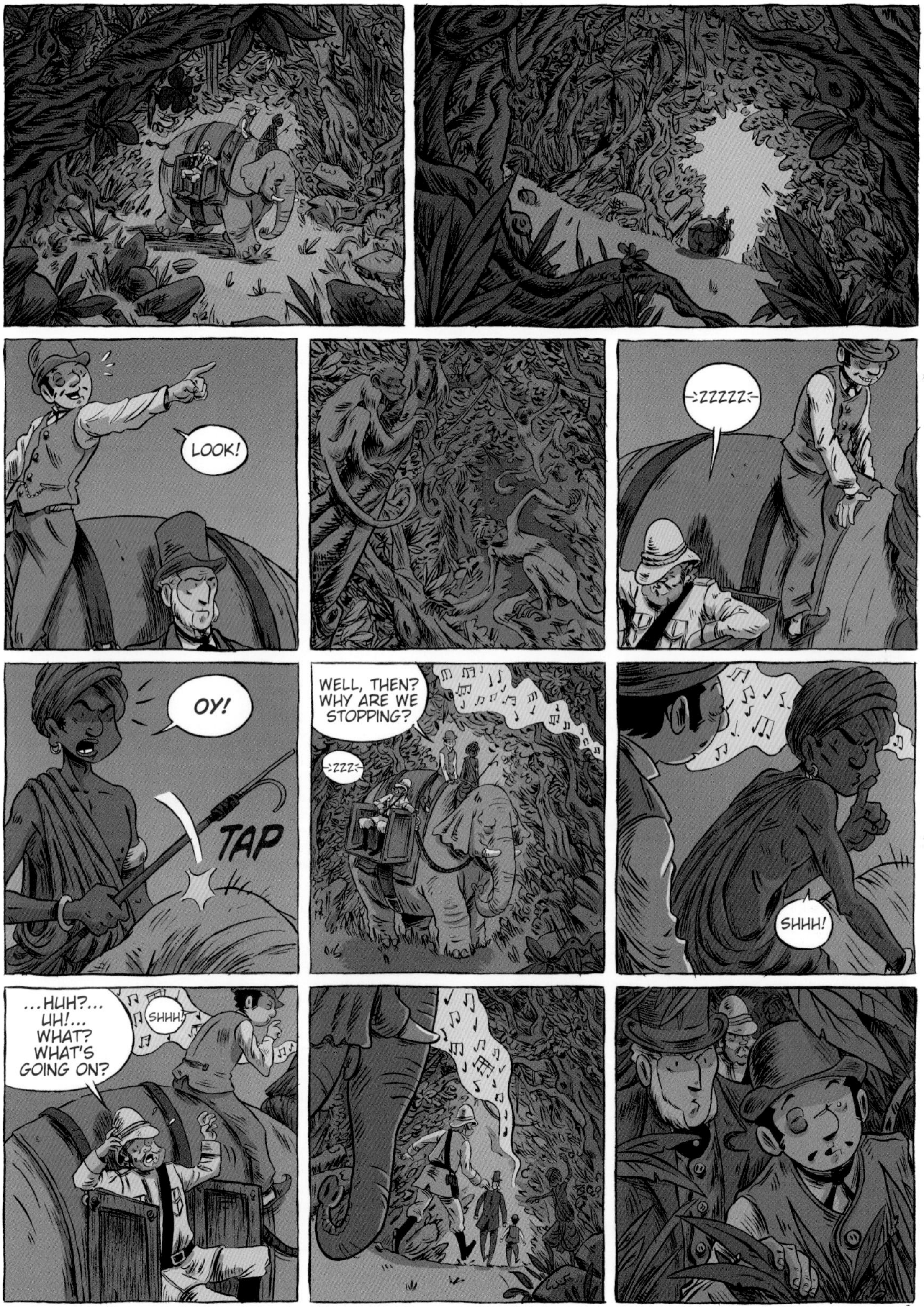
LOOK!
ZZZZZ
OY!
TAP
WELL, THEN? WHY ARE WE STOPPING?
ZZZ
SHHH!
...HUH?... UH!... WHAT? WHAT'S GOING ON?
SHHH!

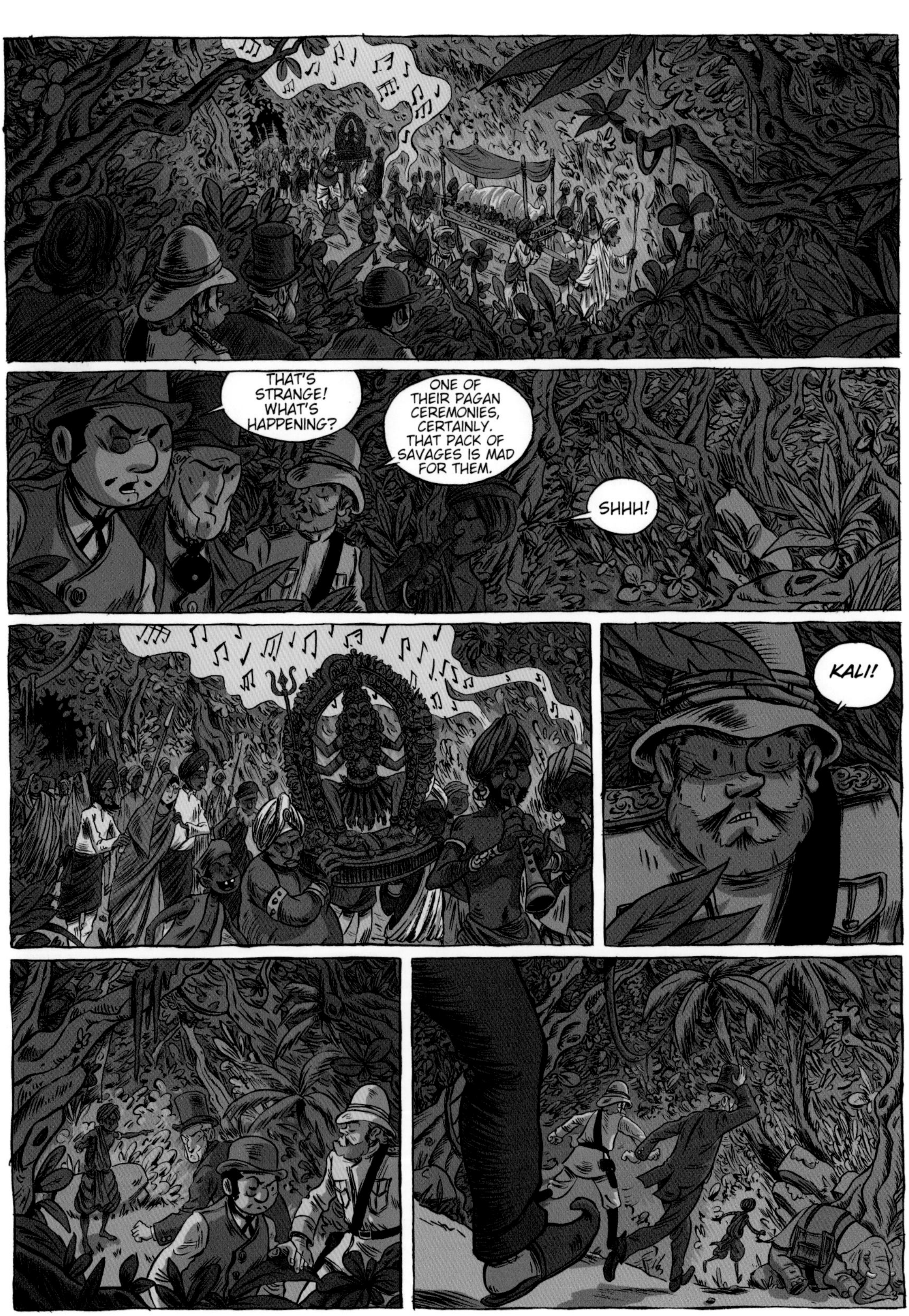
THAT'S STRANGE! WHAT'S HAPPENING?
ONE OF THEIR PAGAN CEREMONIES, CERTAINLY. THAT PACK OF SAVAGES IS MAD FOR THEM.
SHHH!
KALI!

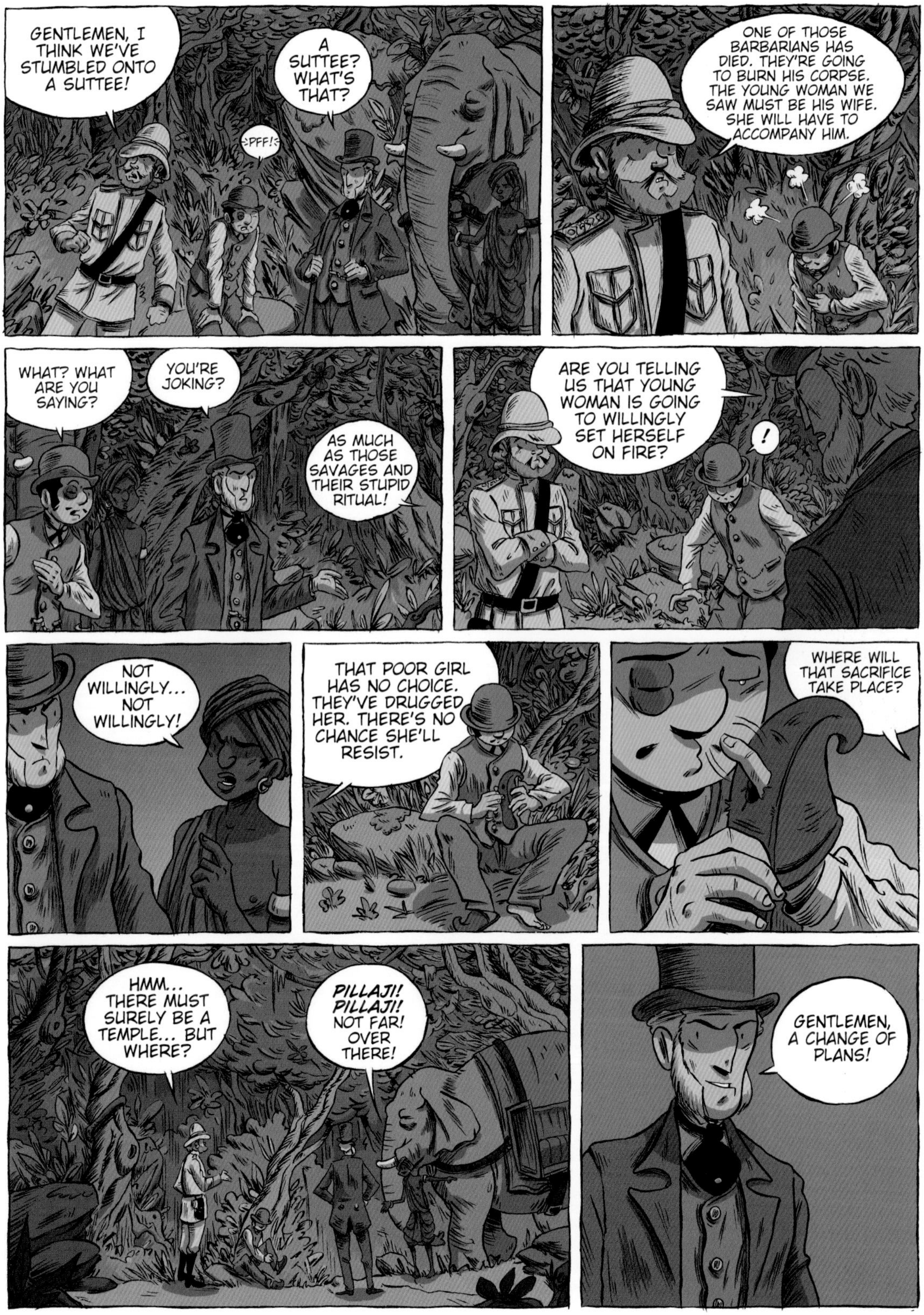

GENTLEMEN, I THINK WE'VE STUMBLED ONTO A SUTTEE!
PFF!
A SUTTEE? WHAT'S THAT?
ONE OF THOSE BARBARIANS HAS DIED. THEY'RE GOING TO BURN HIS CORPSE. THE YOUNG WOMAN WE SAW MUST BE HIS WIFE. SHE WILL HAVE TO ACCOMPANY HIM.
WHAT? WHAT ARE YOU SAYING?
YOU'RE JOKING?
AS MUCH AS THOSE SAVAGES AND THEIR STUPID RITUAL!
ARE YOU TELLING US THAT YOUNG WOMAN IS GOING TO WILLINGLY SET HERSELF ON FIRE?
!
NOT WILLINGLY... NOT WILLINGLY!
THAT POOR GIRL HAS NO CHOICE. THEY'VE DRUGGED HER. THERE'S NO CHANCE SHE'LL RESIST.
WHERE WILL THAT SACRIFICE TAKE PLACE?
HMM... THERE MUST SURELY BE A TEMPLE... BUT WHERE?
PILLAJI! PILLAJI! NOT FAR! OVER THERE!
GENTLEMEN, A CHANGE OF PLANS!

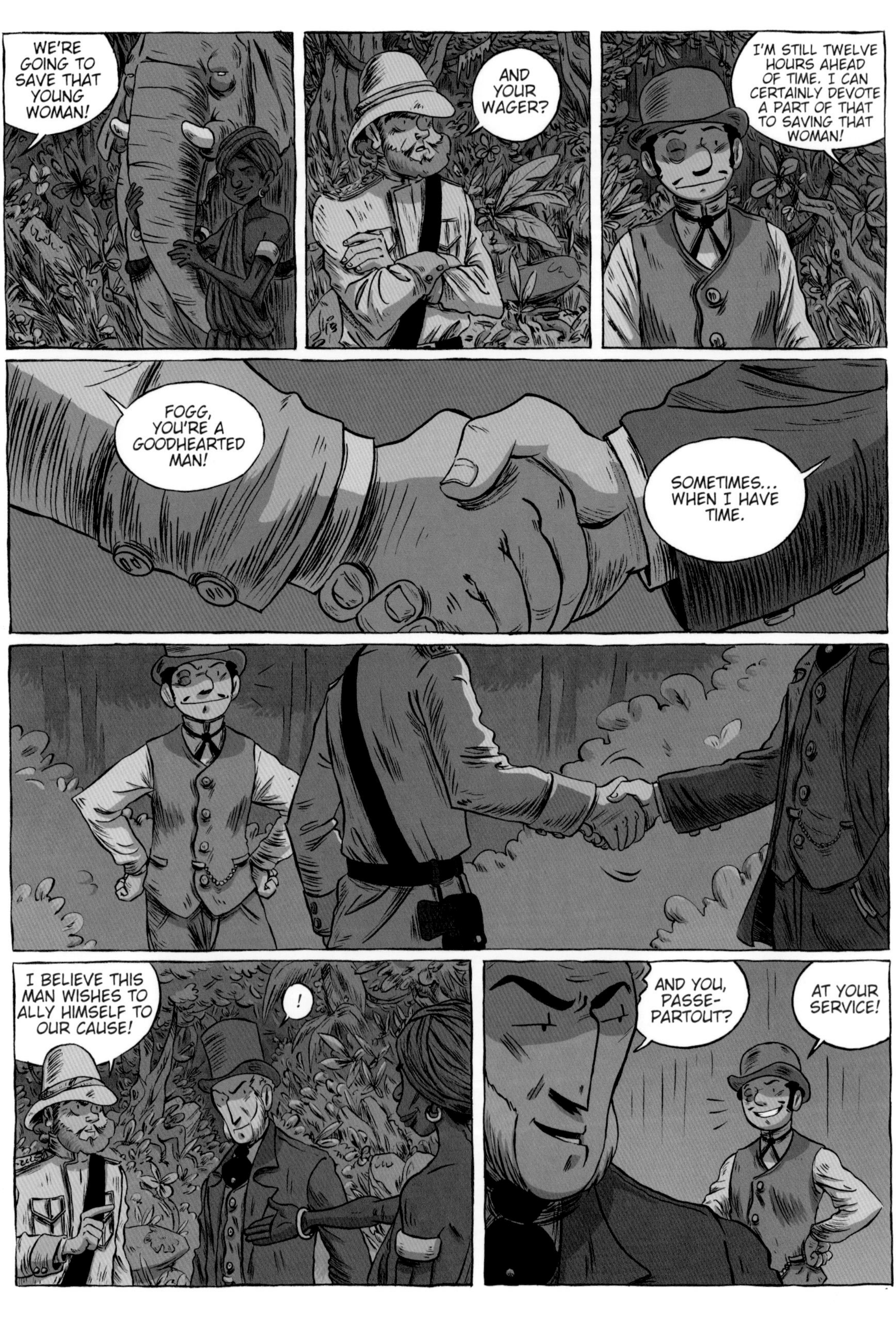
WE'RE GOING TO SAVE THAT YOUNG WOMAN!
AND YOUR WAGER?
I'M STILL TWELVE HOURS AHEAD OF TIME. I CAN CERTAINLY DEVOTE A PART OF THAT TO SAVING THAT WOMAN!
FOGG, YOU'RE A GOODHEARTED MAN!
SOMETIMES... WHEN I HAVE TIME.
I BELIEVE THIS MAN WISHES TO ALLY HIMSELF TO OUR CAUSE!
!
AND YOU, PASSE-PARTOUT?
AT YOUR SERVICE!

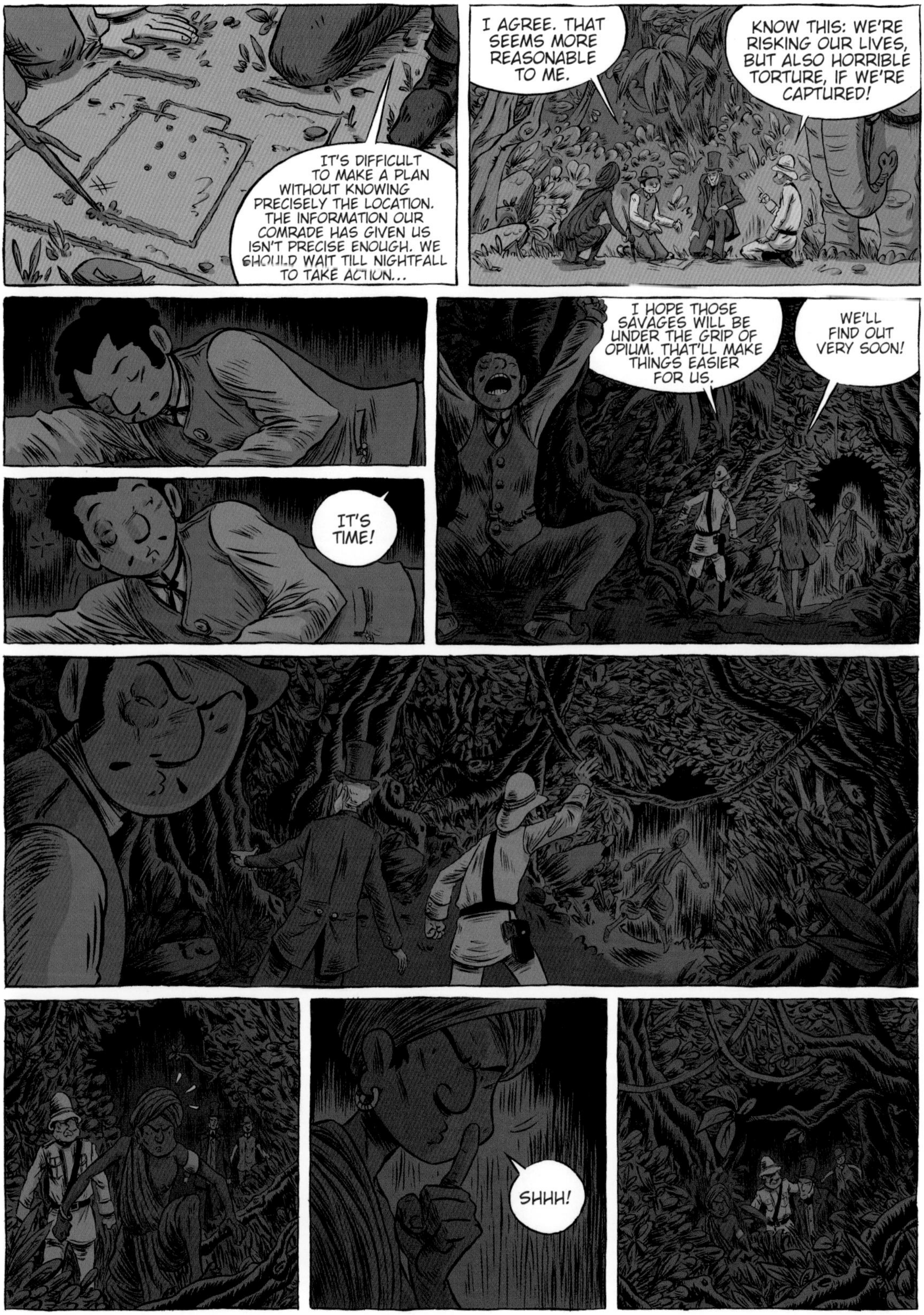
IT'S DIFFICULT TO MAKE A PLAN WITHOUT KNOWING PRECISELY THE LOCATION. THE INFORMATION OUR COMRADE HAS GIVEN US ISN'T PRECISE ENOUGH. WE SHOULD WAIT TILL NIGHTFALL TO TAKE ACTION...
I AGREE. THAT SEEMS MORE REASONABLE TO ME.
KNOW THIS: WE'RE RISKING OUR LIVES, BUT ALSO HORRIBLE TORTURE, IF WE'RE CAPTURED!
IT'S TIME!
I HOPE THOSE SAVAGES WILL BE UNDER THE GRIP OF OPIUM. THAT'LL MAKE THINGS EASIER FOR US.
WE'LL FIND OUT VERY SOON!
SHHH!

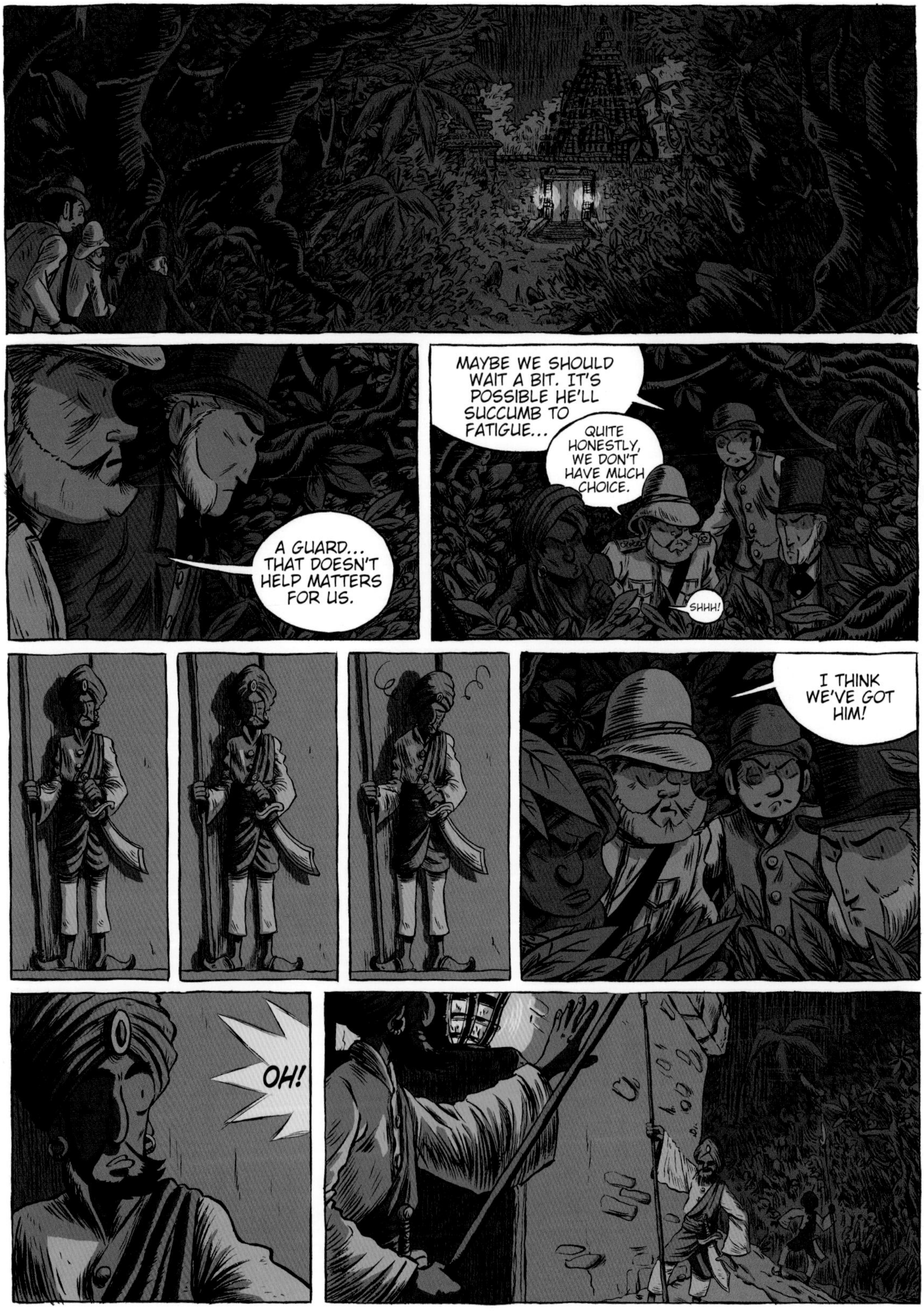
A GUARD... THAT DOESN'T HELP MATTERS FOR US.
MAYBE WE SHOULD WAIT A BIT. IT'S POSSIBLE HE'LL SUCCUMB TO FATIGUE...
QUITE HONESTLY, WE DON'T HAVE MUCH CHOICE.
SHHH!
I THINK WE'VE GOT HIM!
OH!

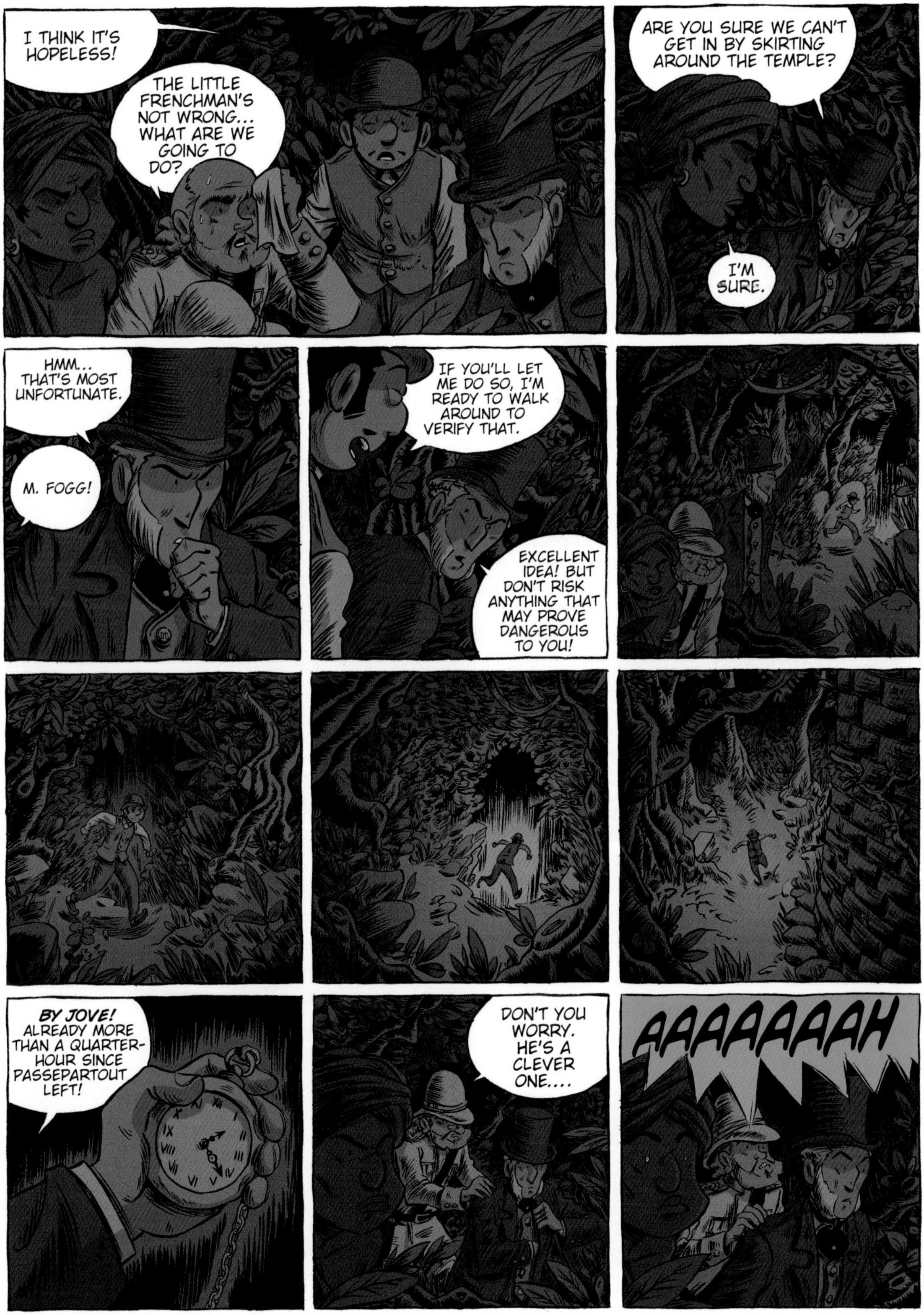
I THINK IT'S HOPELESS!
THE LITTLE FRENCHMAN'S NOT WRONG... WHAT ARE WE GOING TO DO?
ARE YOU SURE WE CAN'T GET IN BY SKIRTING AROUND THE TEMPLE?
I'M SURE.
HMM... THAT'S MOST UNFORTUNATE.
M. FOGG!
IF YOU'LL LET ME DO SO, I'M READY TO WALK AROUND TO VERIFY THAT.
EXCELLENT IDEA! BUT DON'T RISK ANYTHING THAT MAY PROVE DANGEROUS TO YOU!
BY JOVE! ALREADY MORE THAN A QUARTER-HOUR SINCE PASSEPARTOUT LEFT!
DON'T YOU WORRY. HE'S A CLEVER ONE....
AAAAAAAH

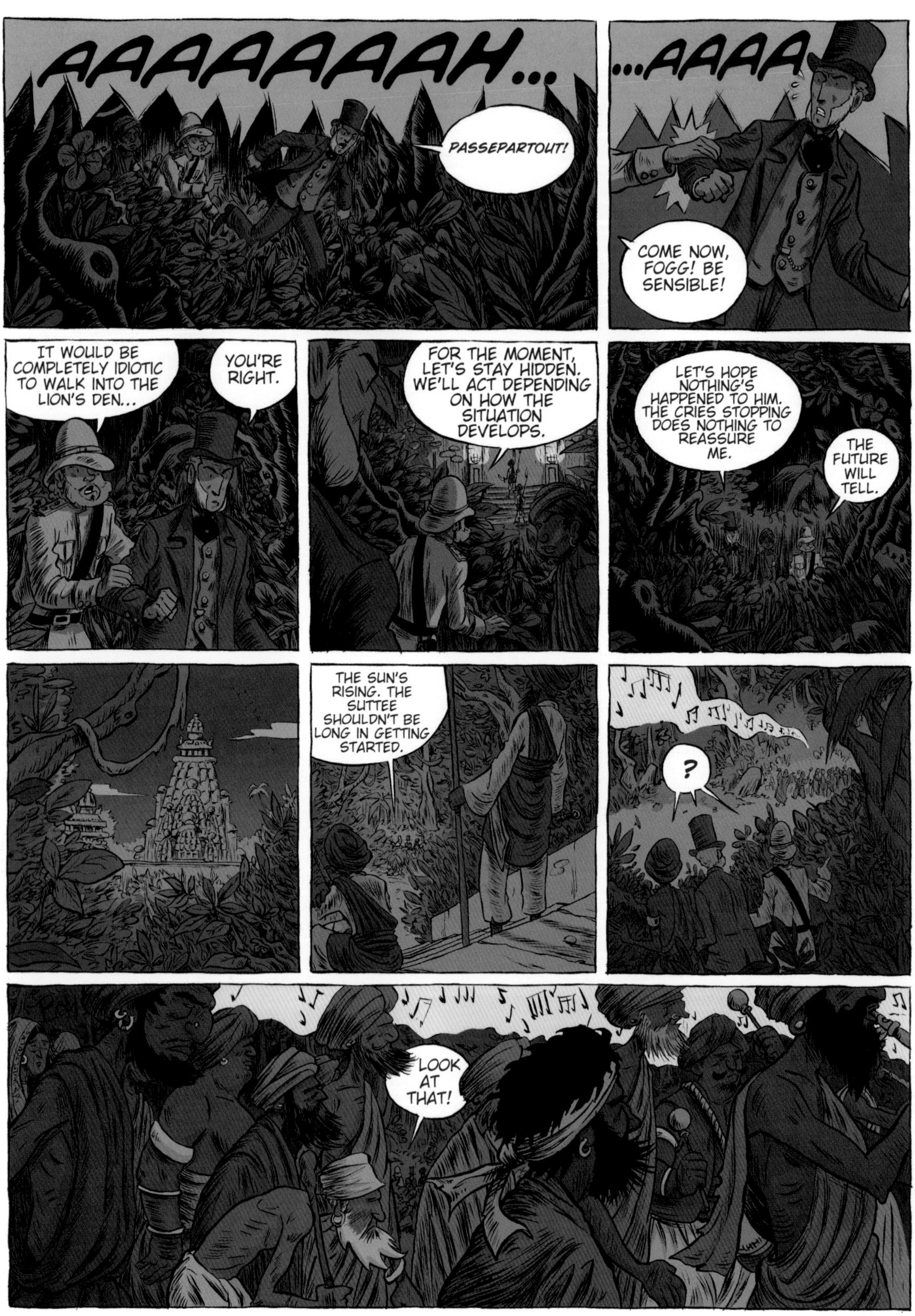
AAAAAAAAH...
PASSEPARTOUT!
...AAAA
COME NOW, FOGG! BE SENSIBLE!
IT WOULD BE COMPLETELY IDIOTIC TO WALK INTO THE LION'S DEN...
YOU'RE RIGHT.
FOR THE MOMENT, LET'S STAY HIDDEN. WE'LL ACT DEPENDING ON HOW THE SITUATION DEVELOPS.
LET'S HOPE NOTHING'S HAPPENED TO HIM. THE CRIES STOPPING DOES NOTHING TO REASSURE ME.
THE FUTURE WILL TELL.
THE SUN'S RISING. THE SUTTEE SHOULDN'T BE LONG IN GETTING STARTED.
?
LOOK AT THAT!

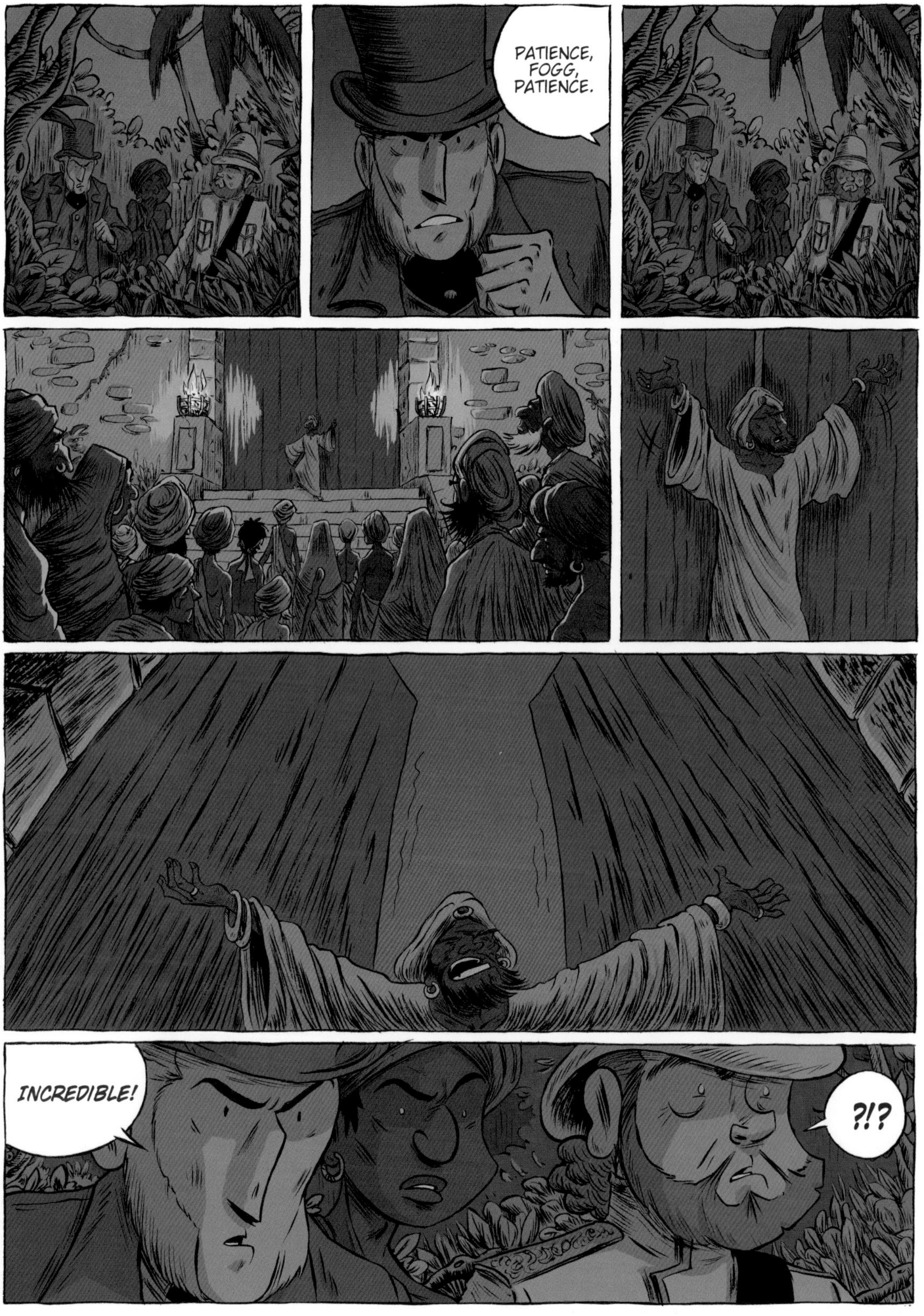
PATIENCE, FOGG, PATIENCE.
INCREDIBLE!
?!?

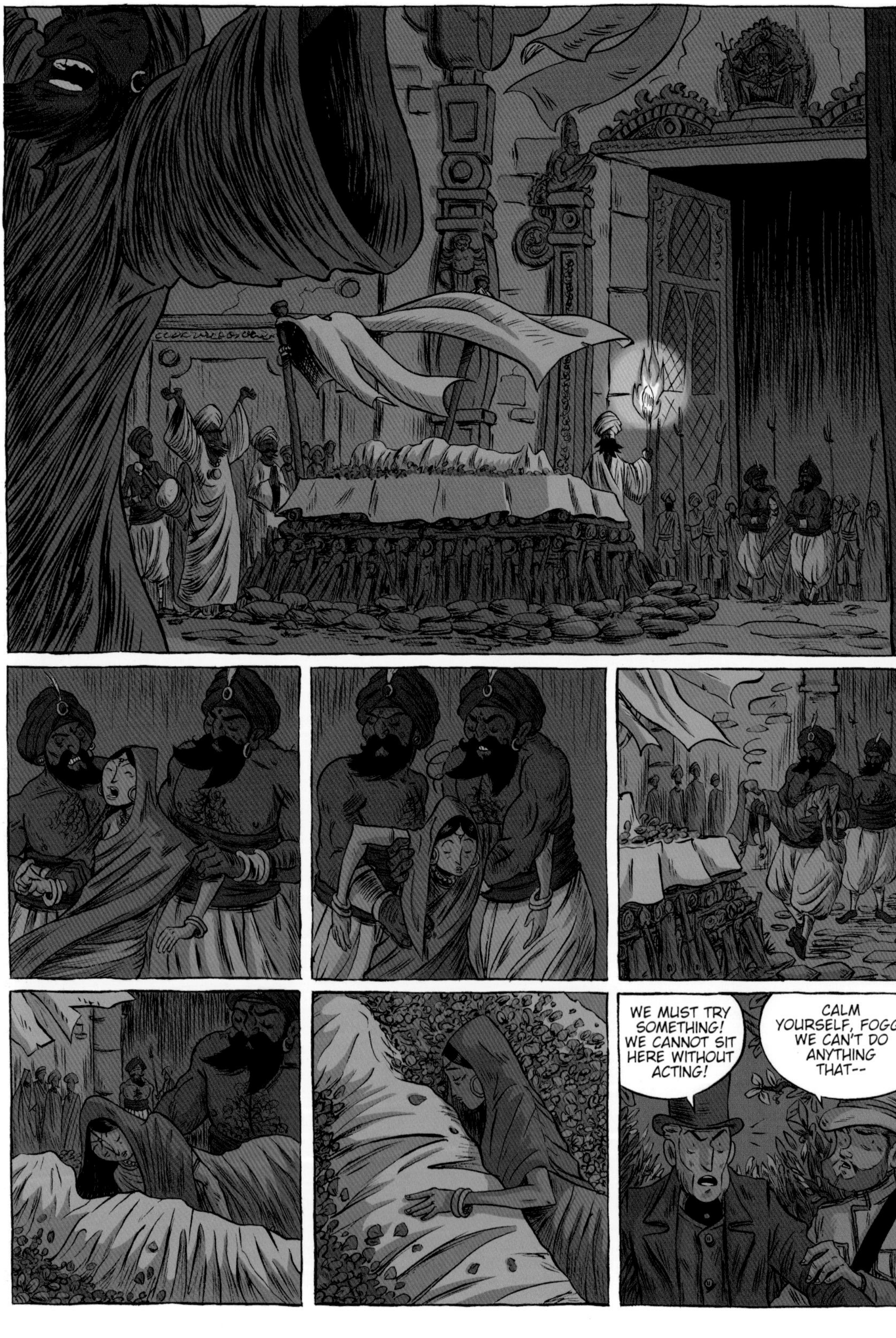
WE MUST TRY SOMETHING! WE CANNOT SIT HERE WITHOUT ACTING!
CALM YOURSELF, FOGG! WE CAN'T DO ANYTHING THAT--

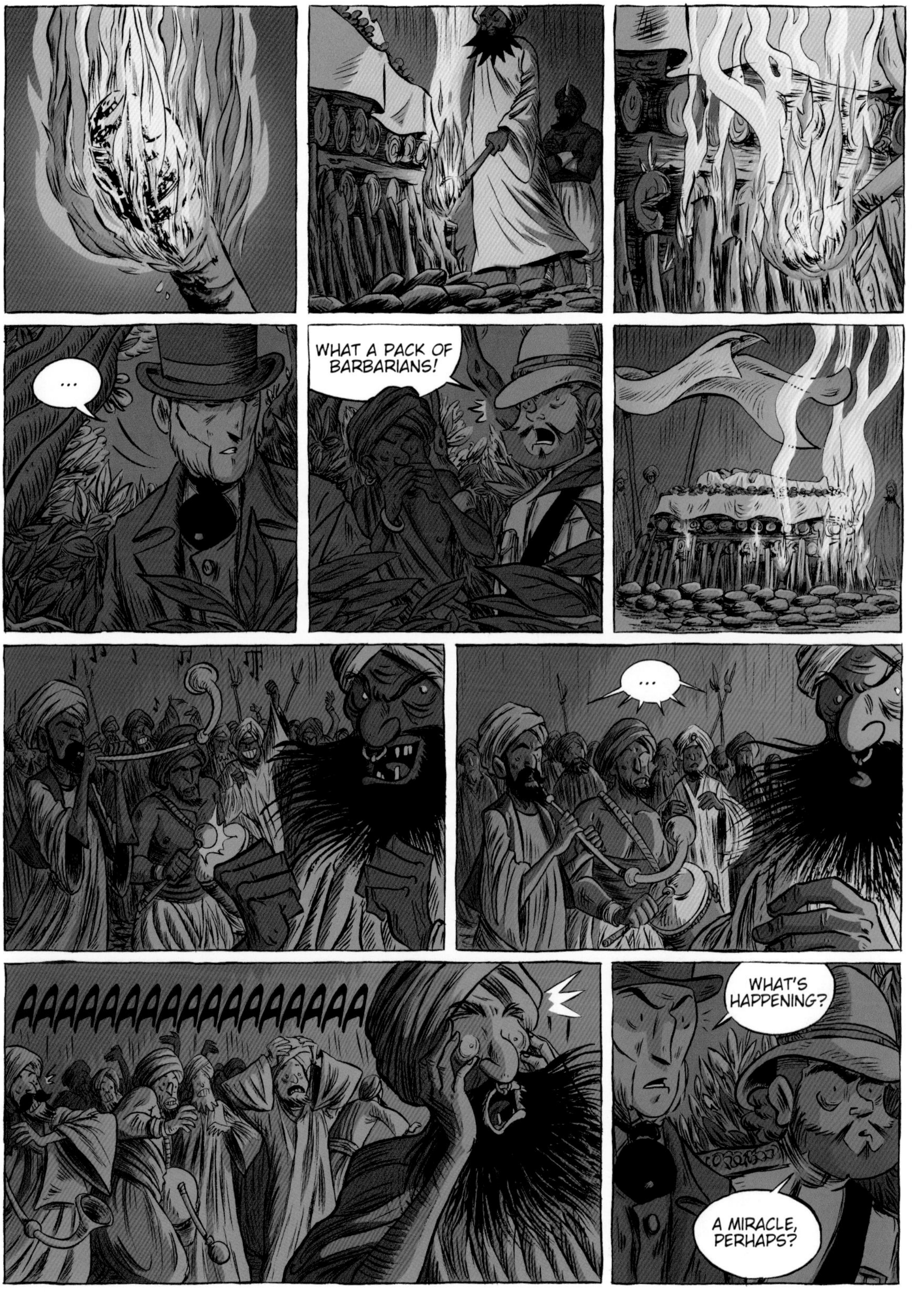
...
WHAT A PACK OF BARBARIANS!
...
AAAAAAAAAAAAAAAAAAA
WHAT'S HAPPENING?
A MIRACLE, PERHAPS?

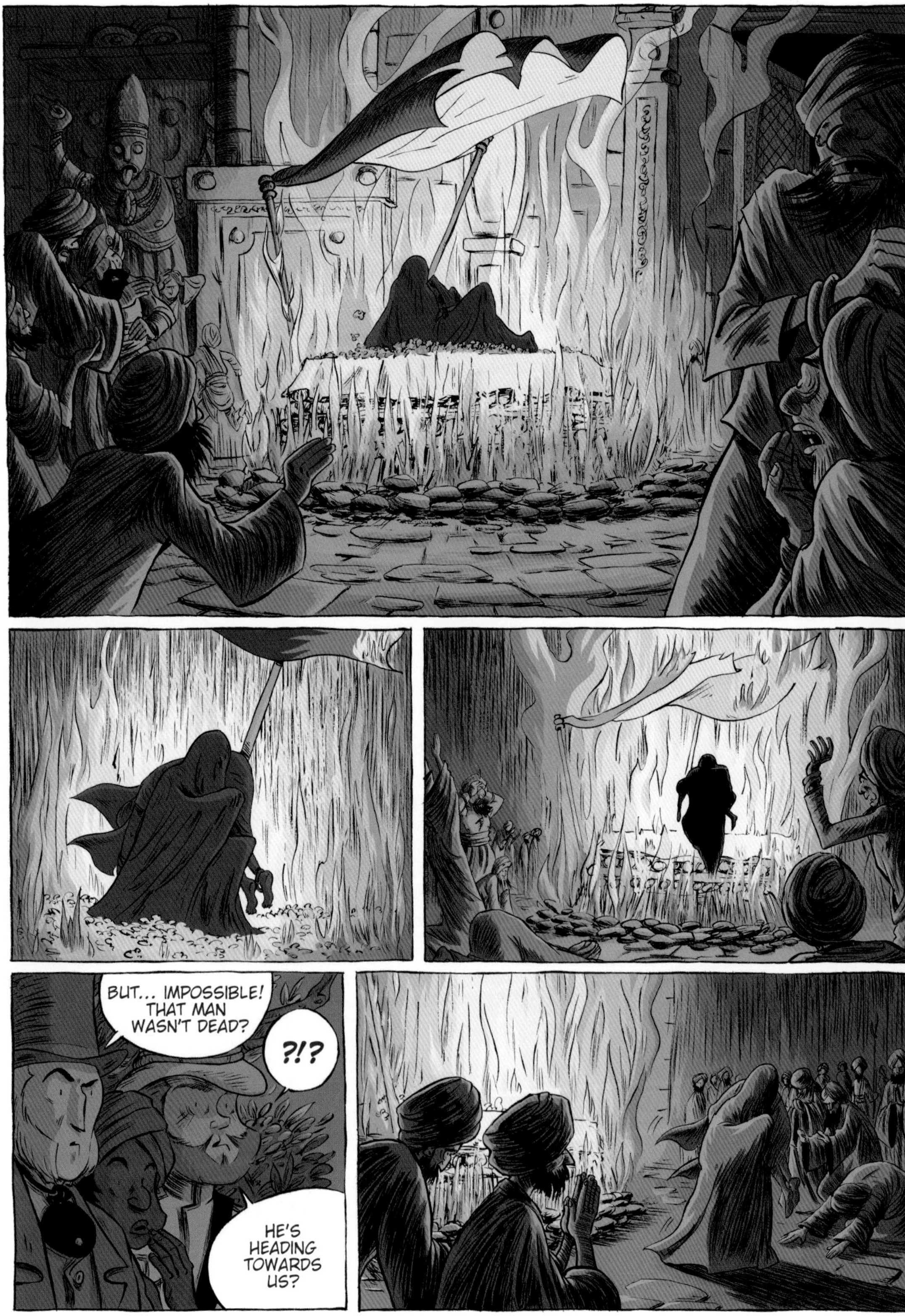

BUT... IMPOSSIBLE! THAT MAN WASN'T DEAD?
?!?
HE'S HEADING TOWARDS US?

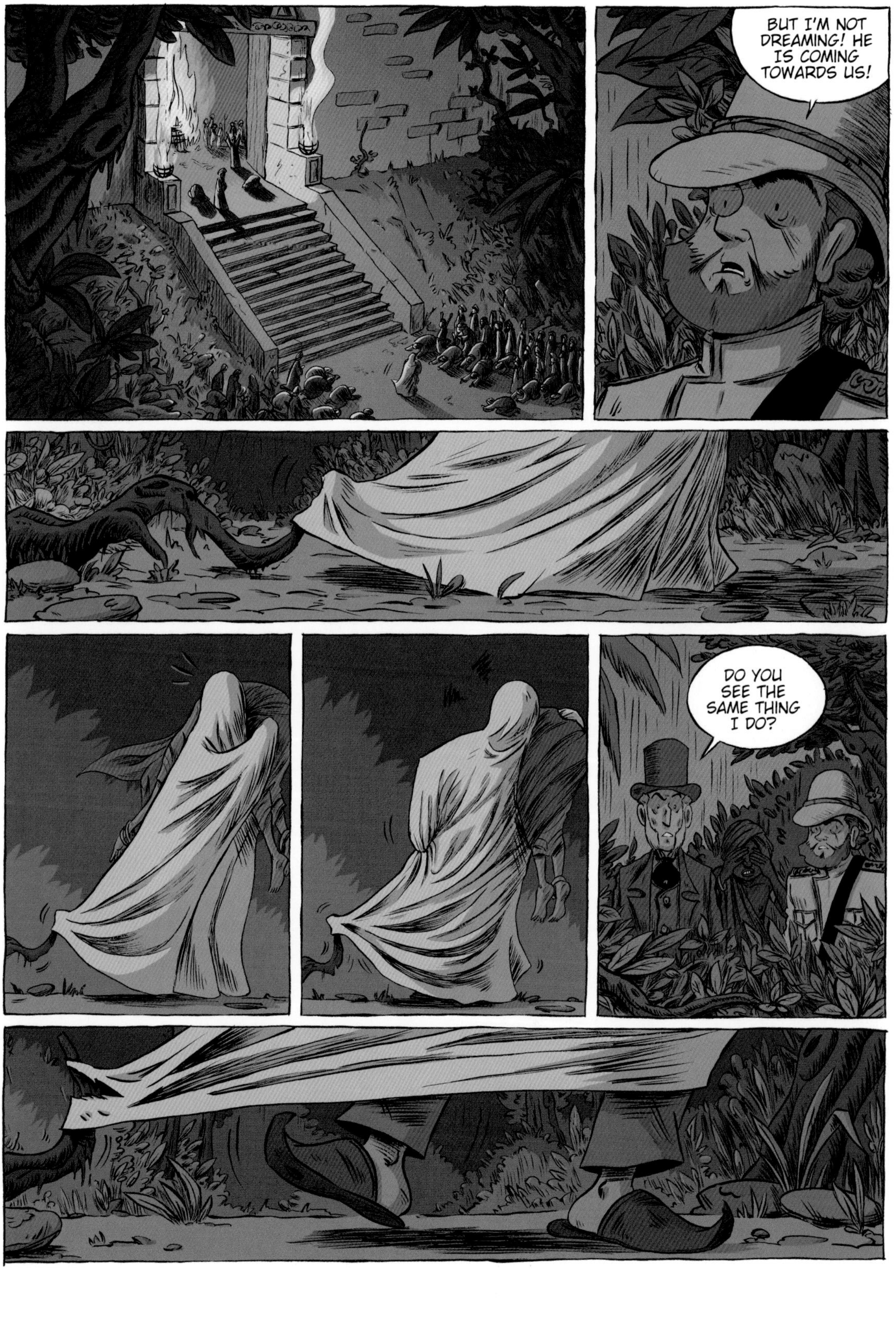
BUT I'M NOT DREAMING! HE IS COMING TOWARDS US!
DO YOU SEE THE SAME THING I DO?

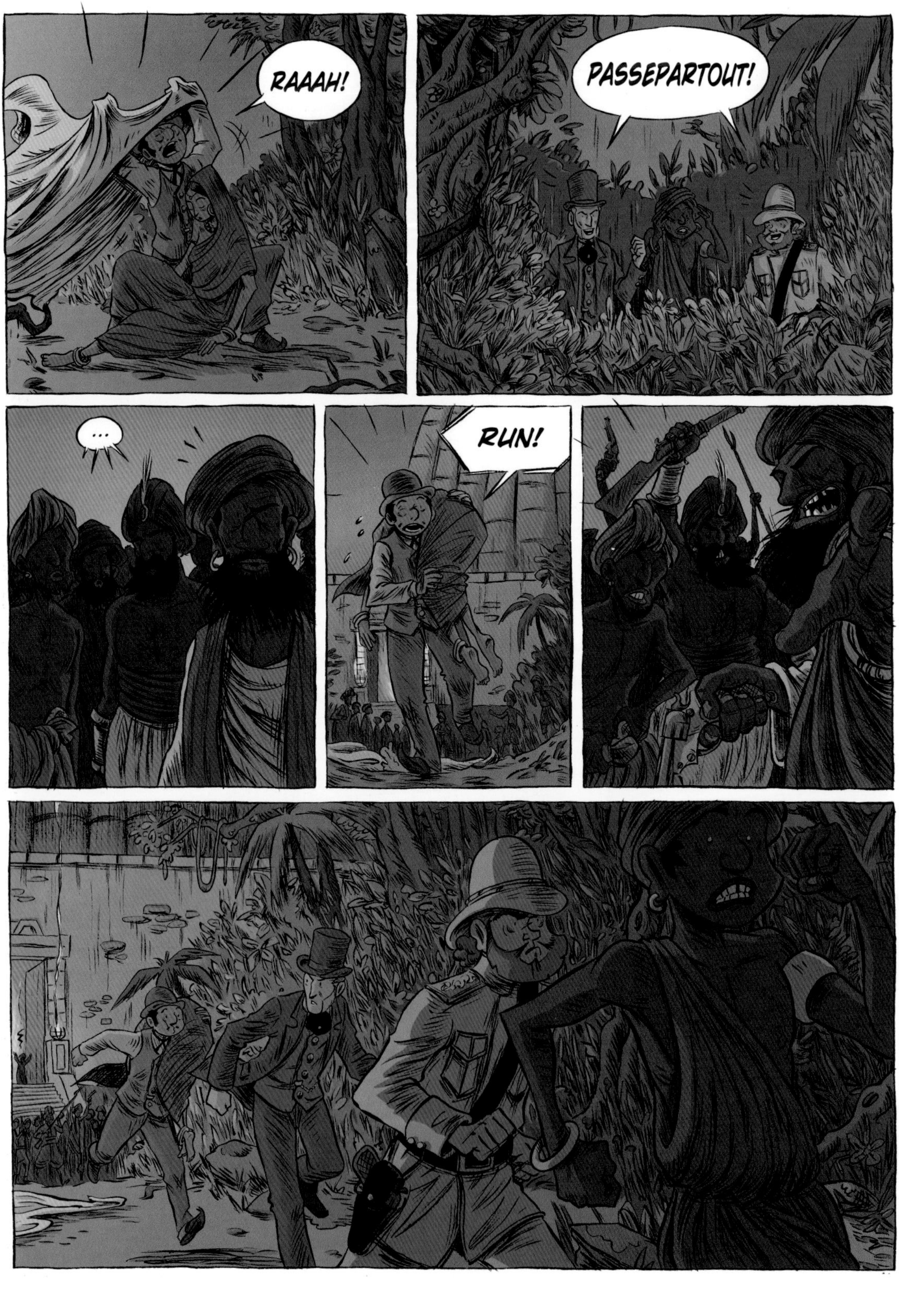
RAAAH!
PASSEPARTOUT!
...
RUN!

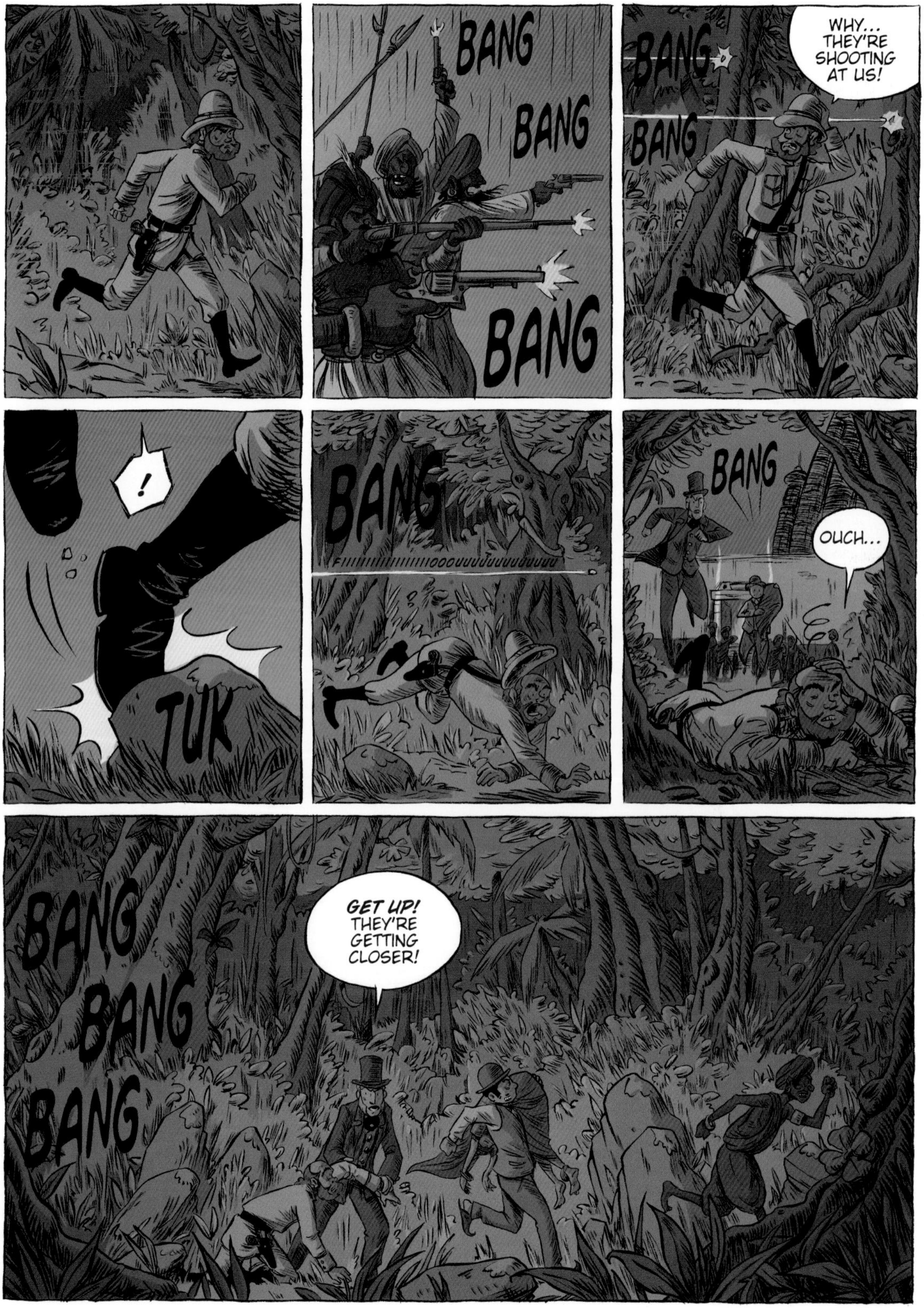
BANG
BANG
BANG
BANG
BANG
WHY... THEY'RE SHOOTING AT US!
!
TUK
BANG
BANG
OUCH...
BANG
BANG
BANG
GET UP! THEY'RE GETTING CLOSER!

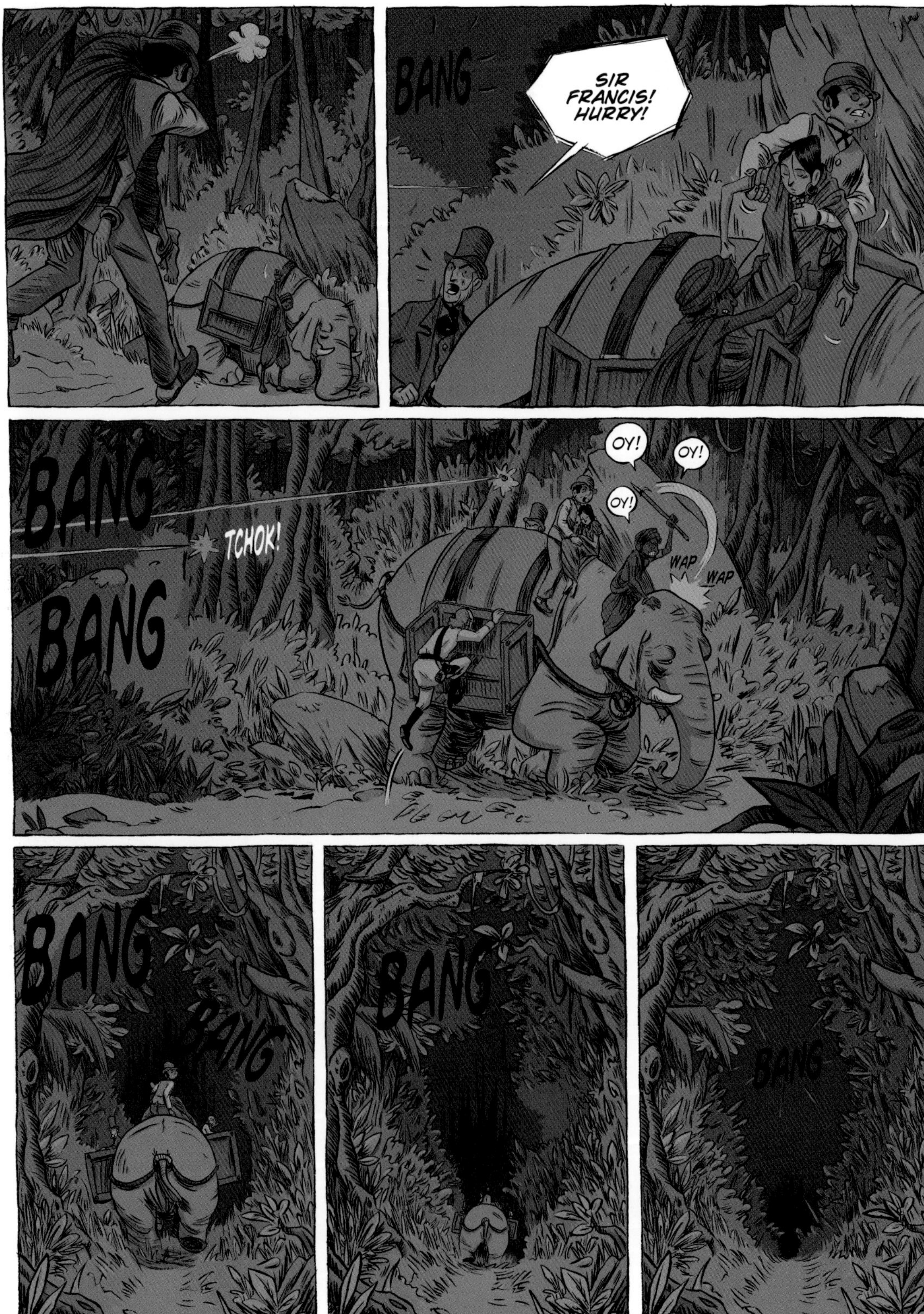
BANG
SIR FRANCIS! HURRY!
CHUCK!
OY!
OY!
OY!
BANG
TCHOK!
BANG
WAP
WAP
BANG
BANG
BANG
BANG

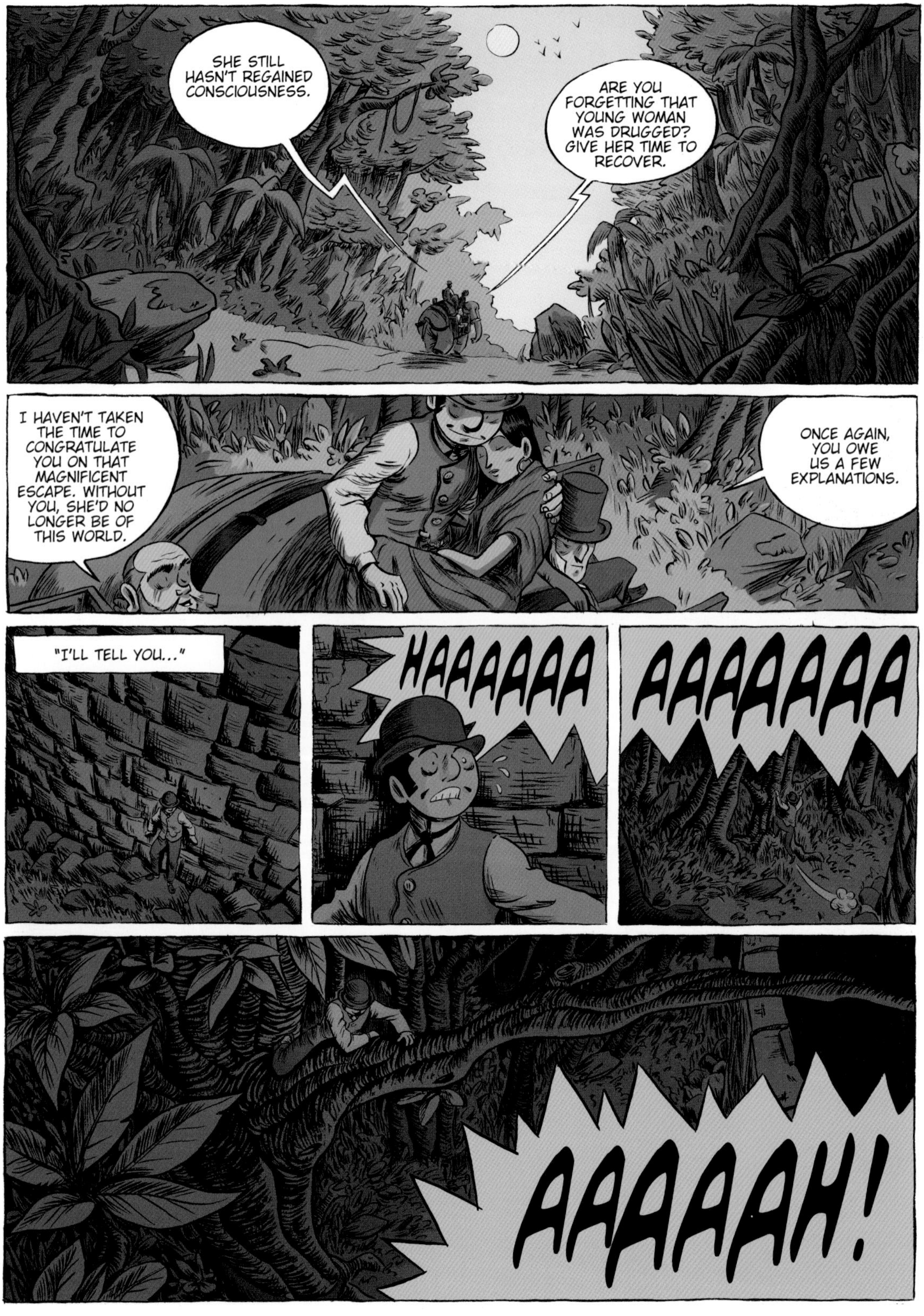
SHE STILL HASN'T REGAINED CONSCIOUSNESS.
ARE YOU FORGETTING THAT YOUNG WOMAN WAS DRUGGED? GIVE HER TIME TO RECOVER.
I HAVEN'T TAKEN THE TIME TO CONGRATULATE YOU ON THAT MAGNIFICENT ESCAPE. WITHOUT YOU, SHE'D NO LONGER BE OF THIS WORLD.
ONCE AGAIN, YOU OWE US A FEW EXPLANATIONS.
"I'LL TELL YOU..."
HAAAAAA
AAAAAAA
AAAAAH!

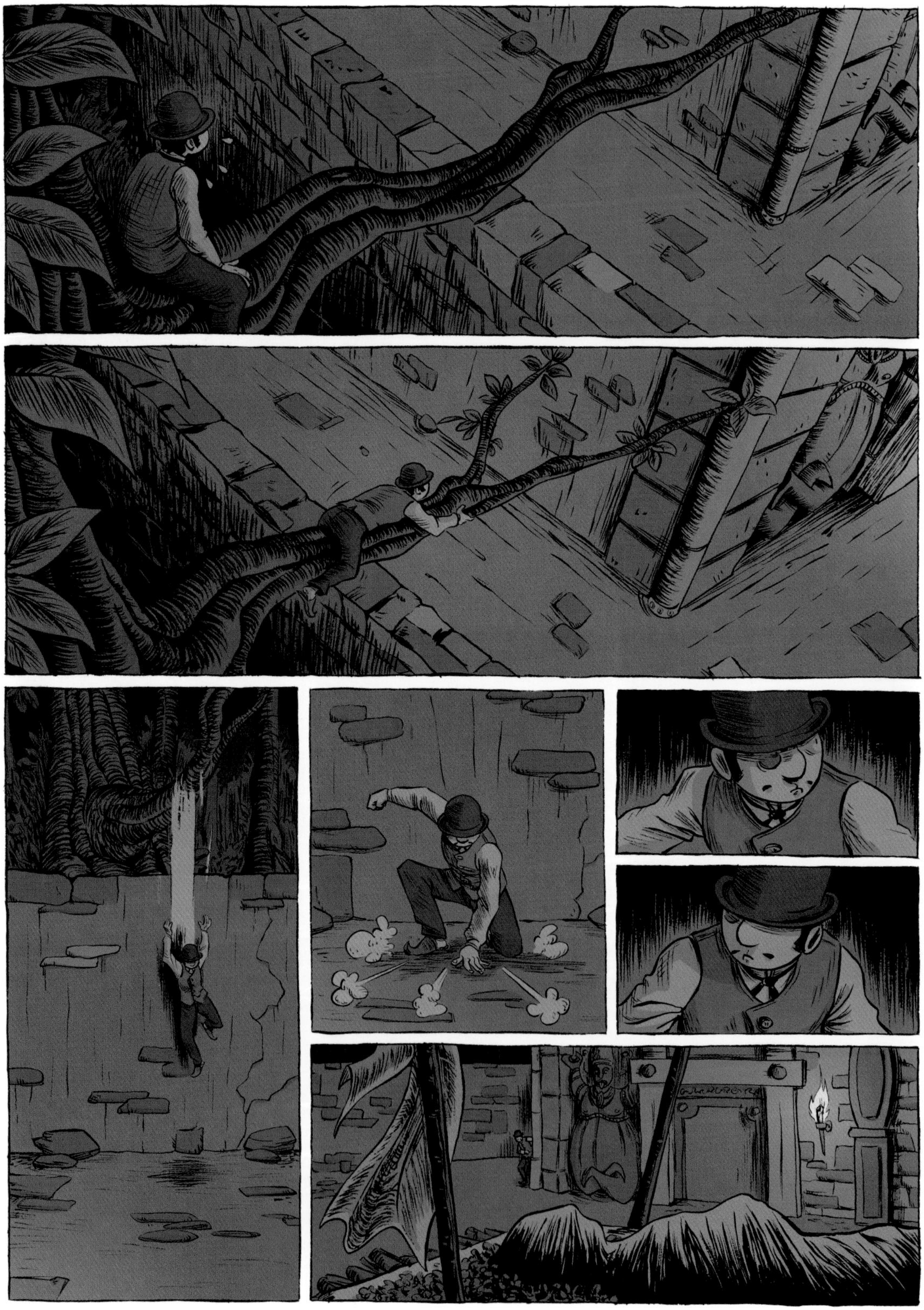

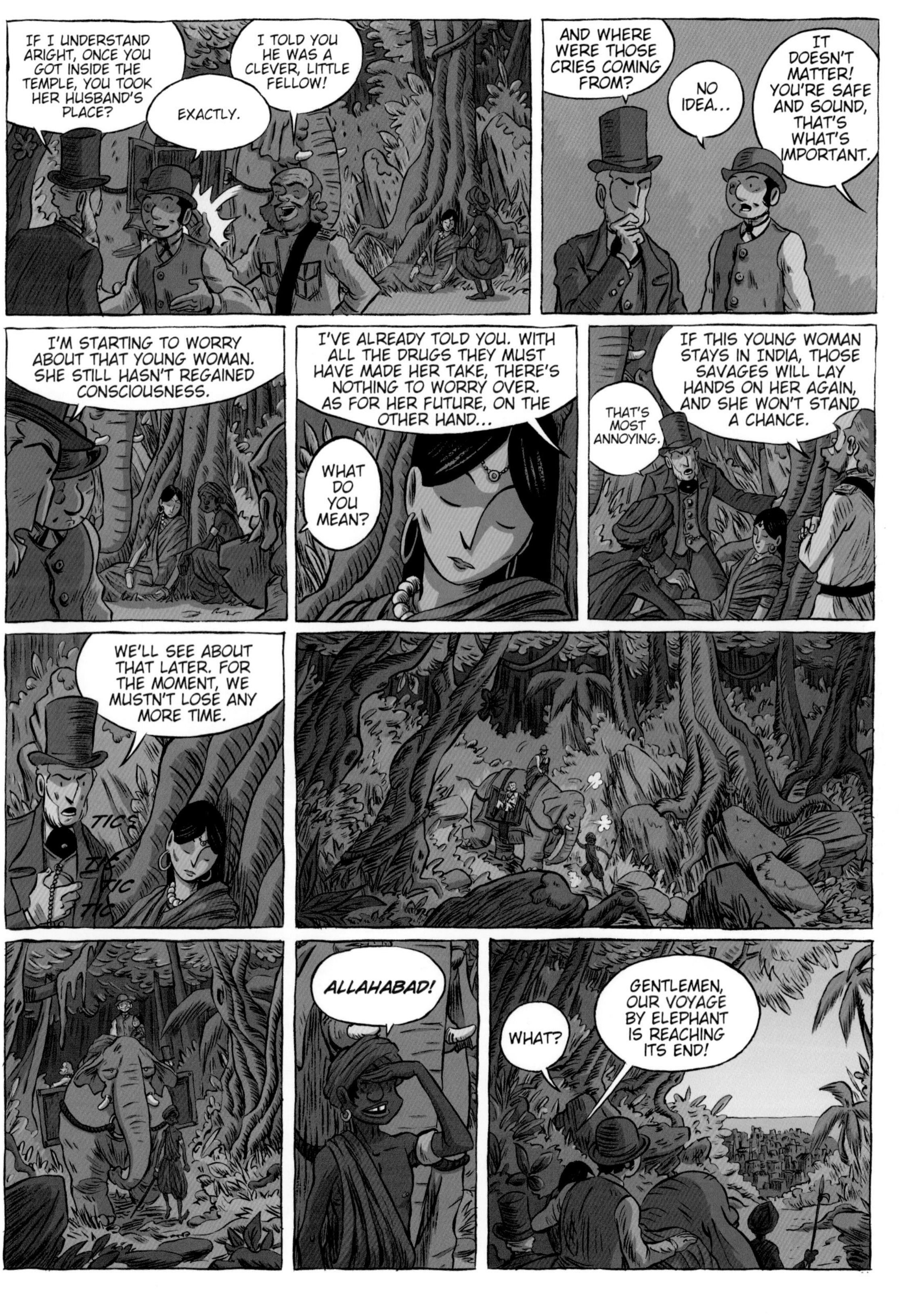
IF I UNDERSTAND ARIGHT, ONCE YOU GOT INSIDE THE TEMPLE, YOU TOOK HER HUSBAND'S PLACE?
EXACTLY.
I TOLD YOU HE WAS A CLEVER, LITTLE FELLOW!
AND WHERE WERE THOSE CRIES COMING FROM?
NO IDEA...
IT DOESN'T MATTER! YOU'RE SAFE AND SOUND, THAT'S WHAT'S IMPORTANT.
I'M STARTING TO WORRY ABOUT THAT YOUNG WOMAN. SHE STILL HASN'T REGAINED CONSCIOUSNESS.
I'VE ALREADY TOLD YOU. WITH ALL THE DRUGS THEY MUST HAVE MADE HER TAKE, THERE'S NOTHING TO WORRY OVER. AS FOR HER FUTURE, ON THE OTHER HAND...
WHAT DO YOU MEAN?
IF THIS YOUNG WOMAN STAYS IN INDIA, THOSE SAVAGES WILL LAY HANDS ON HER AGAIN, AND SHE WON'T STAND A CHANCE.
THAT'S MOST ANNOYING.
WE'LL SEE ABOUT THAT LATER. FOR THE MOMENT, WE MUSTN'T LOSE ANY MORE TIME.
TICS
TIC
TIC
TIC
ALLAHABAD!
WHAT?
GENTLEMEN, OUR VOYAGE BY ELEPHANT IS REACHING ITS END!

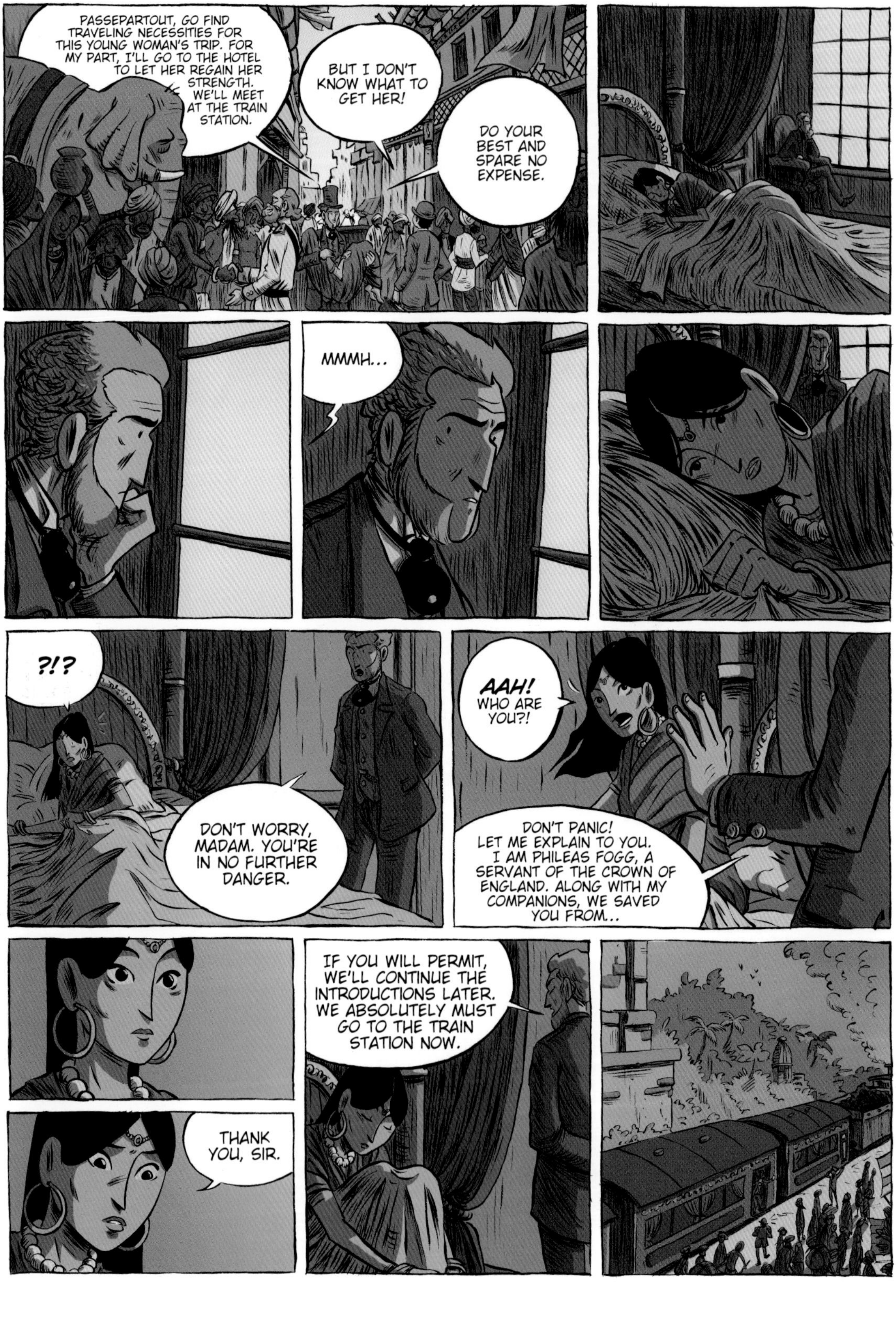
PASSEPARTOUT, GO FIND TRAVELING NECESSITIES FOR THIS YOUNG WOMAN'S TRIP. FOR MY PART, I'LL GO TO THE HOTEL TO LET HER REGAIN HER STRENGTH. WE'LL MEET AT THE TRAIN STATION.
BUT I DON'T KNOW WHAT TO GET HER!
DO YOUR BEST AND SPARE NO EXPENSE.
MMMH...
?!?
DON'T WORRY, MADAM. YOU'RE IN NO FURTHER DANGER.
AAH! WHO ARE YOU?!
DON'T PANIC! LET ME EXPLAIN TO YOU. I AM PHILEAS FOGG, A SERVANT OF THE CROWN OF ENGLAND. ALONG WITH MY COMPANIONS, WE SAVED YOU FROM...
IF YOU WILL PERMIT, WE'LL CONTINUE THE INTRODUCTIONS LATER. WE ABSOLUTELY MUST GO TO THE TRAIN STATION NOW.
THANK YOU, SIR.

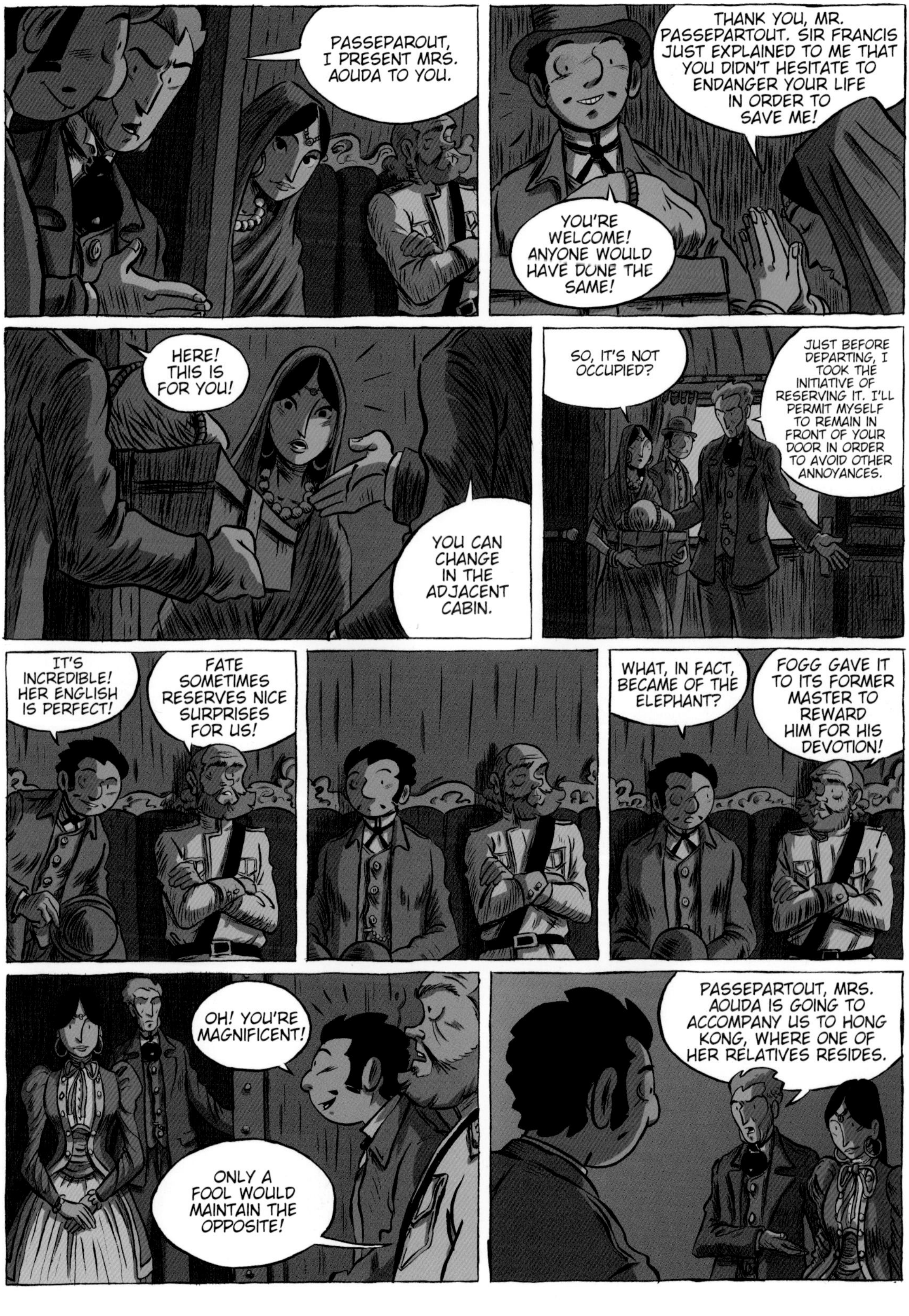
PASSEPAROUT, I PRESENT MRS. AOUDA TO YOU.
THANK YOU, MR. PASSEPARTOUT. SIR FRANCIS JUST EXPLAINED TO ME THAT YOU DIDN'T HESITATE TO ENDANGER YOUR LIFE IN ORDER TO SAVE ME!
YOU'RE WELCOME! ANYONE WOULD HAVE DONE THE SAME!
HERE! THIS IS FOR YOU!
YOU CAN CHANGE IN THE ADJACENT CABIN.
SO, IT'S NOT OCCUPIED?
JUST BEFORE DEPARTING, I TOOK THE INITIATIVE OF RESERVING IT. I'LL PERMIT MYSELF TO REMAIN IN FRONT OF YOUR DOOR IN ORDER TO AVOID OTHER ANNOYANCES.
IT'S INCREDIBLE! HER ENGLISH IS PERFECT!
FATE SOMETIMES RESERVES NICE SURPRISES FOR US!
WHAT, IN FACT, BECAME OF THE ELEPHANT?
FOGG GAVE IT TO ITS FORMER MASTER TO REWARD HIM FOR HIS DEVOTION!
OH! YOU'RE MAGNIFICENT!
ONLY A FOOL WOULD MAINTAIN THE OPPOSITE!
PASSEPARTOUT, MRS. AOUDA IS GOING TO ACCOMPANY US TO HONG KONG, WHERE ONE OF HER RELATIVES RESIDES.

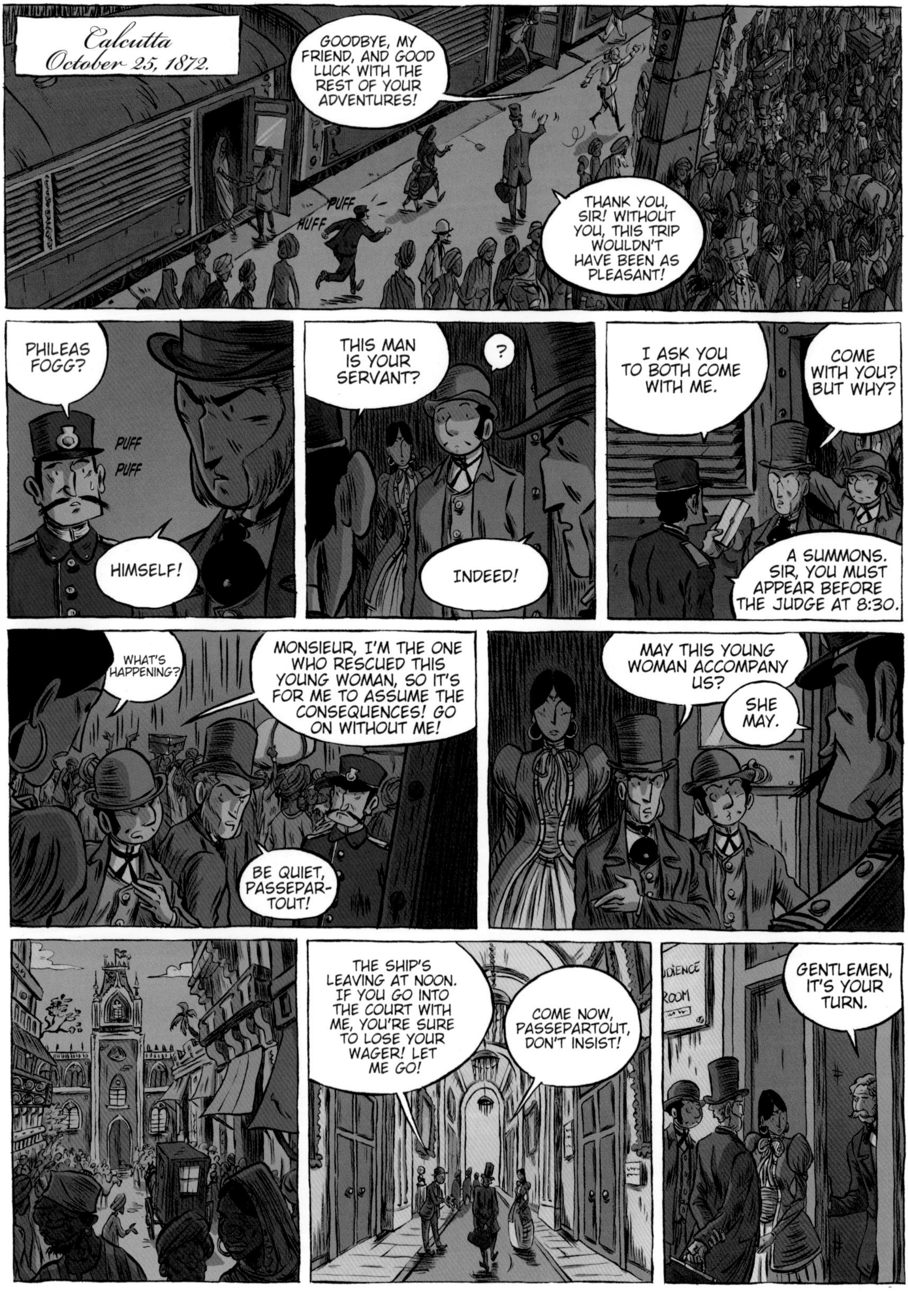
Calcutta
October 25, 1872.
GOODBYE, MY FRIEND, AND GOOD LUCK WITH THE REST OF YOUR ADVENTURES!
PUFF
HUFF
THANK YOU, SIR! WITHOUT YOU, THIS TRIP WOULDN'T HAVE BEEN AS PLEASANT!
PHILEAS FOGG?
PUFF
PUFF
HIMSELF!
THIS MAN IS YOUR SERVANT?
?
INDEED!
I ASK YOU TO BOTH COME WITH ME.
COME WITH YOU? BUT WHY?
A SUMMONS. SIR, YOU MUST APPEAR BEFORE THE JUDGE AT 8:30.
WHAT'S HAPPENING?
MONSIEUR, I'M THE ONE WHO RESCUED THIS YOUNG WOMAN, SO IT'S FOR ME TO ASSUME THE CONSEQUENCES! GO ON WITHOUT ME!
BE QUIET, PASSEPARTOUT!
MAY THIS YOUNG WOMAN ACCOMPANY US?
SHE MAY.
THE SHIP'S LEAVING AT NOON. IF YOU GO INTO THE COURT WITH ME, YOU'RE SURE TO LOSE YOUR WAGER! LET ME GO!
COME NOW, PASSEPARTOUT, DON'T INSIST!
UDIENCE ROOM
GENTLEMEN, IT'S YOUR TURN.

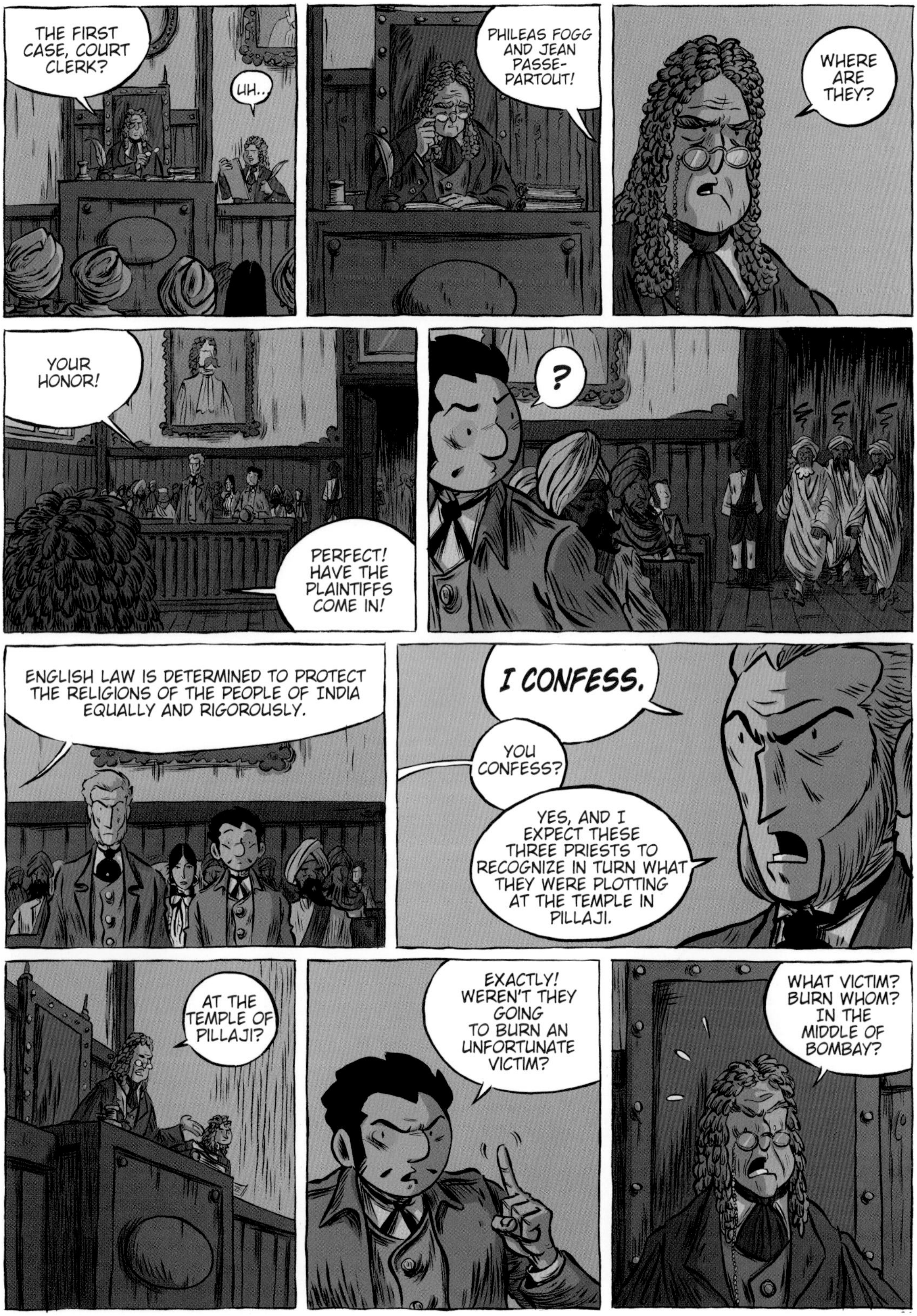
THE FIRST CASE, COURT CLERK?
UH...
PHILEAS FOGG AND JEAN PASSE-PARTOUT!
WHERE ARE THEY?
YOUR HONOR!
PERFECT! HAVE THE PLAINTIFFS COME IN!
?
ENGLISH LAW IS DETERMINED TO PROTECT THE RELIGIONS OF THE PEOPLE OF INDIA EQUALLY AND RIGOROUSLY.
I CONFESS.
YOU CONFESS?
YES, AND I EXPECT THESE THREE PRIESTS TO RECOGNIZE IN TURN WHAT THEY WERE PLOTTING AT THE TEMPLE IN PILLAJI.
AT THE TEMPLE OF PILLAJI?
EXACTLY! WEREN'T THEY GOING TO BURN AN UNFORTUNATE VICTIM?
WHAT VICTIM? BURN WHOM? IN THE MIDDLE OF BOMBAY?

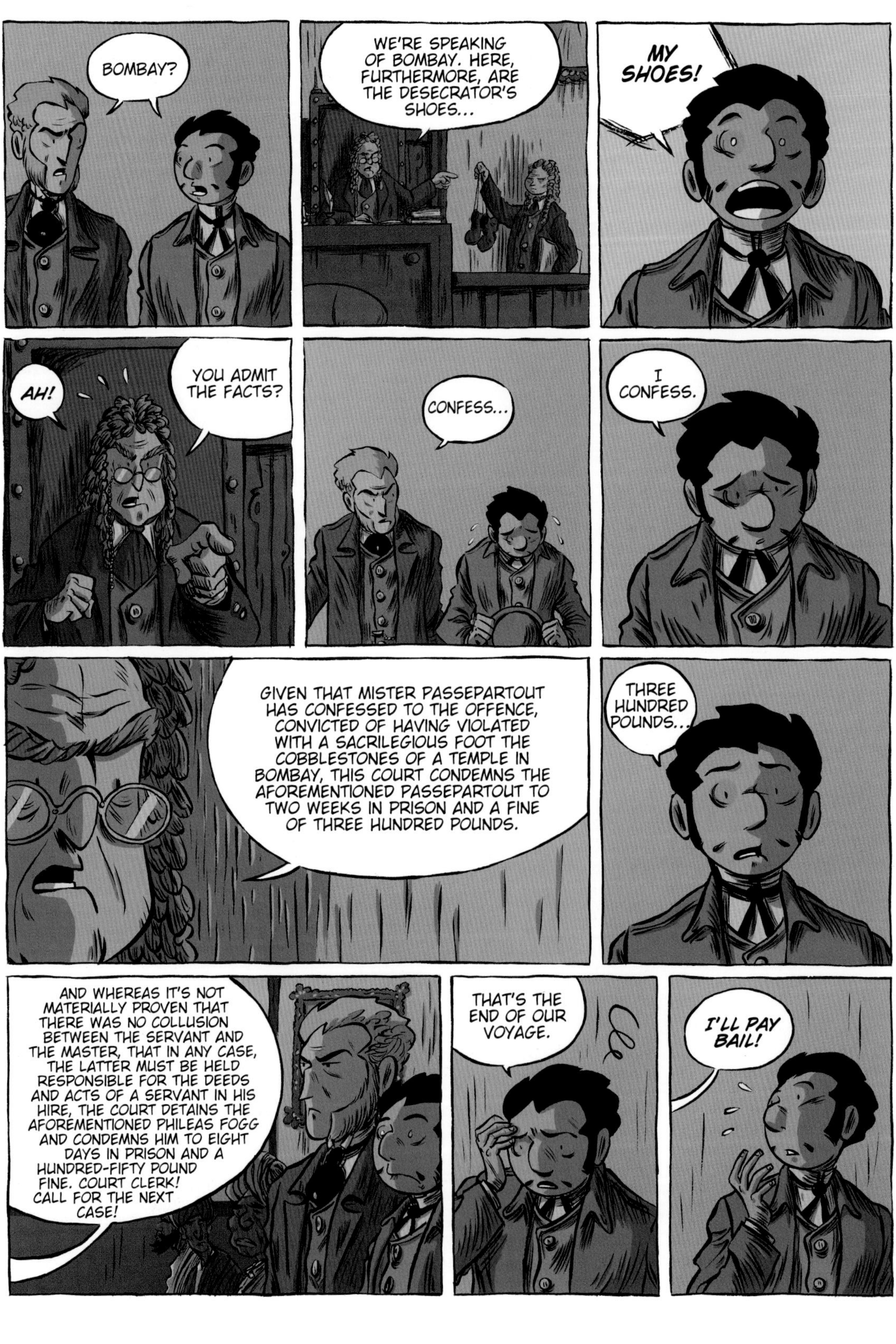
BOMBAY?
WE'RE SPEAKING OF BOMBAY. HERE, FURTHERMORE, ARE THE DESECRATOR'S SHOES...
MY SHOES!
AH!
YOU ADMIT THE FACTS?
CONFESS...
I CONFESS.
GIVEN THAT MISTER PASSEPARTOUT HAS CONFESSED TO THE OFFENCE, CONVICTED OF HAVING VIOLATED WITH A SACRILEGIOUS FOOT THE COBBLESTONES OF A TEMPLE IN BOMBAY, THIS COURT CONDEMNS THE AFOREMENTIONED PASSEPARTOUT TO TWO WEEKS IN PRISON AND A FINE OF THREE HUNDRED POUNDS.
THREE HUNDRED POUNDS...
AND WHEREAS IT'S NOT MATERIALLY PROVEN THAT THERE WAS NO COLLUSION BETWEEN THE SERVANT AND THE MASTER, THAT IN ANY CASE, THE LATTER MUST BE HELD RESPONSIBLE FOR THE DEEDS AND ACTS OF A SERVANT IN HIS HIRE, THE COURT DETAINS THE AFOREMENTIONED PHILEAS FOGG AND CONDEMNS HIM TO EIGHT DAYS IN PRISON AND A HUNDRED-FIFTY POUND FINE. COURT CLERK! CALL FOR THE NEXT CASE!
THAT'S THE END OF OUR VOYAGE.
I'LL PAY BAIL!

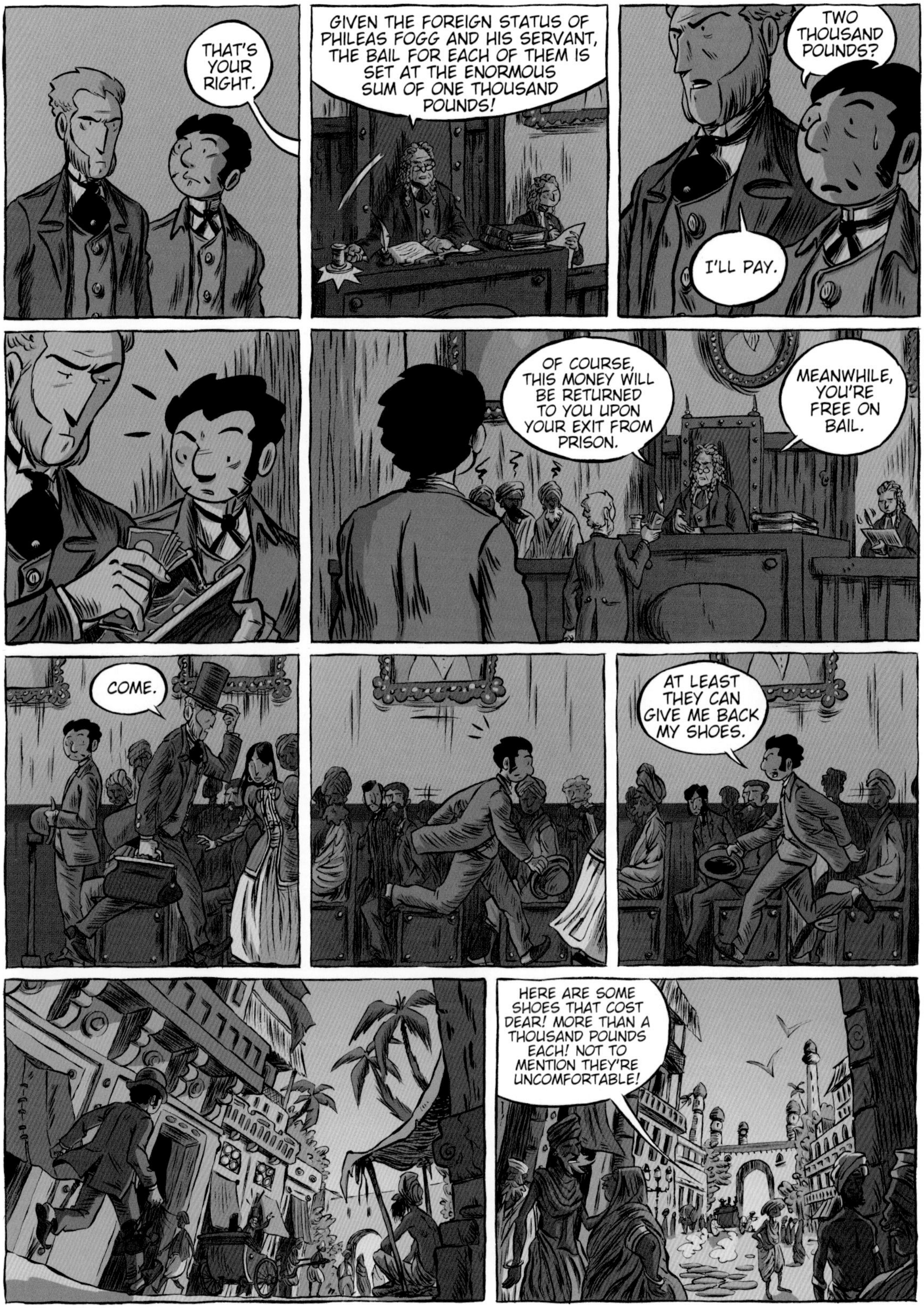
THAT'S YOUR RIGHT.
GIVEN THE FOREIGN STATUS OF PHILEAS FOGG AND HIS SERVANT, THE BAIL FOR EACH OF THEM IS SET AT THE ENORMOUS SUM OF ONE THOUSAND POUNDS!
TWO THOUSAND POUNDS?
I'LL PAY.
OF COURSE, THIS MONEY WILL BE RETURNED TO YOU UPON YOUR EXIT FROM PRISON.
MEANWHILE, YOU'RE FREE ON BAIL.
COME.
AT LEAST THEY CAN GIVE ME BACK MY SHOES.
HERE ARE SOME SHOES THAT COST DEAR! MORE THAN A THOUSAND POUNDS EACH! NOT TO MENTION THEY'RE UNCOMFORTABLE!

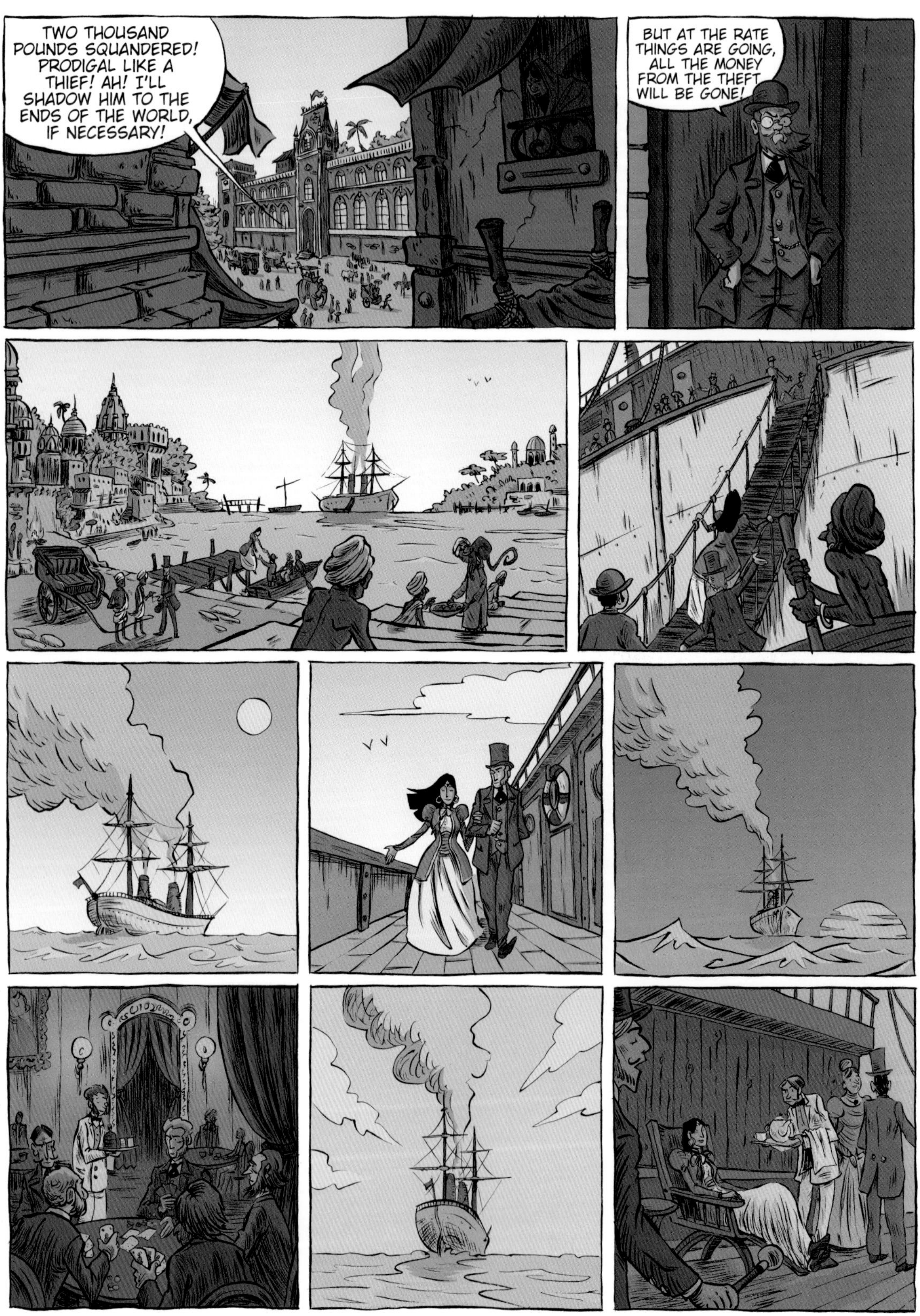
TWO THOUSAND POUNDS SQUANDERED! PRODIGAL LIKE A THIEF! AH! I'LL SHADOW HIM TO THE ENDS OF THE WORLD, IF NECESSARY!
BUT AT THE RATE THINGS ARE GOING, ALL THE MONEY FROM THE THEFT WILL BE GONE!

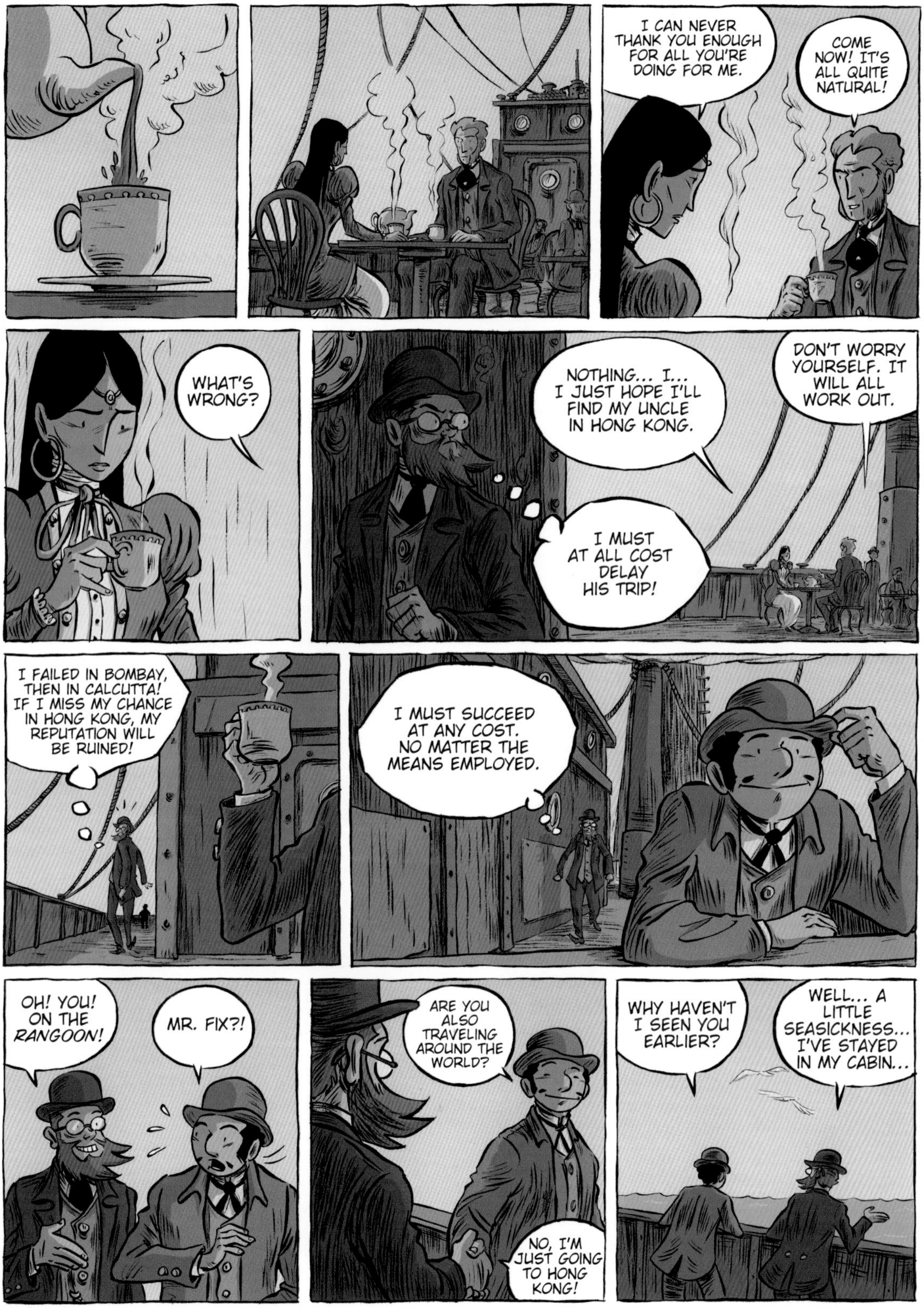
I CAN NEVER THANK YOU ENOUGH FOR ALL YOU'RE DOING FOR ME.
COME NOW! IT'S ALL QUITE NATURAL!
WHAT'S WRONG?
NOTHING... I... I JUST HOPE I'LL FIND MY UNCLE IN HONG KONG.
DON'T WORRY YOURSELF. IT WILL ALL WORK OUT.
I MUST AT ALL COST DELAY HIS TRIP!
I FAILED IN BOMBAY, THEN IN CALCUTTA! IF I MISS MY CHANCE IN HONG KONG, MY REPUTATION WILL BE RUINED!
I MUST SUCCEED AT ANY COST. NO MATTER THE MEANS EMPLOYED.
OH! YOU! ON THE *RANGOON*!
MR. FIX?!
ARE YOU ALSO TRAVELING AROUND THE WORLD?
NO, I'M JUST GOING TO HONG KONG!
WHY HAVEN'T I SEEN YOU EARLIER?
WELL... A LITTLE SEASICKNESS... I'VE STAYED IN MY CABIN...

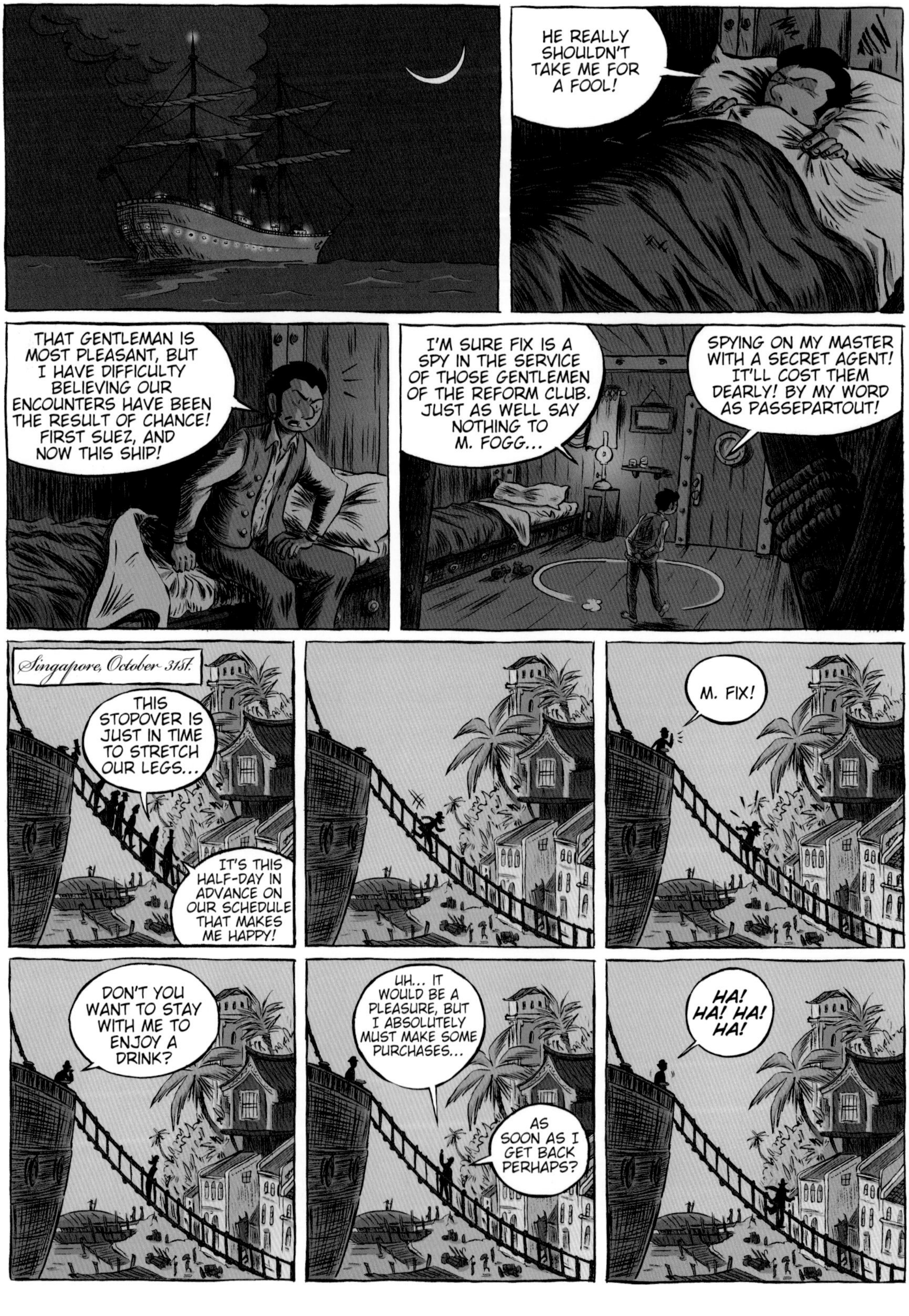
HE REALLY SHOULDN'T TAKE ME FOR A FOOL!
THAT GENTLEMAN IS MOST PLEASANT, BUT I HAVE DIFFICULTY BELIEVING OUR ENCOUNTERS HAVE BEEN THE RESULT OF CHANCE! FIRST SUEZ, AND NOW THIS SHIP!
I'M SURE FIX IS A SPY IN THE SERVICE OF THOSE GENTLEMEN OF THE REFORM CLUB. JUST AS WELL SAY NOTHING TO M. FOGG...
SPYING ON MY MASTER WITH A SECRET AGENT! IT'LL COST THEM DEARLY! BY MY WORD AS PASSEPARTOUT!
Singapore, October 31st.
THIS STOPOVER IS JUST IN TIME TO STRETCH OUR LEGS...
IT'S THIS HALF-DAY IN ADVANCE ON OUR SCHEDULE THAT MAKES ME HAPPY!
M. FIX!
DON'T YOU WANT TO STAY WITH ME TO ENJOY A DRINK?
UH... IT WOULD BE A PLEASURE, BUT I ABSOLUTELY MUST MAKE SOME PURCHASES...
AS SOON AS I GET BACK PERHAPS?
HA! HA! HA! HA!

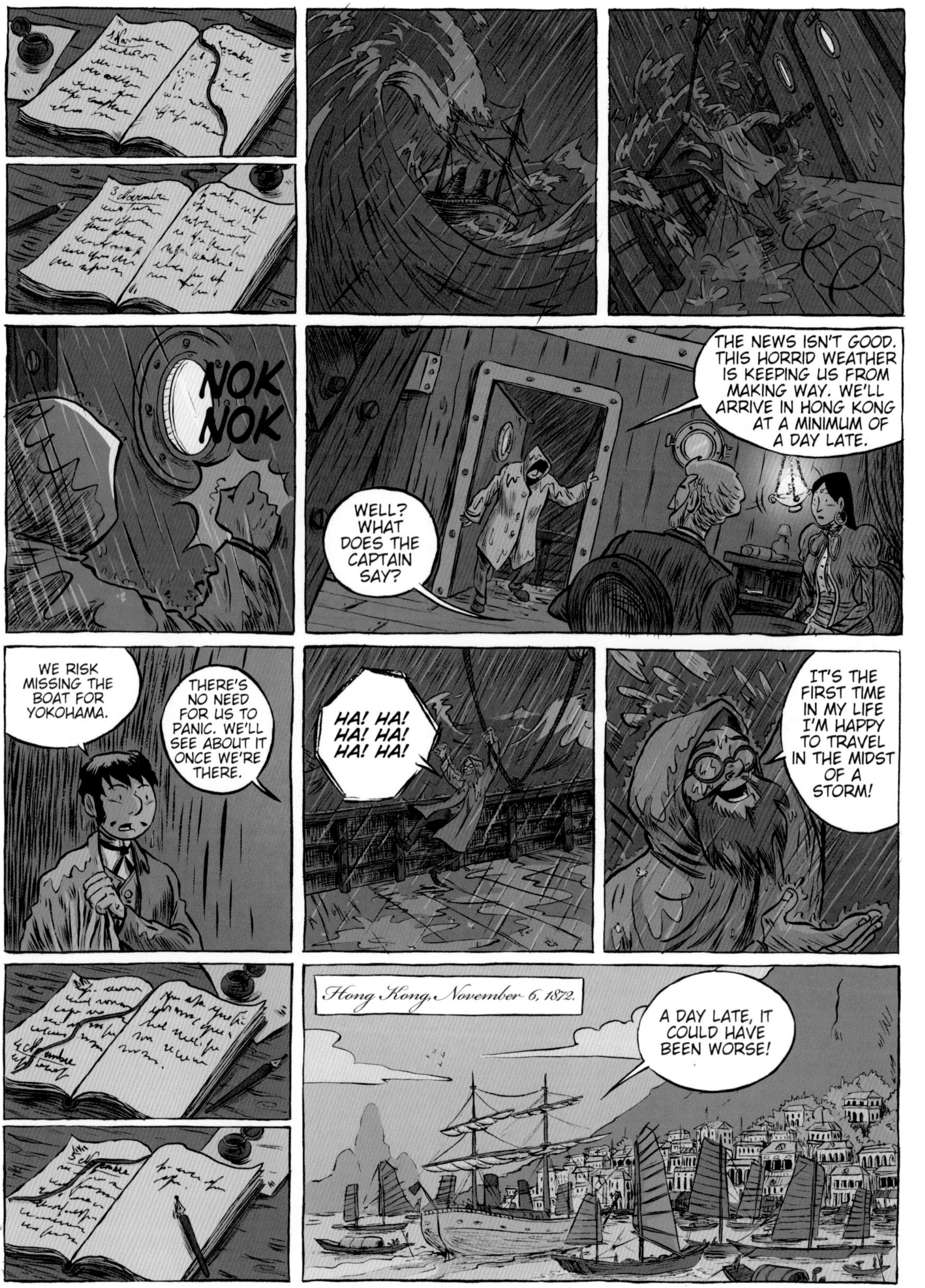
NOK NOK
WELL? WHAT DOES THE CAPTAIN SAY?
THE NEWS ISN'T GOOD. THIS HORRID WEATHER IS KEEPING US FROM MAKING WAY. WE'LL ARRIVE IN HONG KONG AT A MINIMUM OF A DAY LATE.
WE RISK MISSING THE BOAT FOR YOKOHAMA.
THERE'S NO NEED FOR US TO PANIC. WE'LL SEE ABOUT IT ONCE WE'RE THERE.
HA! HA! HA! HA! HA! HA!
IT'S THE FIRST TIME IN MY LIFE I'M HAPPY TO TRAVEL IN THE MIDST OF A STORM!
Hong Kong, November 6, 1872.
A DAY LATE, IT COULD HAVE BEEN WORSE!

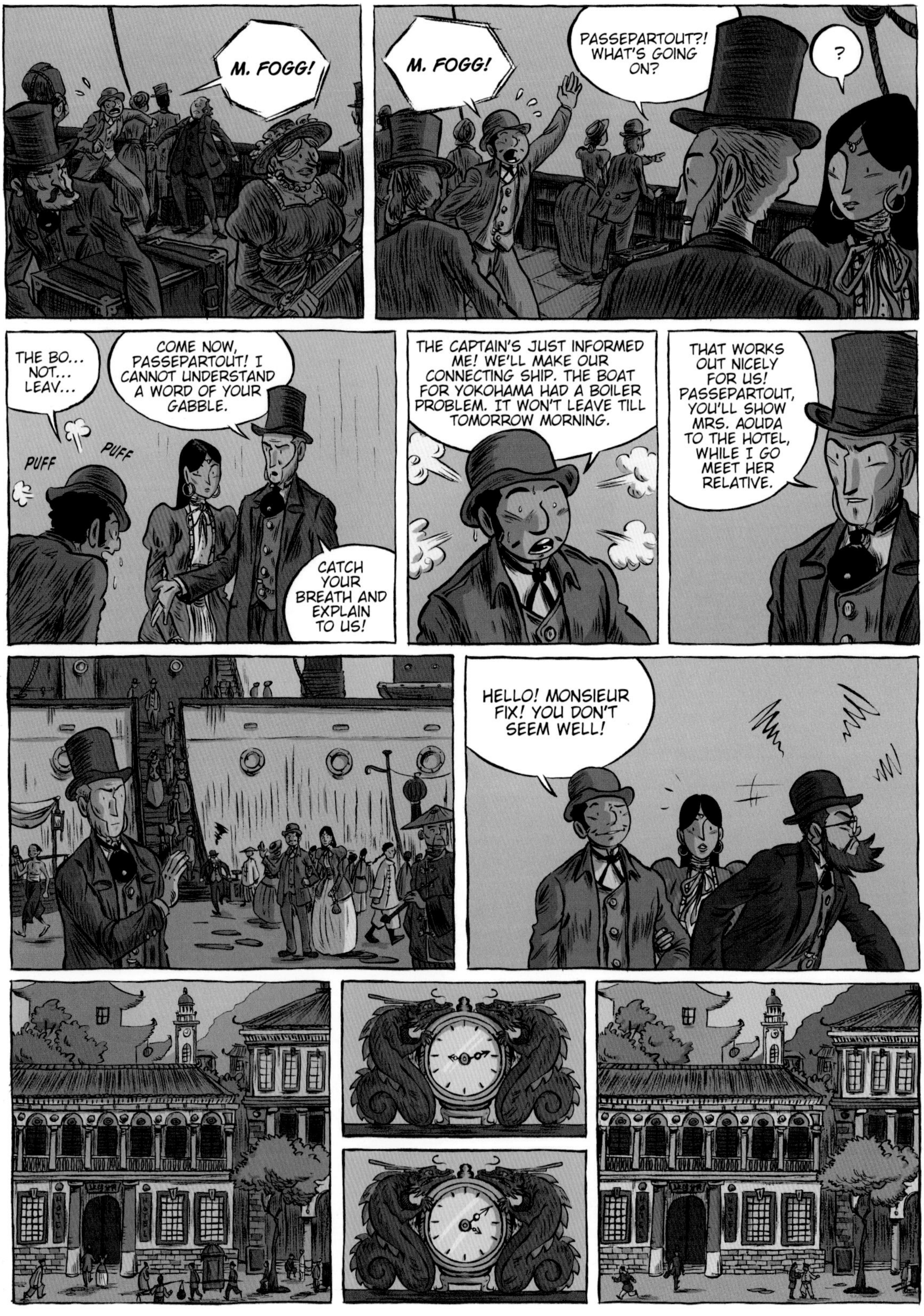
M. FOGG!
M. FOGG!
PASSEPARTOUT?! WHAT'S GOING ON?
?
THE BO... NOT... LEAV...
PUFF
PUFF
COME NOW, PASSEPARTOUT! I CANNOT UNDERSTAND A WORD OF YOUR GABBLE.
CATCH YOUR BREATH AND EXPLAIN TO US!
THE CAPTAIN'S JUST INFORMED ME! WE'LL MAKE OUR CONNECTING SHIP. THE BOAT FOR YOKOHAMA HAD A BOILER PROBLEM. IT WON'T LEAVE TILL TOMORROW MORNING.
THAT WORKS OUT NICELY FOR US! PASSEPARTOUT, YOU'LL SHOW MRS. AOUDA TO THE HOTEL, WHILE I GO MEET HER RELATIVE.
HELLO! MONSIEUR FIX! YOU DON'T SEEM WELL!

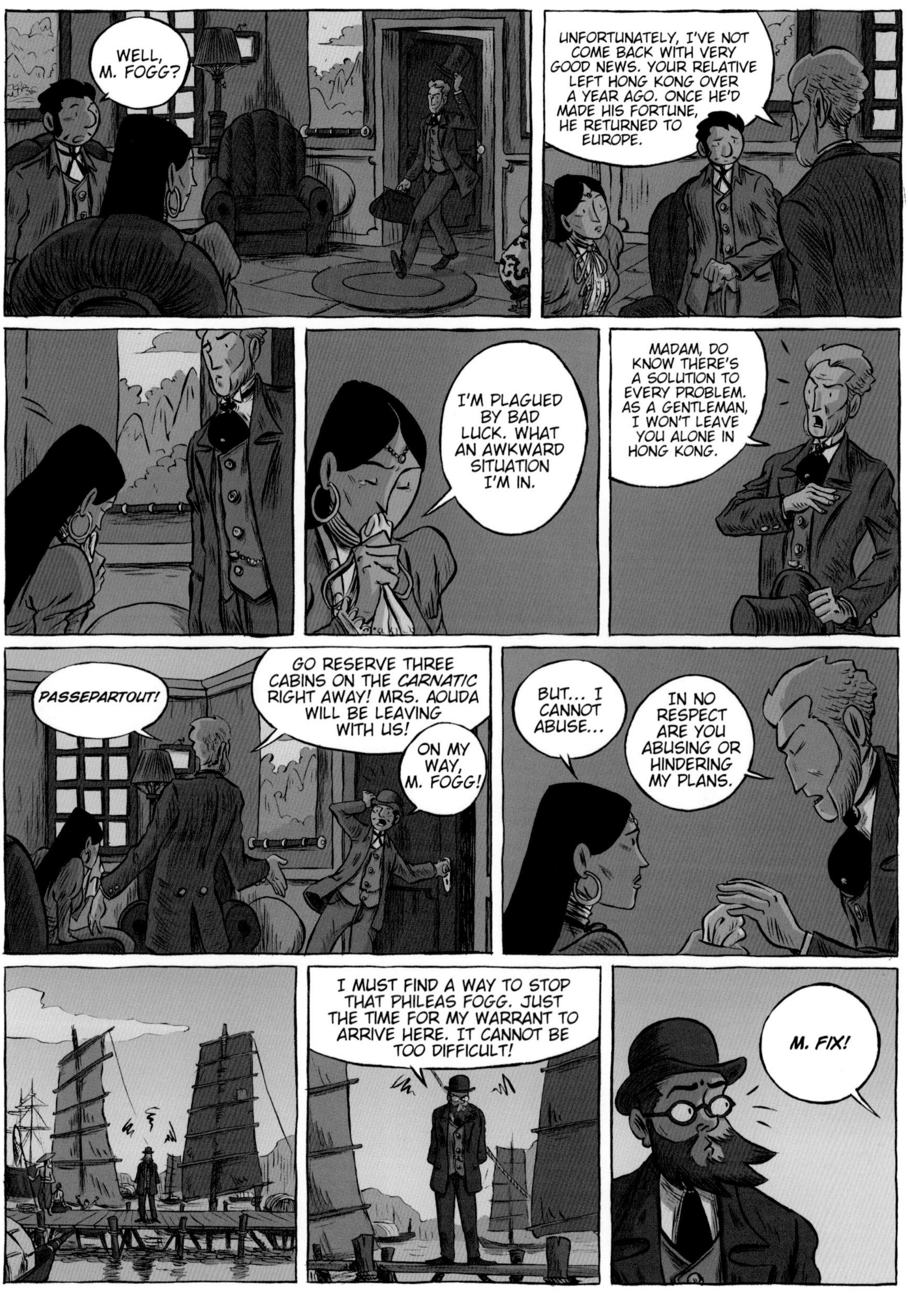
WELL, M. FOGG?
UNFORTUNATELY, I'VE NOT COME BACK WITH VERY GOOD NEWS. YOUR RELATIVE LEFT HONG KONG OVER A YEAR AGO. ONCE HE'D MADE HIS FORTUNE, HE RETURNED TO EUROPE.
I'M PLAGUED BY BAD LUCK. WHAT AN AWKWARD SITUATION I'M IN.
MADAM, DO KNOW THERE'S A SOLUTION TO EVERY PROBLEM. AS A GENTLEMAN, I WON'T LEAVE YOU ALONE IN HONG KONG.
PASSEPARTOUT!
GO RESERVE THREE CABINS ON THE *CARNATIC* RIGHT AWAY! MRS. AOUDA WILL BE LEAVING WITH US!
ON MY WAY, M. FOGG!
BUT... I CANNOT ABUSE...
IN NO RESPECT ARE YOU ABUSING OR HINDERING MY PLANS.
I MUST FIND A WAY TO STOP THAT PHILEAS FOGG. JUST THE TIME FOR MY WARRANT TO ARRIVE HERE. IT CANNOT BE TOO DIFFICULT!
M. FIX!

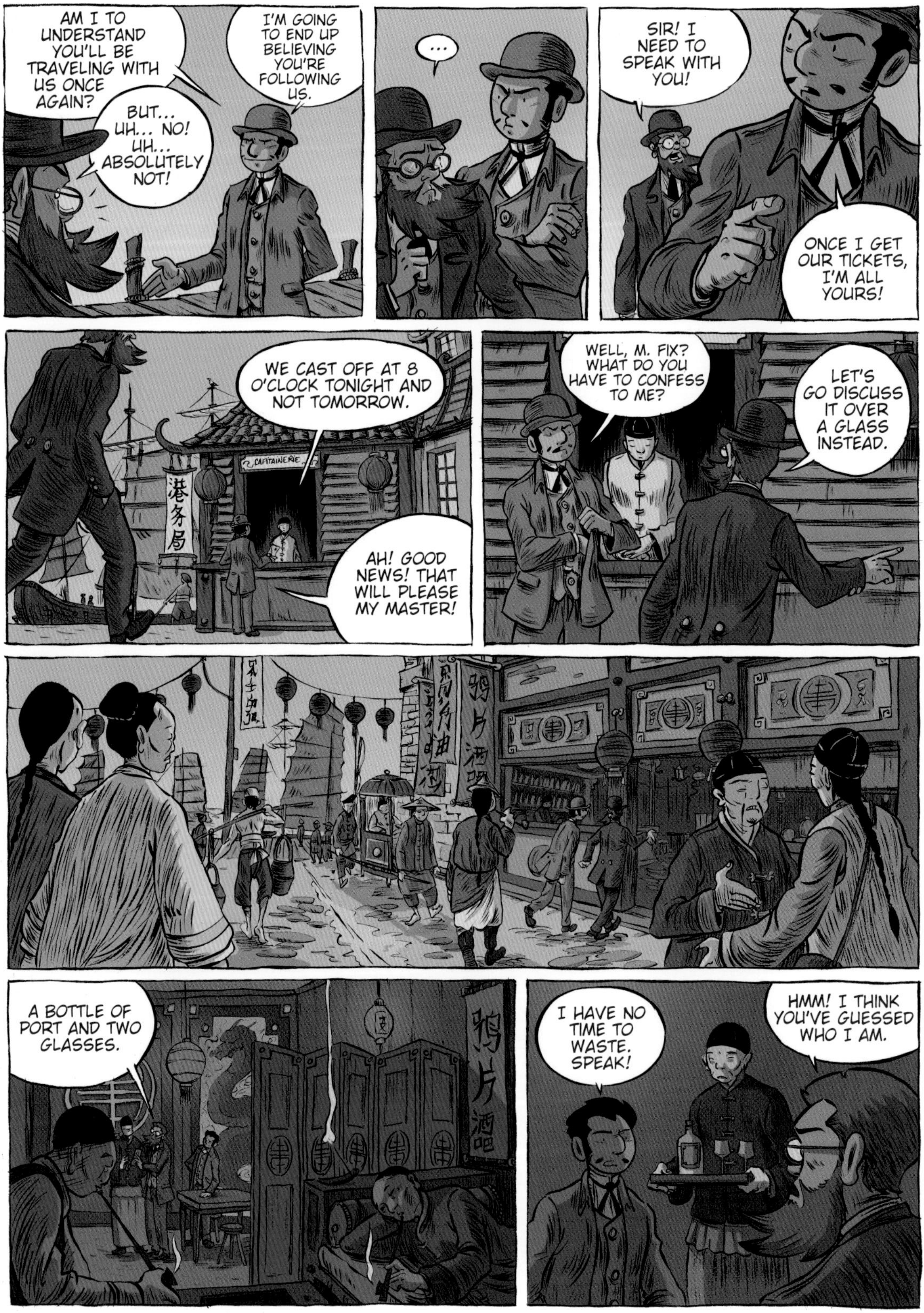
AM I TO UNDERSTAND YOU'LL BE TRAVELING WITH US ONCE AGAIN?
BUT... UH... NO! UH... ABSOLUTELY NOT!
I'M GOING TO END UP BELIEVING YOU'RE FOLLOWING US.
...
SIR! I NEED TO SPEAK WITH YOU!
ONCE I GET OUR TICKETS, I'M ALL YOURS!
WE CAST OFF AT 8 O'CLOCK TONIGHT AND NOT TOMORROW.
CAPITAINERIE
港务局
AH! GOOD NEWS! THAT WILL PLEASE MY MASTER!
WELL, M. FIX? WHAT DO YOU HAVE TO CONFESS TO ME?
LET'S GO DISCUSS IT OVER A GLASS INSTEAD.
A BOTTLE OF PORT AND TWO GLASSES.
I HAVE NO TIME TO WASTE. SPEAK!
HMM! I THINK YOU'VE GUESSED WHO I AM.

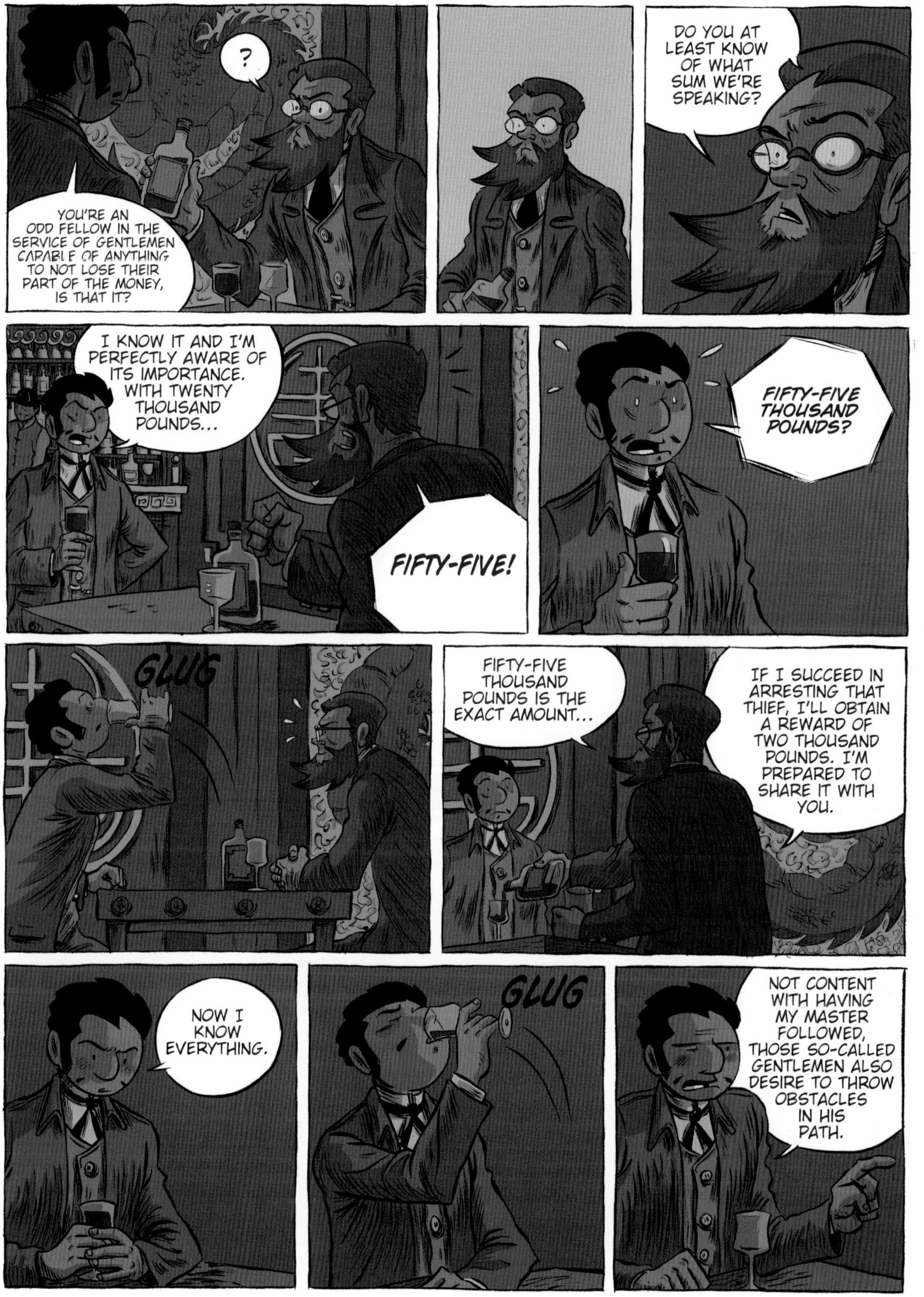
?
YOU'RE AN ODD FELLOW IN THE SERVICE OF GENTLEMEN CAPABLE OF ANYTHING TO NOT LOSE THEIR PART OF THE MONEY, IS THAT IT?
DO YOU AT LEAST KNOW OF WHAT SUM WE'RE SPEAKING?
I KNOW IT AND I'M PERFECTLY AWARE OF ITS IMPORTANCE. WITH TWENTY THOUSAND POUNDS...
FIFTY-FIVE!
FIFTY-FIVE THOUSAND POUNDS?
GLUG
FIFTY-FIVE THOUSAND POUNDS IS THE EXACT AMOUNT...
IF I SUCCEED IN ARRESTING THAT THIEF, I'LL OBTAIN A REWARD OF TWO THOUSAND POUNDS. I'M PREPARED TO SHARE IT WITH YOU.
NOW I KNOW EVERYTHING.
GLUG
NOT CONTENT WITH HAVING MY MASTER FOLLOWED, THOSE SO-CALLED GENTLEMEN ALSO DESIRE TO THROW OBSTACLES IN HIS PATH.

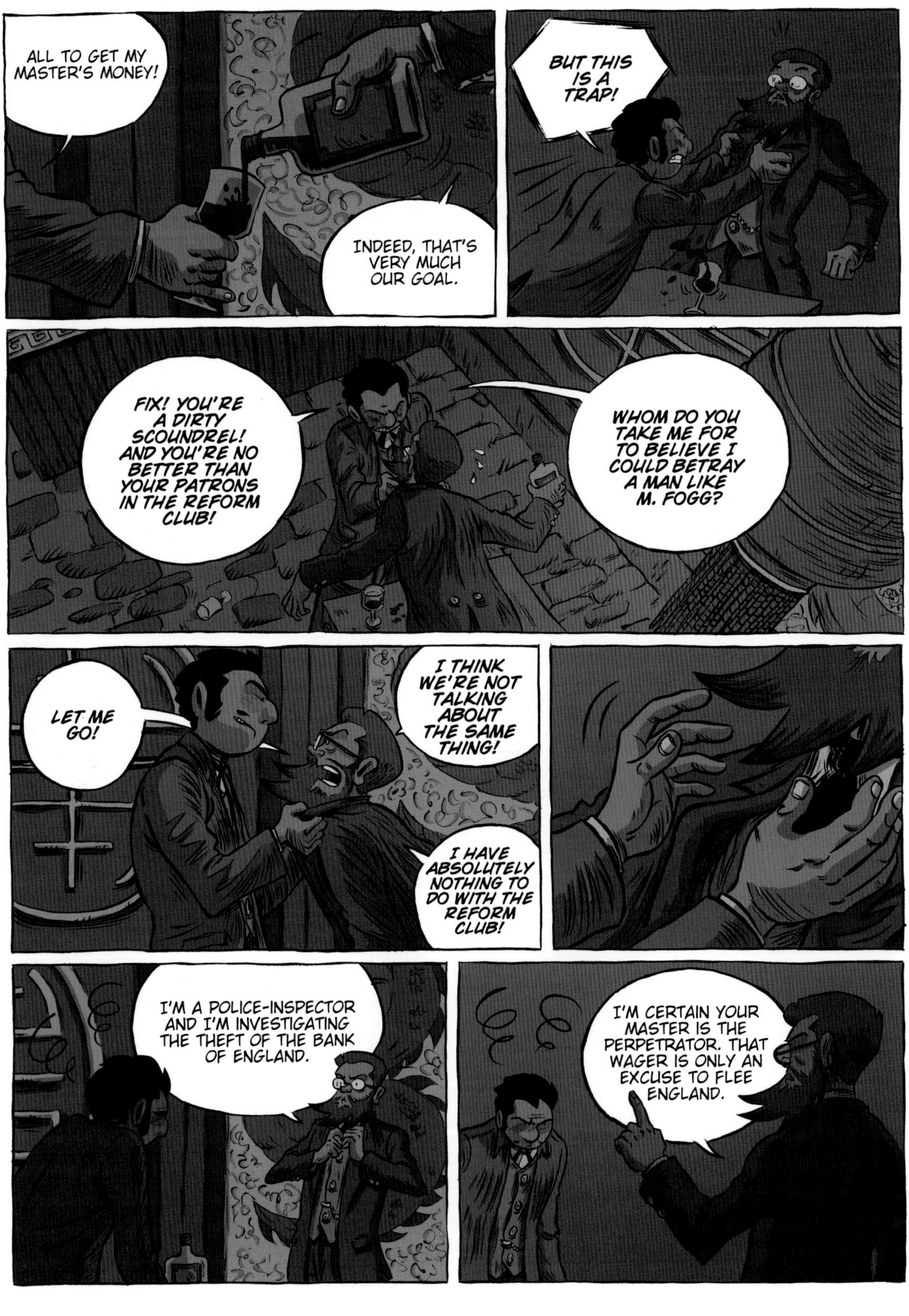
ALL TO GET MY MASTER'S MONEY!
INDEED, THAT'S VERY MUCH OUR GOAL.
BUT THIS IS A TRAP!
FIX! YOU'RE A DIRTY SCOUNDREL! AND YOU'RE NO BETTER THAN YOUR PATRONS IN THE REFORM CLUB!
WHOM DO YOU TAKE ME FOR TO BELIEVE I COULD BETRAY A MAN LIKE M. FOGG?
LET ME GO!
I THINK WE'RE NOT TALKING ABOUT THE SAME THING!
I HAVE ABSOLUTELY NOTHING TO DO WITH THE REFORM CLUB!
I'M A POLICE-INSPECTOR AND I'M INVESTIGATING THE THEFT OF THE BANK OF ENGLAND.
I'M CERTAIN YOUR MASTER IS THE PERPETRATOR. THAT WAGER IS ONLY AN EXCUSE TO FLEE ENGLAND.

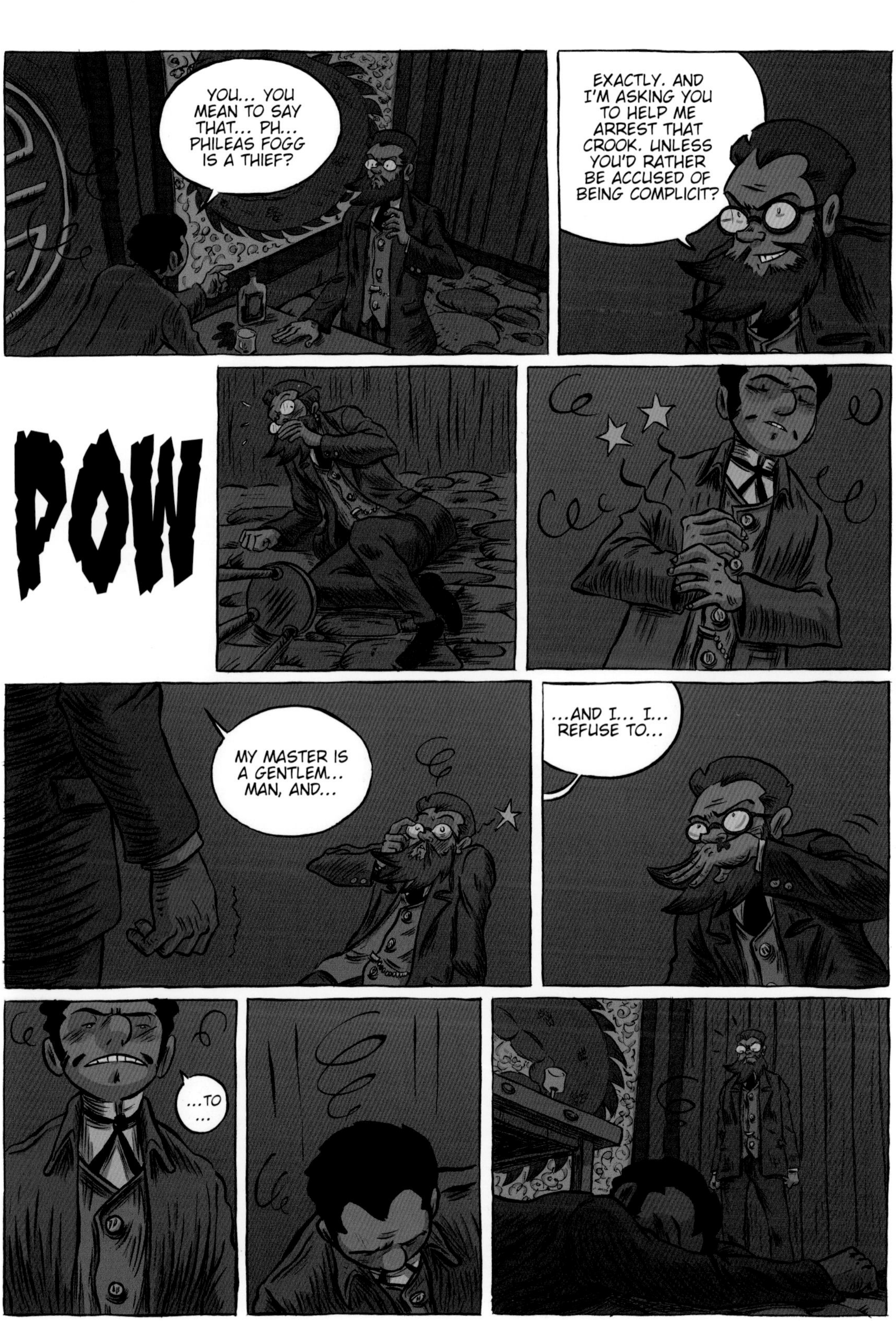
YOU... YOU MEAN TO SAY THAT... PH... PHILEAS FOGG IS A THIEF?
EXACTLY. AND I'M ASKING YOU TO HELP ME ARREST THAT CROOK. UNLESS YOU'D RATHER BE ACCUSED OF BEING COMPLICIT?
POW
MY MASTER IS A GENTLEM... MAN, AND...
...AND I... I... REFUSE TO...
...TO ...

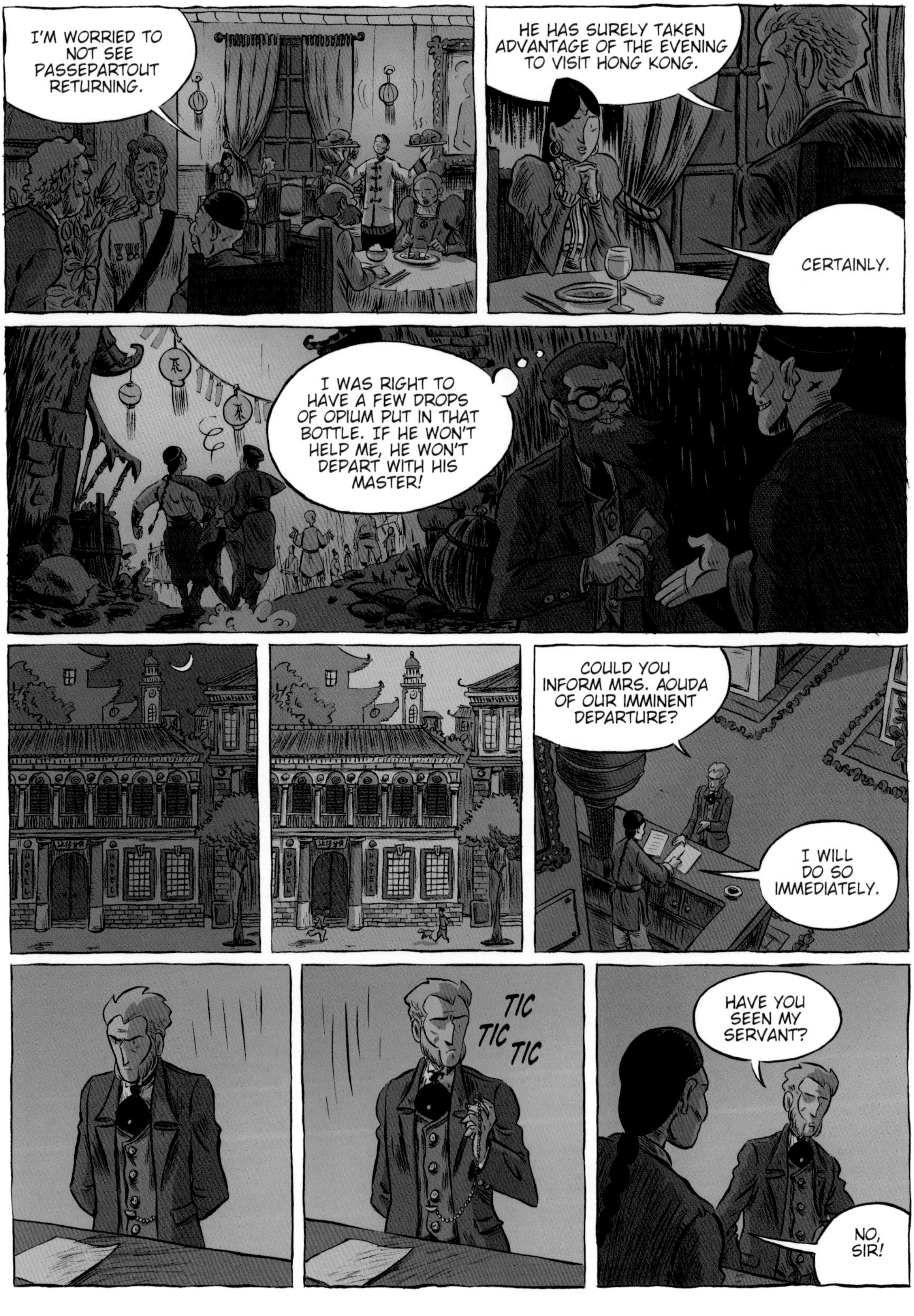
I'M WORRIED TO NOT SEE PASSEPARTOUT RETURNING.
HE HAS SURELY TAKEN ADVANTAGE OF THE EVENING TO VISIT HONG KONG.
CERTAINLY.
I WAS RIGHT TO HAVE A FEW DROPS OF OPIUM PUT IN THAT BOTTLE. IF HE WON'T HELP ME, HE WON'T DEPART WITH HIS MASTER!
COULD YOU INFORM MRS. AOUDA OF OUR IMMINENT DEPARTURE?
I WILL DO SO IMMEDIATELY.
TIC
TIC TIC
HAVE YOU SEEN MY SERVANT?
NO, SIR!

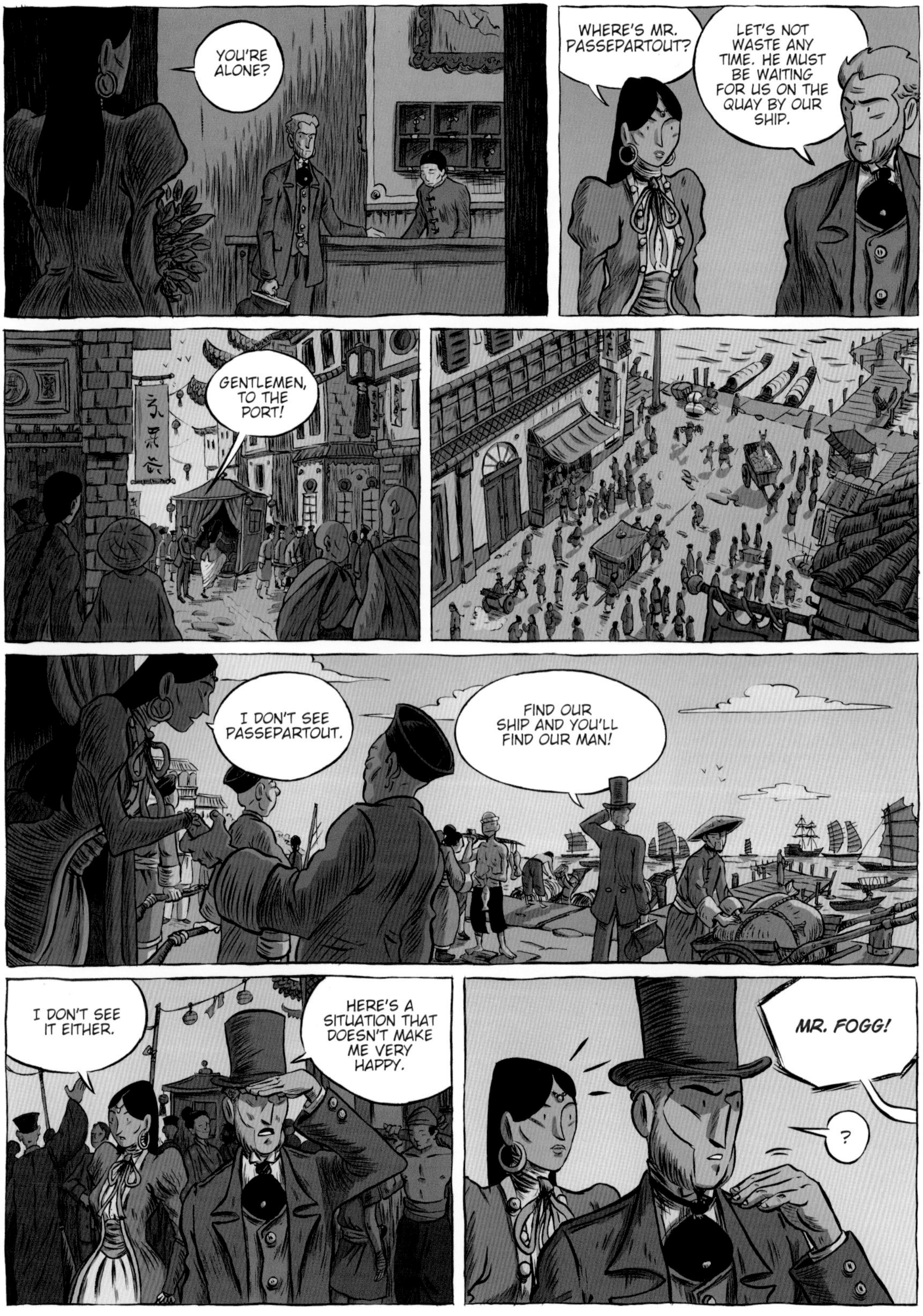
YOU'RE ALONE?
WHERE'S MR. PASSEPARTOUT?
LET'S NOT WASTE ANY TIME. HE MUST BE WAITING FOR US ON THE QUAY BY OUR SHIP.
GENTLEMEN, TO THE PORT!
I DON'T SEE PASSEPARTOUT.
FIND OUR SHIP AND YOU'LL FIND OUR MAN!
I DON'T SEE IT EITHER.
HERE'S A SITUATION THAT DOESN'T MAKE ME VERY HAPPY.
MR. FOGG!
?

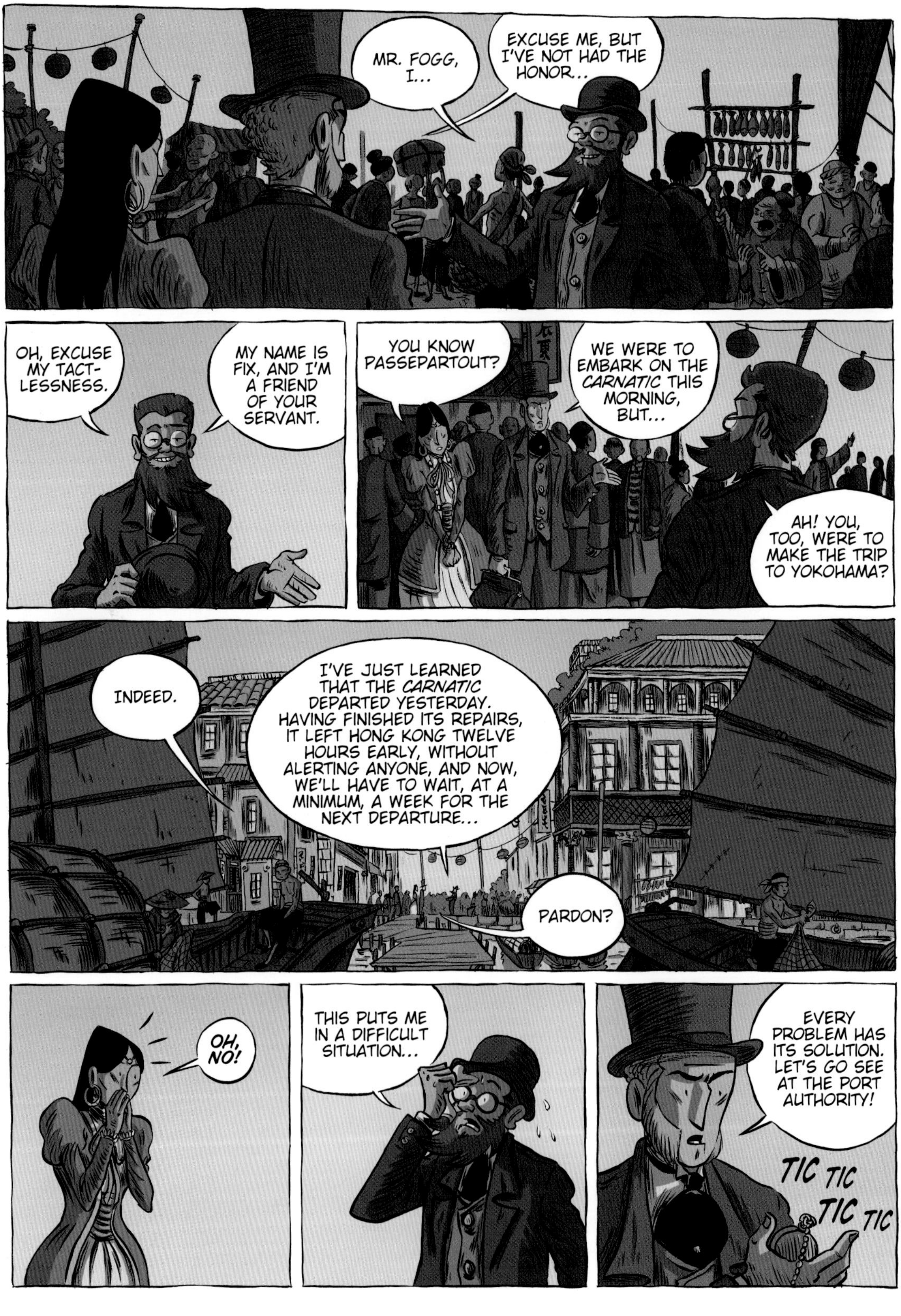
MR. FOGG, I...
EXCUSE ME, BUT I'VE NOT HAD THE HONOR...
OH, EXCUSE MY TACT-LESSNESS.
MY NAME IS FIX, AND I'M A FRIEND OF YOUR SERVANT.
YOU KNOW PASSEPARTOUT?
WE WERE TO EMBARK ON THE *CARNATIC* THIS MORNING, BUT...
AH! YOU, TOO, WERE TO MAKE THE TRIP TO YOKOHAMA?
INDEED.
I'VE JUST LEARNED THAT THE *CARNATIC* DEPARTED YESTERDAY. HAVING FINISHED ITS REPAIRS, IT LEFT HONG KONG TWELVE HOURS EARLY, WITHOUT ALERTING ANYONE, AND NOW, WE'LL HAVE TO WAIT, AT A MINIMUM, A WEEK FOR THE NEXT DEPARTURE...
PARDON?
OH, NO!
THIS PUTS ME IN A DIFFICULT SITUATION...
EVERY PROBLEM HAS ITS SOLUTION. LET'S GO SEE AT THE PORT AUTHORITY!
TIC TIC TIC TIC

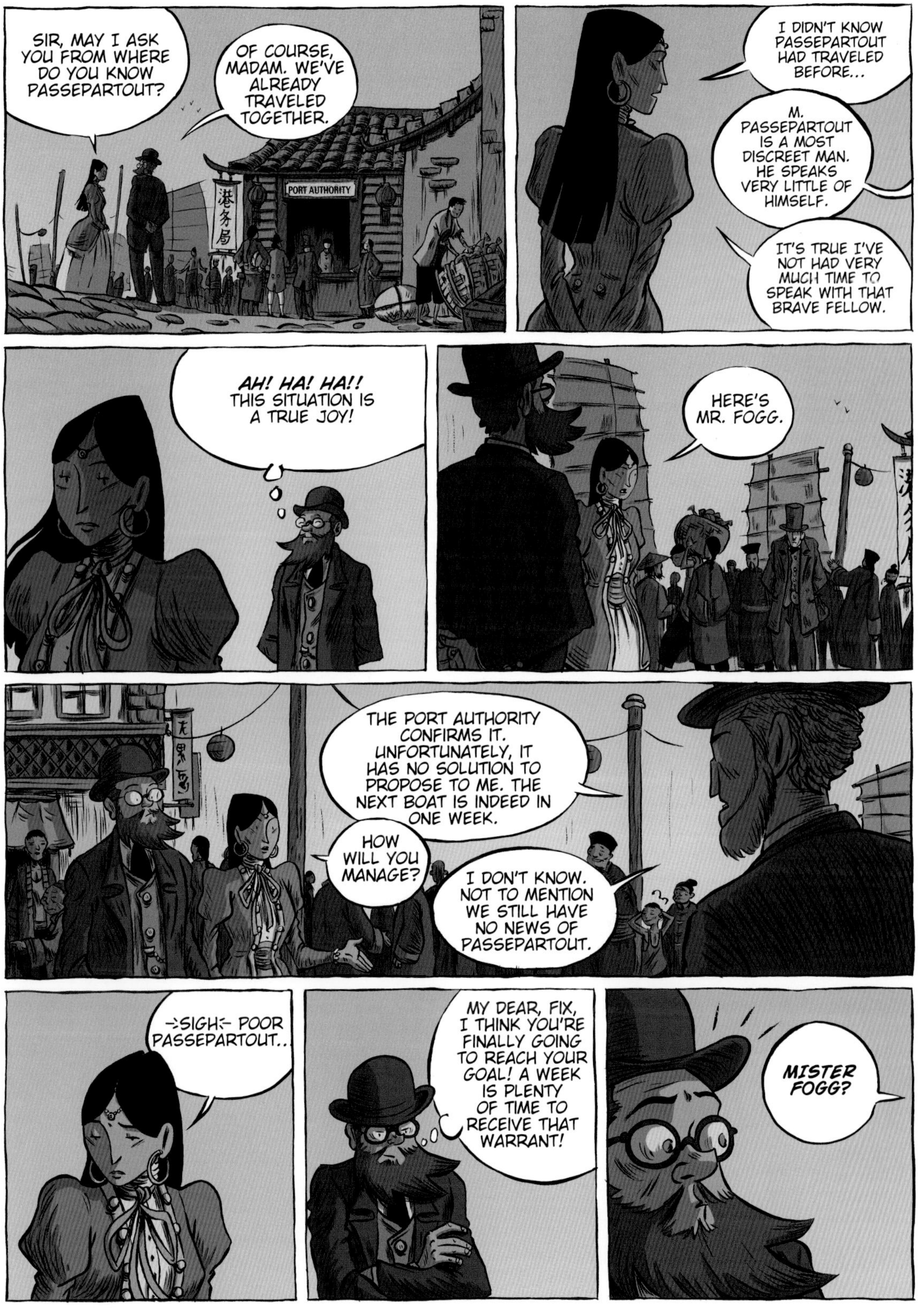
SIR, MAY I ASK YOU FROM WHERE DO YOU KNOW PASSEPARTOUT?
OF COURSE, MADAM. WE'VE ALREADY TRAVELED TOGETHER.
PORT AUTHORITY
港务局
I DIDN'T KNOW PASSEPARTOUT HAD TRAVELED BEFORE...
M. PASSEPARTOUT IS A MOST DISCREET MAN. HE SPEAKS VERY LITTLE OF HIMSELF.
IT'S TRUE I'VE NOT HAD VERY MUCH TIME TO SPEAK WITH THAT BRAVE FELLOW.
AH! HA! HA!! THIS SITUATION IS A TRUE JOY!
HERE'S MR. FOGG.
THE PORT AUTHORITY CONFIRMS IT. UNFORTUNATELY, IT HAS NO SOLUTION TO PROPOSE TO ME. THE NEXT BOAT IS INDEED IN ONE WEEK.
HOW WILL YOU MANAGE?
I DON'T KNOW. NOT TO MENTION WE STILL HAVE NO NEWS OF PASSEPARTOUT.
-SIGH- POOR PASSEPARTOUT...
MY DEAR, FIX, I THINK YOU'RE FINALLY GOING TO REACH YOUR GOAL! A WEEK IS PLENTY OF TIME TO RECEIVE THAT WARRANT!
MISTER FOGG?

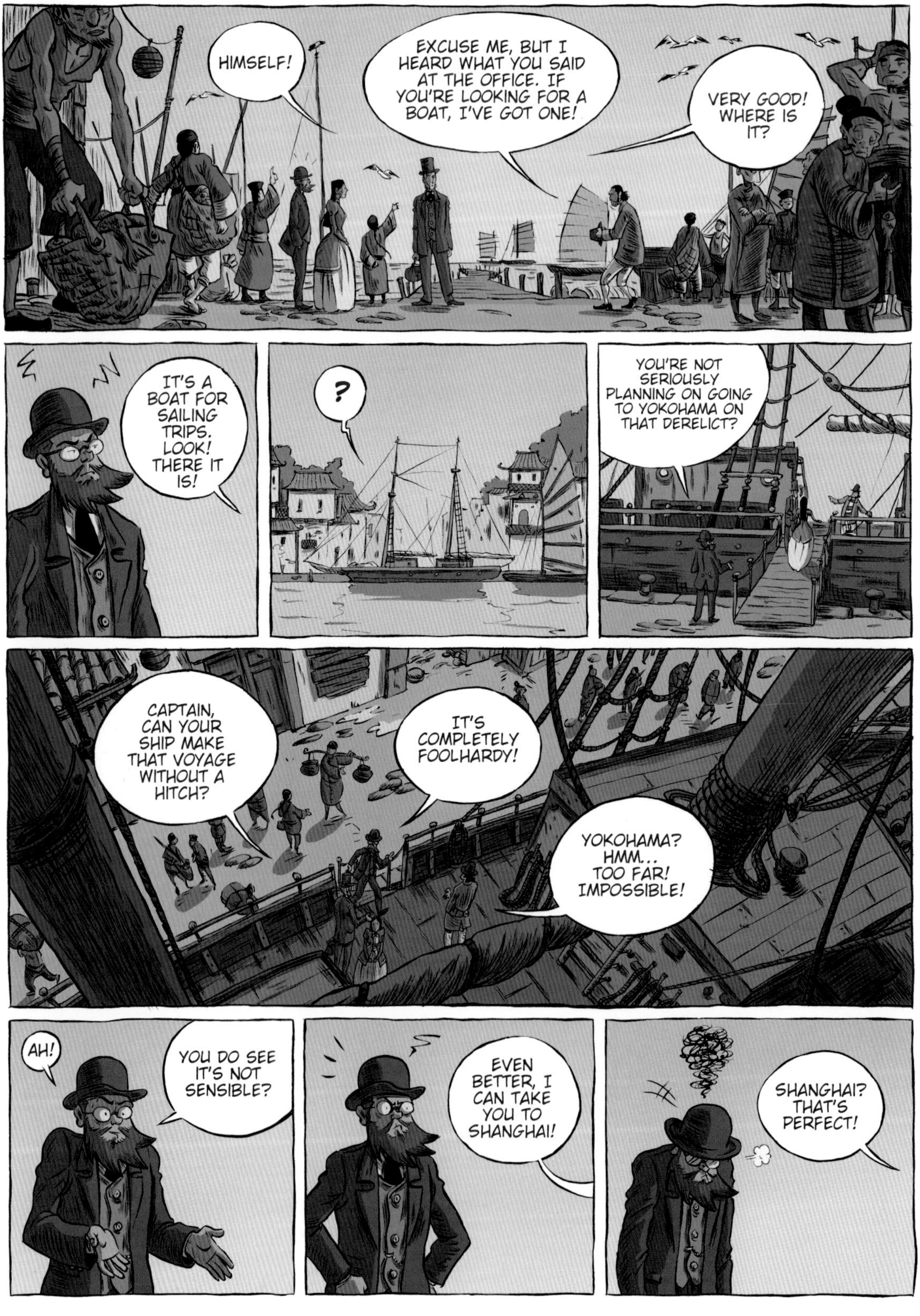
HIMSELF!
EXCUSE ME, BUT I HEARD WHAT YOU SAID AT THE OFFICE. IF YOU'RE LOOKING FOR A BOAT, I'VE GOT ONE!
VERY GOOD! WHERE IS IT?
IT'S A BOAT FOR SAILING TRIPS. LOOK! THERE IT IS!
?
YOU'RE NOT SERIOUSLY PLANNING ON GOING TO YOKOHAMA ON THAT DERELICT?
CAPTAIN, CAN YOUR SHIP MAKE THAT VOYAGE WITHOUT A HITCH?
IT'S COMPLETELY FOOLHARDY!
YOKOHAMA? HMM... TOO FAR! IMPOSSIBLE!
AH!
YOU DO SEE IT'S NOT SENSIBLE?
EVEN BETTER, I CAN TAKE YOU TO SHANGHAI!
SHANGHAI? THAT'S PERFECT!

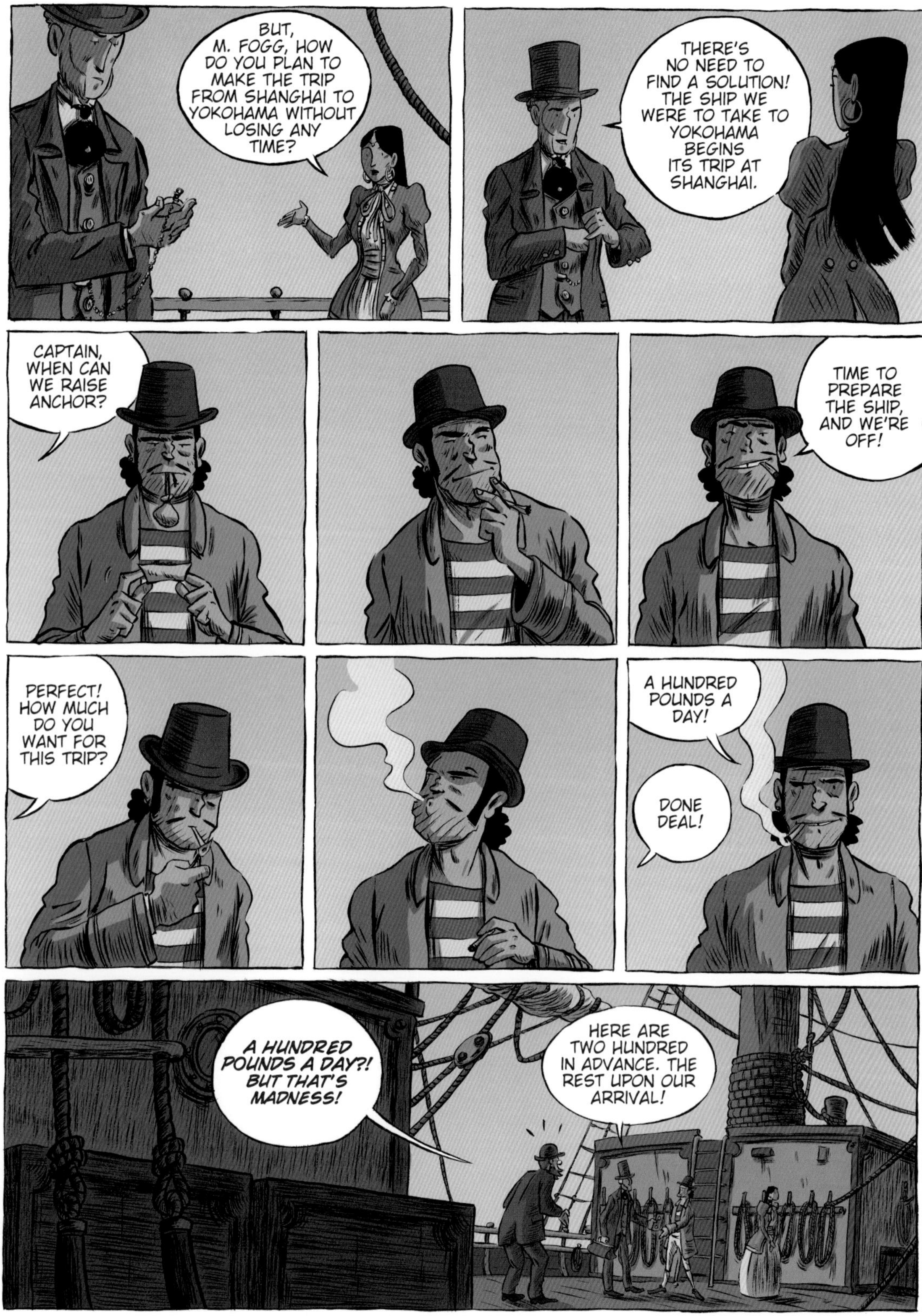
BUT, M. FOGG, HOW DO YOU PLAN TO MAKE THE TRIP FROM SHANGHAI TO YOKOHAMA WITHOUT LOSING ANY TIME?
THERE'S NO NEED TO FIND A SOLUTION! THE SHIP WE WERE TO TAKE TO YOKOHAMA BEGINS ITS TRIP AT SHANGHAI.
CAPTAIN, WHEN CAN WE RAISE ANCHOR?
TIME TO PREPARE THE SHIP, AND WE'RE OFF!
PERFECT! HOW MUCH DO YOU WANT FOR THIS TRIP?
A HUNDRED POUNDS A DAY!
DONE DEAL!
A HUNDRED POUNDS A DAY?! BUT THAT'S MADNESS!
HERE ARE TWO HUNDRED IN ADVANCE. THE REST UPON OUR ARRIVAL!

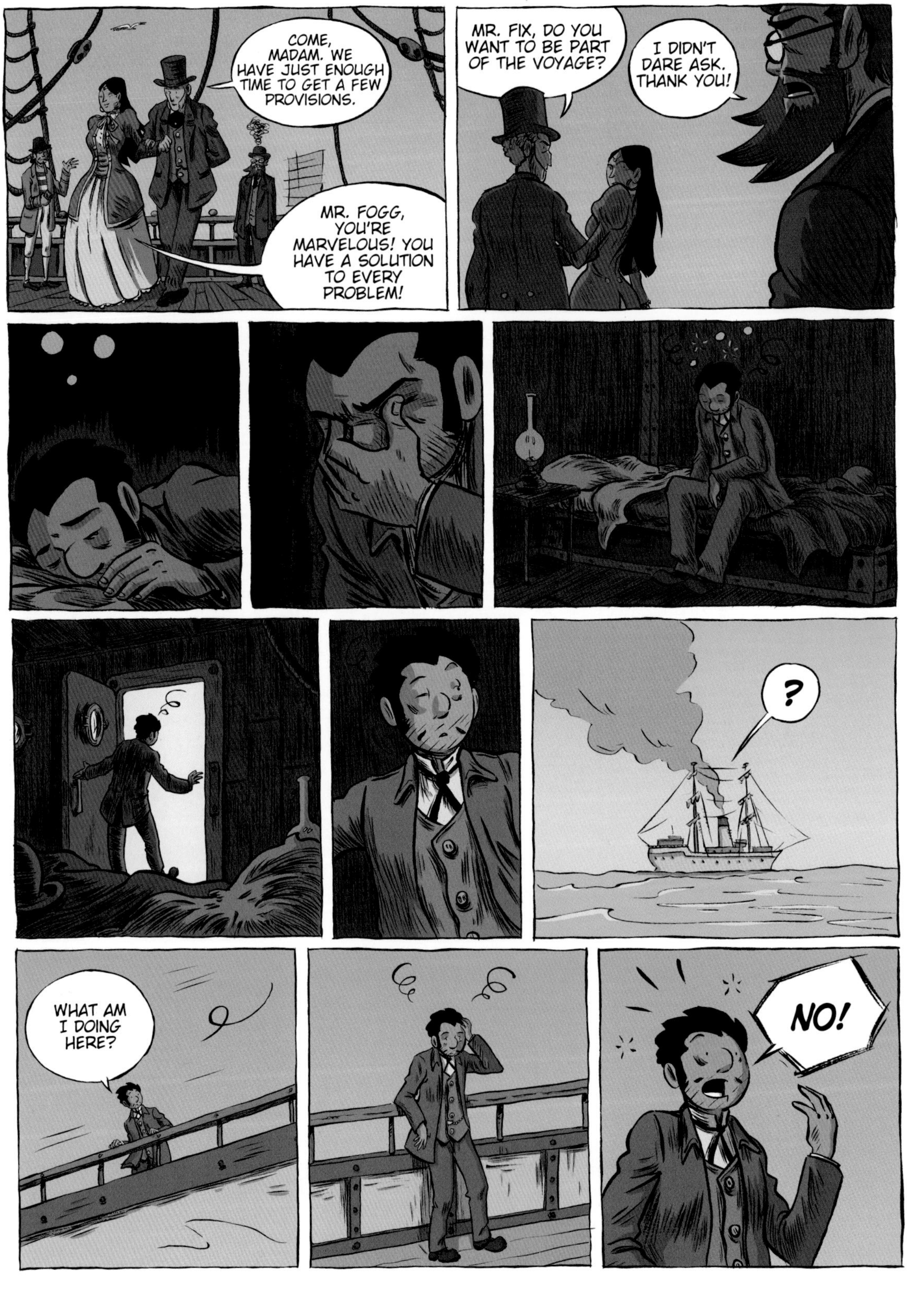
COME, MADAM. WE HAVE JUST ENOUGH TIME TO GET A FEW PROVISIONS.
MR. FOGG, YOU'RE MARVELOUS! YOU HAVE A SOLUTION TO EVERY PROBLEM!
MR. FIX, DO YOU WANT TO BE PART OF THE VOYAGE?
I DIDN'T DARE ASK. THANK YOU!
?
WHAT AM I DOING HERE?
NO!

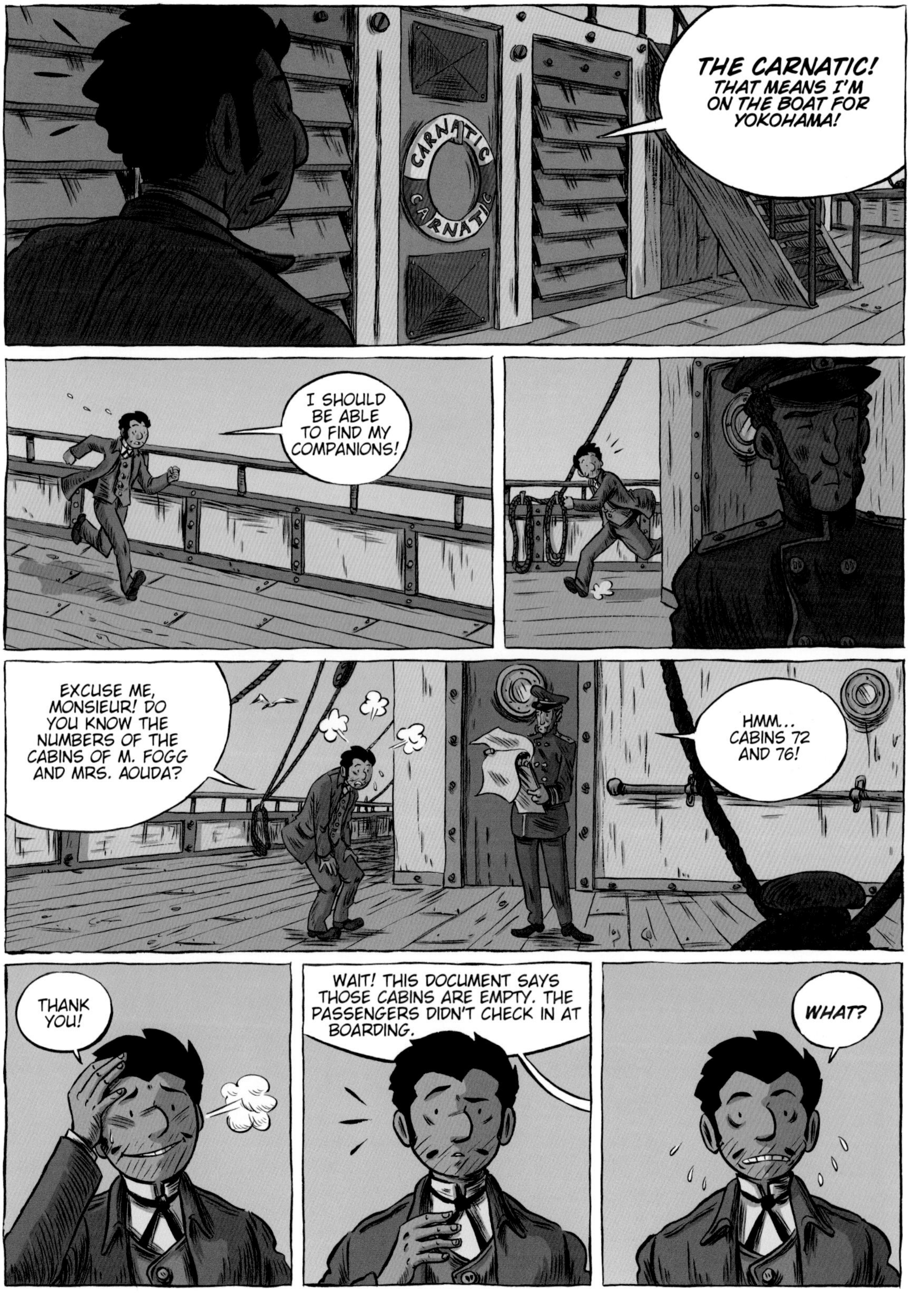
THE CARNATIC!
THAT MEANS I'M ON THE BOAT FOR YOKOHAMA!
CARNATIC
CARNATIC
I SHOULD BE ABLE TO FIND MY COMPANIONS!
EXCUSE ME, MONSIEUR! DO YOU KNOW THE NUMBERS OF THE CABINS OF M. FOGG AND MRS. AOUDA?
HMM... CABINS 72 AND 76!
THANK YOU!
WAIT! THIS DOCUMENT SAYS THOSE CABINS ARE EMPTY. THE PASSENGERS DIDN'T CHECK IN AT BOARDING.
WHAT?

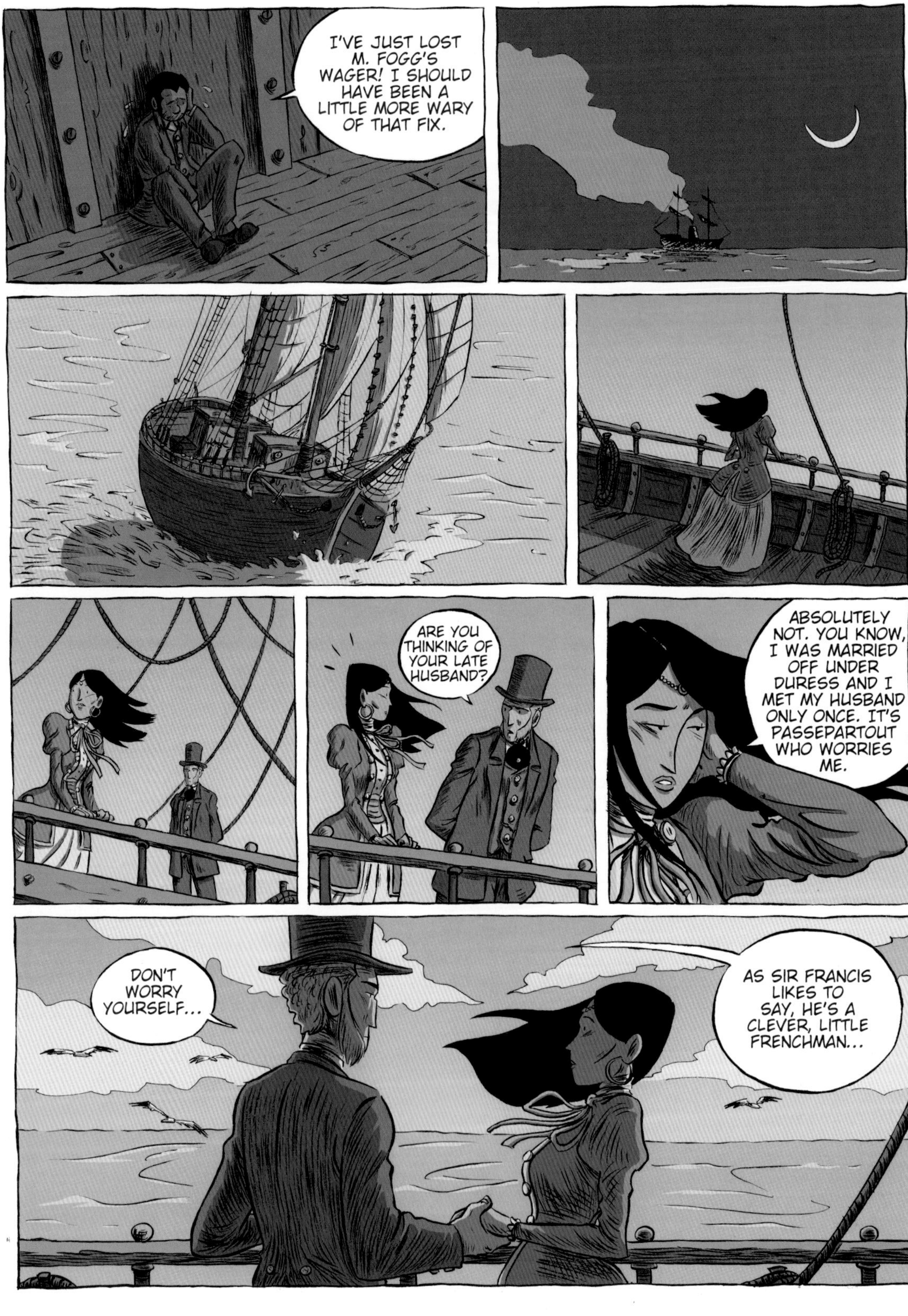
I'VE JUST LOST M. FOGG'S WAGER! I SHOULD HAVE BEEN A LITTLE MORE WARY OF THAT FIX.
ARE YOU THINKING OF YOUR LATE HUSBAND?
ABSOLUTELY NOT. YOU KNOW, I WAS MARRIED OFF UNDER DURESS AND I MET MY HUSBAND ONLY ONCE. IT'S PASSEPARTOUT WHO WORRIES ME.
DON'T WORRY YOURSELF...
AS SIR FRANCIS LIKES TO SAY, HE'S A CLEVER, LITTLE FRENCHMAN...

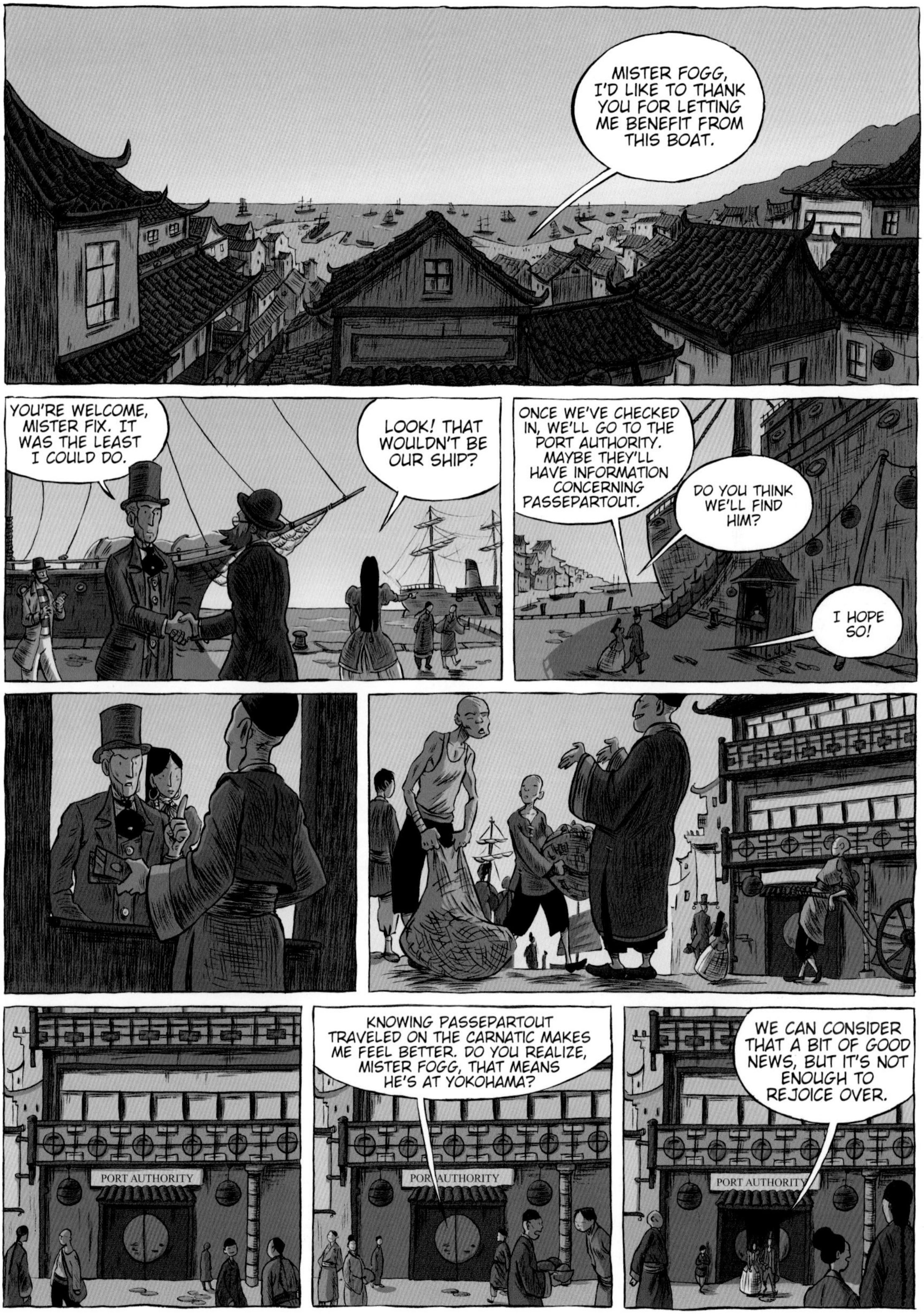
MISTER FOGG, I'D LIKE TO THANK YOU FOR LETTING ME BENEFIT FROM THIS BOAT.
YOU'RE WELCOME, MISTER FIX. IT WAS THE LEAST I COULD DO.
LOOK! THAT WOULDN'T BE OUR SHIP?
ONCE WE'VE CHECKED IN, WE'LL GO TO THE PORT AUTHORITY. MAYBE THEY'LL HAVE INFORMATION CONCERNING PASSEPARTOUT.
DO YOU THINK WE'LL FIND HIM?
I HOPE SO!
PORT AUTHORITY
KNOWING PASSEPARTOUT TRAVELED ON THE CARNATIC MAKES ME FEEL BETTER. DO YOU REALIZE, MISTER FOGG, THAT MEANS HE'S AT YOKOHAMA?
PORT AUTHORITY
WE CAN CONSIDER THAT A BIT OF GOOD NEWS, BUT IT'S NOT ENOUGH TO REJOICE OVER.
PORT AUTHORITY

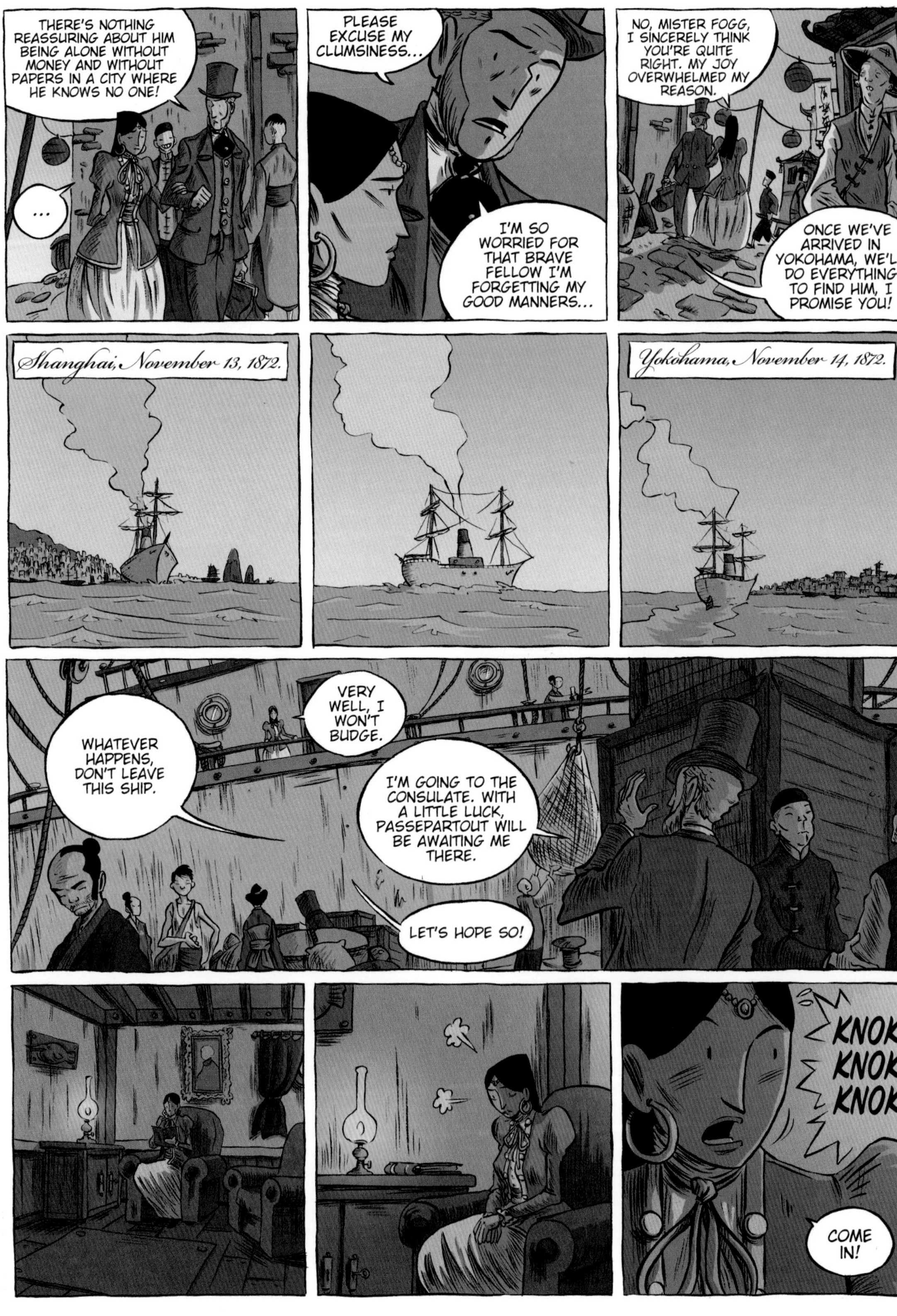
THERE'S NOTHING REASSURING ABOUT HIM BEING ALONE WITHOUT MONEY AND WITHOUT PAPERS IN A CITY WHERE HE KNOWS NO ONE!
...
PLEASE EXCUSE MY CLUMSINESS...
I'M SO WORRIED FOR THAT BRAVE FELLOW I'M FORGETTING MY GOOD MANNERS...
NO, MISTER FOGG, I SINCERELY THINK YOU'RE QUITE RIGHT. MY JOY OVERWHELMED MY REASON.
ONCE WE'VE ARRIVED IN YOKOHAMA, WE'LL DO EVERYTHING TO FIND HIM, I PROMISE YOU!
Shanghai, November 13, 1872.
Yokohama, November 14, 1872.
WHATEVER HAPPENS, DON'T LEAVE THIS SHIP.
VERY WELL, I WON'T BUDGE.
I'M GOING TO THE CONSULATE. WITH A LITTLE LUCK, PASSEPARTOUT WILL BE AWAITING ME THERE.
LET'S HOPE SO!
KNOK KNOK KNOK
COME IN!

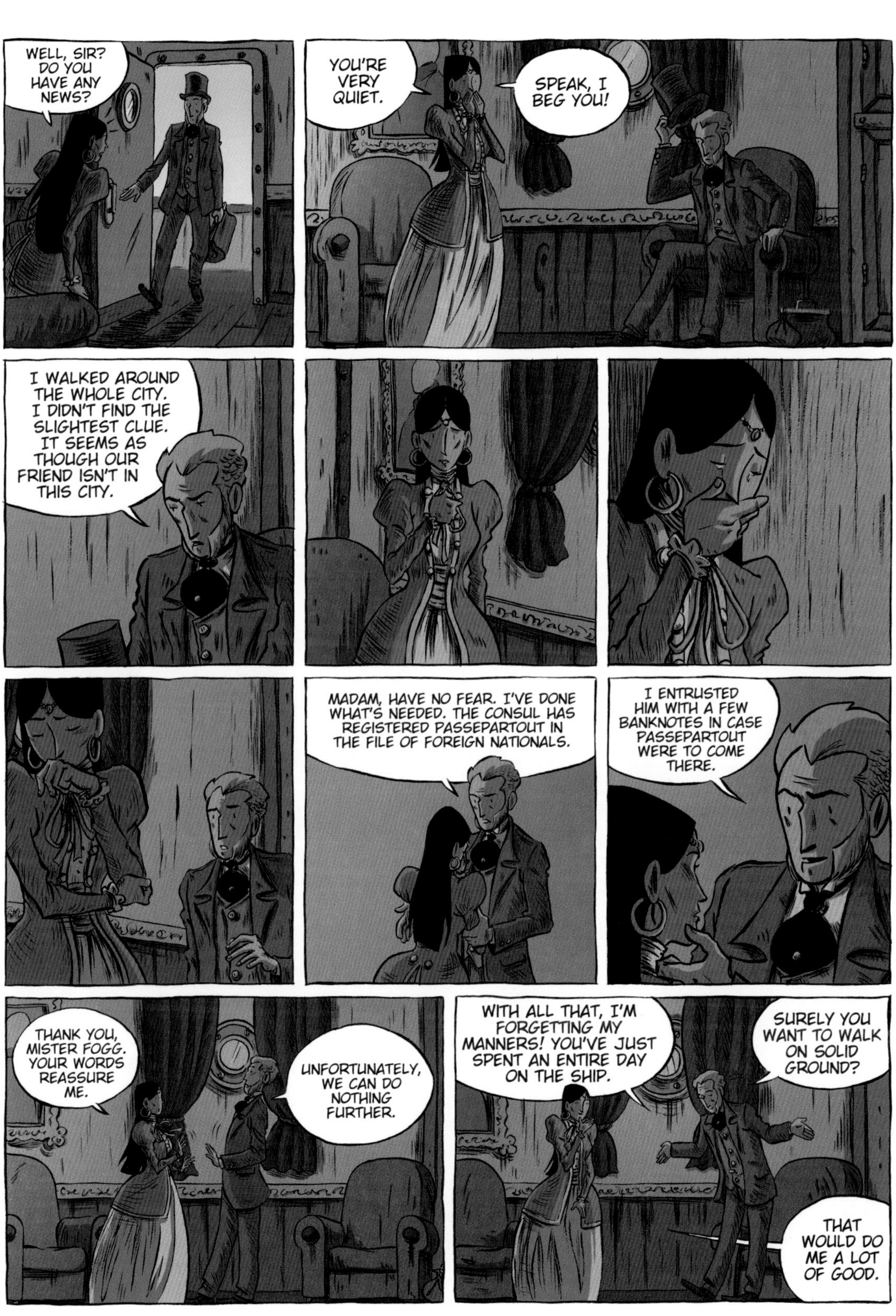
WELL, SIR? DO YOU HAVE ANY NEWS?
YOU'RE VERY QUIET.
SPEAK, I BEG YOU!
I WALKED AROUND THE WHOLE CITY. I DIDN'T FIND THE SLIGHTEST CLUE. IT SEEMS AS THOUGH OUR FRIEND ISN'T IN THIS CITY.
MADAM, HAVE NO FEAR. I'VE DONE WHAT'S NEEDED. THE CONSUL HAS REGISTERED PASSEPARTOUT IN THE FILE OF FOREIGN NATIONALS.
I ENTRUSTED HIM WITH A FEW BANKNOTES IN CASE PASSEPARTOUT WERE TO COME THERE.
THANK YOU, MISTER FOGG. YOUR WORDS REASSURE ME.
UNFORTUNATELY, WE CAN DO NOTHING FURTHER.
WITH ALL THAT, I'M FORGETTING MY MANNERS! YOU'VE JUST SPENT AN ENTIRE DAY ON THE SHIP.
SURELY YOU WANT TO WALK ON SOLID GROUND?
THAT WOULD DO ME A LOT OF GOOD.

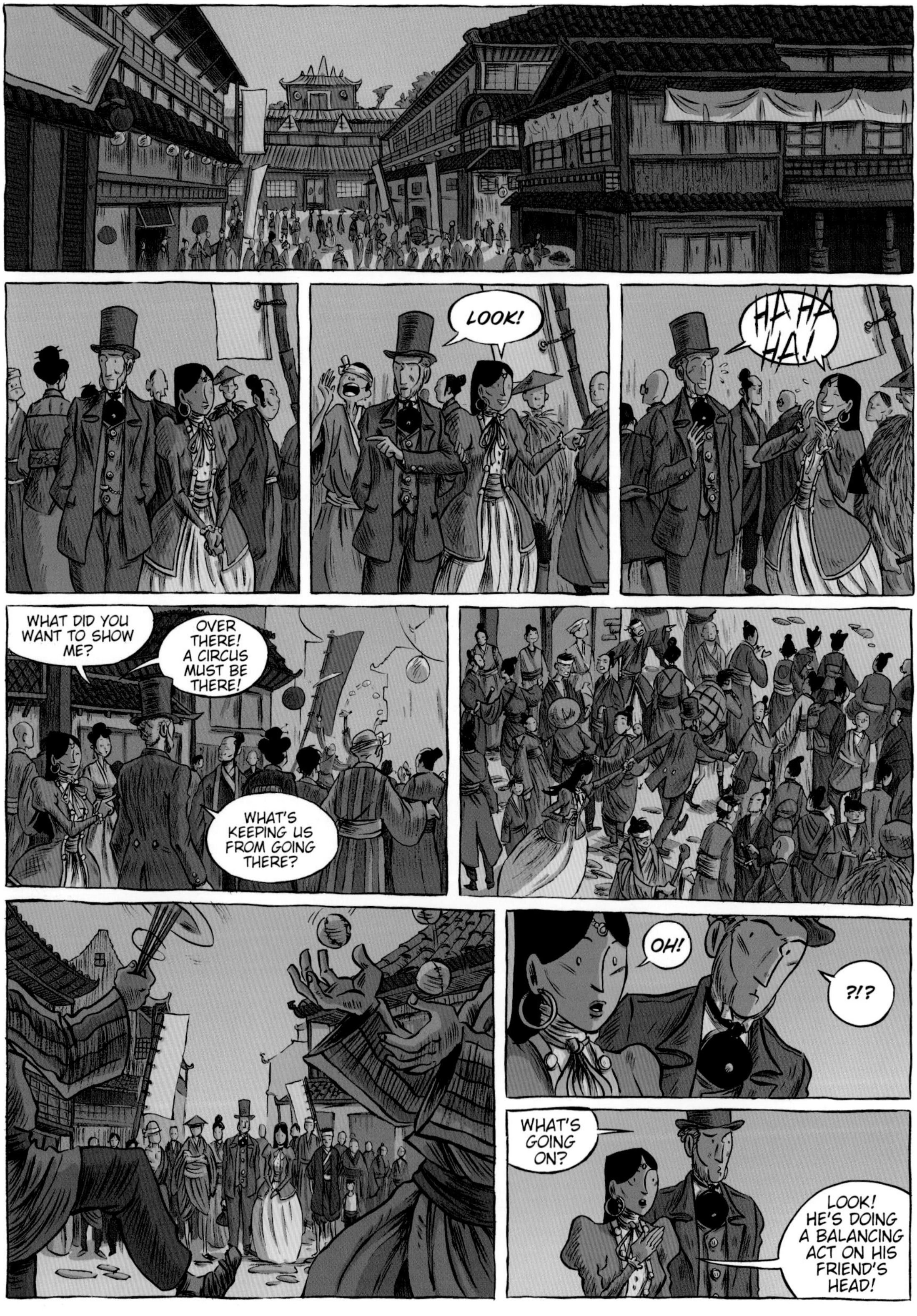
LOOK!
HA HA HA!
WHAT DID YOU WANT TO SHOW ME?
OVER THERE! A CIRCUS MUST BE THERE!
WHAT'S KEEPING US FROM GOING THERE?
OH!
?!?
WHAT'S GOING ON?
LOOK! HE'S DOING A BALANCING ACT ON HIS FRIEND'S HEAD!

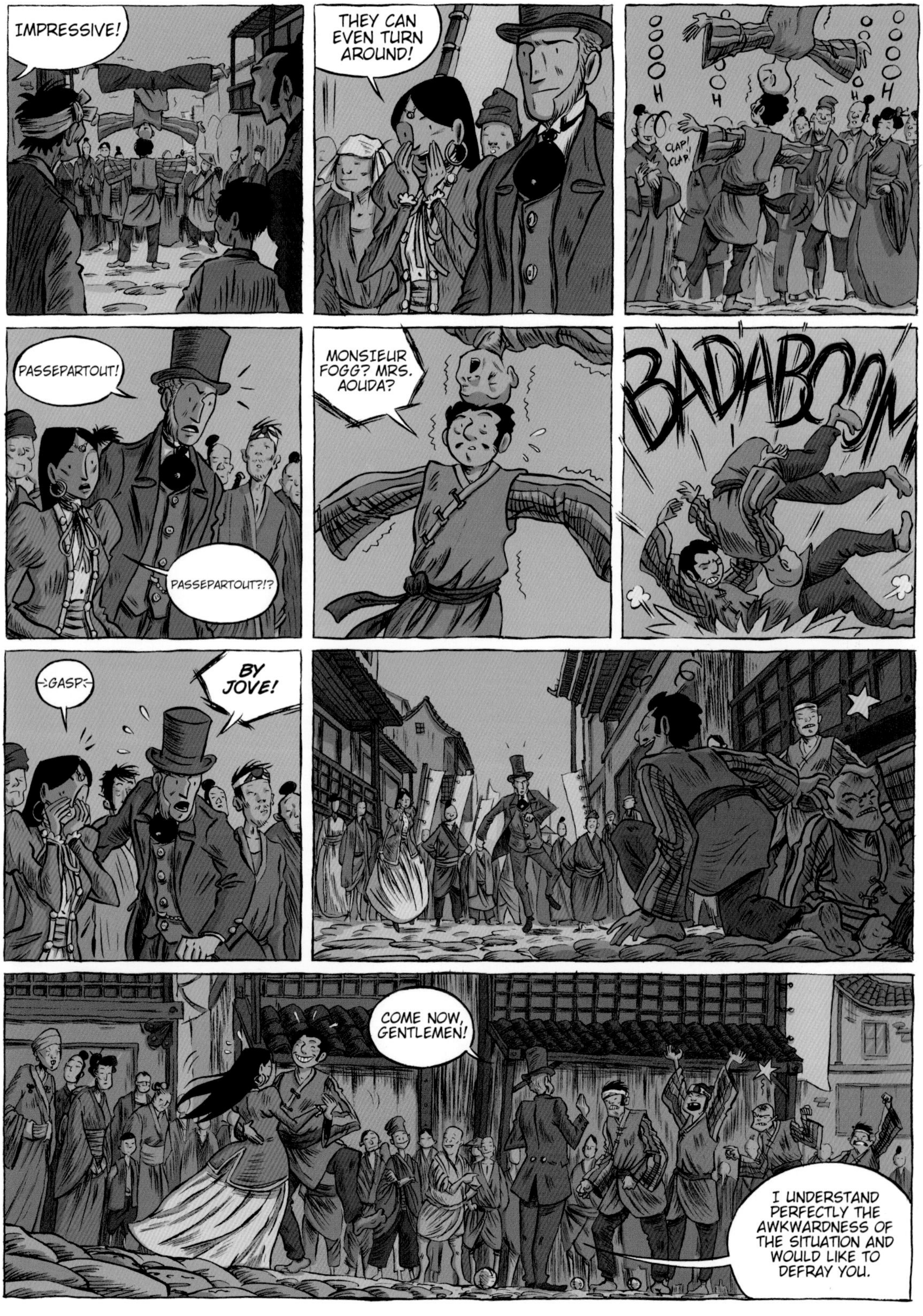
IMPRESSIVE!
THEY CAN EVEN TURN AROUND!
OOOOH
OOH
OOH
OOOOH
CLAP! CLAP!
PASSEPARTOUT!
PASSEPARTOUT?!?
MONSIEUR FOGG? MRS. AOUDA?
BADABOOM
GASP
BY JOVE!
COME NOW, GENTLEMEN!
I UNDERSTAND PERFECTLY THE AWKWARDNESS OF THE SITUATION AND WOULD LIKE TO DEFRAY YOU.

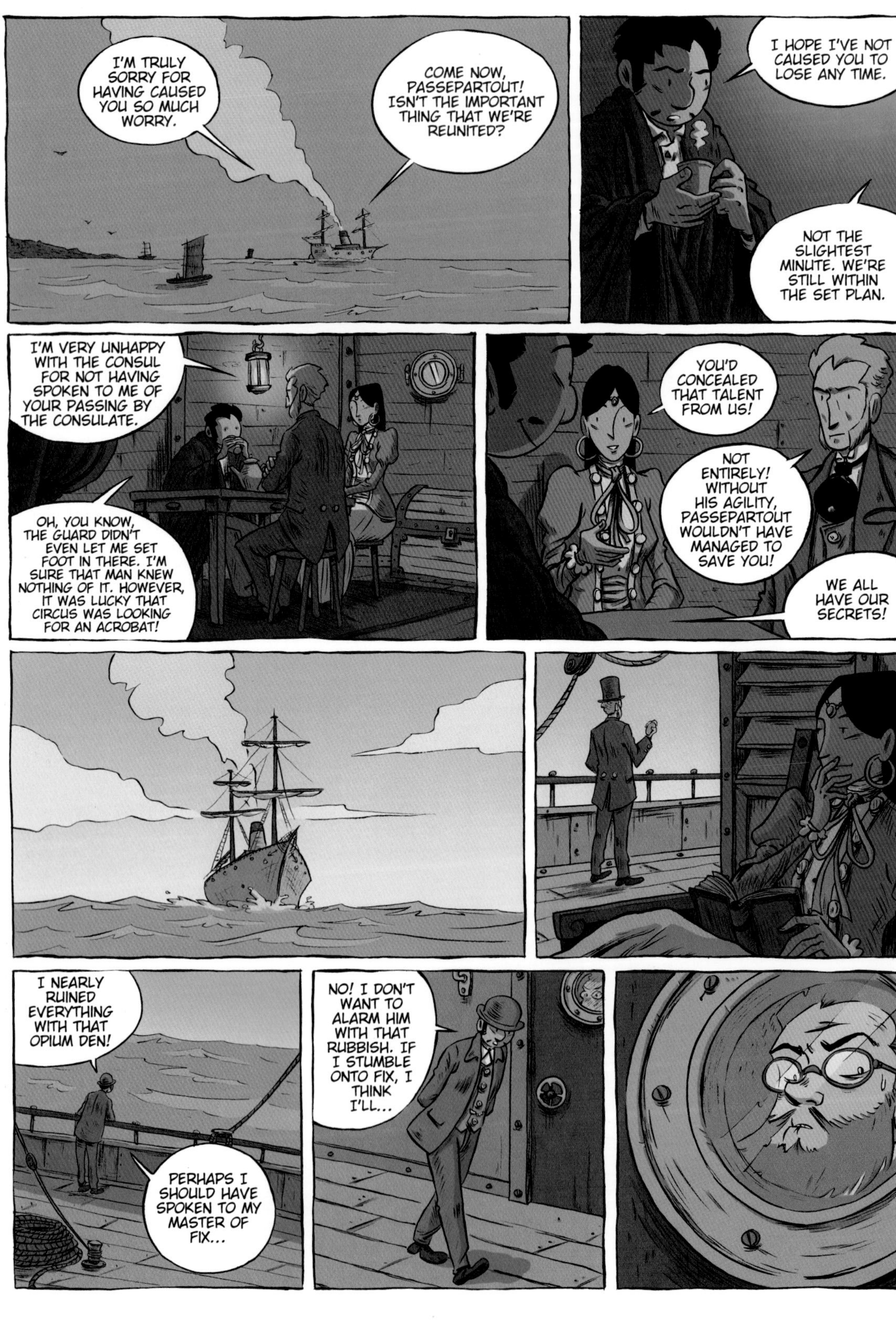
I'M TRULY SORRY FOR HAVING CAUSED YOU SO MUCH WORRY.
COME NOW, PASSEPARTOUT! ISN'T THE IMPORTANT THING THAT WE'RE REUNITED?
I HOPE I'VE NOT CAUSED YOU TO LOSE ANY TIME.
NOT THE SLIGHTEST MINUTE. WE'RE STILL WITHIN THE SET PLAN.
I'M VERY UNHAPPY WITH THE CONSUL FOR NOT HAVING SPOKEN TO ME OF YOUR PASSING BY THE CONSULATE.
OH, YOU KNOW, THE GUARD DIDN'T EVEN LET ME SET FOOT IN THERE. I'M SURE THAT MAN KNEW NOTHING OF IT. HOWEVER, IT WAS LUCKY THAT CIRCUS WAS LOOKING FOR AN ACROBAT!
YOU'D CONCEALED THAT TALENT FROM US!
NOT ENTIRELY! WITHOUT HIS AGILITY, PASSEPARTOUT WOULDN'T HAVE MANAGED TO SAVE YOU!
WE ALL HAVE OUR SECRETS!
I NEARLY RUINED EVERYTHING WITH THAT OPIUM DEN!
PERHAPS I SHOULD HAVE SPOKEN TO MY MASTER OF FIX...
NO! I DON'T WANT TO ALARM HIM WITH THAT RUBBISH. IF I STUMBLE ONTO FIX, I THINK I'LL...

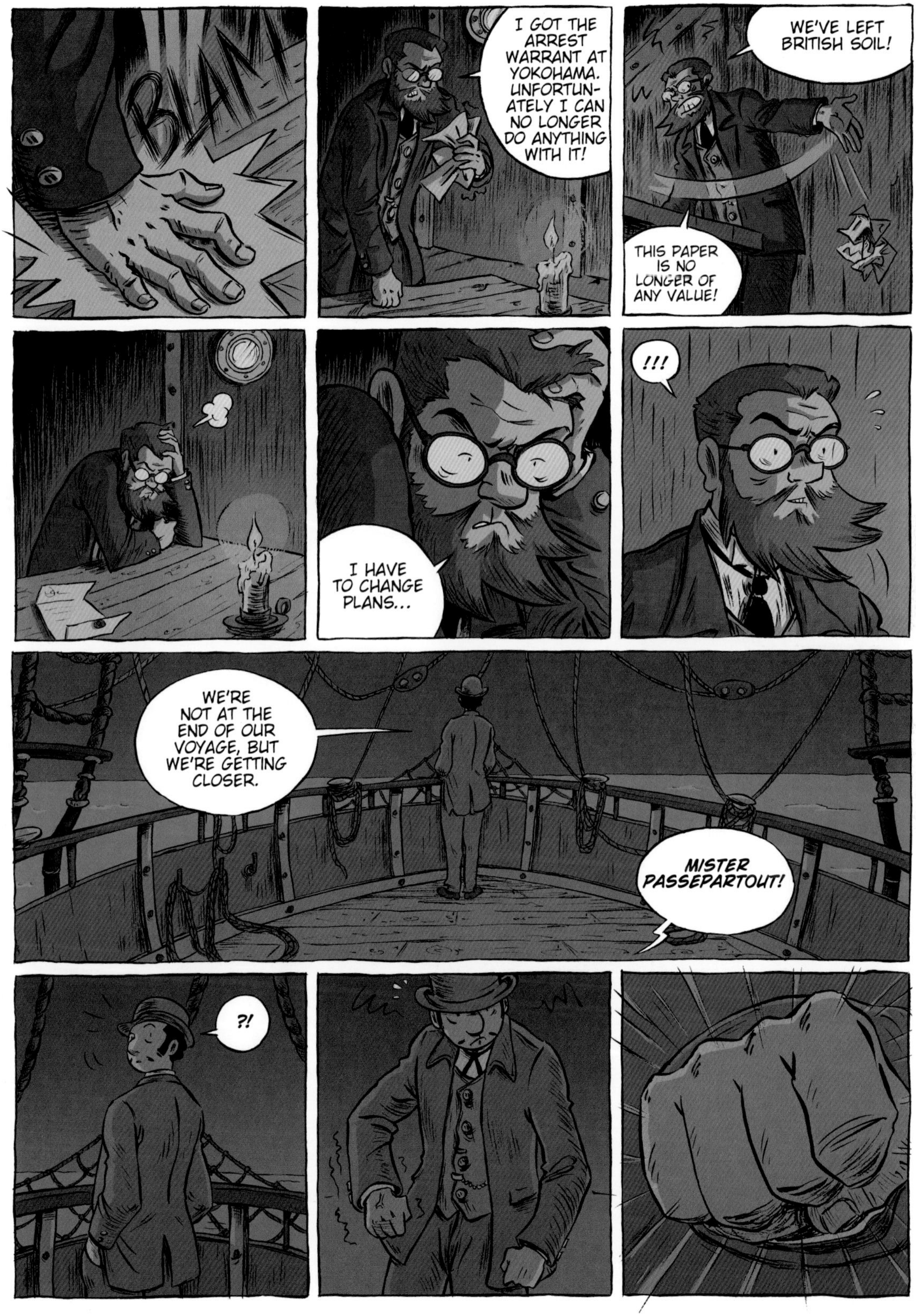
BLAM
I GOT THE ARREST WARRANT AT YOKOHAMA. UNFORTUNATELY I CAN NO LONGER DO ANYTHING WITH IT!
WE'VE LEFT BRITISH SOIL!
THIS PAPER IS NO LONGER OF ANY VALUE!
I HAVE TO CHANGE PLANS...
!!!
WE'RE NOT AT THE END OF OUR VOYAGE, BUT WE'RE GETTING CLOSER.
MISTER PASSEPARTOUT!
?!

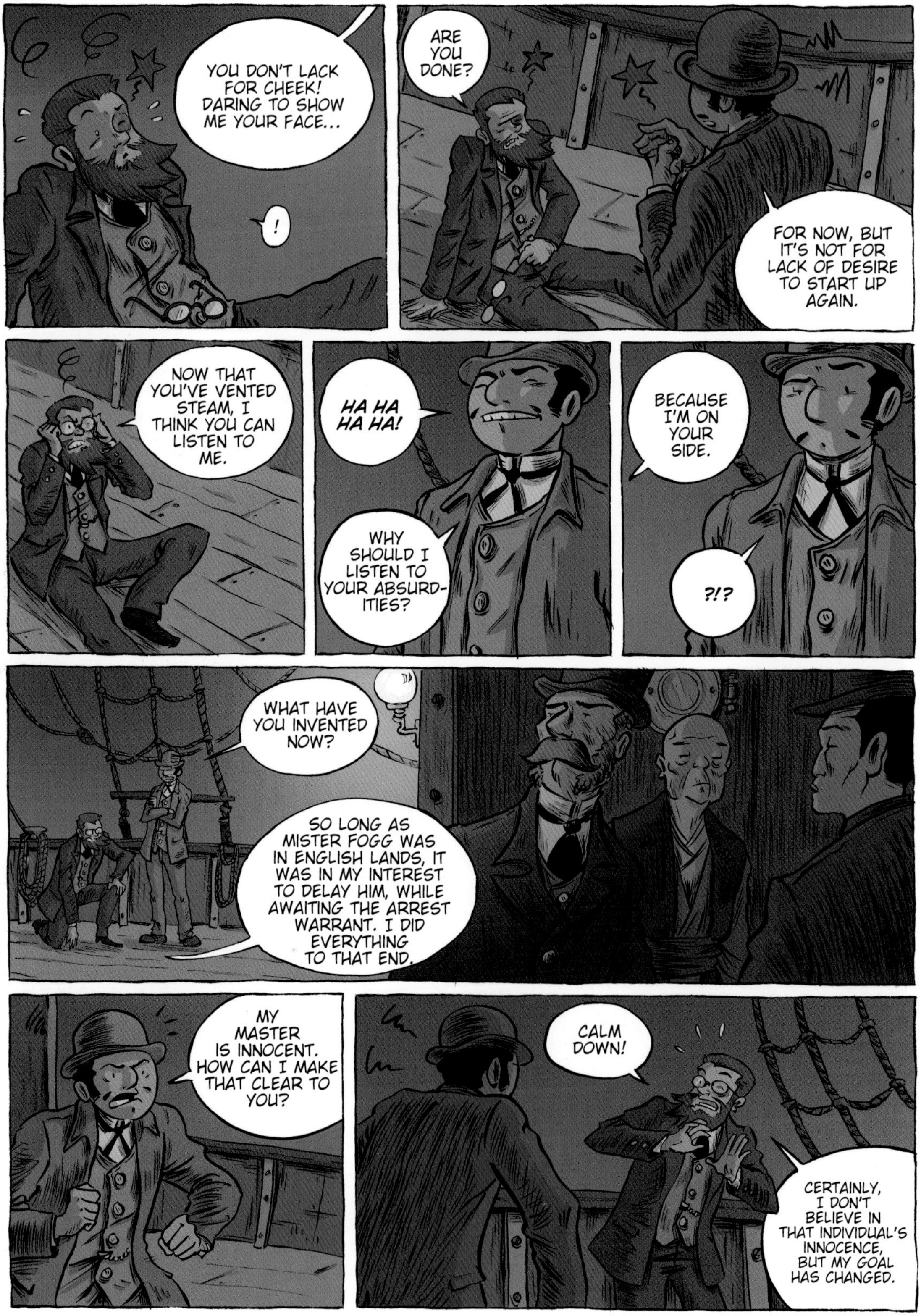
YOU DON'T LACK FOR CHEEK! DARING TO SHOW ME YOUR FACE...
!
ARE YOU DONE?
FOR NOW, BUT IT'S NOT FOR LACK OF DESIRE TO START UP AGAIN.
NOW THAT YOU'VE VENTED STEAM, I THINK YOU CAN LISTEN TO ME.
HA HA HA HA!
WHY SHOULD I LISTEN TO YOUR ABSURD-ITIES?
BECAUSE I'M ON YOUR SIDE.
?!?
WHAT HAVE YOU INVENTED NOW?
SO LONG AS MISTER FOGG WAS IN ENGLISH LANDS, IT WAS IN MY INTEREST TO DELAY HIM, WHILE AWAITING THE ARREST WARRANT. I DID EVERYTHING TO THAT END.
MY MASTER IS INNOCENT. HOW CAN I MAKE THAT CLEAR TO YOU?
CALM DOWN!
CERTAINLY, I DON'T BELIEVE IN THAT INDIVIDUAL'S INNOCENCE, BUT MY GOAL HAS CHANGED.

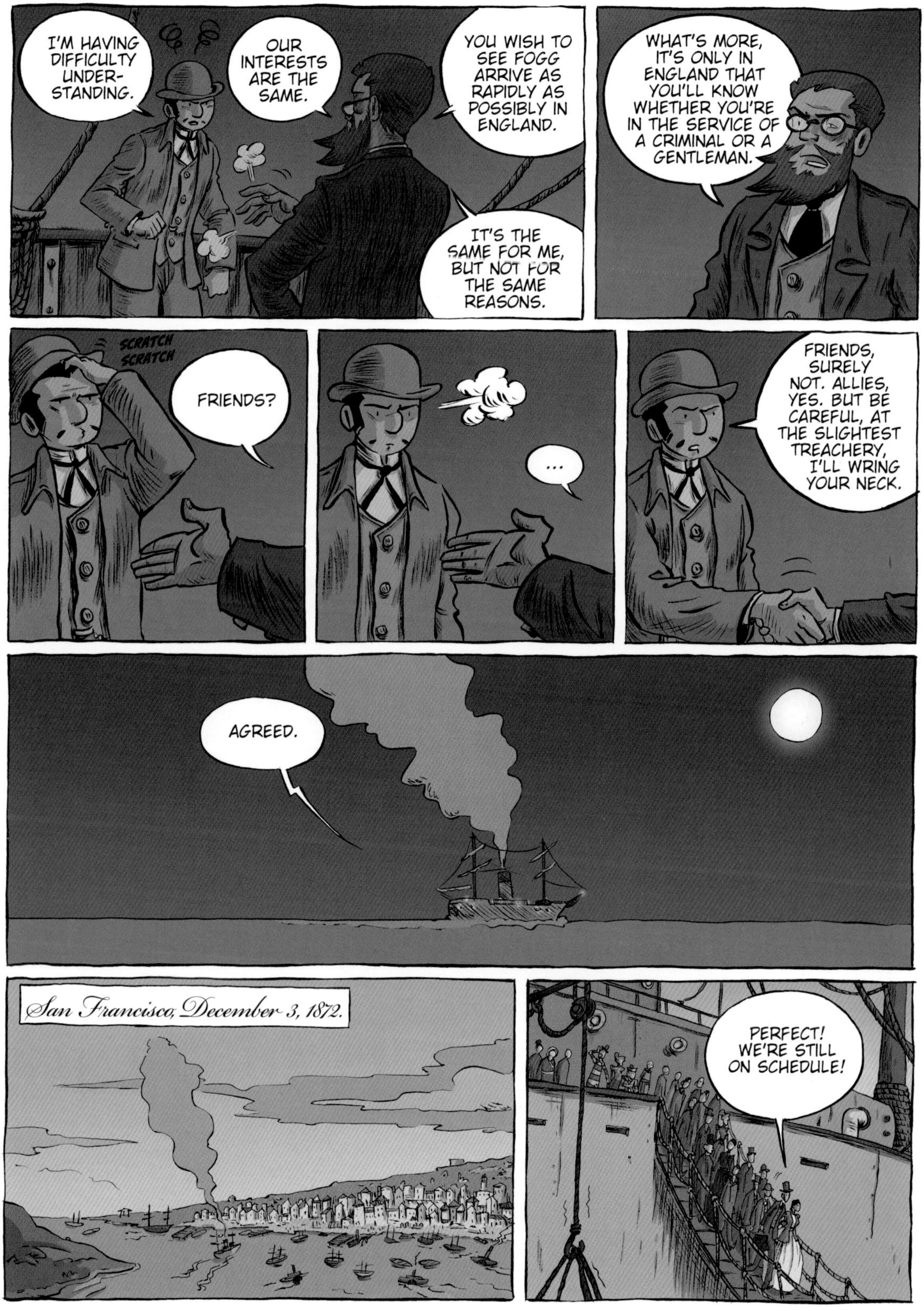
I'M HAVING DIFFICULTY UNDER-STANDING.
OUR INTERESTS ARE THE SAME.
YOU WISH TO SEE FOGG ARRIVE AS RAPIDLY AS POSSIBLY IN ENGLAND.
IT'S THE SAME FOR ME, BUT NOT FOR THE SAME REASONS.
WHAT'S MORE, IT'S ONLY IN ENGLAND THAT YOU'LL KNOW WHETHER YOU'RE IN THE SERVICE OF A CRIMINAL OR A GENTLEMAN.
SCRATCH SCRATCH
FRIENDS?
...
FRIENDS, SURELY NOT. ALLIES, YES. BUT BE CAREFUL, AT THE SLIGHTEST TREACHERY, I'LL WRING YOUR NECK.
AGREED.
San Francisco, December 3, 1872.
PERFECT! WE'RE STILL ON SCHEDULE!

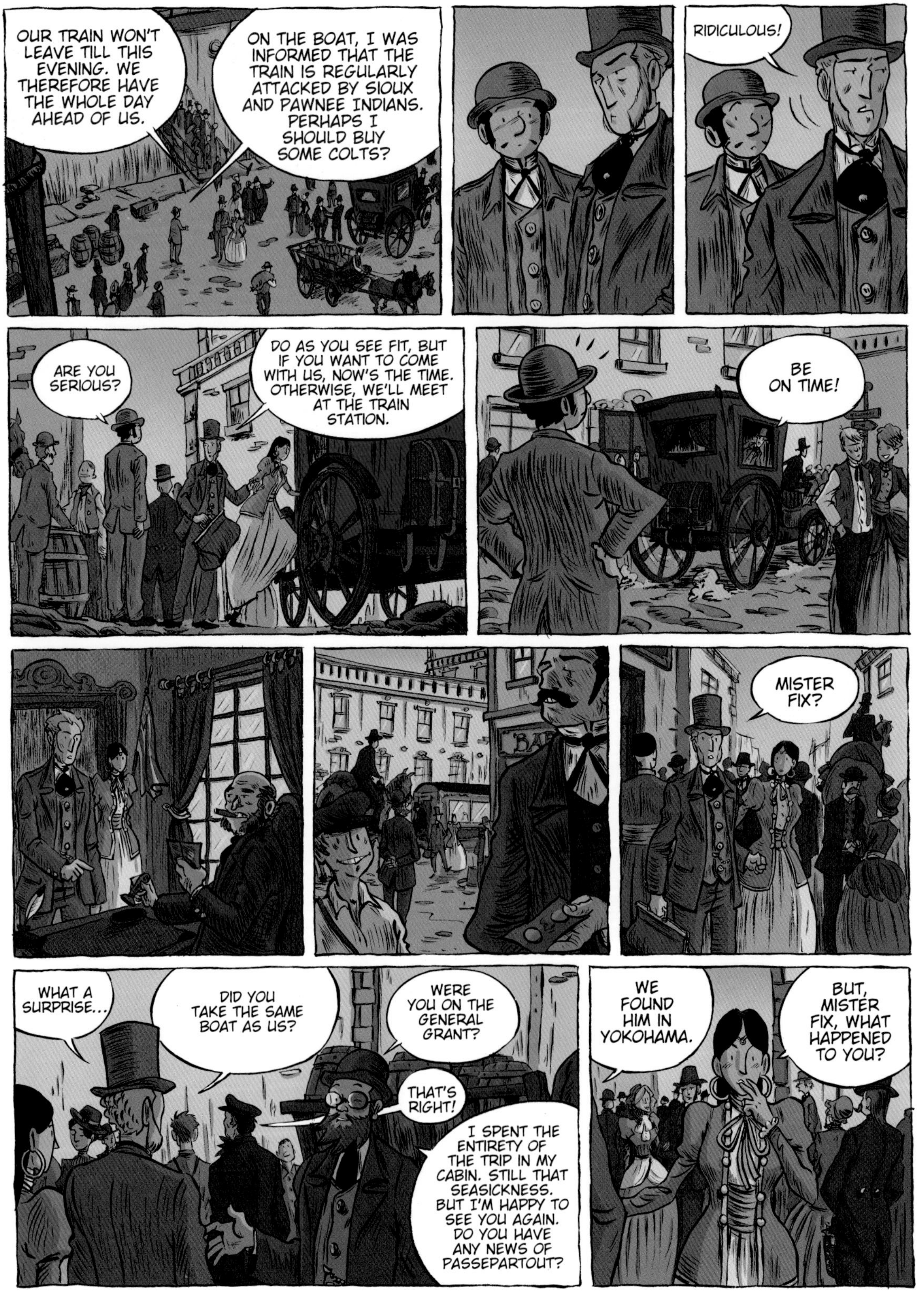

OUR TRAIN WON'T LEAVE TILL THIS EVENING. WE THEREFORE HAVE THE WHOLE DAY AHEAD OF US.
ON THE BOAT, I WAS INFORMED THAT THE TRAIN IS REGULARLY ATTACKED BY SIOUX AND PAWNEE INDIANS. PERHAPS I SHOULD BUY SOME COLTS?
RIDICULOUS!
ARE YOU SERIOUS?
DO AS YOU SEE FIT, BUT IF YOU WANT TO COME WITH US, NOW'S THE TIME. OTHERWISE, WE'LL MEET AT THE TRAIN STATION.
BE ON TIME!
MISTER FIX?
WHAT A SURPRISE...
DID YOU TAKE THE SAME BOAT AS US?
WERE YOU ON THE GENERAL GRANT?
THAT'S RIGHT!
I SPENT THE ENTIRETY OF THE TRIP IN MY CABIN. STILL THAT SEASICKNESS. BUT I'M HAPPY TO SEE YOU AGAIN. DO YOU HAVE ANY NEWS OF PASSEPARTOUT?
WE FOUND HIM IN YOKOHAMA.
BUT, MISTER FIX, WHAT HAPPENED TO YOU?

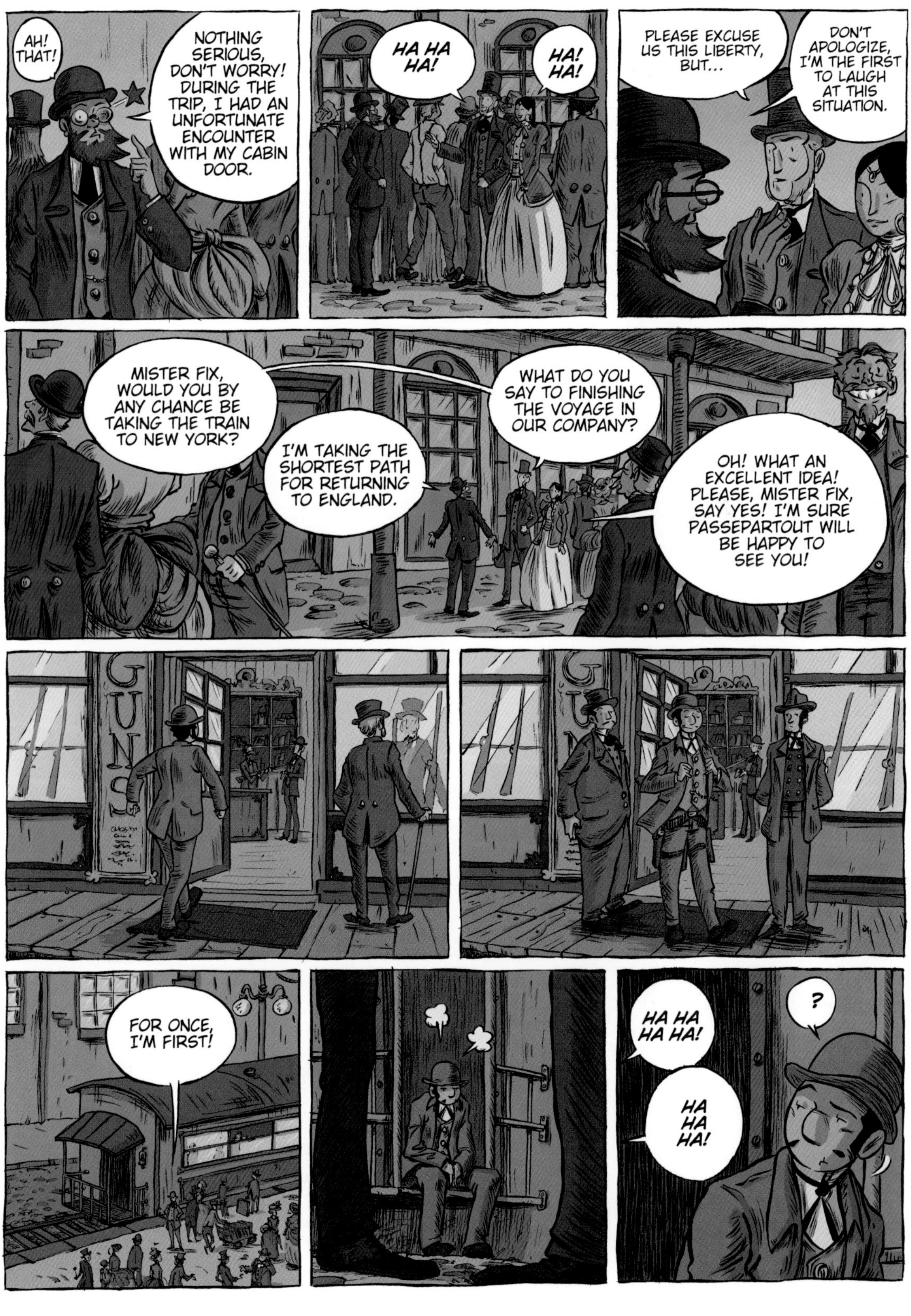
AH! THAT!
NOTHING SERIOUS, DON'T WORRY! DURING THE TRIP, I HAD AN UNFORTUNATE ENCOUNTER WITH MY CABIN DOOR.
HA HA HA!
HA! HA!
PLEASE EXCUSE US THIS LIBERTY, BUT...
DON'T APOLOGIZE, I'M THE FIRST TO LAUGH AT THIS SITUATION.
MISTER FIX, WOULD YOU BY ANY CHANCE BE TAKING THE TRAIN TO NEW YORK?
WHAT DO YOU SAY TO FINISHING THE VOYAGE IN OUR COMPANY?
I'M TAKING THE SHORTEST PATH FOR RETURNING TO ENGLAND.
OH! WHAT AN EXCELLENT IDEA! PLEASE, MISTER FIX, SAY YES! I'M SURE PASSEPARTOUT WILL BE HAPPY TO SEE YOU!
GUNS
FOR ONCE, I'M FIRST!
HA HA HA HA!
?
HA HA HA!

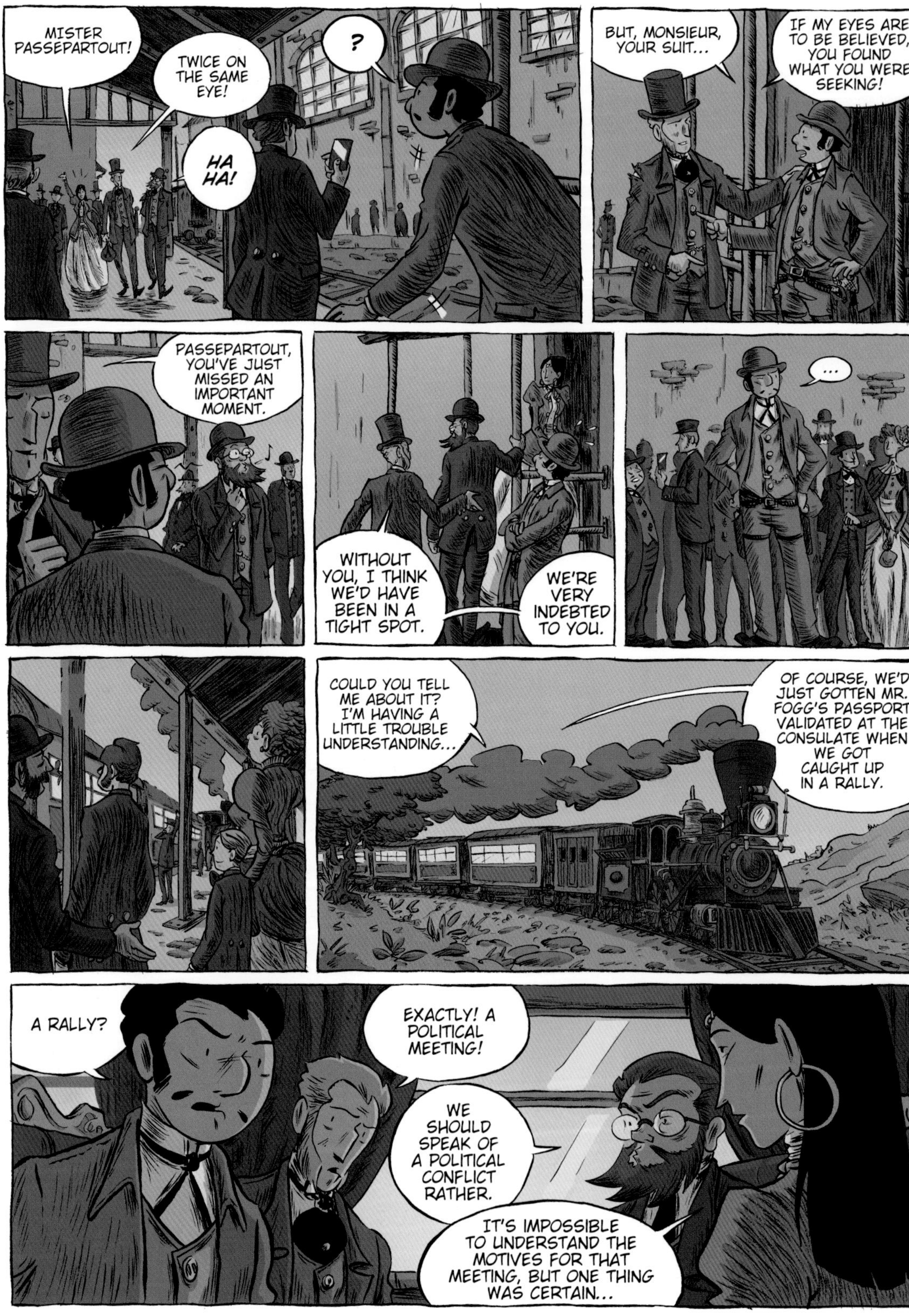
MISTER PASSEPARTOUT!
TWICE ON THE SAME EYE!
HA HA!
?
BUT, MONSIEUR, YOUR SUIT...
IF MY EYES ARE TO BE BELIEVED, YOU FOUND WHAT YOU WERE SEEKING!
PASSEPARTOUT, YOU'VE JUST MISSED AN IMPORTANT MOMENT.
WITHOUT YOU, I THINK WE'D HAVE BEEN IN A TIGHT SPOT.
WE'RE VERY INDEBTED TO YOU.
...
COULD YOU TELL ME ABOUT IT? I'M HAVING A LITTLE TROUBLE UNDERSTANDING...
OF COURSE, WE'D JUST GOTTEN MR. FOGG'S PASSPORT VALIDATED AT THE CONSULATE WHEN WE GOT CAUGHT UP IN A RALLY.
A RALLY?
EXACTLY! A POLITICAL MEETING!
WE SHOULD SPEAK OF A POLITICAL CONFLICT RATHER.
IT'S IMPOSSIBLE TO UNDERSTAND THE MOTIVES FOR THAT MEETING, BUT ONE THING WAS CERTAIN...

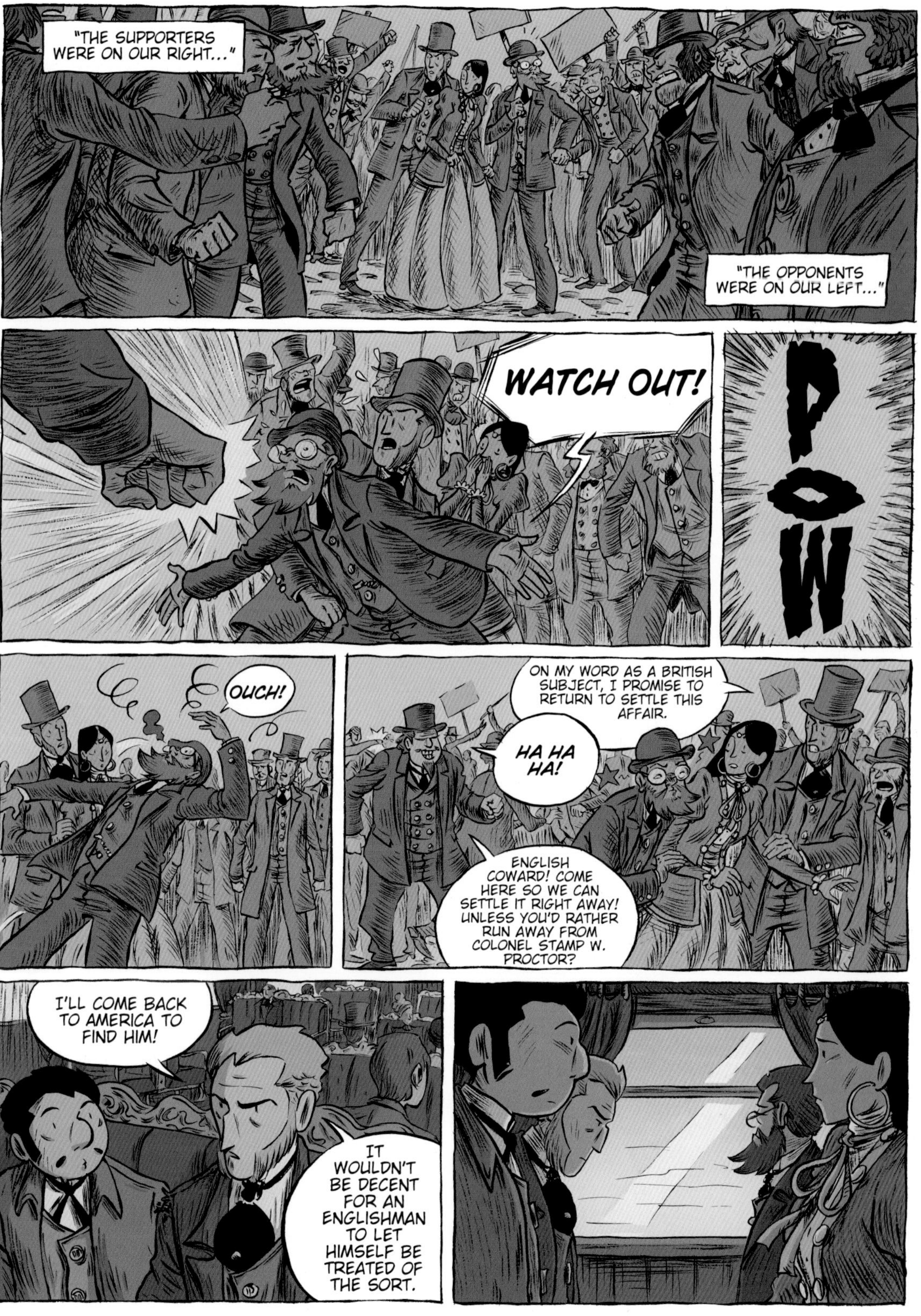
"THE SUPPORTERS WERE ON OUR RIGHT..."
"THE OPPONENTS WERE ON OUR LEFT..."
WATCH OUT!
POW
OUCH!
ON MY WORD AS A BRITISH SUBJECT, I PROMISE TO RETURN TO SETTLE THIS AFFAIR.
HA HA HA!
ENGLISH COWARD! COME HERE SO WE CAN SETTLE IT RIGHT AWAY! UNLESS YOU'D RATHER RUN AWAY FROM COLONEL STAMP W. PROCTOR?
I'LL COME BACK TO AMERICA TO FIND HIM!
IT WOULDN'T BE DECENT FOR AN ENGLISHMAN TO LET HIMSELF BE TREATED OF THE SORT.

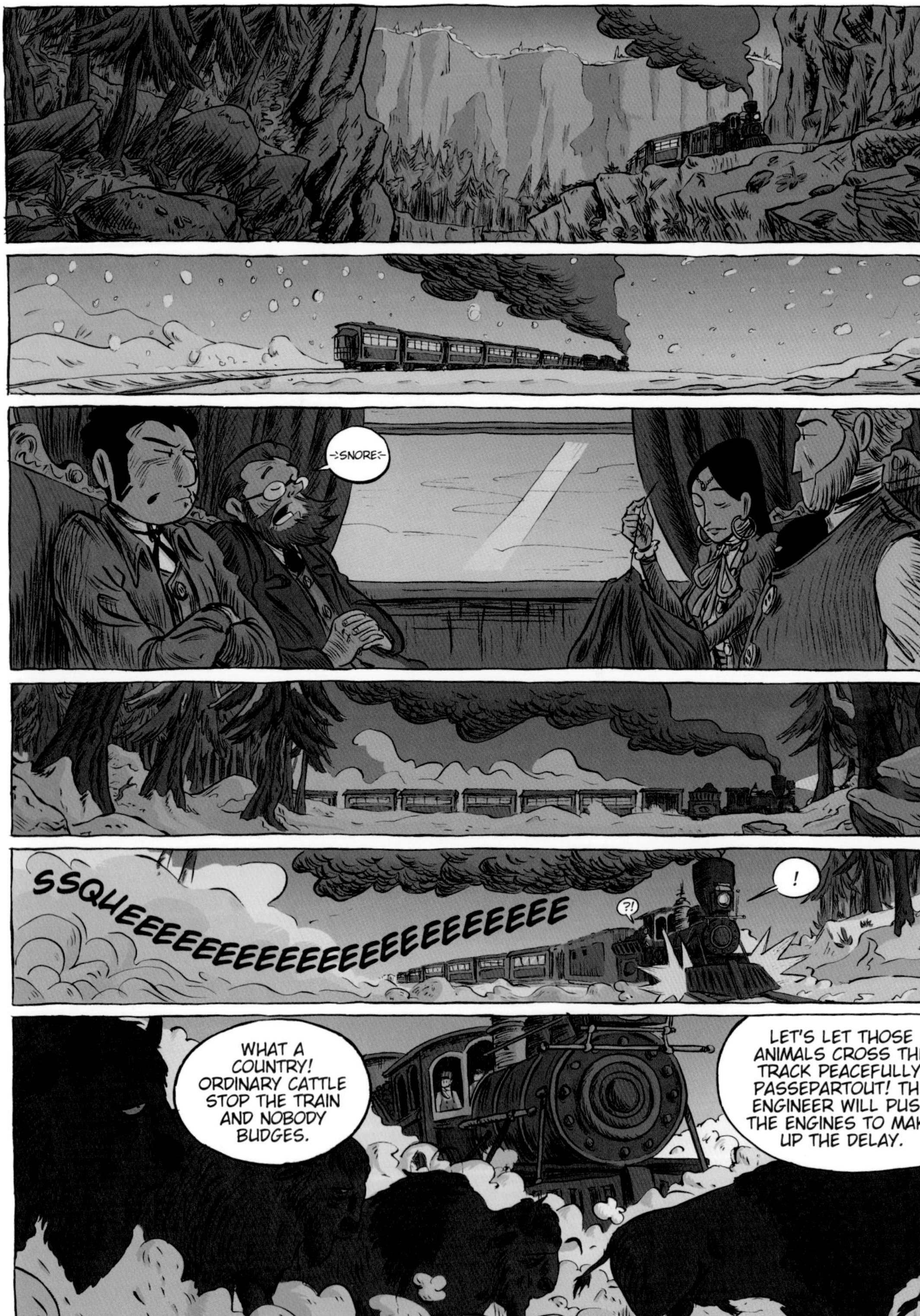

SNORE
SSQUEEEEEEEEEEEEEEEEEEEEEEEEE
?!
!
WHAT A COUNTRY! ORDINARY CATTLE STOP THE TRAIN AND NOBODY BUDGES.
LET'S LET THOSE ANIMALS CROSS THE TRACK PEACEFULLY, PASSEPARTOUT! THE ENGINEER WILL PUSH THE ENGINES TO MAKE UP THE DELAY.

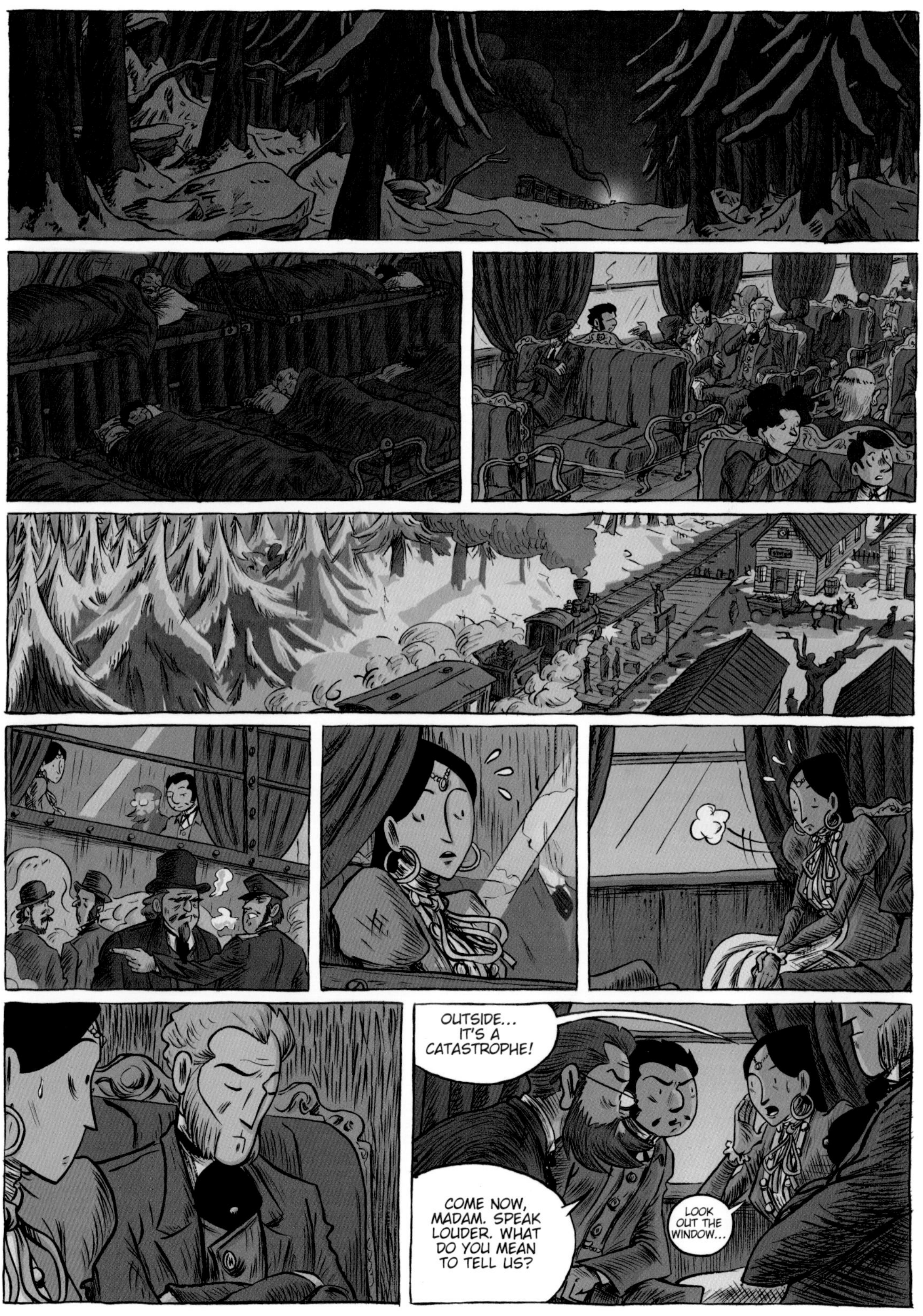
OUTSIDE... IT'S A CATASTROPHE!
COME NOW, MADAM. SPEAK LOUDER. WHAT DO YOU MEAN TO TELL US?
LOOK OUT THE WINDOW...

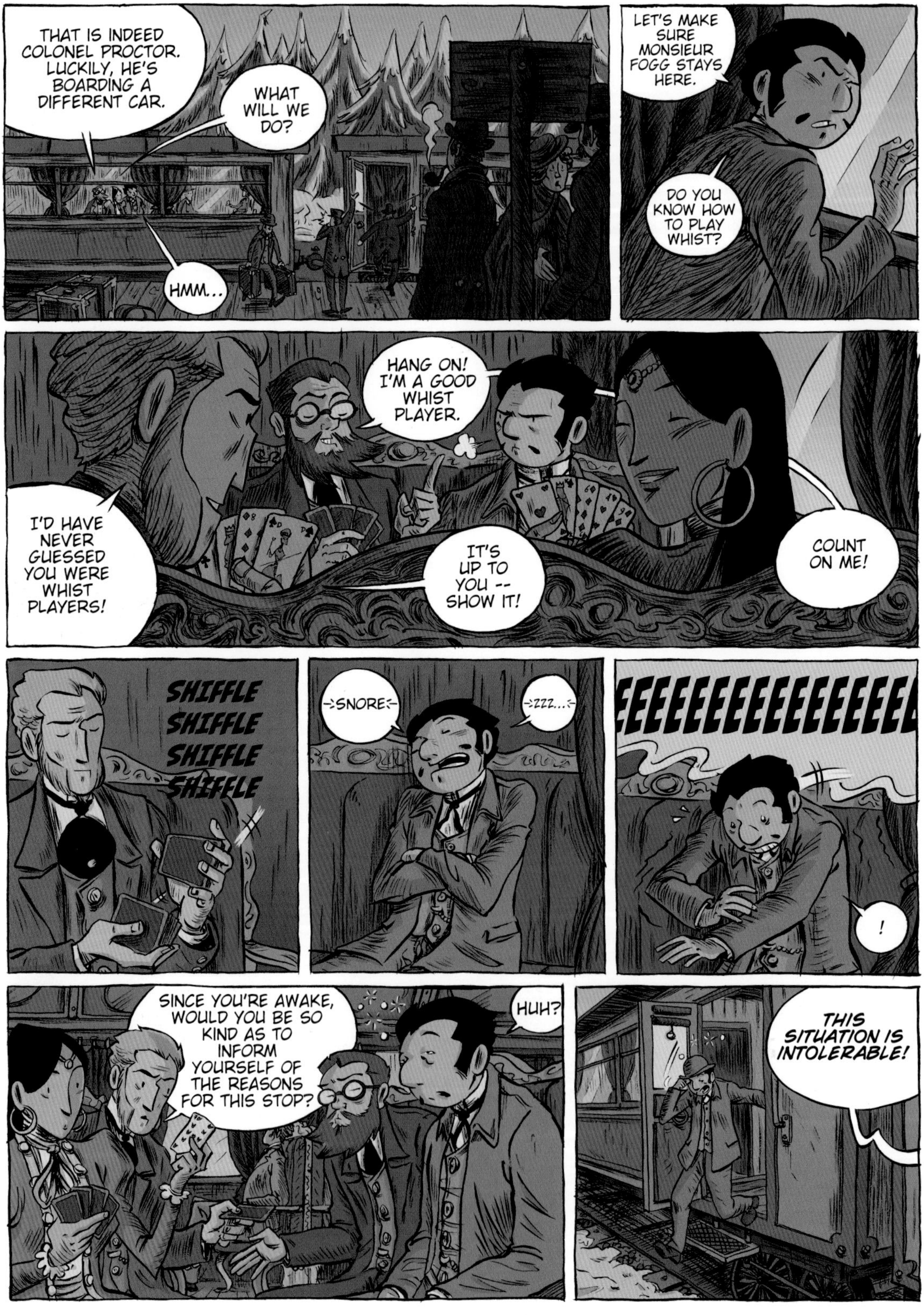
THAT IS INDEED COLONEL PROCTOR. LUCKILY, HE'S BOARDING A DIFFERENT CAR.
WHAT WILL WE DO?
HMM...
LET'S MAKE SURE MONSIEUR FOGG STAYS HERE.
DO YOU KNOW HOW TO PLAY WHIST?
HANG ON! I'M A GOOD WHIST PLAYER.
I'D HAVE NEVER GUESSED YOU WERE WHIST PLAYERS!
IT'S UP TO YOU -- SHOW IT!
COUNT ON ME!
SHIFFLE SHIFFLE SHIFFLE SHIFFLE
SNORE
ZZZ...
EEEEEEEEEEEEEEEE
!
SINCE YOU'RE AWAKE, WOULD YOU BE SO KIND AS TO INFORM YOURSELF OF THE REASONS FOR THIS STOP?
HUH?
THIS SITUATION IS INTOLERABLE!

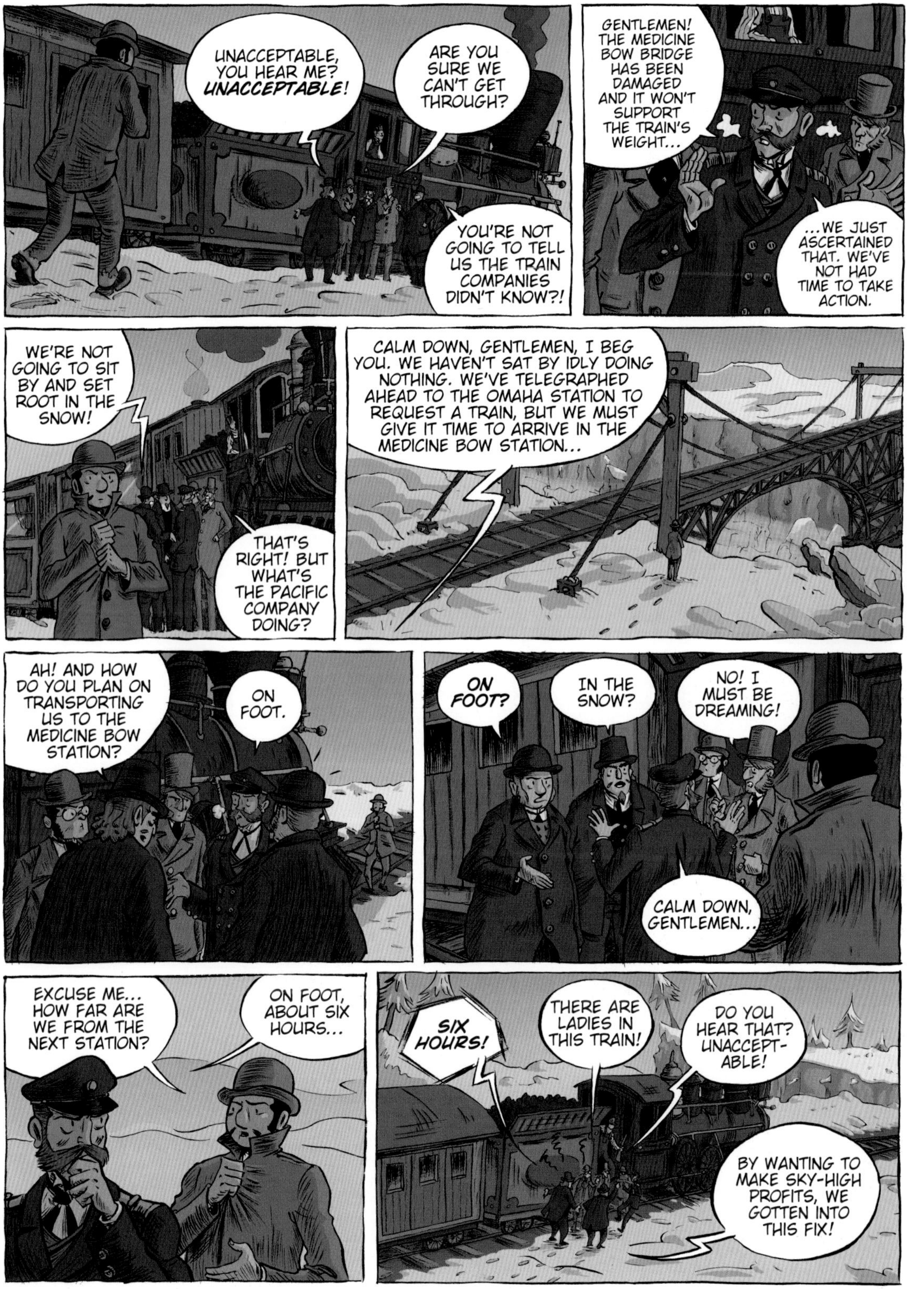
UNACCEPTABLE, YOU HEAR ME? UNACCEPTABLE!
ARE YOU SURE WE CAN'T GET THROUGH?
YOU'RE NOT GOING TO TELL US THE TRAIN COMPANIES DIDN'T KNOW?!
GENTLEMEN! THE MEDICINE BOW BRIDGE HAS BEEN DAMAGED AND IT WON'T SUPPORT THE TRAIN'S WEIGHT...
...WE JUST ASCERTAINED THAT. WE'VE NOT HAD TIME TO TAKE ACTION.
WE'RE NOT GOING TO SIT BY AND SET ROOT IN THE SNOW!
THAT'S RIGHT! BUT WHAT'S THE PACIFIC COMPANY DOING?
CALM DOWN, GENTLEMEN, I BEG YOU. WE HAVEN'T SAT BY IDLY DOING NOTHING. WE'VE TELEGRAPHED AHEAD TO THE OMAHA STATION TO REQUEST A TRAIN, BUT WE MUST GIVE IT TIME TO ARRIVE IN THE MEDICINE BOW STATION...
AH! AND HOW DO YOU PLAN ON TRANSPORTING US TO THE MEDICINE BOW STATION?
ON FOOT.
ON FOOT?
IN THE SNOW?
NO! I MUST BE DREAMING!
CALM DOWN, GENTLEMEN...
EXCUSE ME... HOW FAR ARE WE FROM THE NEXT STATION?
ON FOOT, ABOUT SIX HOURS...
SIX HOURS!
THERE ARE LADIES IN THIS TRAIN!
DO YOU HEAR THAT? UNACCEPT-ABLE!
BY WANTING TO MAKE SKY-HIGH PROFITS, WE GOTTEN INTO THIS FIX!

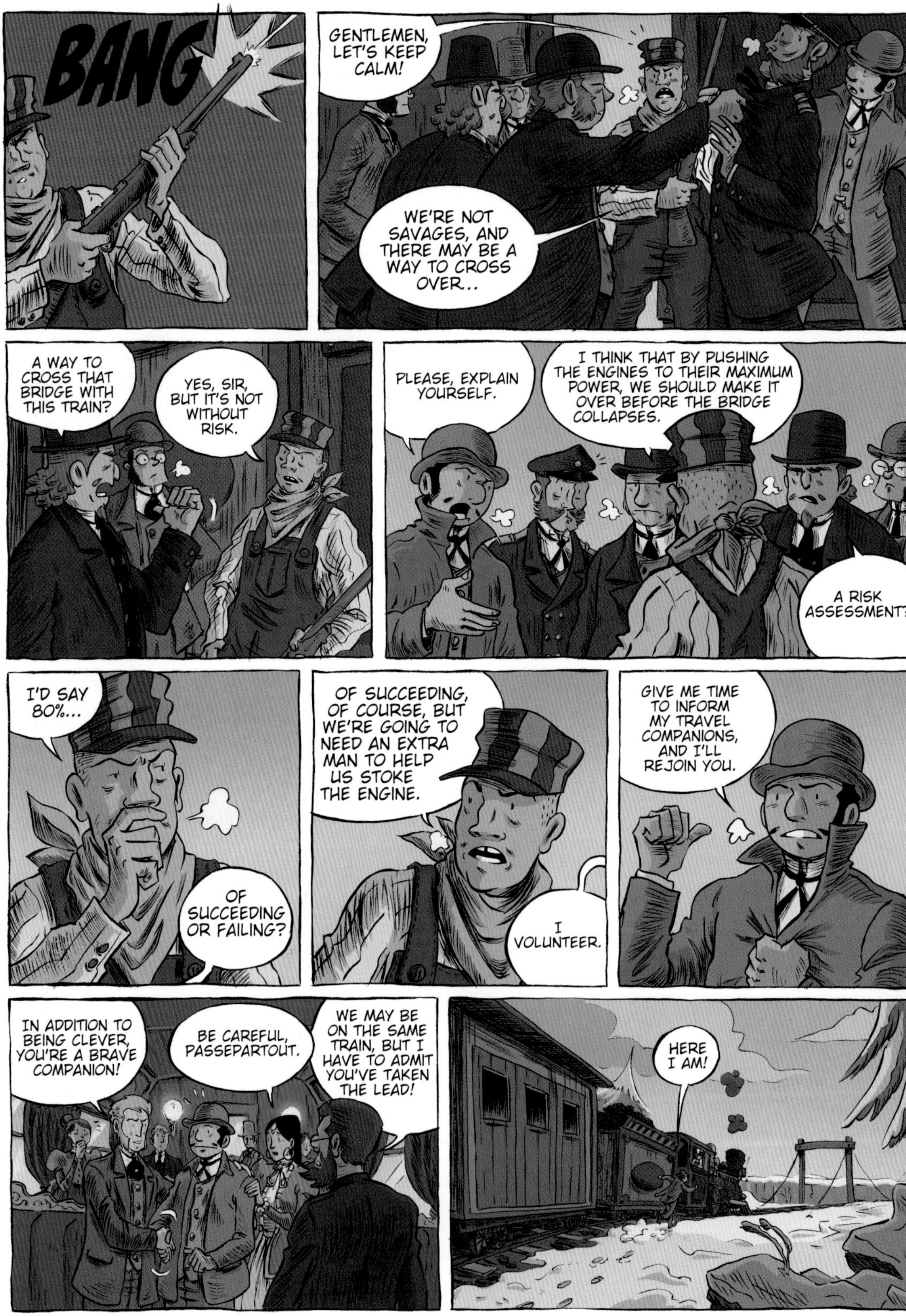
BANG
GENTLEMEN, LET'S KEEP CALM!
WE'RE NOT SAVAGES, AND THERE MAY BE A WAY TO CROSS OVER...
A WAY TO CROSS THAT BRIDGE WITH THIS TRAIN?
YES, SIR, BUT IT'S NOT WITHOUT RISK.
PLEASE, EXPLAIN YOURSELF.
I THINK THAT BY PUSHING THE ENGINES TO THEIR MAXIMUM POWER, WE SHOULD MAKE IT OVER BEFORE THE BRIDGE COLLAPSES.
A RISK ASSESSMENT?
I'D SAY 80%...
OF SUCCEEDING OR FAILING?
OF SUCCEEDING, OF COURSE, BUT WE'RE GOING TO NEED AN EXTRA MAN TO HELP US STOKE THE ENGINE.
I VOLUNTEER.
GIVE ME TIME TO INFORM MY TRAVEL COMPANIONS, AND I'LL REJOIN YOU.
IN ADDITION TO BEING CLEVER, YOU'RE A BRAVE COMPANION!
BE CAREFUL, PASSEPARTOUT.
WE MAY BE ON THE SAME TRAIN, BUT I HAVE TO ADMIT YOU'VE TAKEN THE LEAD!
HERE I AM!

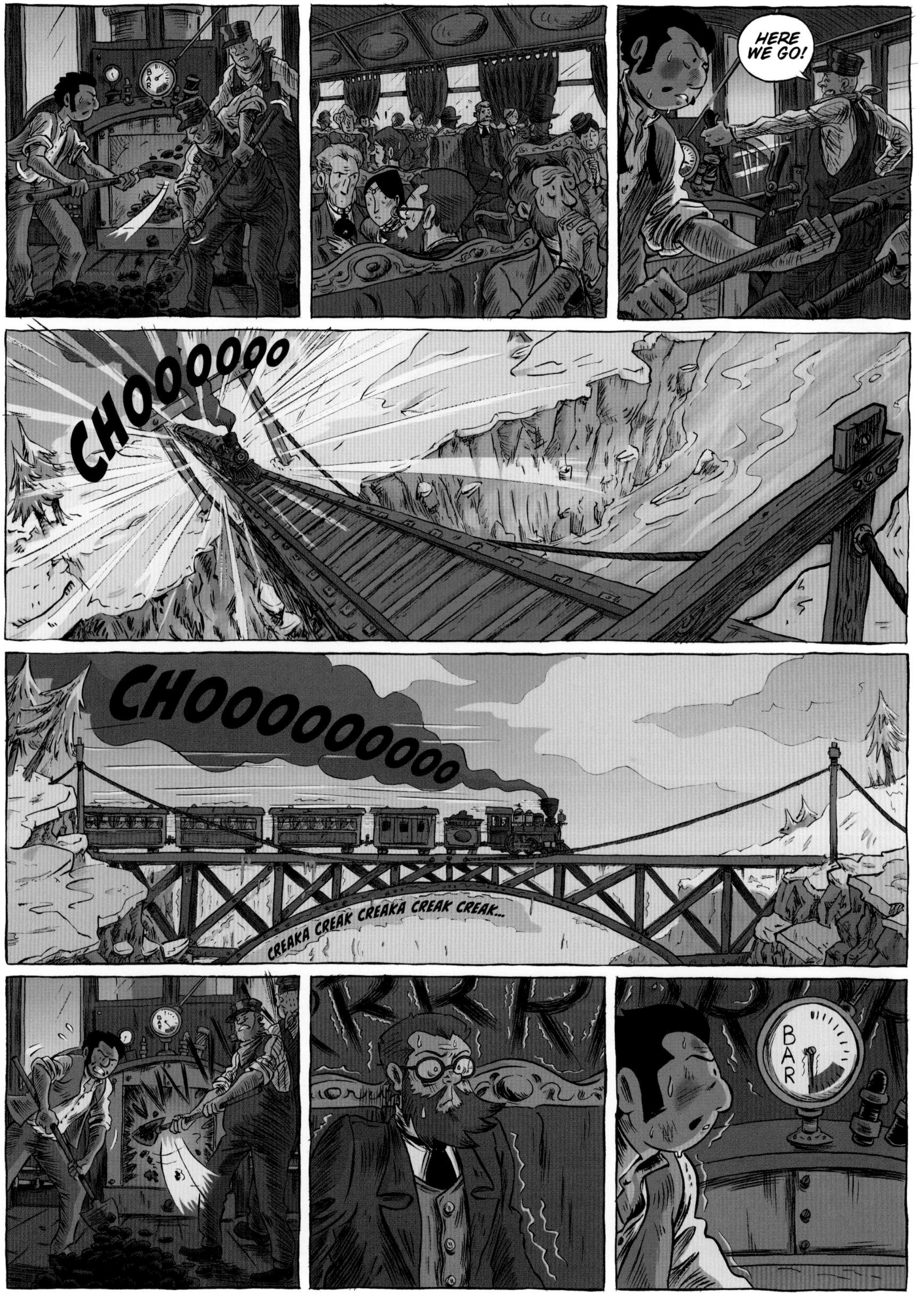
HERE WE GO!
CHOOOOOO
CHOOOOOOOOOO
CREAKA CREAK CREAKA CREAK CREAK...

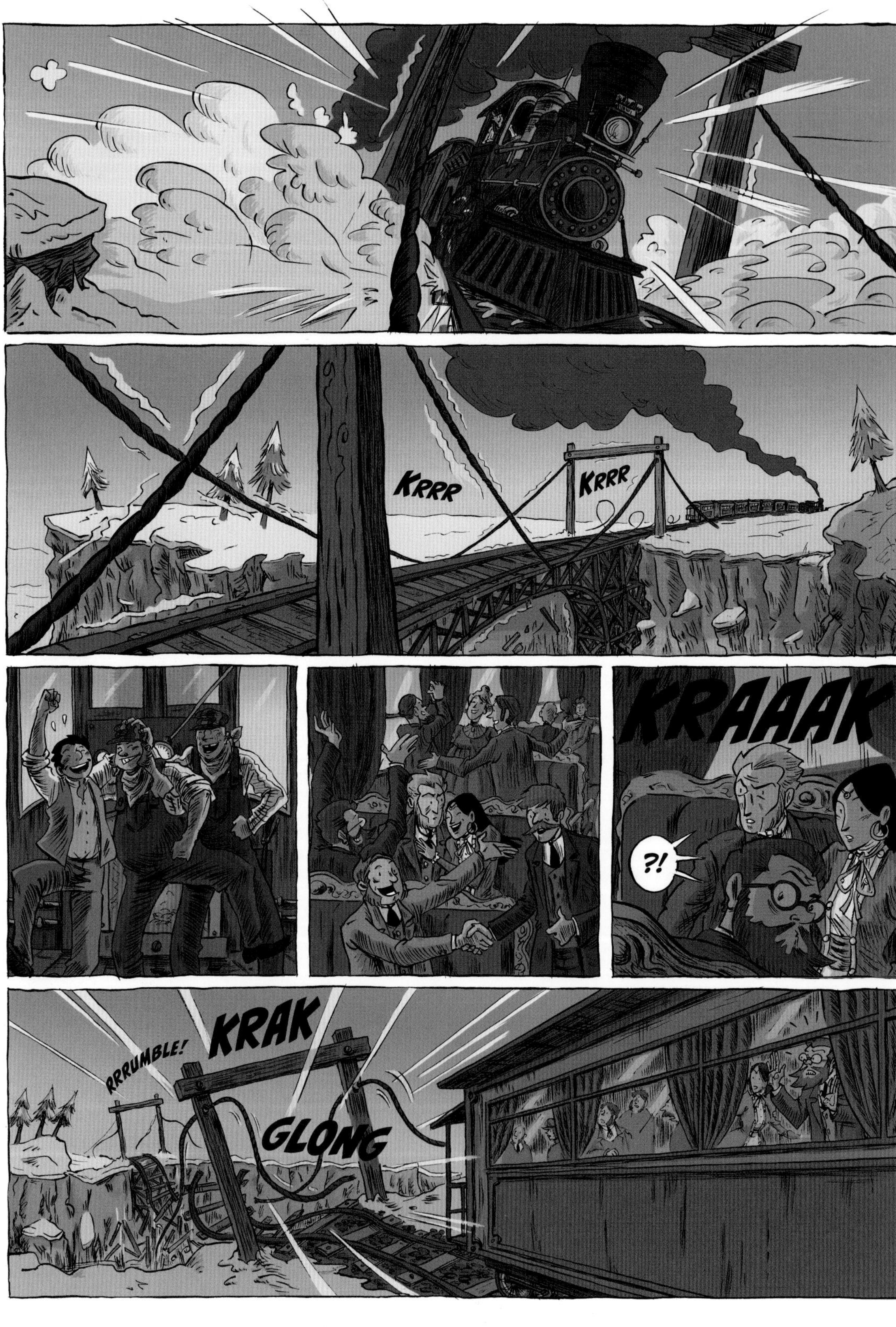
KRRR
KRRR
KRAAAK
?!
RRRUMBLE!
KRAK
GLONG

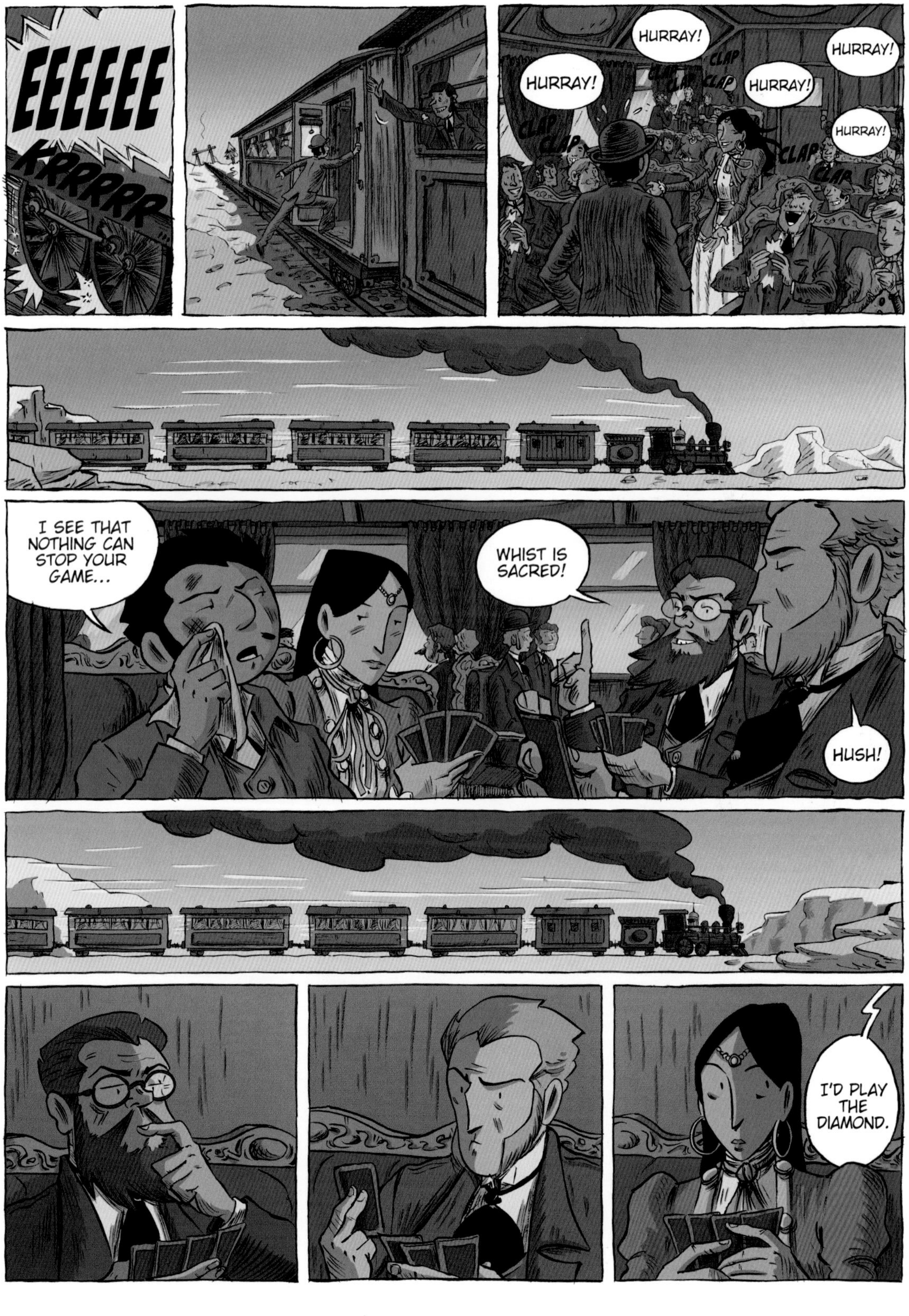
EEEEEE
KRRRRRR
HURRAY!
HURRAY!
CLAP CLAP
HURRAY!
HURRAY!
HURRAY!
I SEE THAT NOTHING CAN STOP YOUR GAME...
WHIST IS SACRED!
HUSH!
I'D PLAY THE DIAMOND.

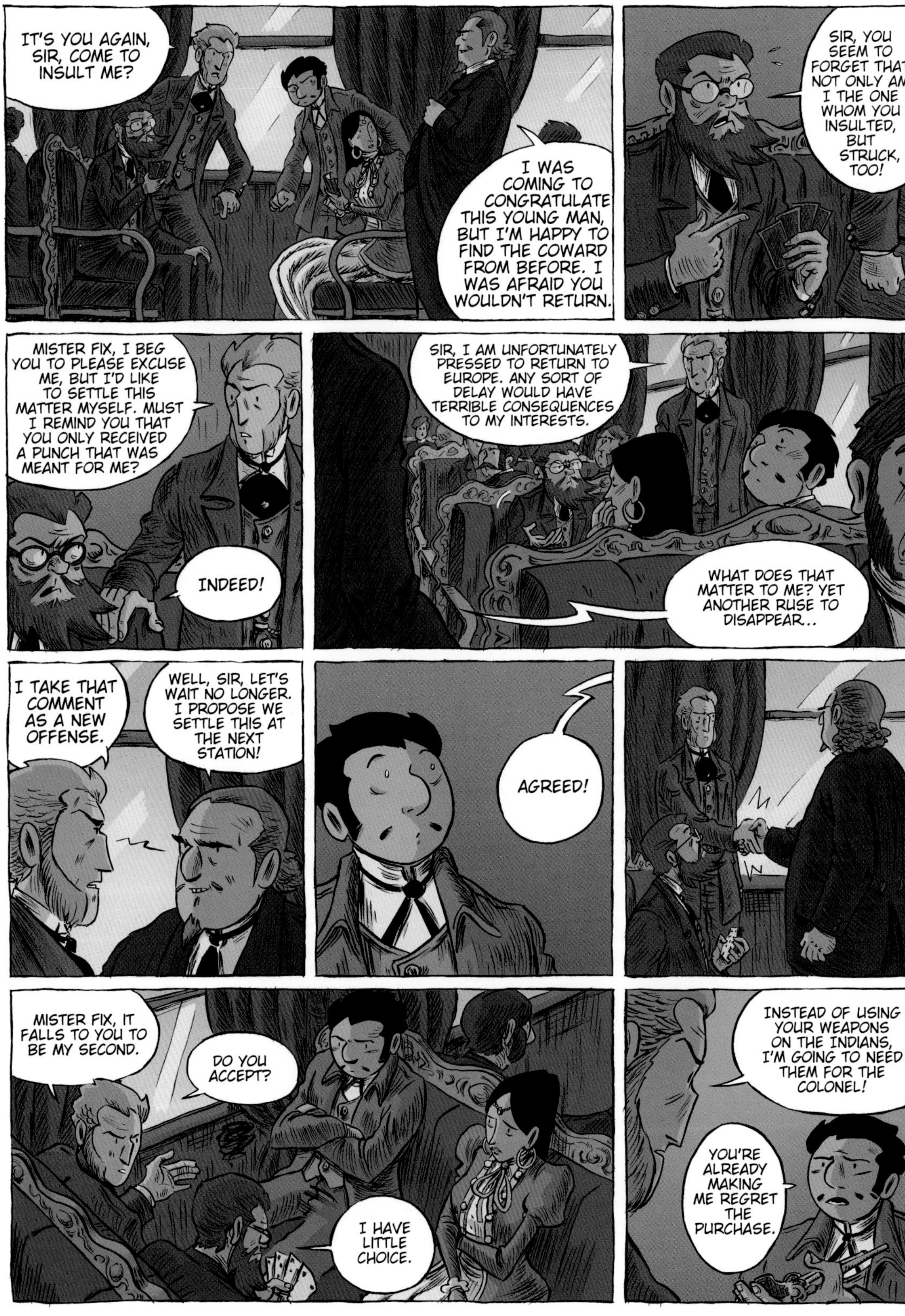
IT'S YOU AGAIN, SIR, COME TO INSULT ME?
I WAS COMING TO CONGRATULATE THIS YOUNG MAN, BUT I'M HAPPY TO FIND THE COWARD FROM BEFORE. I WAS AFRAID YOU WOULDN'T RETURN.
SIR, YOU SEEM TO FORGET THAT NOT ONLY AM I THE ONE WHOM YOU INSULTED, BUT STRUCK, TOO!
MISTER FIX, I BEG YOU TO PLEASE EXCUSE ME, BUT I'D LIKE TO SETTLE THIS MATTER MYSELF. MUST I REMIND YOU THAT YOU ONLY RECEIVED A PUNCH THAT WAS MEANT FOR ME?
INDEED!
SIR, I AM UNFORTUNATELY PRESSED TO RETURN TO EUROPE. ANY SORT OF DELAY WOULD HAVE TERRIBLE CONSEQUENCES TO MY INTERESTS.
WHAT DOES THAT MATTER TO ME? YET ANOTHER RUSE TO DISAPPEAR...
I TAKE THAT COMMENT AS A NEW OFFENSE.
WELL, SIR, LET'S WAIT NO LONGER. I PROPOSE WE SETTLE THIS AT THE NEXT STATION!
AGREED!
MISTER FIX, IT FALLS TO YOU TO BE MY SECOND.
DO YOU ACCEPT?
I HAVE LITTLE CHOICE.
INSTEAD OF USING YOUR WEAPONS ON THE INDIANS, I'M GOING TO NEED THEM FOR THE COLONEL!
YOU'RE ALREADY MAKING ME REGRET THE PURCHASE.

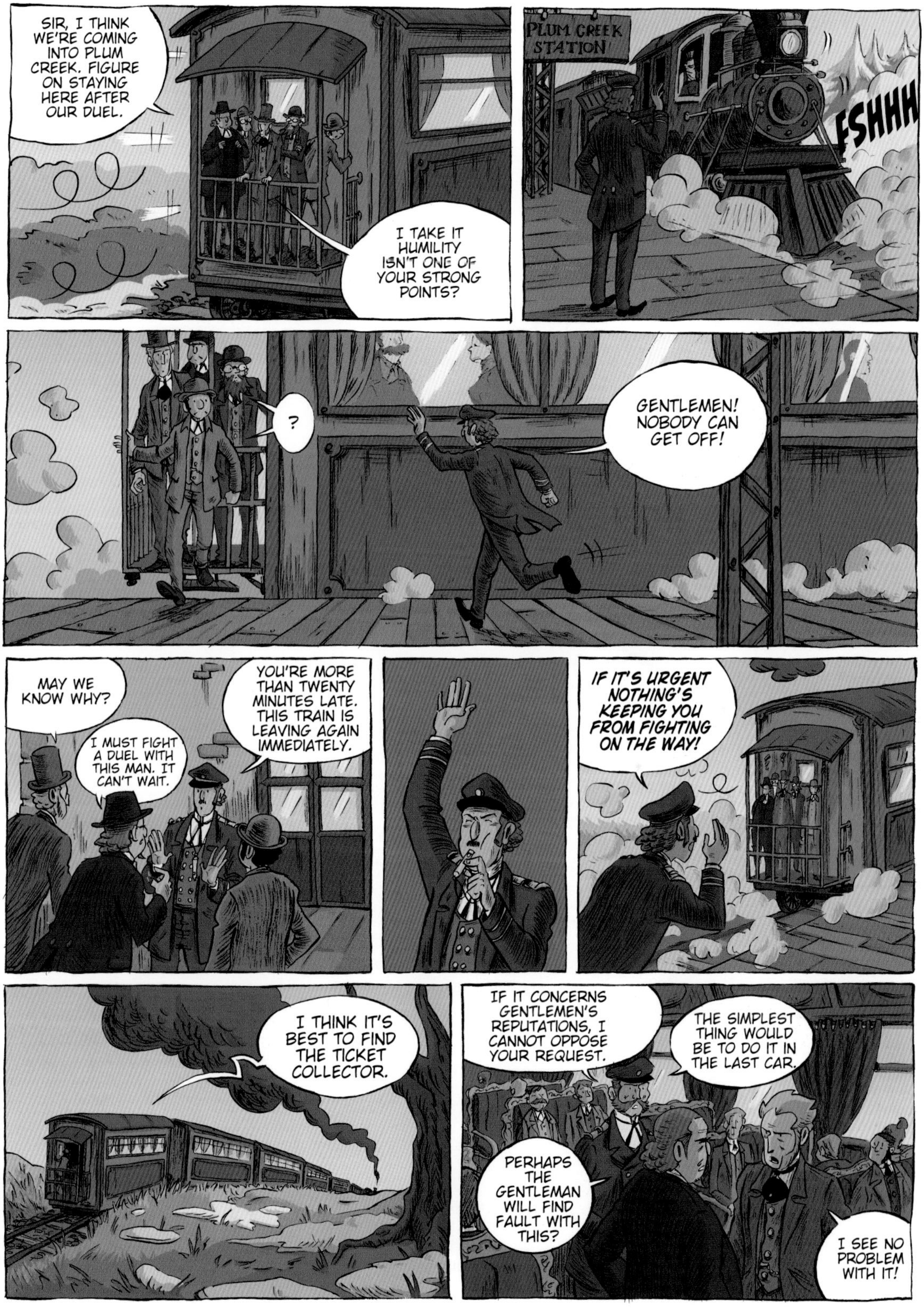
SIR, I THINK WE'RE COMING INTO PLUM CREEK. FIGURE ON STAYING HERE AFTER OUR DUEL.
I TAKE IT HUMILITY ISN'T ONE OF YOUR STRONG POINTS?
PLUM CREEK STATION
FSHHH
?
GENTLEMEN! NOBODY CAN GET OFF!
MAY WE KNOW WHY?
I MUST FIGHT A DUEL WITH THIS MAN. IT CAN'T WAIT.
YOU'RE MORE THAN TWENTY MINUTES LATE. THIS TRAIN IS LEAVING AGAIN IMMEDIATELY.
IF IT'S URGENT NOTHING'S KEEPING YOU FROM FIGHTING ON THE WAY!
I THINK IT'S BEST TO FIND THE TICKET COLLECTOR.
IF IT CONCERNS GENTLEMEN'S REPUTATIONS, I CANNOT OPPOSE YOUR REQUEST.
THE SIMPLEST THING WOULD BE TO DO IT IN THE LAST CAR.
PERHAPS THE GENTLEMAN WILL FIND FAULT WITH THIS?
I SEE NO PROBLEM WITH IT!

I BEG YOU, BE CAREFUL.

COME NOW, PASSEPARTOUT.

DO YOU THINK PRUDENCE IS THE BEST ADVICE TO GIVE TO A MAN WHO'S GOING TO DEFEND HIS HONOR?

WE'LL SOON BE ABLE TO RESUME OUR VOYAGE.

GENTLEMEN, I'M GOING TO ASK YOU TO GO ONTO THE PLATFORM TO LET OUR TWO MEN SETTLE THEIR DISPUTE.

YOU MUSTN'T OPEN FIRE BEFORE MY WHISTLE. GENTLEMEN, MAY THE BEST MAN LIVE!

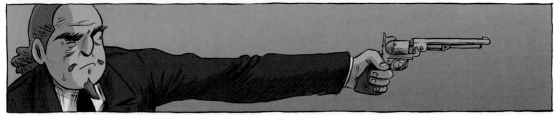

WHY YOU WAITING TO WHISTLE?

I'M WAITING FOR THE RIGHT MOMENT.

BANG

TCHAK

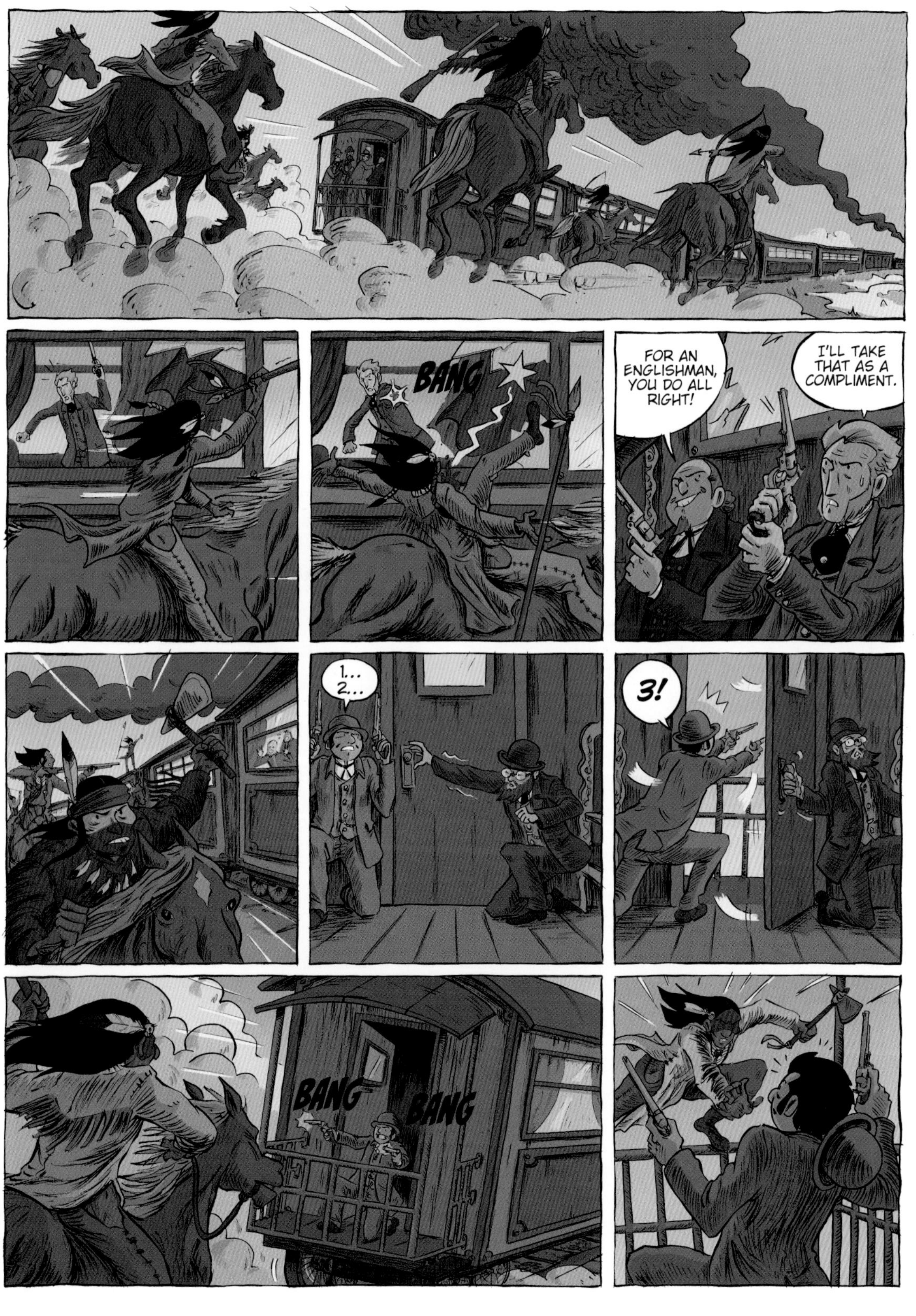
BANG
FOR AN ENGLISHMAN, YOU DO ALL RIGHT!
I'LL TAKE THAT AS A COMPLIMENT.
1... 2...
3!
BANG
BANG

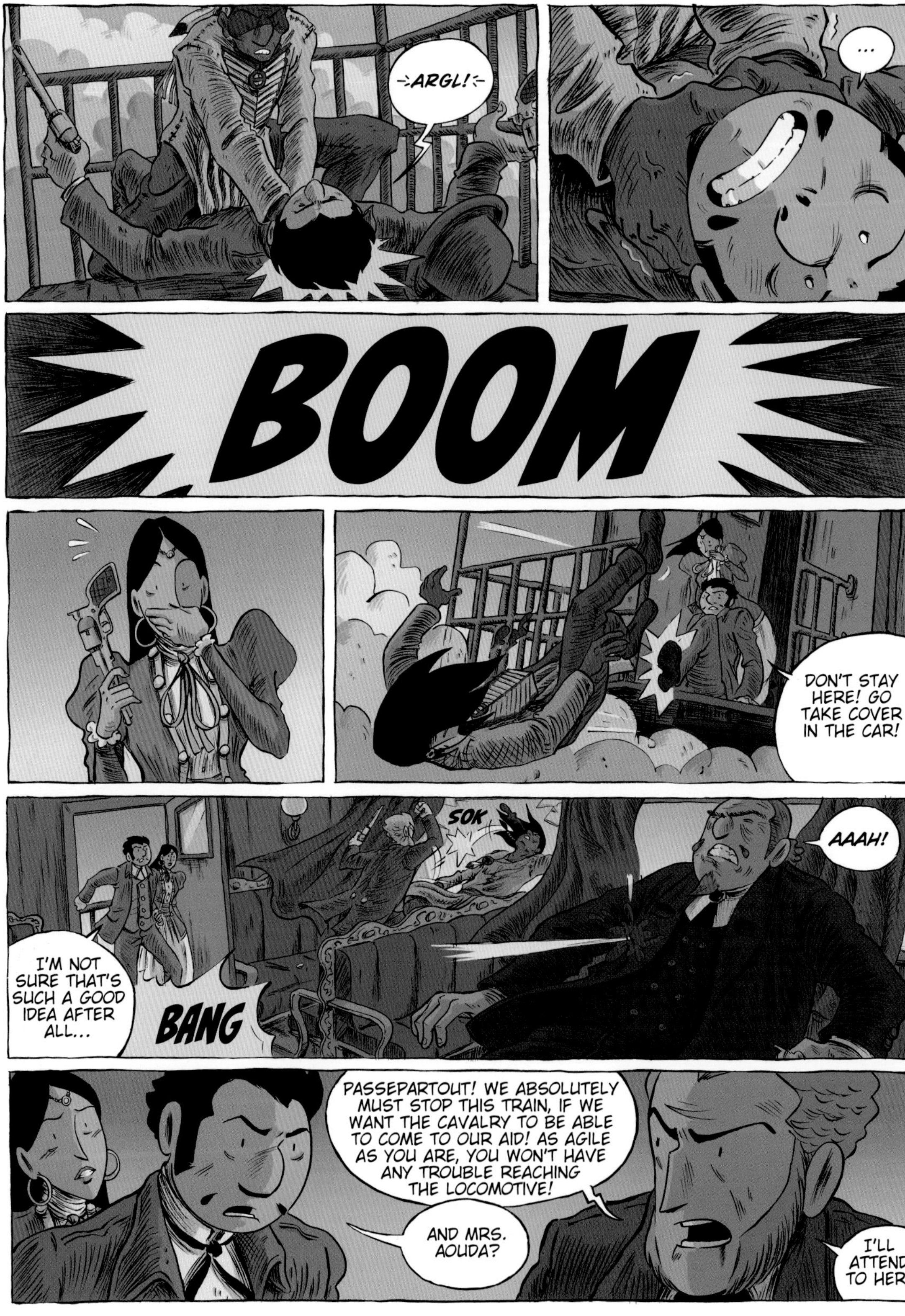
ARGL!
...
BOOM
DON'T STAY HERE! GO TAKE COVER IN THE CAR!
SOK
AAAH!
I'M NOT SURE THAT'S SUCH A GOOD IDEA AFTER ALL...
BANG
PASSEPARTOUT! WE ABSOLUTELY MUST STOP THIS TRAIN, IF WE WANT THE CAVALRY TO BE ABLE TO COME TO OUR AID! AS AGILE AS YOU ARE, YOU WON'T HAVE ANY TROUBLE REACHING THE LOCOMOTIVE!
AND MRS. AOUDA?
I'LL ATTEND TO HER!

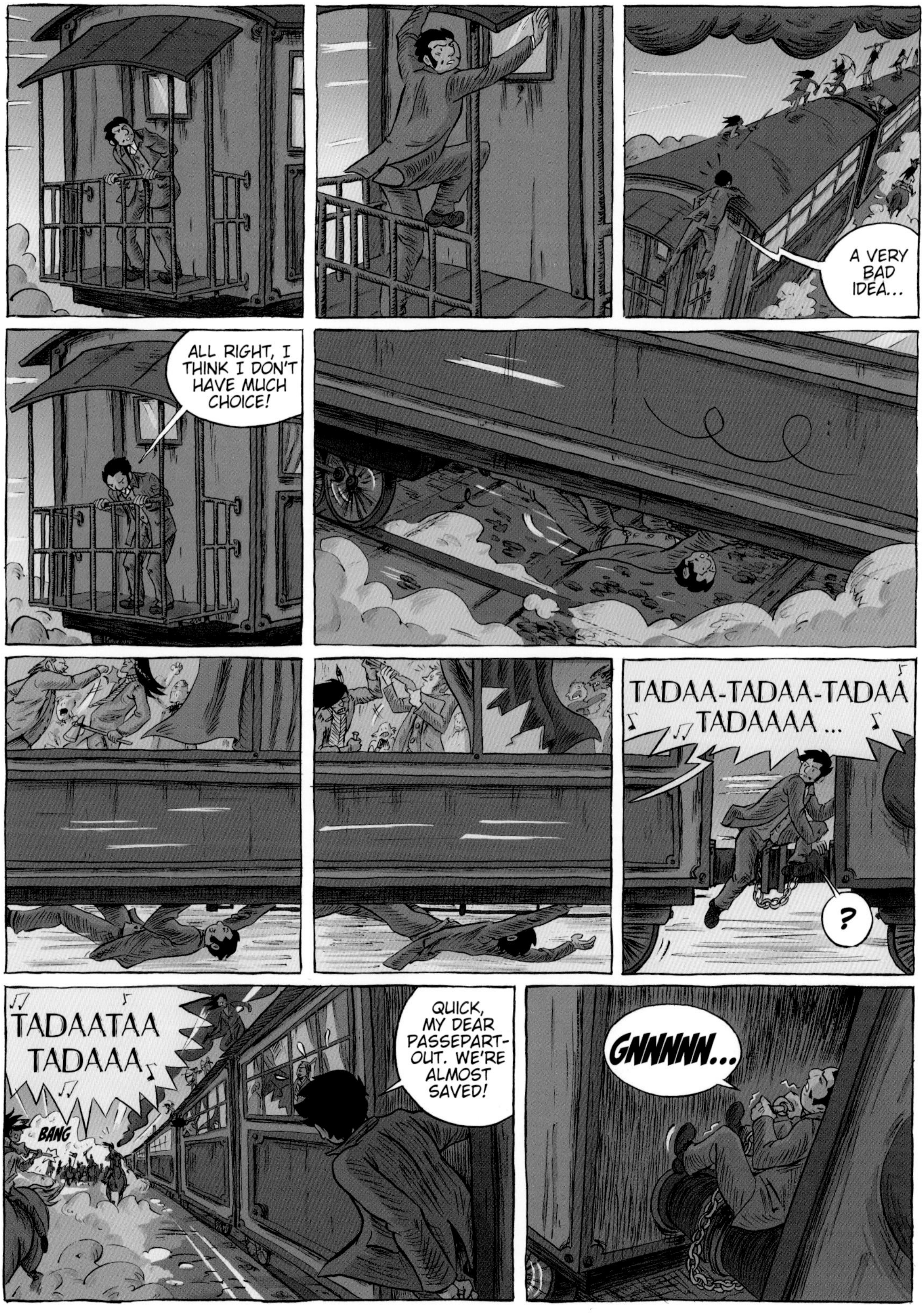
A VERY BAD IDEA...
ALL RIGHT, I THINK I DON'T HAVE MUCH CHOICE!
TADAA-TADAA-TADAA TADAAAA ...
?
TADAATAA TADAAA
BANG
QUICK, MY DEAR PASSEPART-OUT. WE'RE ALMOST SAVED!
GNNNNN...

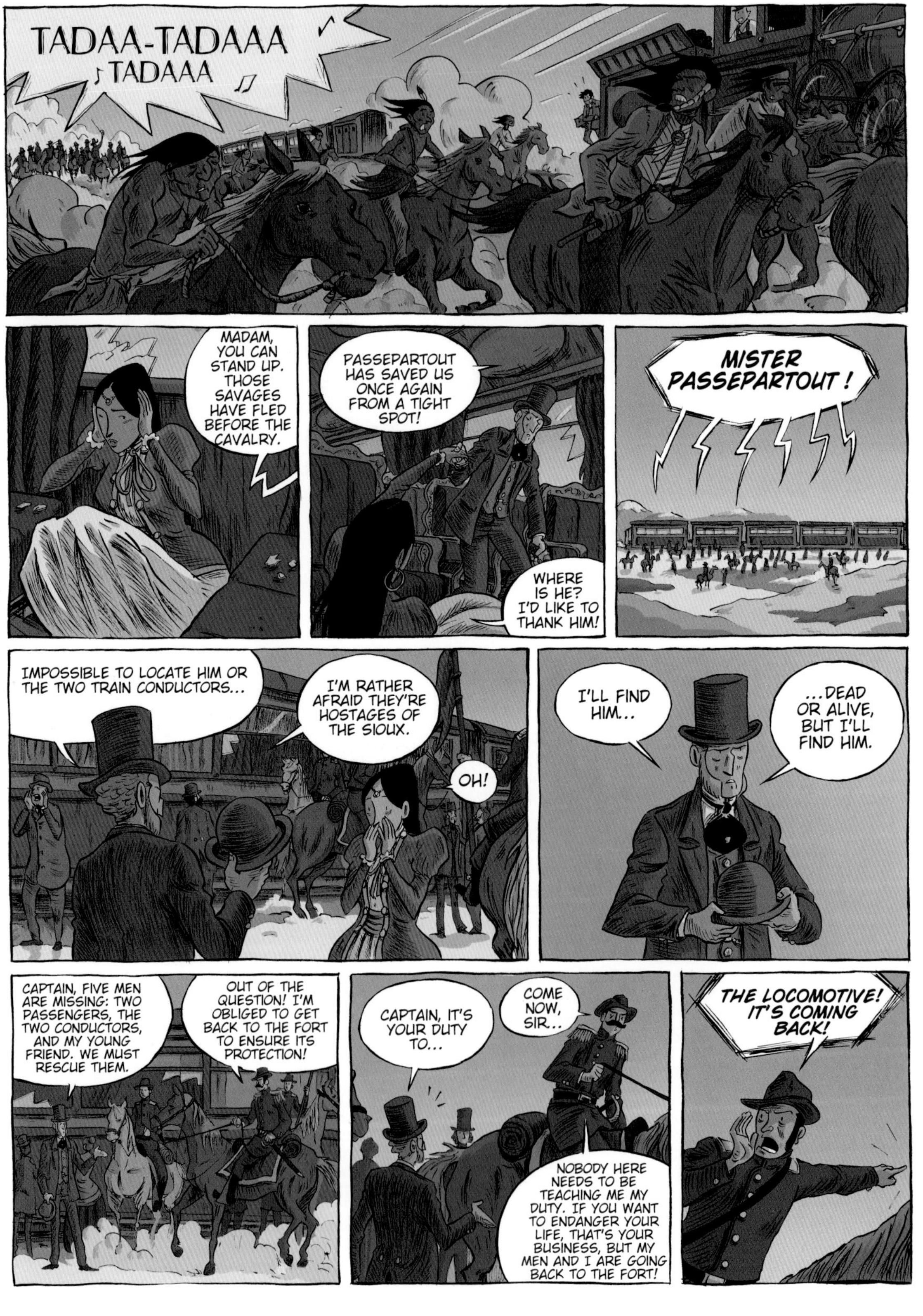
TADAA-TADAAA
TADAAA
MADAM, YOU CAN STAND UP. THOSE SAVAGES HAVE FLED BEFORE THE CAVALRY.
PASSEPARTOUT HAS SAVED US ONCE AGAIN FROM A TIGHT SPOT!
WHERE IS HE? I'D LIKE TO THANK HIM!
MISTER PASSEPARTOUT !
IMPOSSIBLE TO LOCATE HIM OR THE TWO TRAIN CONDUCTORS...
I'M RATHER AFRAID THEY'RE HOSTAGES OF THE SIOUX.
OH!
I'LL FIND HIM...
...DEAD OR ALIVE, BUT I'LL FIND HIM.
CAPTAIN, FIVE MEN ARE MISSING: TWO PASSENGERS, THE TWO CONDUCTORS, AND MY YOUNG FRIEND. WE MUST RESCUE THEM.
OUT OF THE QUESTION! I'M OBLIGED TO GET BACK TO THE FORT TO ENSURE ITS PROTECTION!
CAPTAIN, IT'S YOUR DUTY TO...
COME NOW, SIR...
NOBODY HERE NEEDS TO BE TEACHING ME MY DUTY. IF YOU WANT TO ENDANGER YOUR LIFE, THAT'S YOUR BUSINESS, BUT MY MEN AND I ARE GOING BACK TO THE FORT!
THE LOCOMOTIVE! IT'S COMING BACK!

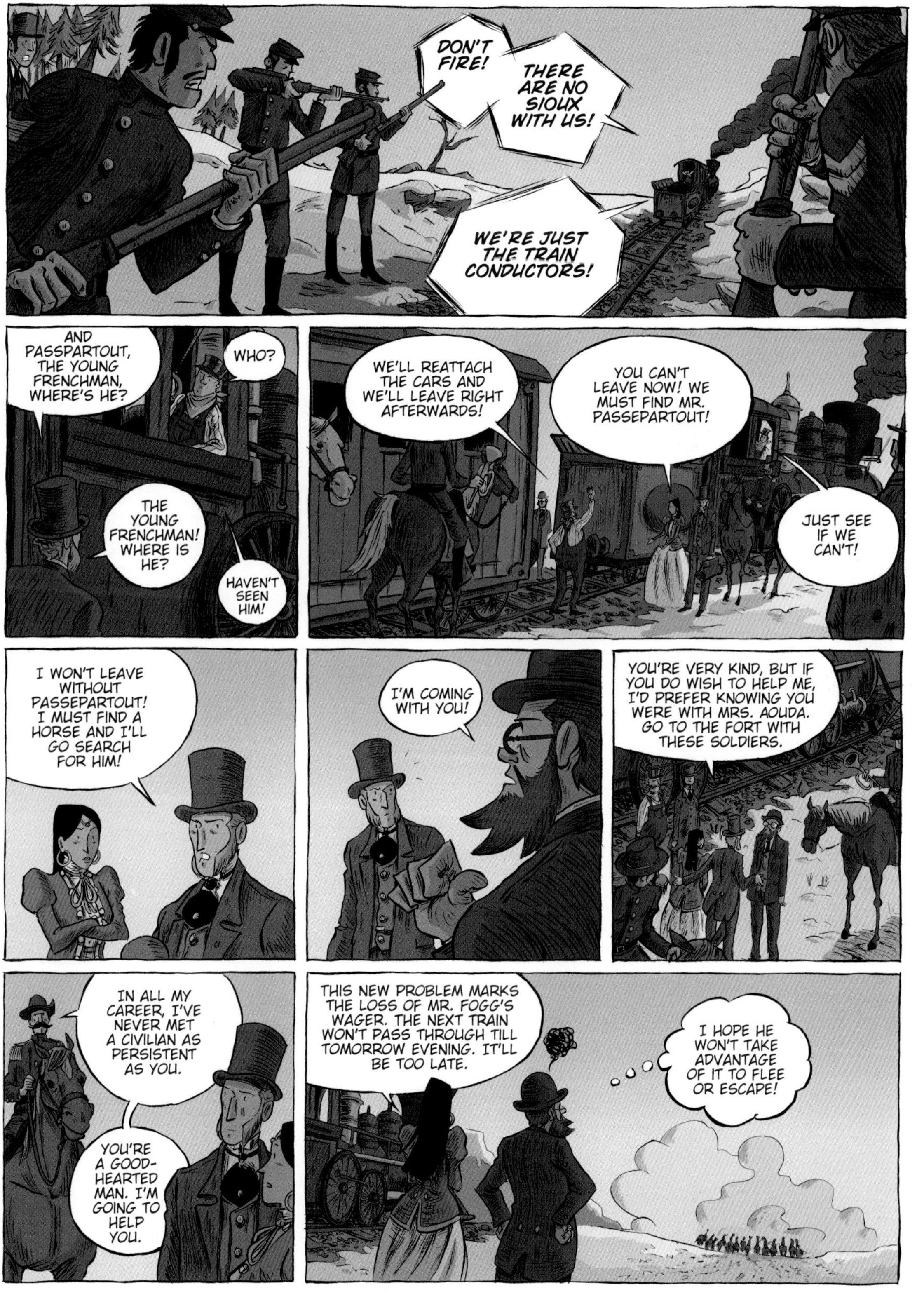
DON'T FIRE!
THERE ARE NO SIOUX WITH US!
WE'RE JUST THE TRAIN CONDUCTORS!
AND PASSPARTOUT, THE YOUNG FRENCHMAN, WHERE'S HE?
WHO?
THE YOUNG FRENCHMAN! WHERE IS HE?
HAVEN'T SEEN HIM!
WE'LL REATTACH THE CARS AND WE'LL LEAVE RIGHT AFTERWARDS!
YOU CAN'T LEAVE NOW! WE MUST FIND MR. PASSEPARTOUT!
JUST SEE IF WE CAN'T!
I WON'T LEAVE WITHOUT PASSEPARTOUT! I MUST FIND A HORSE AND I'LL GO SEARCH FOR HIM!
I'M COMING WITH YOU!
YOU'RE VERY KIND, BUT IF YOU DO WISH TO HELP ME, I'D PREFER KNOWING YOU WERE WITH MRS. AOUDA. GO TO THE FORT WITH THESE SOLDIERS.
IN ALL MY CAREER, I'VE NEVER MET A CIVILIAN AS PERSISTENT AS YOU.
YOU'RE A GOOD-HEARTED MAN. I'M GOING TO HELP YOU.
THIS NEW PROBLEM MARKS THE LOSS OF MR. FOGG'S WAGER. THE NEXT TRAIN WON'T PASS THROUGH TILL TOMORROW EVENING. IT'LL BE TOO LATE.
I HOPE HE WON'T TAKE ADVANTAGE OF IT TO FLEE OR ESCAPE!

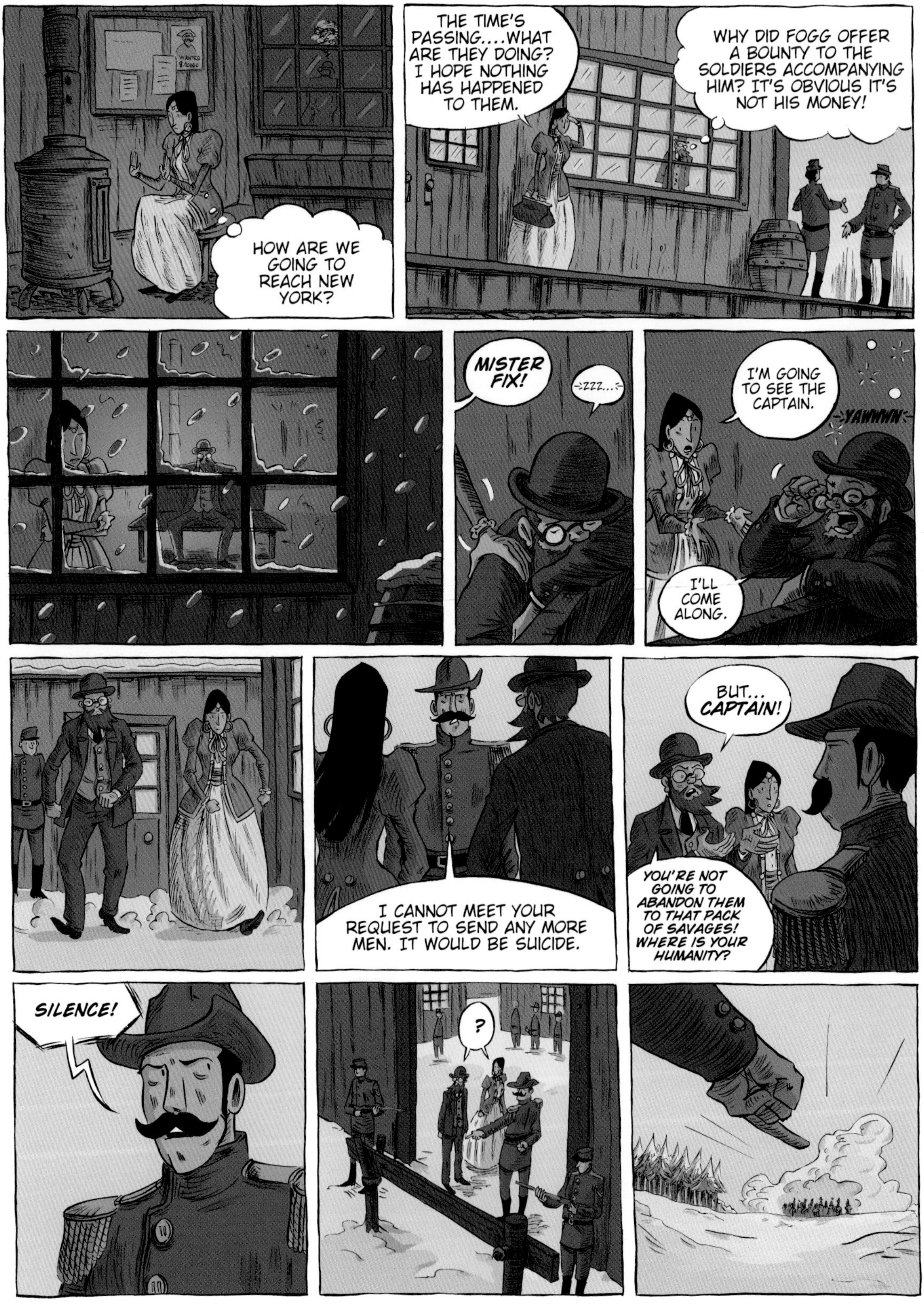
HOW ARE WE GOING TO REACH NEW YORK?
THE TIME'S PASSING....WHAT ARE THEY DOING? I HOPE NOTHING HAS HAPPENED TO THEM.
WHY DID FOGG OFFER A BOUNTY TO THE SOLDIERS ACCOMPANYING HIM? IT'S OBVIOUS IT'S NOT HIS MONEY!
MISTER FIX!
ZZZ...
I'M GOING TO SEE THE CAPTAIN.
YAWWWN
I'LL COME ALONG.
I CANNOT MEET YOUR REQUEST TO SEND ANY MORE MEN. IT WOULD BE SUICIDE.
BUT... CAPTAIN!
YOU'RE NOT GOING TO ABANDON THEM TO THAT PACK OF SAVAGES! WHERE IS YOUR HUMANITY?
SILENCE!
?

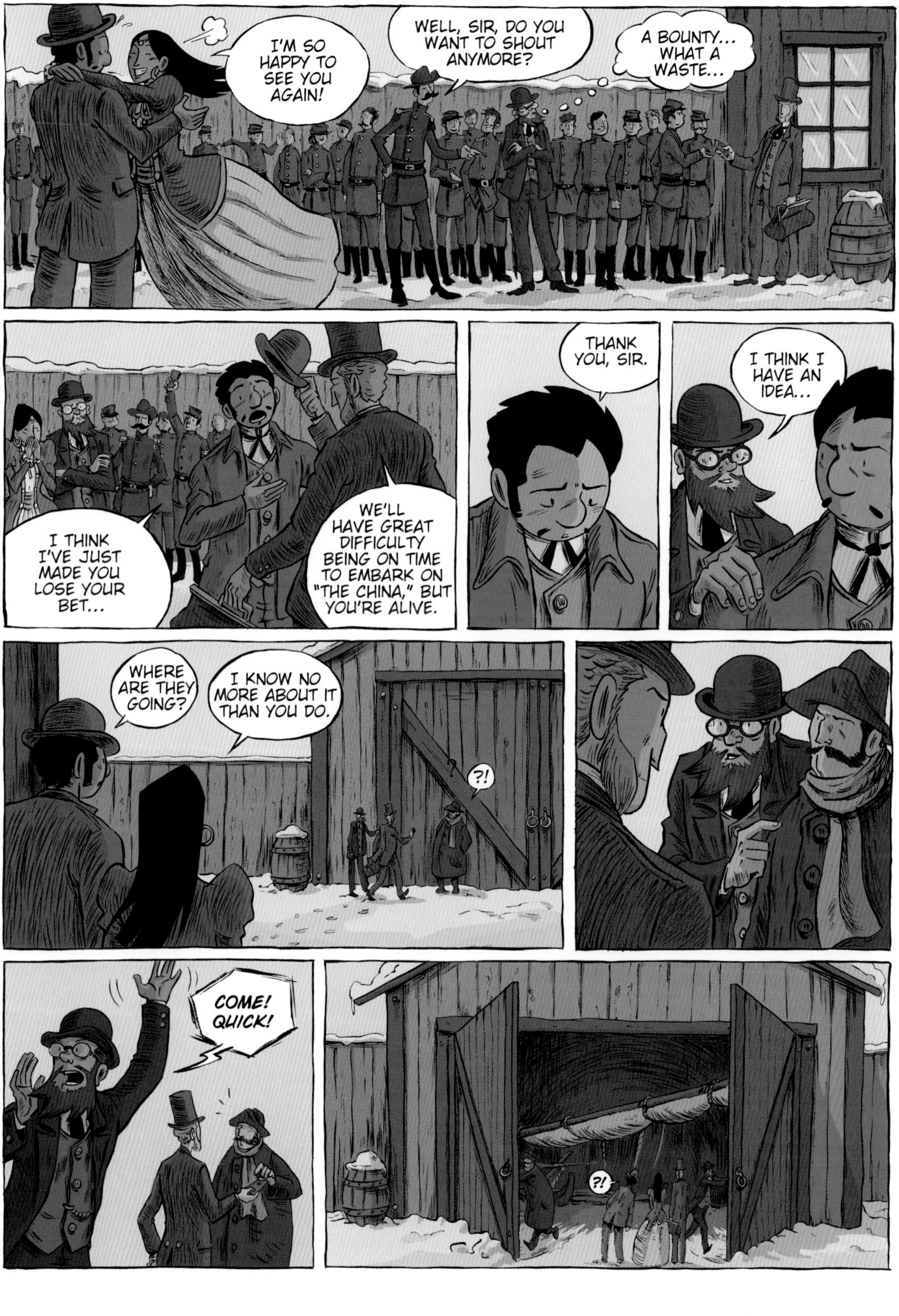
I'M SO HAPPY TO SEE YOU AGAIN!
WELL, SIR, DO YOU WANT TO SHOUT ANYMORE?
A BOUNTY... WHAT A WASTE...
I THINK I'VE JUST MADE YOU LOSE YOUR BET...
WE'LL HAVE GREAT DIFFICULTY BEING ON TIME TO EMBARK ON "THE CHINA," BUT YOU'RE ALIVE.
THANK YOU, SIR.
I THINK I HAVE AN IDEA...
WHERE ARE THEY GOING?
I KNOW NO MORE ABOUT IT THAN YOU DO.
?!
COME! QUICK!
?!

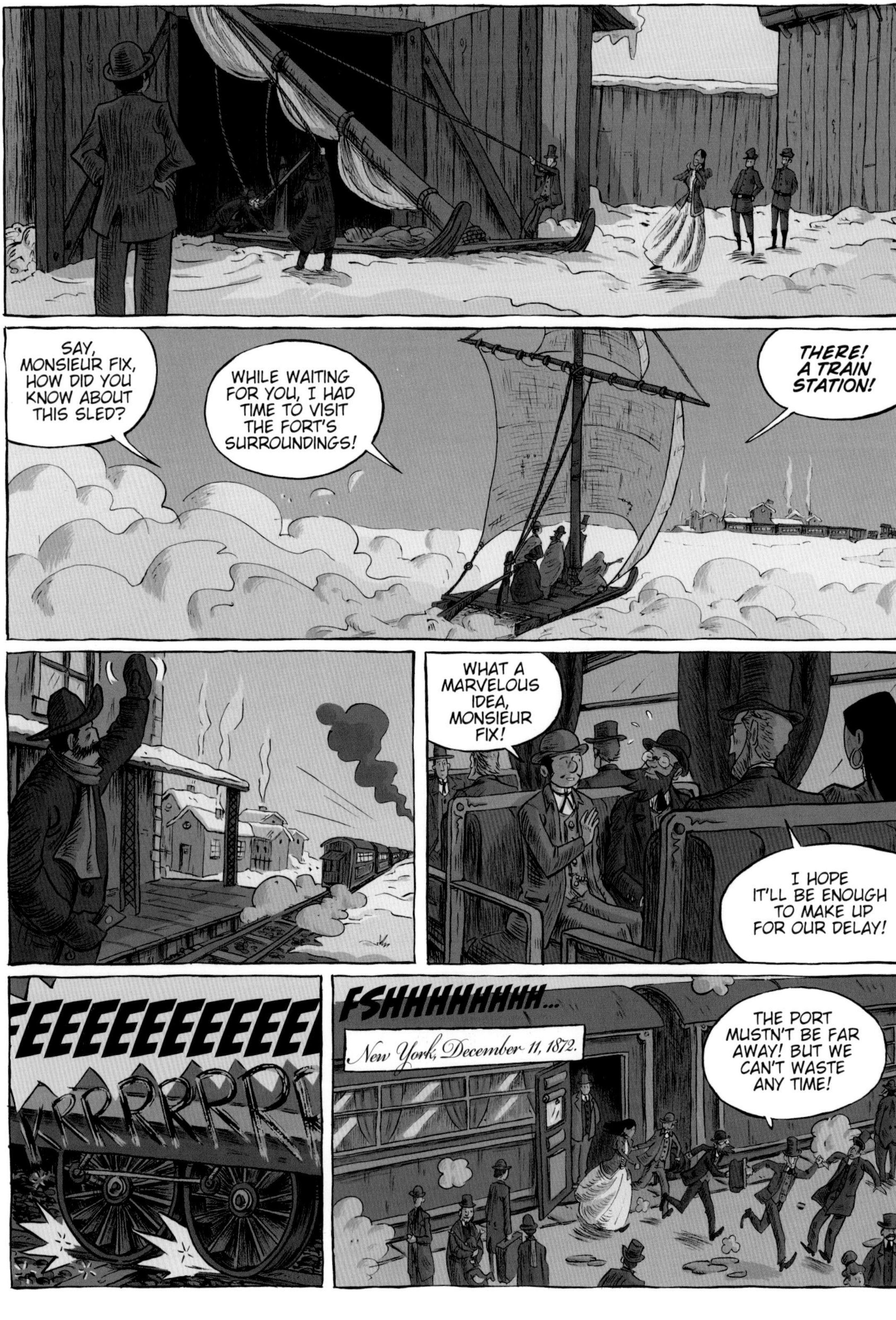
SAY, MONSIEUR FIX, HOW DID YOU KNOW ABOUT THIS SLED?
WHILE WAITING FOR YOU, I HAD TIME TO VISIT THE FORT'S SURROUNDINGS!
THERE! A TRAIN STATION!
WHAT A MARVELOUS IDEA, MONSIEUR FIX!
I HOPE IT'LL BE ENOUGH TO MAKE UP FOR OUR DELAY!
FEEEEEEEEEEE
KRRRRRRR
FSHHHHHHHH...
New York, December 11, 1872.
THE PORT MUSTN'T BE FAR AWAY! BUT WE CAN'T WASTE ANY TIME!

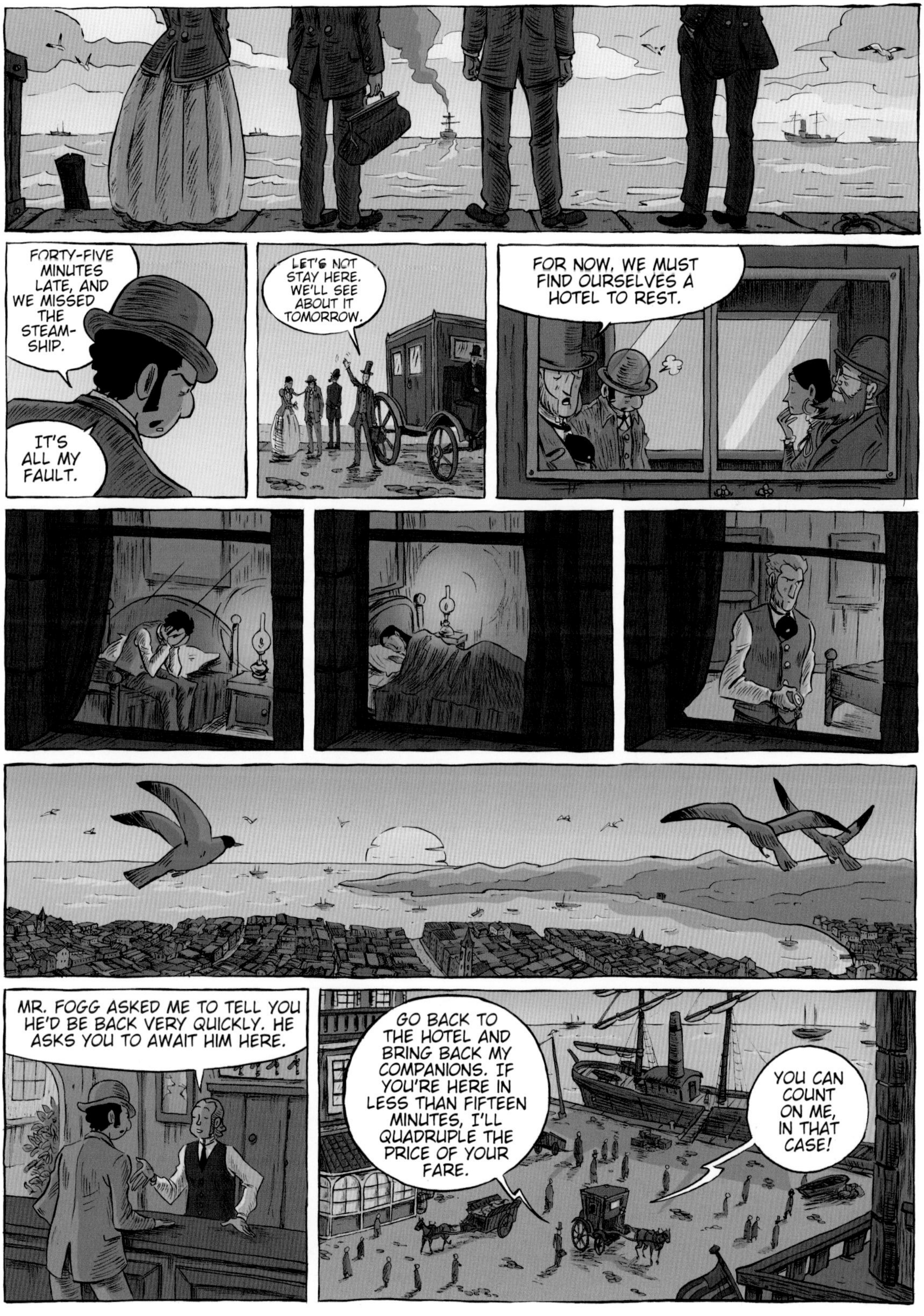

FORTY-FIVE MINUTES LATE, AND WE MISSED THE STEAMSHIP.
IT'S ALL MY FAULT.
LET'S NOT STAY HERE. WE'LL SEE ABOUT IT TOMORROW.
FOR NOW, WE MUST FIND OURSELVES A HOTEL TO REST.
MR. FOGG ASKED ME TO TELL YOU HE'D BE BACK VERY QUICKLY. HE ASKS YOU TO AWAIT HIM HERE.
GO BACK TO THE HOTEL AND BRING BACK MY COMPANIONS. IF YOU'RE HERE IN LESS THAN FIFTEEN MINUTES, I'LL QUADRUPLE THE PRICE OF YOUR FARE.
YOU CAN COUNT ON ME, IN THAT CASE!

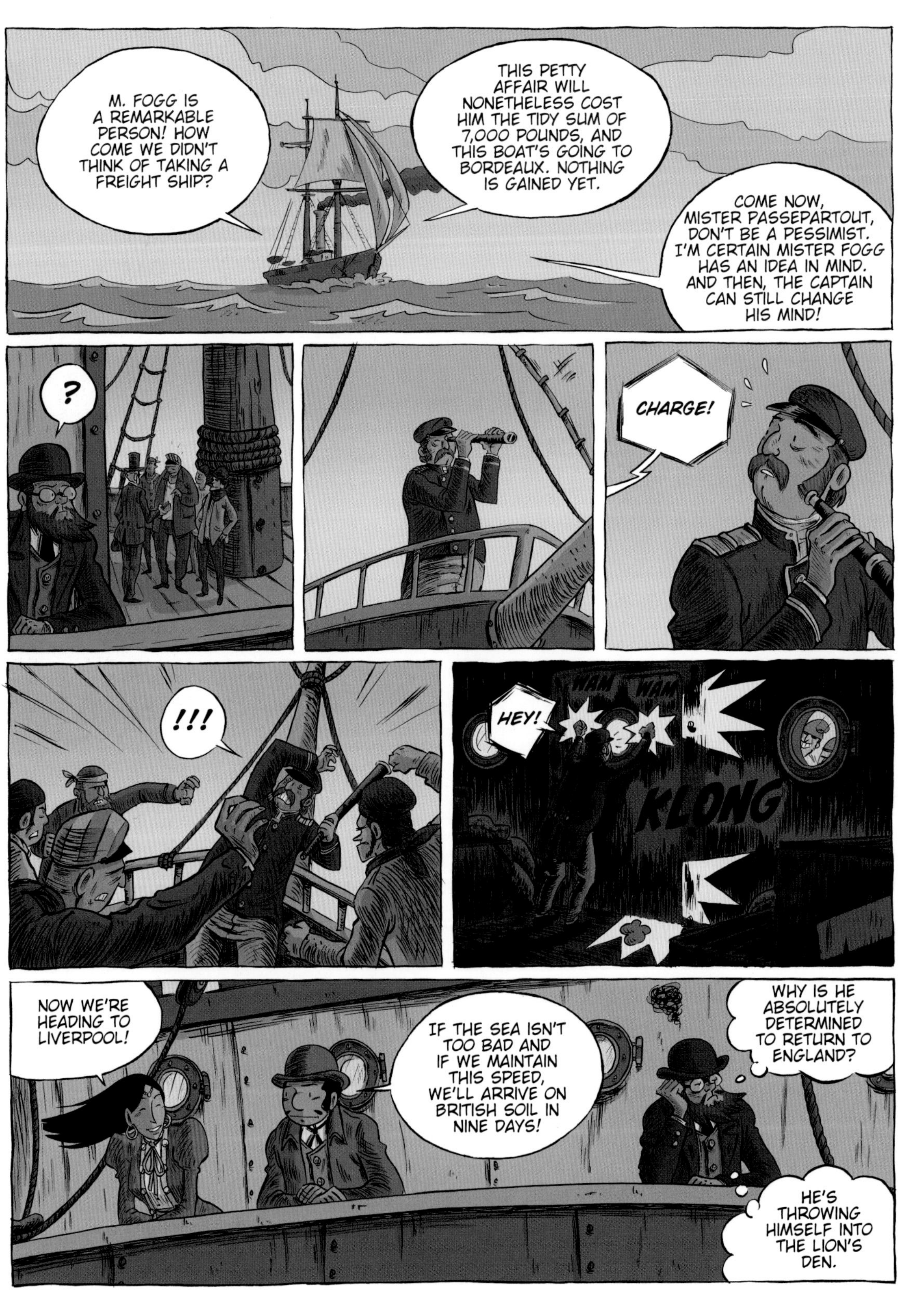

M. FOGG IS A REMARKABLE PERSON! HOW COME WE DIDN'T THINK OF TAKING A FREIGHT SHIP?
THIS PETTY AFFAIR WILL NONETHELESS COST HIM THE TIDY SUM OF 7,000 POUNDS, AND THIS BOAT'S GOING TO BORDEAUX. NOTHING IS GAINED YET.
COME NOW, MISTER PASSEPARTOUT, DON'T BE A PESSIMIST. I'M CERTAIN MISTER FOGG HAS AN IDEA IN MIND. AND THEN, THE CAPTAIN CAN STILL CHANGE HIS MIND!
?
CHARGE!
!!!
HEY!
WAM
WAM
KLONG
NOW WE'RE HEADING TO LIVERPOOL!
IF THE SEA ISN'T TOO BAD AND IF WE MAINTAIN THIS SPEED, WE'LL ARRIVE ON BRITISH SOIL IN NINE DAYS!
WHY IS HE ABSOLUTELY DETERMINED TO RETURN TO ENGLAND?
HE'S THROWING HIMSELF INTO THE LION'S DEN.

Newfoundland

New York

OH BOY, OH BOY, OH BOY...

HH... HHH...

>BRRFFF...<

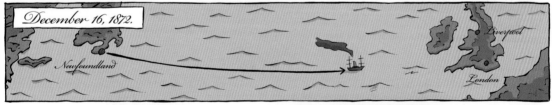

December 16, 1872.

Newfoundland

Liverpool

London

THINGS ARE PROCEEDING IMPECCABLY! WE'RE ON TIME!

I DIDN'T DARE ASK THE QUESTION! THAT'S EXCELLENT NEWS!

I DON'T UNDERSTAND IT ONE BIT. I DON'T UNDERSTAND IT ONE BIT!!

SIR! SIR!

?!

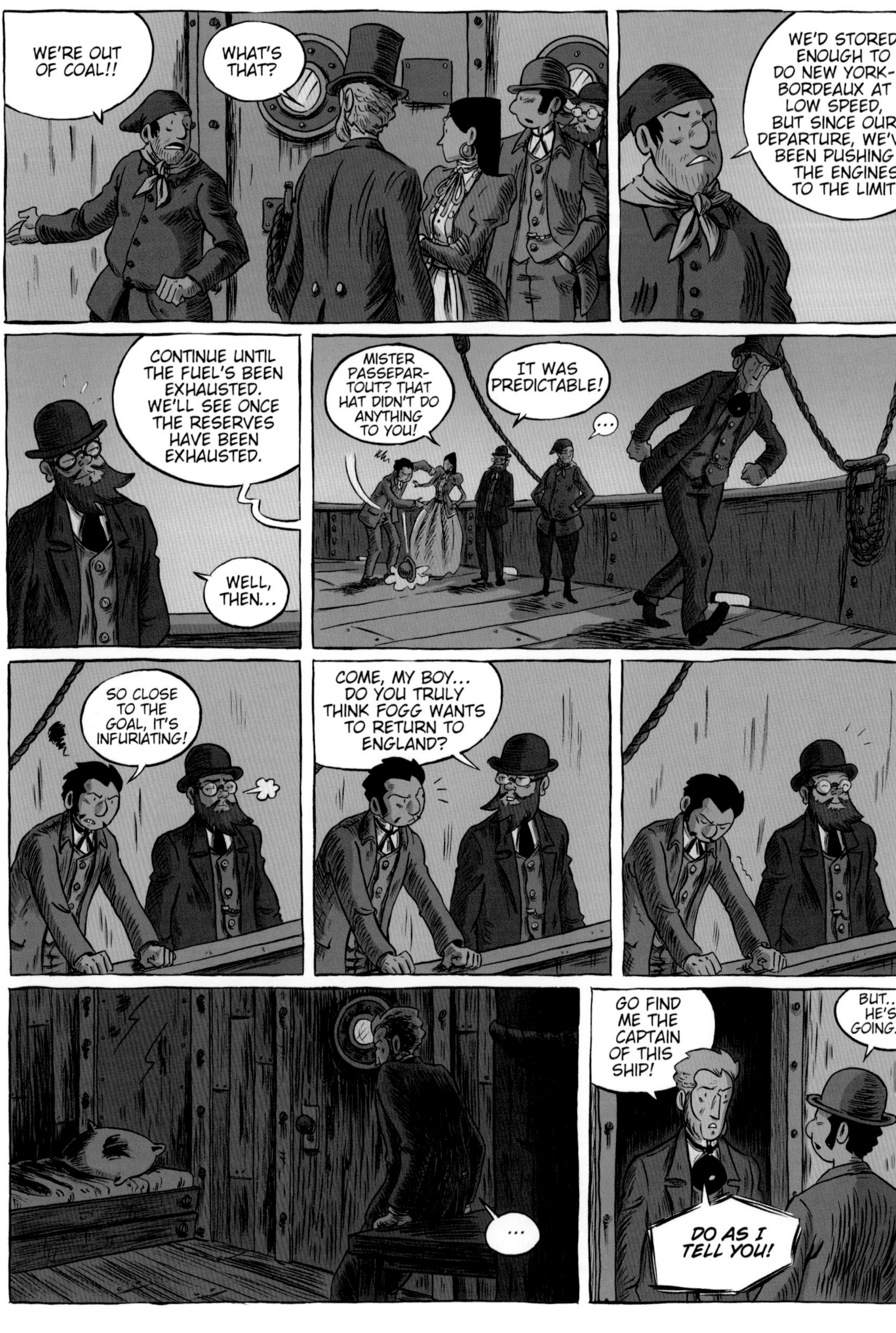

WE'RE OUT OF COAL!!
WHAT'S THAT?
WE'D STORED ENOUGH TO DO NEW YORK-BORDEAUX AT LOW SPEED, BUT SINCE OUR DEPARTURE, WE'VE BEEN PUSHING THE ENGINES TO THE LIMIT.
CONTINUE UNTIL THE FUEL'S BEEN EXHAUSTED. WE'LL SEE ONCE THE RESERVES HAVE BEEN EXHAUSTED.
WELL, THEN...
MISTER PASSEPARTOUT? THAT HAT DIDN'T DO ANYTHING TO YOU!
IT WAS PREDICTABLE!
...
SO CLOSE TO THE GOAL, IT'S INFURIATING!
COME, MY BOY... DO YOU TRULY THINK FOGG WANTS TO RETURN TO ENGLAND?
...
GO FIND ME THE CAPTAIN OF THIS SHIP!
BUT... HE'S GOING...
DO AS I TELL YOU!

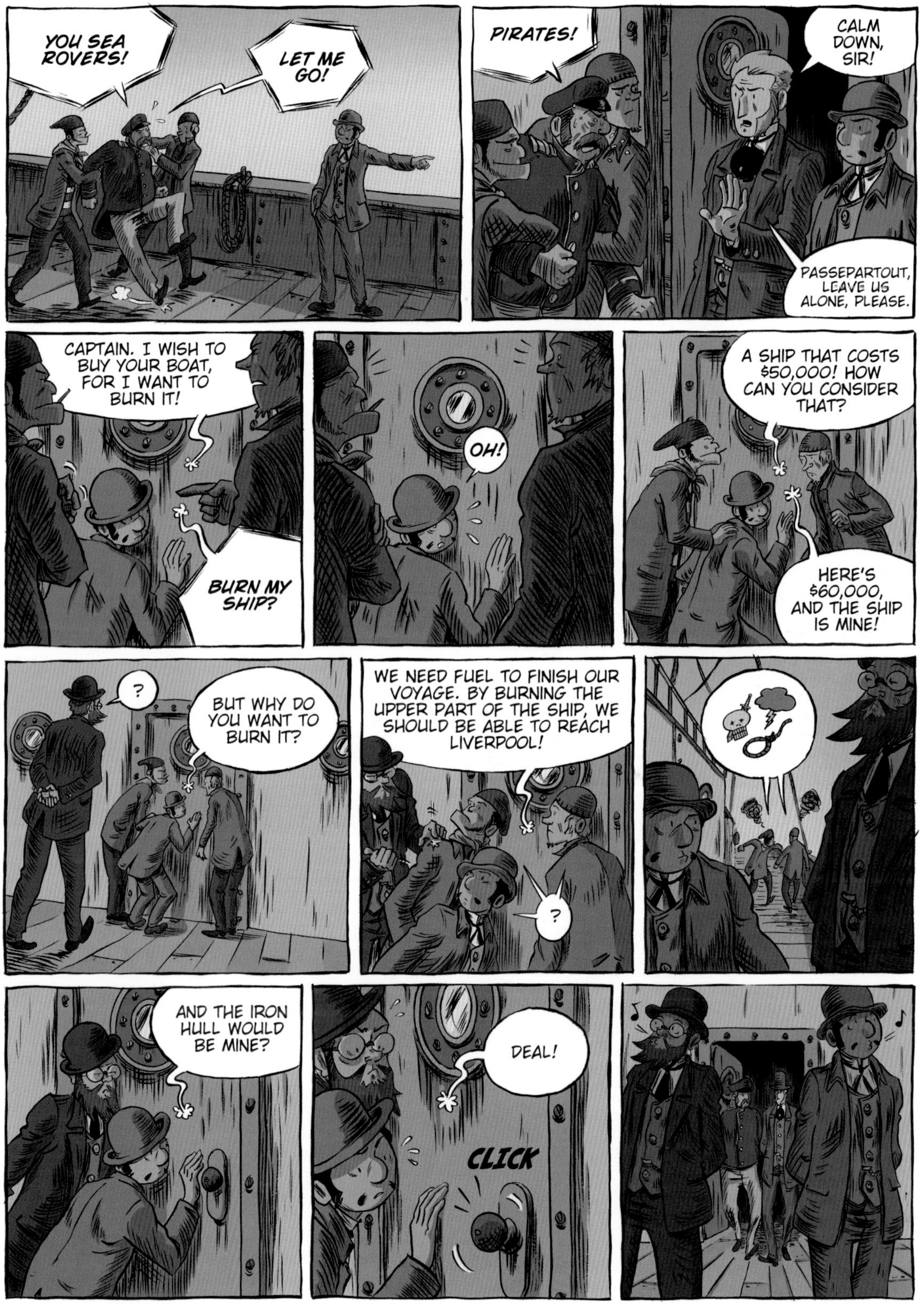
YOU SEA ROVERS!
LET ME GO!
PIRATES!
CALM DOWN, SIR!
PASSEPARTOUT, LEAVE US ALONE, PLEASE.
CAPTAIN. I WISH TO BUY YOUR BOAT, FOR I WANT TO BURN IT!
BURN MY SHIP?
OH!
A SHIP THAT COSTS $50,000! HOW CAN YOU CONSIDER THAT?
HERE'S $60,000, AND THE SHIP IS MINE!
?
BUT WHY DO YOU WANT TO BURN IT?
WE NEED FUEL TO FINISH OUR VOYAGE. BY BURNING THE UPPER PART OF THE SHIP, WE SHOULD BE ABLE TO REACH LIVERPOOL!
?
AND THE IRON HULL WOULD BE MINE?
DEAL!
CLICK

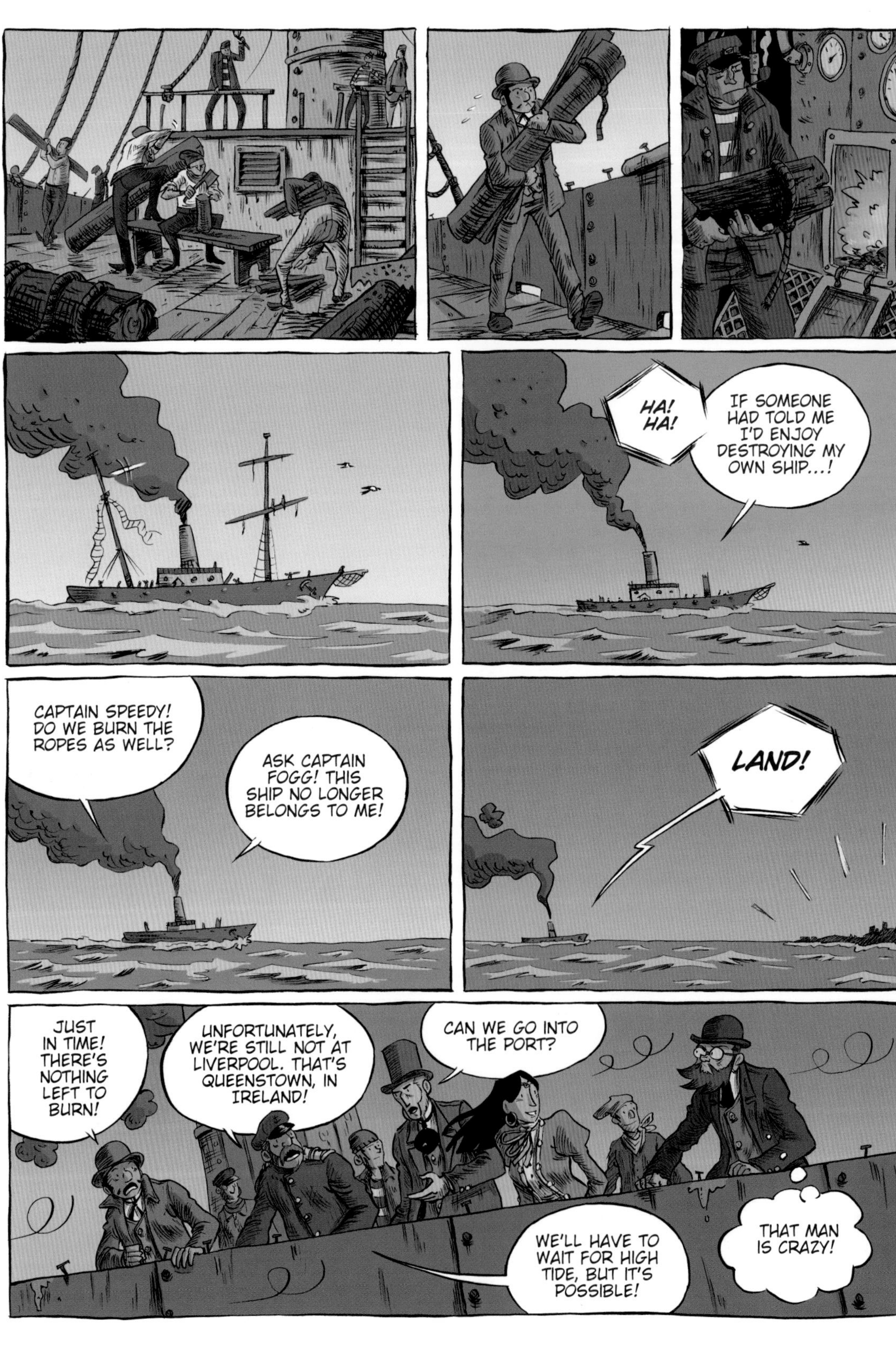
HA! HA!
IF SOMEONE HAD TOLD ME I'D ENJOY DESTROYING MY OWN SHIP...!
CAPTAIN SPEEDY! DO WE BURN THE ROPES AS WELL?
ASK CAPTAIN FOGG! THIS SHIP NO LONGER BELONGS TO ME!
LAND!
JUST IN TIME! THERE'S NOTHING LEFT TO BURN!
UNFORTUNATELY, WE'RE STILL NOT AT LIVERPOOL. THAT'S QUEENSTOWN, IN IRELAND!
CAN WE GO INTO THE PORT?
WE'LL HAVE TO WAIT FOR HIGH TIDE, BUT IT'S POSSIBLE!
THAT MAN IS CRAZY!

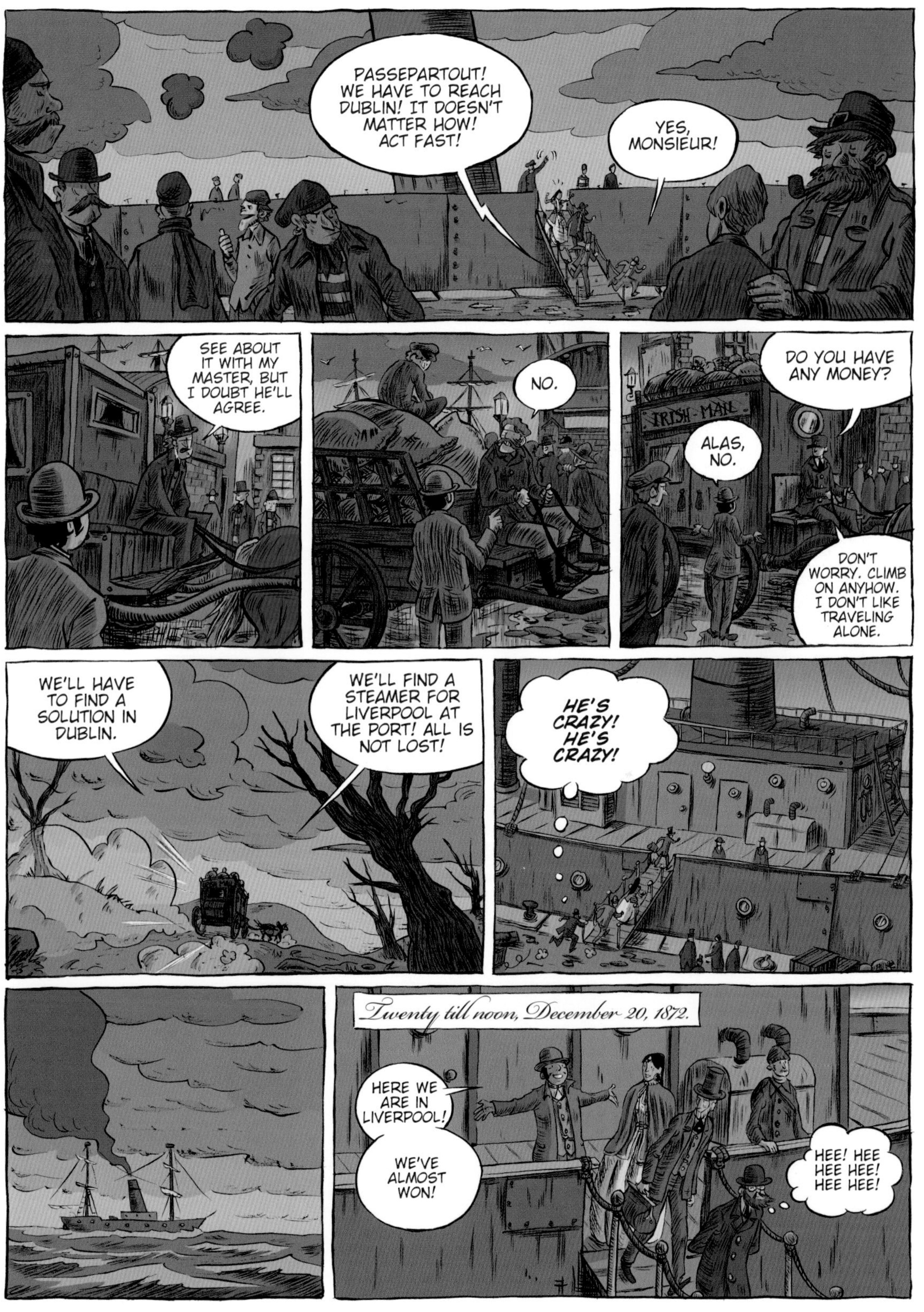
PASSEPARTOUT! WE HAVE TO REACH DUBLIN! IT DOESN'T MATTER HOW! ACT FAST!
YES, MONSIEUR!
SEE ABOUT IT WITH MY MASTER, BUT I DOUBT HE'LL AGREE.
NO.
DO YOU HAVE ANY MONEY?
IRISH MAIL
ALAS, NO.
DON'T WORRY. CLIMB ON ANYHOW. I DON'T LIKE TRAVELING ALONE.
WE'LL HAVE TO FIND A SOLUTION IN DUBLIN.
WE'LL FIND A STEAMER FOR LIVERPOOL AT THE PORT! ALL IS NOT LOST!
HE'S CRAZY! HE'S CRAZY!
Twenty till noon, December 20, 1872.
HERE WE ARE IN LIVERPOOL!
WE'VE ALMOST WON!
HEE! HEE HEE HEE! HEE HEE!

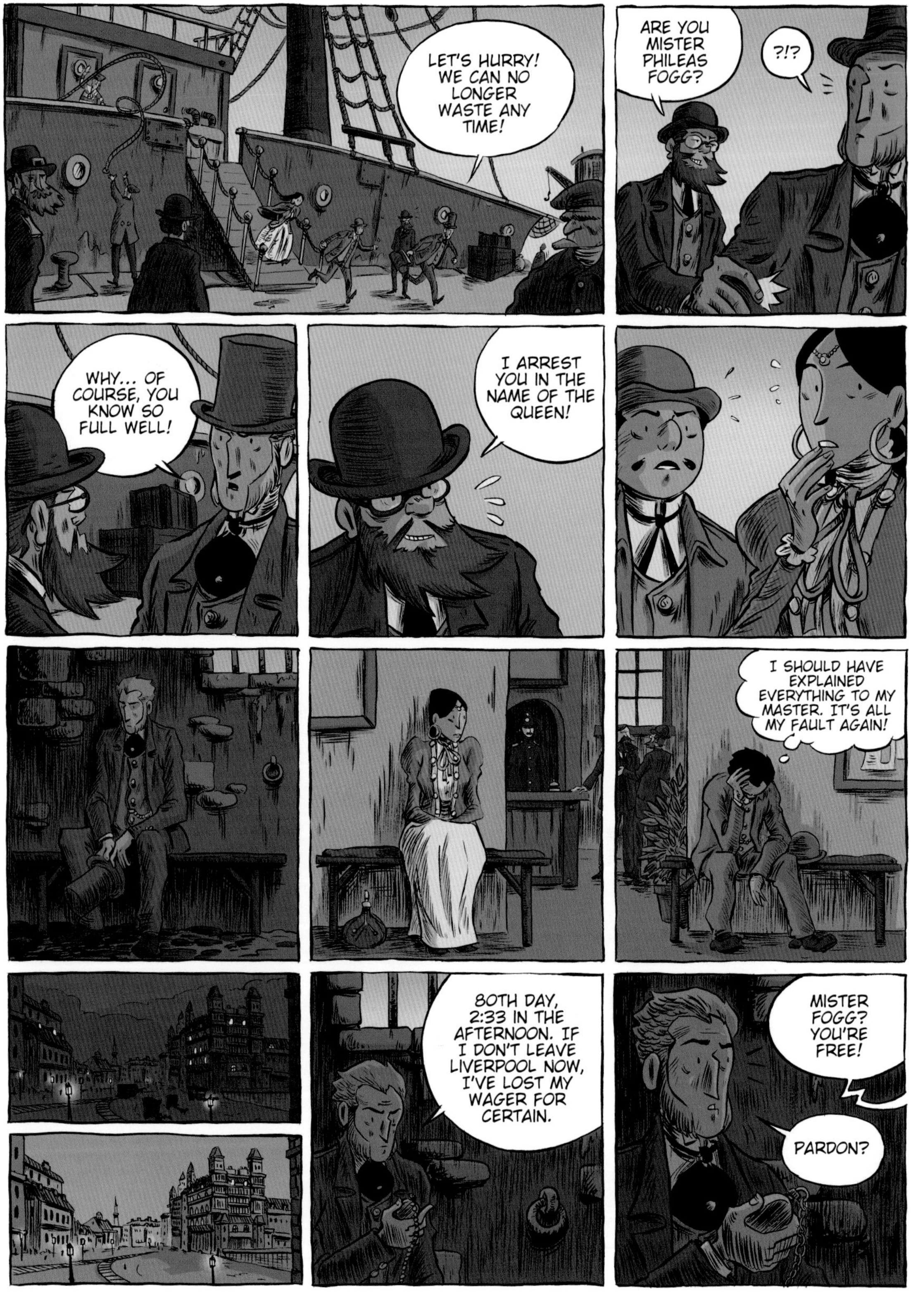
LET'S HURRY! WE CAN NO LONGER WASTE ANY TIME!
ARE YOU MISTER PHILEAS FOGG?
?!?
WHY... OF COURSE, YOU KNOW SO FULL WELL!
I ARREST YOU IN THE NAME OF THE QUEEN!
I SHOULD HAVE EXPLAINED EVERYTHING TO MY MASTER. IT'S ALL MY FAULT AGAIN!
80TH DAY, 2:33 IN THE AFTERNOON. IF I DON'T LEAVE LIVERPOOL NOW, I'VE LOST MY WAGER FOR CERTAIN.
MISTER FOGG? YOU'RE FREE!
PARDON?

I'M SORRY, I MADE A MISTAKE. THE THIEF HAS ALREADY BEEN ARRESTED AND...

LET'S NOT WASTE ANY TIME! COME!

WAIT, I NEED 2 SECONDS!

?

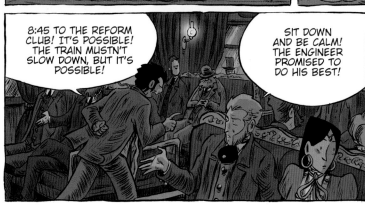

8:45 TO THE REFORM CLUB! IT'S POSSIBLE! THE TRAIN MUSTN'T SLOW DOWN, BUT IT'S POSSIBLE!

SIT DOWN AND BE CALM! THE ENGINEER PROMISED TO DO HIS BEST!

LONDON!

WE'VE ARRIVED!

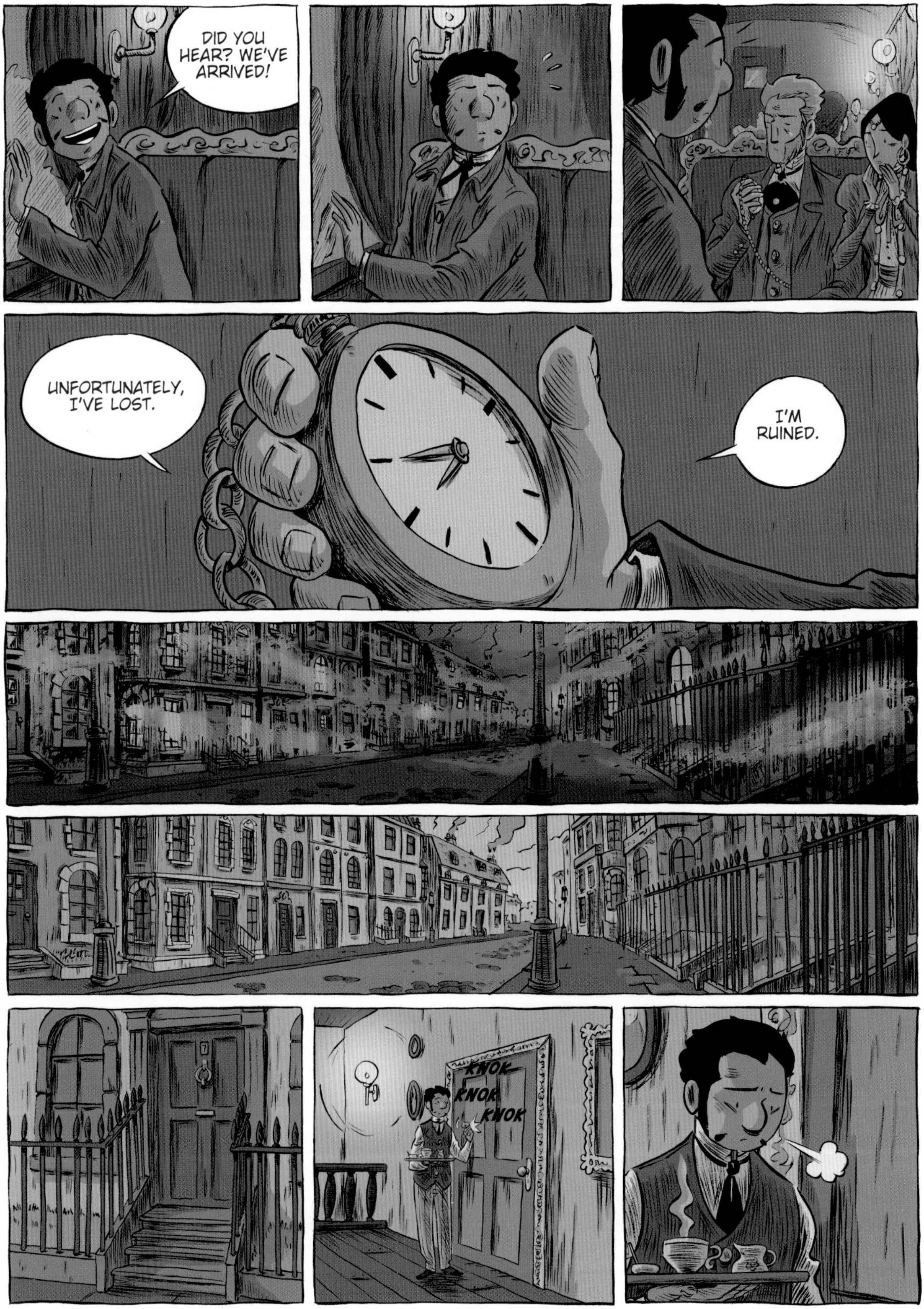
DID YOU HEAR? WE'VE ARRIVED!
UNFORTUNATELY, I'VE LOST.
I'M RUINED.
KNOK
KNOK
KNOK

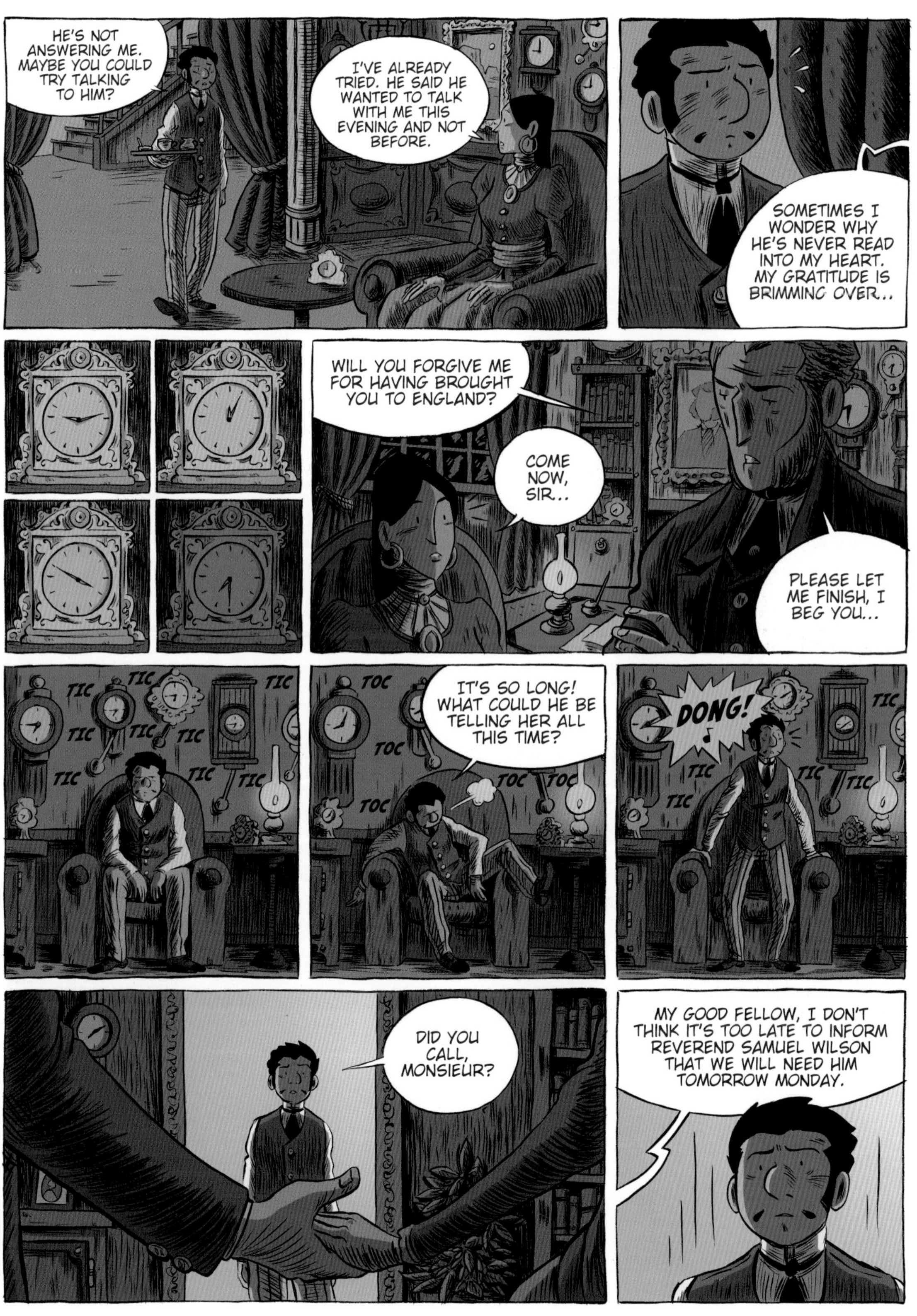

HE'S NOT ANSWERING ME. MAYBE YOU COULD TRY TALKING TO HIM?
I'VE ALREADY TRIED. HE SAID HE WANTED TO TALK WITH ME THIS EVENING AND NOT BEFORE.
SOMETIMES I WONDER WHY HE'S NEVER READ INTO MY HEART. MY GRATITUDE IS BRIMMING OVER...
WILL YOU FORGIVE ME FOR HAVING BROUGHT YOU TO ENGLAND?
COME NOW, SIR...
PLEASE LET ME FINISH, I BEG YOU...
TIC TIC TIC TIC TIC TIC TIC TIC
TOC TOC TOC TOC TOC
IT'S SO LONG! WHAT COULD HE BE TELLING HER ALL THIS TIME?
DONG!
TIC TIC TIC TIC
DID YOU CALL, MONSIEUR?
MY GOOD FELLOW, I DON'T THINK IT'S TOO LATE TO INFORM REVEREND SAMUEL WILSON THAT WE WILL NEED HIM TOMORROW MONDAY.

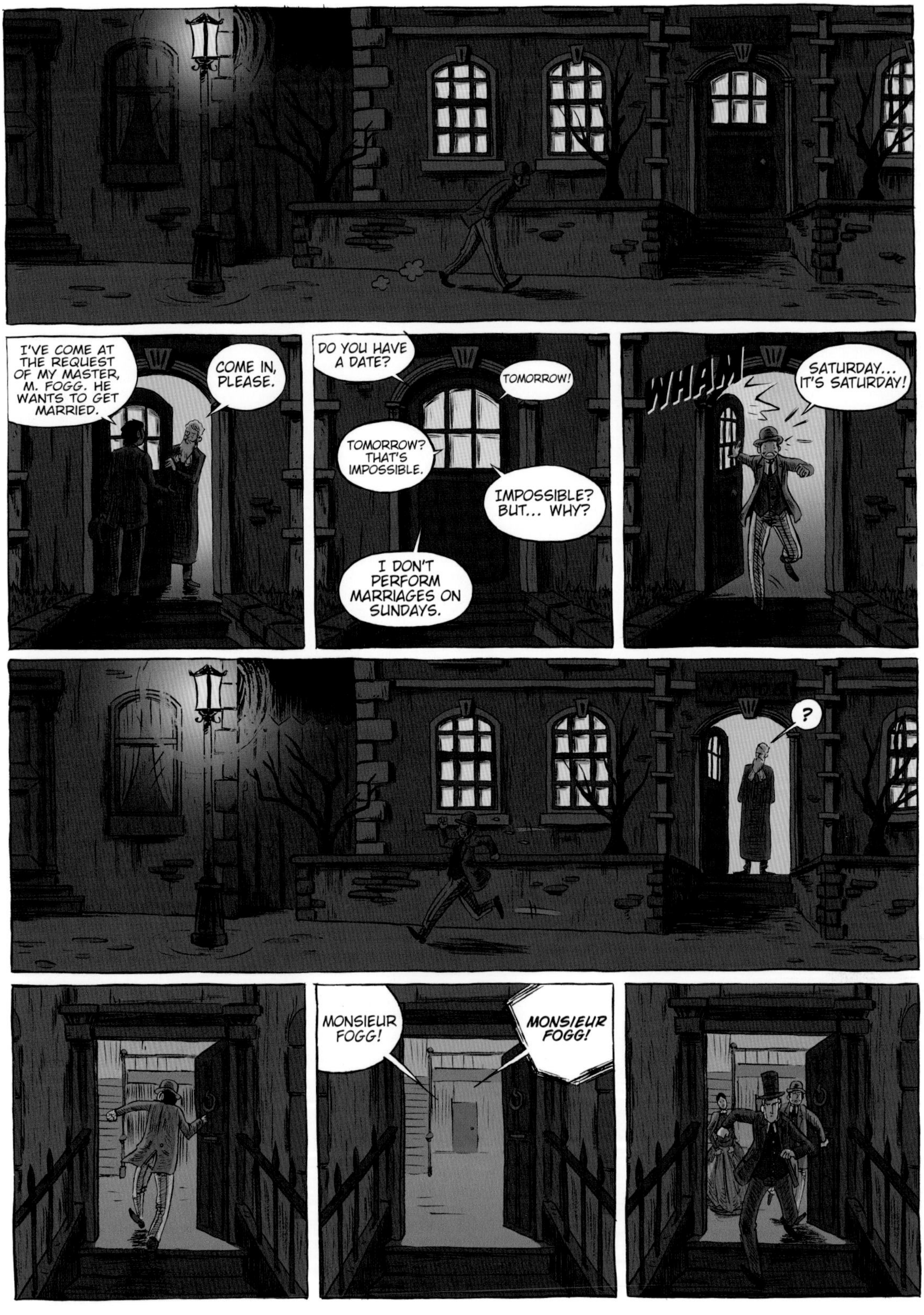

I'VE COME AT THE REQUEST OF MY MASTER, M. FOGG. HE WANTS TO GET MARRIED.
COME IN, PLEASE.
DO YOU HAVE A DATE?
TOMORROW!
TOMORROW? THAT'S IMPOSSIBLE.
IMPOSSIBLE? BUT... WHY?
I DON'T PERFORM MARRIAGES ON SUNDAYS.
WHAM
SATURDAY... IT'S SATURDAY!
?
MONSIEUR FOGG!
MONSIEUR FOGG!

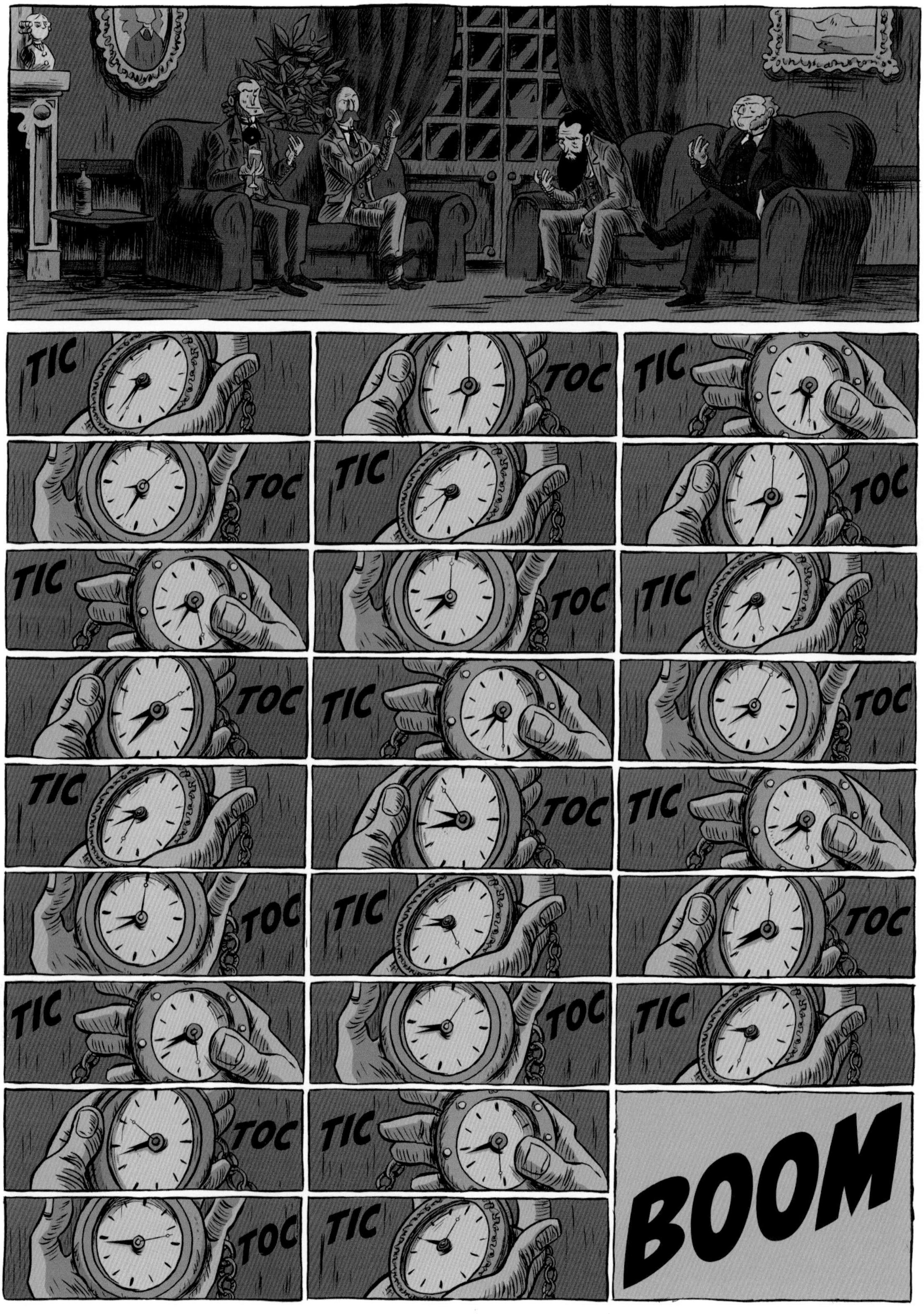
TIC
TOC
TIC
TOC
TIC
TOC
TIC
TOC
TIC
TOC
TIC
TOC
TIC
TOC
TIC
TOC
TIC
TOC
TIC
TOC
TIC
TOC
TIC
TOC
TIC
BOOM

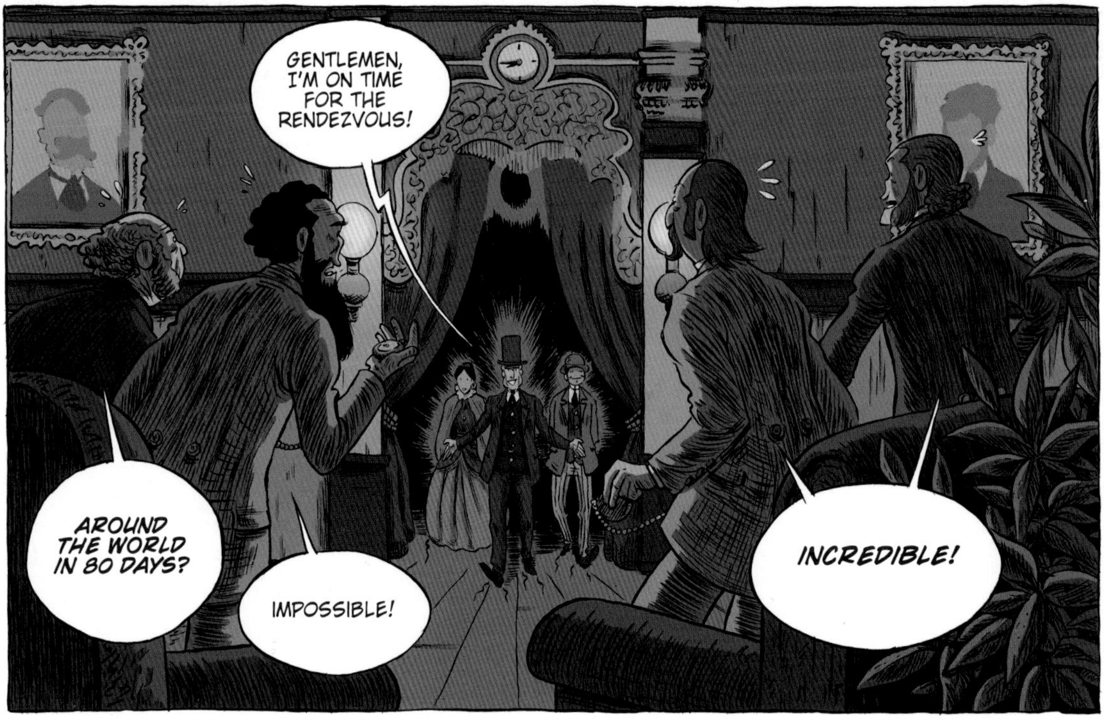
GENTLEMEN, I'M ON TIME FOR THE RENDEZVOUS!
AROUND THE WORLD IN 80 DAYS?
IMPOSSIBLE!
INCREDIBLE!

"And now, how could such an exact, meticulous man have committed that error of a day? Why did he think it was Saturday evening, December 21st, when he arrived in London, when it was but Friday, December 20th, only seventy-nine days after his departure?

Here's the reason for that mistake. It's quite simple.

Without suspecting it, Phileas Fogg had gained a day on his itinerary, and that solely because he'd done the tour of the world by going east, and he would, on the contrary, have lost that day by going in the opposite direction, that is, west.

Indeed, by heading east, Phileas Fogg was going ahead of the sun and, consequently, the days shrank by four minutes each time he traversed degrees in that direction. For the earth's circumference is divided into three hundred and sixty degrees, and those three hundred and sixty degrees, multiplied by four minutes, gives precisely twenty-four hours, that is, the day gained unconsciously.

In other words, whereas Phileas Fogg, while traveling east, saw the sun reach its meridian eighty times, his colleagues back in London, only saw it happening seventy-nine times. That's why, that very day, which was Saturday and not Sunday, as Mr. Fogg believed, the former were waiting for him in the lounge of the Reform Club."

The End.

NOW THAT YOU HAVE READ THE CLASSICS Illustrated EDITION, DON'T MISS THE ADDED ENJOYMENT OF READING THE ORIGINAL, OBTAINABLE AT YOUR SCHOOL OR PUBLIC LIBRARY

Afterword

"Around the World in 80 Days" is the most famous of Jules Verne's novels. Others could steal this first place from it, "Twenty Thousand Leagues Under the Sea," "Journey to the Center of the Earth," and "Five Weeks in a Balloon"... but the success of "Around the World..." remains unequaled in its era and ever since. Adapted for the stage after its success as a series in the newspaper *Le Temps* in 1872 and its appearance as a book with the Hetzel publishing house, the play toured the world as quickly as did its hero Phileas Fogg. It was a spectacle whose splendor critical reviews describe to us with many ballets, extras, flashy decors, and an elephant on the stage, when not a locomotive or even a balloon that, for its part, is not in the novel.

This passion for "Around the World in 80 Days," which brought riches to Jules Verne, marks a more profound phenomenon than an epic play's glitter, sequins, and rhinestones, a phenomenon which still moves us all. Phileas Fogg's wager isn't so much one with his friends in the Reform Club, but a wager with time. It is more a sort of a challenge even than a wager, and that challenge against time is what still moves us, for the race has become almost banal. Nowadays, we all must race around, just like Passepartout in the streets of Bombay. But when the novel first appeared, it revealed that new social fact: we were entering a world where it was necessary to chase time, which had become money. That financial evolution, since Jules Verne's day, has only accelerated. Those with a mastery of it seem to be of a cold and imperturbable resolution. Like that of Phileas Fogg? It's not at all sure. Faceless companies are far from Phileas's panache.

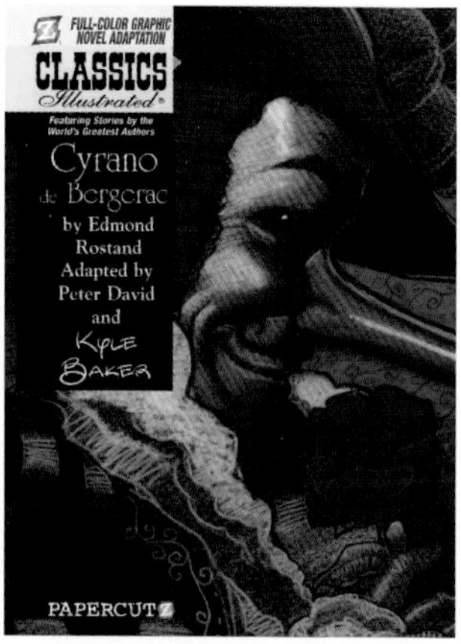

FULL-COLOR GRAPHIC NOVEL ADAPTATION
CLASSICS Illustrated
Featuring Stories by the World's Greatest Authors
Cyrano de Bergerac
by Edmond Rostand
Adapted by Peter David and
KYLE BAKER
PAPERCUT

CLASSICS ILLUSTRATED #10 "Cyrano de Bergerac," featured the short essay, "A Word About Cyrano's Panache," by Ken Wong.

For here's Jules Verne's secret. Thirty years before the success, every bit as phenomenal, of Edmond Rostand's "Cyrano de Bergerac," the entire success of Phileas Fogg's adventure lies in panache. What makes the beauty of the gesture is not that race against time, which Jules Verne already guessed was rather banal, but the panache of its author: Phileas, a man who never hurries and who stakes the entire fortune at his disposal at the end of a wager. Money serves for acting, not for enriching oneself. It's the beauty of the gesture and his humanity which create the success of the trip around the world in a record time. With Phileas, never cynical, Jules Verne drew upon the strength of our most powerful symbols.

Phileas Fogg the Englishman and Passepartout the Frenchman are an association of measured whimsy and fantasy, in a comedy whose success has lasted for a century and a half. Today, as soon as an advertisement, a movie, a trip start with "Around the World in..." we think of Jules Verne's novel, a voyage that's become a myth, of a geographical and planetary dimension that gives us the entire earth for horizon.

Jean-Paul Dekiss
Director of the Centre International Jules Verne

JULES VERNE (1828-1905)

The son of a bourgeois family in Nantes, Jules Verne is destined for a career as a lawyer, but his preferences lean towards literature. His law degree obtained, he turns towards the theatre. In Paris, he meets Alexandre Dumas who, in 1850, will stage his first play, "Les Pailles rompues" ("The Broken Straws"). Refusing to follow in the footsteps of his father, who is a lawyer, he prefers to devote himself to the study of science and writing. He thus publishes his first stories and, in 1852, is employed as a secretary at the Théâtre-Lyrique. In 1862, Jules Verne publishes with Hetzel the novel "Five Weeks in a Balloon." Its success is immense. Between 1864 and 1869 appear "Journey to the Center of the Earth," then "From the Earth to the Moon," and "Twenty-Thousand Leagues Under the Sea." His series "Extraordinary Adventures" will count sixty-four volumes. Mobilized during the Franco-Prussian War of 1872, he nevertheless continues writing. In 1872, he publishes "Around the World in 80 Days" and in 1876 "Michel Strogoff." He then moves to Amiens, where he is elected a city councilor and becomes an ardent defender of Esperanto. He writes more than 80 novels, not including numerous poems, plays, and works for the general public.

WATCH OUT FOR PAPERCUT**Z** ™

The special celebration of the 70th Anniversary of CLASSICS ILLUSTRATED continues with this edition of CLASSICS ILLUSTRATED DELUXE's all-new, 138-page adaptation of Jules Verne's "Around the World in 80 Days." I'm your jet-lagged editor-in-chief, Jim Salicrup, here to squeeze in a few words about CLASSICS ILLUSTRATED and Papercutz.

First, if you're like millions of others and are part of the social network known as Facebook, may I suggest "liking" this page:

http://www.facebook.com/pages/Classics-Illustrated-A-Cultural-History-2d-Ed/221247977894633

It's the official Facebook page for William B. Jones's "Classics Illustrated: A Cultural History"—the second edition! Besides getting a peek at sample artwork from the book and a link to the book's publisher, McFarland, you'll also find information on author signings and interviews. If you're a fan or any version of CLASSICS ILLUSTRATED, especially the original comicbook incarnation, this book is a major must-have! As one of the two listed CLASSICS ILLUSTRATED historians credited in each Papercutz edition of CLASSICS ILLUSTRATED and CLASSICS ILLUSTRATED DELUXE, Bill has been very supportive of our efforts and generous with his help (he wrote the wonderful historical articles about CLASSICS ILLUSTRATED founder Albert Lewis Kanter featured in our premiere volumes). The first edition of his book was incredibly researched and wonderfully written. The new second edition promises to be even more informative.

And if Mr. Jones's book gets you jonesing (sorry, I couldn't resist) for a taste of the original CLASSICS ILLUSTRATED (or CLASSIC COMICS, as it was originally dubbed), then you can either hunt for back issues from your favorite comicbook shops or online back issue dealers, or you can check out the hardcover facsimile editions published by our good friends over at www.jacklakeproductions.com.

In the meantime, let us know what you think of this adaptation of "Around the World in 80 Days"—you can email me at salicrup@papercutz.com, or send a letter to me at Papercutz, 40 Exchange Pl., Ste. 1308, New York, NY 10005. Next up in CLASSICS ILLUSTRATED DELUXE #8—"Oliver Twist"! Our longest adaptation yet! Don't miss it!

Thanks, *Jim*